SHADOW KILL is a work of fiction. [illegible] businesses, locations and incidents are either products of the author's imagination or used in a fictitious manner. Any resemblance to actual persons, living or dead, is coincidental.

CHAPTER 1

The man John Kovac was hunting swerved to avoid a puddle, muttering to himself in his native Japanese. He crashed into a row of pushbikes, then trudged forward again.

The clatter in the otherwise quiet alley was explosive, but no lights came on.

They were alone. Just Kovac and his target.

The man's name was Yoshinori Yamada. He was five nine, 170 pounds, with a gait that left both feet sticking out a little.

Like a penguin, Kovac thought.

Yamada was in the yakuza, but there were no tattoos. There was no little finger chopped off at the first joint, either. The guy was a suit, a salaryman practically, with a gift for finding young women and putting them to work in alleys just like this one. He wouldn't be mourned.

The quiet returned, broken now only by Yamada's drunken mumbling and a faint buzzing overhead.

Kovac glanced up. No one in the topmost windows and no one behind him... The buzzing sound wasn't a drone. It was coming from a thick nest of electrical wiring clumped to a street pole. Wires fanning up to roofs and down to red, purple and yellow snack bar signs, and all of it reflected in the fluorescent puddles underfoot.

Yamada lurched towards the next alley. He was still handsome, albeit in a baby-faced, pop-idol kind of way. A seducer of minor repute until his fifth or sixth scotch, and after that just another drunk wending his way home. Five more years of drinking like this and the charm would be all gone. The teeth too, probably.

Not that Kovac would give Yamada five years.

Kovac ran through the plan in a series of mental images. Two more alleys, then the enclosed concrete staircase, which was often slippery. Then the front door, which was never locked. Then his knife and a polite request to undress. A bath for one, a shot of succinylcholine, a quick and peaceful drowning with zero thrashing and splashing. Then out again, watching for the slippery stairs again, walking again. A cab with a driver in white gloves, an airport lounge, and a first-class ticket. He'd be out of Japan before dawn.

The plan was fine.

Yamada entered the next alley.

Kovac waited, listening. He knew every detail of this alley he was yet to enter, and it sounded like Yamada was letting the low, tiled wall on the left prop him up as he walked.

Kovac pulled his black, down jacket tighter but didn't zip it. He wanted quick access to his knife.

The plan was fine.

This next alley would be fine.

So why did it feel off?

He sensed it in his chest, a heavy mass like a ball of snakes, sending up all kinds of signals.

He rolled his head to loosen up his neck, twice clockwise.

A few hundred people drowned in bathtubs in Japan every year, mostly in the winter months like now. They weren't all drownings of course. They were cardiac arrests. But Japanese authorities were nothing if not literal. The deaths were recorded as drownings, which made drownings here banal.

Useful, Kovac reminded himself. It was a rare day that Kovac utilized a sniper rifle or even a knife, though his years as a Navy SEAL had left him expert with both. "Natural causes" was his Plan A.

And the plan was fine.

The snakes settled a bit.

Kovac started moving again, faster now. He entered the next alley. And immediately saw the plan was shot.

Yamada was gone.

CHAPTER 2

The assassin tasked with ending John Kovac's life was waiting at the end of the alley. He was at the top of the enclosed concrete staircase, a staircase he had found a little slippery. He blinked hard. He was jet-lagged, and his eyes still hurt from the dry cabin air. In point of fact, his entire body hurt. He was a tall man, too tall for Economy, and yet too new to this game for Business. The flight to Japan had cost him valuable rest and, worse than that, focus.

The man's name was Sukhomlinov. He wasn't unskilled, but he was no John Kovac. This was a job he had thought long and hard about before finally accepting. It would make his career or end his life. The next five minutes would decide which.

He tested Yoshinori Yamada's front door.

Unlocked, just as he had been told it would be.

He let himself in and shut the door again. Lingered just behind it. He had a knife and a pistol and enough of the plan to know what Kovac intended to do. A drowning, with a minimum of thrashing and splashing.

From there, the plan was a cab to the airport. But that would never happen. Once Kovac was inside this apartment, Sukhomlinov would make sure he never left.

For a few minutes, there was silence. Then Sukhomlinov heard footsteps. They were uneven, but coming towards the staircase, coming up it maybe?

Yes. He could hear the echo on the enclosed concrete.

He retreated a little deeper into Yamada's apartment. It was an old place with a low roof and a checkerboard wood-veneer floor. There were a few tatami mats, too, with strewn liquor bottles.

Not a man living his best life.

Not even a man getting by.

A drunk.

A small orange cat watched Sukhomlinov from its perch atop a microwave. Cautious, all-knowing cat eyes. Sukhomlinov considered wringing its neck and putting it out of sight. But it was a cat, not a dog. Barely older than a kitten, too. He doubted it would alert anyone to his presence.

He made his way through into the bathroom. It was a molded, plastic unit with a sewer pipe in the center of the floor. Sukhomlinov wondered where this pipe exited, because if everything went according to plan it would end up full of blood.

The sort of thing Kovac would've thought of before now.

The tub had a single shower curtain with a print featuring sailboats. Sukhomlinov extended it out a little, then stepped around it and into the tub. He took out his pistol and racked the slide. He screwed on a silencer and flicked the safety off.

The end of the tub was sloped, which pushed him further forward than he had expected. He had to extend the shower curtain even further out on its rail to hide. He noted the slimy feel of the plastic. The bathroom smelled strongly of urine.

He listened as the front door opened, its base making contact with a warp in the wood-veneer. *Sccccreeaaaah.* He heard Yamada enter, heard him go for a flimsy-sounding cabinet in the kitchen. There was another scrape, different from the first. It sounded like a metal lid on glass this time, like a bottle of spirits being opened. Liquid was poured, then perfect silence again. A glass was slammed back down onto a table, like a gunshot. A small glass, Sukhomlinov thought to himself, probably a shot glass.

Sukhomlinov listened for Kovac, despite knowing better. He wouldn't hear Kovac.

Still behind the shower curtain, he half-raised his pistol.

And waited.

Yamada soon burst in. Sukhomlinov didn't shoot. He remained perfectly still as Yamada did battle with his pants and started pissing directly into the toilet water.

Sukhomlinov had chosen the bathroom on the assumption Kovac would be more relaxed by the time he made it this deep into the apartment. Kovac's focus would be narrowing as he closed in on his prey, as he got to work on his plan.

But Sukhomlinov hadn't counted on the extent of Yamada's drunkenness. The loud pissing continued, and still no Kovac.

Sukhomlinov was vulnerable. There was no mirror in this little bathroom, nothing that would reveal him. But if Yamada turned, he would see a man with a pistol at the far end of his bathtub. Sukhomlinov would have no choice but to shoot him, which would alert Kovac to the threat. And if that happened, Sukhomlinov knew he wouldn't get out of this apartment alive.

He remained perfectly still, less sure of his plan now.

Did Kovac already know he was here? Was Sukhomlinov already into the last few seconds of his life?

Yamada's aim wandered, sometimes striking the bowl, sometimes striking the floor. Sukhomlinov knew why. Even from this angle, he could see that Yamada was cocking his head and closing one eye, trying desperately to aim. The man was seeing double.

Sukhomlinov tried to reassure himself. To drown Yamada, Kovac had to subdue Yamada. And to frame it as a heart attack, he needed to subdue Yamada with a minimum of force. Which meant time and concentration. And that's when Sukhomlinov would take his shot.

Yamada zipped up.

Yamada flushed.

Yamada left the bathroom.

Still no Kovac.

Sukhomlinov gave it another two minutes, his anticipation growing with every second that passed. He experienced a frustration that eventually verged on rage. Logically, he knew to stay put. Logically, there was no reason to abandon the bathtub. It provided him with security. It provided him with an element of surprise.

Another three minutes passed.

Then two more.

Sukhomlinov's lower back was beginning to hurt and the calf muscle in his left leg was threatening to cramp. It was the slope of the bathtub. It left him in a sort of crouch, his toes angling down as if on starting blocks. He couldn't keep this up all night, and what was the point, anyway? Kovac wasn't coming. Either Masuda had misled him, or the plan had changed.

It was rage now, and intolerable.

It took over.

He stepped around the shower curtain, over the sewer pipe and slipped out of the bathroom. Pistol up, he scanned the apartment. No Kovac.

Yamada was lying splayed on his tatami floor, his eyes closed, singing to himself under his breath.

Sukhomlinov crossed the room and locked the front door.

Yamada's eyes snapped open at the sound of the lock. He

struggled to pull himself up into a seated crouch. He looked like a child pretending to bobsled. He spotted the pistol and cowered. His hands came up, palms trembling.

Sukhomlinov flicked the gun towards the bathroom. In Japanese, he said: 'Run the water, fill the bathtub.'

'I did what Masuda wanted. I led him there.'

'Led who?'

'The foreigner.'

'Led him where?'

'The snack bar. I threw the tracking device on the roof, like Masuda told me.'

'Fill the bathtub.'

Yamada struggled to his feet. He glanced back towards the orange cat pleadingly. It didn't help. It remained exactly where it was, staring, not even blinking.

Yamada went into the bathroom. He filled the bathtub. He tested the temperature with his fingers, over and over, like maybe he would get to enjoy this bath. He wasn't thinking straight.

Sukhomlinov said: 'Get undressed, get in the bathtub.'

Yamada did as ordered, putting two trembling palms over his genitals and keeping them there the whole time. He sat in the bathtub exactly the way he had sat on the tatami, like he was bobsledding.

Sukhomlinov didn't have succinylcholine. The quick-acting skeletal muscle relaxant would've been useful right now. It would've rendered Yamada incapable of staying upright in the bathtub and facilitated a drowning that was all but devoid of evidence.

He said: 'Put your head underwater.'

Yamada frowned. For a long beat, he didn't move. Then,

reluctantly, he rolled sideways. He went over like a cargo ship, his whole body capsizing.

He had rolled towards Sukhomlinov, which made things easy.

Sukhomlinov put his left knee to the edge of the bathtub and swung his right leg over the side. His right knee came down between Yamada's shoulder and chin, on the side of his neck. Sukhomlinov twisted so that his own body was almost parallel with the bathtub's edge, which enabled him to exert a lot more force – all of it down onto his right knee and Yamada's neck and jaw. Yamada was still lying on his side. His hands came up, but they had to reach backward now. On his side, pinned as he was, the angles were all against him. He could reach Sukhomlinov's thigh, but there was no way for him to apply leverage.

Sukhomlinov waited for the bubbles. Ten seconds. Twenty seconds. Thirty. Yamada held out a lot longer than Sukhomlinov would've guessed. He forced his knee down even harder, looking to induce panic, and sure enough, bubbles exploded to the surface. Yamada shouted underwater, flailing.

Sukhomlinov saw him inhale, sucking water deep into his lungs, into all the narrow passageways and sacs.

Game over.

Sukhomlinov gave it another minute, then eased the pressure and raised his knee. A minute after that he was out of the apartment and making his way carefully down the slippery concrete staircase.

He wasn't sure how he felt about it. He was sending a message to Kovac, which was reckless. He had let his rage get the better of him, always his greatest weakness. He had blown the element of surprise.

But maybe it was for the best. He needed to stop mythologizing Kovac. He needed to believe in himself, and that started here. He had opened a dialogue now, announcing his presence if not his intentions.

And why not? He brought skills of his own to this duel, along with a ruthlessness Kovac could never match. If everything Masuda had told him about Kovac was true – if Kovac believed in innocence, in justice, in mercy – Sukhomlinov would exploit that.

He stepped sideways into shadow and felt his breathing drop to almost nothing. He checked his pistol again and let his eyes adjust to the gloom. He listened, waiting for the adrenaline to subside.

CHAPTER 3

John Kovac had never left the shadows. He had been standing for close on fifteen minutes in this new alley, his back to a roller door.

The entire alley was snack bars, though only one was open. Kovac had been waiting for Yamada to come out of this bar, but now he was unsure. He ran through it again. Yamada might've taken a different route home, cutting left a few feet on from where Kovac now stood and winding his way back to his apartment. But why would he? That wasn't his routine. It was also a longer route. In Kovac's experience, drunks chose the path of least resistance, especially when that path included alcohol.

The odds favored Yamada being in the one snack bar in this alley that was open. But fifteen minutes was still fifteen minutes. It was a serious delay now – one that could eventually jeopardize Kovac making his flight.

He pulled out an earpiece with an inbuilt mic. He put it in his ear then placed an end-to-end encrypted call through his phone to his handler, Bishop. One touch. The earpiece only rang one number, because Kovac only had one employer. It had been that way since the day he said adios to Uncle Sam and entered the private sector.

The call connected. Under his breath, Kovac said: 'I've lost the subject.'

'Understood. Give me thirty seconds.'

Kovac stayed on the line.

He heard Bishop typing.

A long pause.

Then Bishop's voice again: 'Tracking device shows the subject in a bar.'

'Opposite me, right?'

'Opposite you.'

Kovac tapped the earpiece again, ending the call.

He decided in an instant. The plan needed to change.

He checked his surroundings one last time then crossed the street. He slid back the snack bar's opaque glass door and slipped inside. He was instantly blasted by hot air from a space-aged kerosene heater. The thing was lit up orange, snarling at him. He moved past it, feeling the heat pass over the side of his leg.

Two girls in tight black dresses chanted what Kovac guessed was some kind of greeting. They were behind the bar. One was in her twenties with her hair down. The other was a little older, hair up. Both had stunning figures, perfectly accentuated by their dresses.

The bar was faux oak, with lighting that made the varnish shine yellow in spots. There were bottles of sake and assorted clear spirits on the bar itself, and bottles of dark spirits on three sets of shelves behind the women.

The room was larger than Kovac had expected. In the middle of it, a group of yakuza thugs in their thirties and forties were groping five other women, all younger than the two at the bar. Eight people in all, at one long table which looked like it had been made by pulling three smaller tables together. One of the women was blonde, a foreigner.

Further back, at the only other table in the room, there was one more man. Older. Meaner looking. He was sitting alone, studying Kovac. He was the local Yakuza boss, Ken Masuda, the one slated to receive Kovac's message. Kovac recognized him from photos.

But no Yamada.

Kovac's heartbeat picked up a little. It was all one hell of a coincidence… Yamada missing and his boss sitting here like he was waiting for Kovac to walk in.

'Anyone speak English?' Kovac asked, making sure each word was loud and slurred. He was a foreigner in a bar that never saw tourists; there was no point trying to blend in. On the off chance this was a coincidence, he wanted to lower expectations.

All eyes were on him now, and he let his body sway just a little, giving the subtle illusion of intoxication.

No one spoke.

'*Ingrish*?' he asked again, obnoxiously now, imitating the local pronunciation of the word while making a mental note to keep an eye on the bathroom door. If things turned nasty, which they now seemed certain to do, it was possible Yamada was in that bathroom.

'*Ingrish*?' he asked again. Kovac was American by birth but Australian by upbringing. Normally he didn't have much of an accent. In his homeland, people were always asking him if he was American. But he could turn the Aussie accent on when he wanted to.

Still no answer, though all conversation had cut out. All groping, too.

Progress of a sort.

Kovac's eyes finally adjusted to the gloom. He took a seat at the bar, sitting sideways so he could monitor the two women behind it and everyone else simultaneously. He saw his reflection. He looked like a regular guy, albeit big. Six two, solid. But to see him with his shirt off, it was a different story. Kovac was 35, but not in a bored-wife-and-three-kids-at-home kind of a way. He maintained the 200-pound physique of a fighter because his work demanded it. Traveling across time zones, in airports, in hotels, it didn't matter. He had his routines, all ingrained and so conditioned he couldn't call a day done until he had worked up a sweat. Jujitsu, boxing, Muay Thai, it didn't matter what, so much as how often. Kovac was a big believer in the fundamentals, in repetition, in preparation, in consistency at any cost. And he was grateful for all of that now, along with ten years' experience killing people for a living. It was just the sort of resume a man wanted going into a bar fight.

But how much did these guys know about him? And more to the point, how did they know anything? Kovac worked alone, he worked in the shadows; yet he was increasingly certain the four males in this bar knew exactly who he was. Perhaps even who he worked for. He was compromised. That much was clear. And this was an ambush.

He checked for cameras and wasn't surprised to find the place devoid of them. What middle-aged man wanted to be recorded with his red, grinning face buried between a pair of teenage breasts?

'I'll have a beer,' he said to the closer of the two women standing behind the bar. 'And what do these guys drink? Something for them, too – on me.'

The three men from the large middle table were rising, all getting up onto their feet and adjusting their black suit jackets.

They wearily pulled out knives – almost with a roll of the eyes, like they did this every day – and started forward.

CHAPTER 4

Kovac pretended not to notice the knives and eyed the toilet door. Small, plastic, out of keeping with the rest of the venue. There was a chance there was a fourth thug in there. Yamada, most likely. Or a clone of the three who were closing in on him now. But if not, this was the entire party. There were no other doors, and no kitchen either.

Kovac didn't have the authority to kill the boss. Ken Masuda was something of a whale in Australian gambling circles. But these other three... these other three were a gift. They were still coming at Kovac now, knives out. If Kovac could survive the next few minutes, he wouldn't need to hunt down Yamada. Yamada had only ever been a warning, a message to Masuda.

Under their black suit jackets, the thugs were all in white, V-neck tees that revealed tattooed chests. Their hair was slicked back with some kind of product, like they'd spent all morning in front of a mirror getting every last strand glued in place. Masuda, still seated in the back corner of the bar, was a bit classier. At sixty-something, he had a shiny purple tie on, and a blood-red Fedora sitting on the table in front of him. He was watching intently, more like a man in a movie theater than a bar.

Kovac stood. He reached back for the bar and feigned misjudging it.

The men stopped – at first surprised, then smirking. They were amused by Kovac's clumsy recovery when his hand found more air than bar.

Kovac righted himself again, eyes on the bar like he was confused, like it had moved.

One of them indicated for Kovac to walk over to Masuda by jerking his head towards his boss.

The woman behind the bar hadn't poured Kovac a beer. She now made for the main door. The other woman followed her, then most of the women from the tables, too. They all quietly put on extra layers of clothing and exited into the night. Only the blonde girl stayed.

Icy night air swirled in from the street outside, overpowering the heater. Without the other women, the bar suddenly felt still and cold. Kovac wanted this last girl gone, too – the blonde. The further away she was from this, the better.

The girl was in her late teens, as still as a wax statue. She sat with her head down, her palms together as if in prayer. But the praying hands were both locked tightly between her knees. She was terrified.

Masuda motioned for her to come and sit with him by tapping his knee.

She stood, uncurling her body to reveal a total height that almost matched Kovac's. She was thin, but with the muscle and taught fresh skin of youth. Her dress was almost the same purple as Masuda's tie. Almost as shiny, too.

She crossed to him, wobbly on high-heels, and sat on his lap. Even after she sat, Kovac could recall the exact shape of her body. Her dress hid absolutely nothing.

Youth and beauty, age and corruption. The juxtaposition was sharp.

They wanted Kovac in the corner, that much was clear. They wanted him at the table with their boss. If he sat there like a good boy, like the tall blonde maybe, on Masuda's other knee, they could talk about what Kovac wanted for Christmas, and one of the thugs could sneak a blade into his kidneys. That was their plan. Corner him, trap him, stab him to death.

He was going to pass on their plan.

Kovac turned and stumbled drunkenly out of the bar. It was like stepping out into a meat fridge. But he ignored the cold. He was now completely focused. The instant the door clicked shut, he cut sideways, easing his back up against the damp wall. He was just to the right of the doorframe. He could see his breath again. He took in a deep lungful of air and held it. The door would open towards him, and as soon as it was open, it would hide him. He saw the handle move as the thugs came out. They had been slow to follow, doubtless thrown by the abrupt departure. It had taken them a moment to remember that they wanted him in the bar; that he didn't have permission to just up and stumble out. Perhaps Masuda had needed to remind them. Whatever the case, they were now all piling out – and all expecting him to be twenty or thirty feet into the alley. They were looking to run down a drunk.

Masuda hadn't given them a bio then.

Kovac came at the first from behind the open door, appearing out of nowhere and stabbing him in the heart. The man dropped dead on the spot. Straight down as soon as the knife came out: knees, hips, shoulders, like a cut puppet.

His buddy tripped on him. This second thug had been pushing hard. He was short, a real charger, all enthusiasm. He had momentum so Kovac let him go. He was going to end up on his hands and knees, and that suited Kovac just fine. Turning, kneeling, standing: all these things took time.

Time Kovac now used to deal with the third guy.

Kovac didn't over-think it. The first guy had cleared the doorway before going down so Kovac hip-and-shouldered the door. He jammed the third guy between door and frame, like a mousetrap. This last guy was right-handed. That meant his knife was inside the bar, thumping against the inside of the door, completely harmless. Kovac buried his own knife into the side of the man's neck. Once, twice, three times. There was a lot of blood and noise, as there always was when Kovac chose to involve a neck. He was going to end up with splatter on him, which would mean a change of clothes; but that was low on his priority list right now. He still had the little charger to deal with.

He released the door again and got a fistful of the third guy's once-white, now red V-neck. He pulled the choking, dying mass forward. He harnessed gravity to do it, flinging the third guy hard down onto the little charger.

The little charger hadn't completely fallen, but he had come close enough. The third man, propelled by Kovac, hit him with the force and weight of a mini-fridge and sent him reeling back into the alley.

Kovac strode out to him. For all his years of doing this to people, one thing he had never quite mastered was throwing knives. The little charger had rolled onto his stomach, preparing to rise onto his hands and knees. Kovac stood on his arm before this could happen: specifically, on the elbow of the arm which led to the knife. He put his own knife into the charger's kidneys.

The man howled, getting his free arm around behind him, his hand to Kovac's hand. His thumb and fingers snapped like a crab claw, trying for any kind of purchase and finding none. Kovac, one leg bent, one straight, like a man stretching before a run, kept the majority of his body weight on his front foot, on the pinned elbow. He twisted his blade even as he checked to make sure Masuda wasn't on his way out, perhaps with a gun in hand.

He wasn't.

'Who told you about me?' he hissed.

The man said something in panicky Japanese.

'Who told you?' Kovac demanded again, slowing the words.

More panicky Japanese.

Given the language barrier, interrogation was a waste of time. Kovac left his knife where it was and straightened. He circled the guy, who now got a grip on the blade in his kidneys. He started to remove it, screamed, stopped, then tried again. Screamed again.

Kovac took his knife back and finished him off. It wasn't something he enjoyed doing, but he had a message to deliver, and he was on a schedule.

He checked for Masuda again, checked the street.

Nothing.

Just him and three dead guys.

He searched his three kills one by one, hoping for a pistol. *No dice.* This was Japan. It had some of the strictest gun laws in the world and the gangsters here were all making do with knives, just as he was.

He took their phones and checked each. To the last, they wanted fingerprints. He grabbed dead hands and entered the prints before going to the settings for each and deactivating the screen locks. Then he turned all three phones off and pocketed them in his jacket.

He checked the snack bar and street again.

No one coming.

He risked thumbing through the men's wallets but there was nothing of interest. Cash, coins and – in the case of the little charger – condoms.

Optimistic.

Kovac tossed the wallets aside.

He stood for a moment, wondering about Yamada. Was

Yamada still in the vicinity? If so, he was probably worth finishing off, too. Kovac was nothing if not a perfectionist.

He circled the outside of the snack bar and located the small window and fan denoting the bathroom. He dragged a cinder block across coarse gravel and used it to step up and cautiously look through.

No Yamada.

Which meant there was no good reason to go back in – or even to stick around. Ken Masuda would find his message on his doorstep, and it would be easy to figure out who tipped him off by monitoring him in coming days. Kovac had the three phones as a starting point. He would watch Masuda's every move, record his every word for later translation, then spider-web his associates.

He slipped into a narrow gap between two buildings behind the bar. He had to turn almost sideways to manage it. He started shuffling away, planning to enter the next street along and disappear. He didn't want to be here when police turned up. Unfair as it was, there wasn't a lot of trust for foreigners in this country.

And that was when he heard it – the girl back inside the bar, screaming.

CHAPTER 5

Kovac didn't owe her. He knew exactly who he was, what he had done in the past, and what he did for a living now. He didn't improve people's lives, he ended them.

Even so, he knew this particular scream. He had heard it before, countless times in fact, but mostly long ago. He'd heard it on the night that changed his life forever, the night that arguably had left him standing here. He had that girl's face fresh in his mind now. The girl from back then, but somehow the girl from tonight, too. For an instant, they were one in the same, fused. But he wasn't the same. Not even close. He had been aware of this change for a long time now. He didn't feel the cold fury of old, which had defined him as a teenager, and which had stalked him well into his twenties. He actually pitied this girl tonight and – job to do or not – he hated the idea of leaving her with a man like Masuda.

'Bastard,' he growled, unsure whether he meant the word for himself or Masuda.

He allowed himself to think it through. Why was she screaming?

As Kovac saw it, there were a few possibilities.

One, Masuda was scared. He had heard something at the front door and now his pet thugs had failed to come back on command. Maybe he'd opened the front door for a peek and received his message. He had realized he was a crime boss in a small room with a bathroom and nowhere else to hide. The building was one of the few in the street which didn't have an upstairs level. It was a cheap build, little more than a frame. It looked like it went back to the 70s or 80s. Perhaps originally it was a ma and pa restaurant or bar. At some point though, Masuda had taken it over. He had ripped out the interior and replaced it with a new one. He had added the faux wood and leather décor – a shot at Western class. It was likely lucrative now, too. Snack bars had a simple business model: get women who are down on their luck to sit and be fondled by patrons who pay five or ten times the going rate for a drink. Soft prostitution, really, and probably just one of a hundred similar businesses Masuda owned. Now Masuda found himself trapped in a hell of his own making, with no way to know Kovac planned to spare him. Maybe he figured a hostage would give him a shot at survival as he exited.

Or maybe Masuda had no intention of exiting…

This brought Kovac to possibility two. Masuda was just trying to keep Kovac around while he waited for reinforcements. Either more thugs or even police. The man had access to both.

There was a third and final possibility. It was a theory premised on the idea Masuda was far dumber than he looked. Masuda figured his thugs were taking their time working Kovac over and he was taking the chance to push the blonde for more than the usual groping.

Whichever of the three it was, there was only one right course of action. *Walk away*. Kovac didn't need to confront Masuda right now. It was better not to, in fact. He couldn't kill the man, which put him at a disadvantage in any confrontation. Then there was the surveillance. If he went after Masuda now, humbled him, humiliated him, he'd alter Masuda's behavior in the coming days and weeks. Maybe he'd still find out who gave Masuda the drop on him, but then again maybe not.

The girl was still screaming.

Kovac let out a long, frustrated sigh. Could he help this girl and help himself in the process? Execution was a no-go, but if he could get Masuda to a different location the options would open up again. Torture would be back on the table, for one. He could get the information he needed here and now and save himself the time. He might even still make his flight.

He shuffled sideways, back towards the bar, and crossed the gravel space at the rear. He needed to assume Masuda was armed. He ran a hand quietly over the outside wall. The structure had definitely been put up on the cheap. It felt like most urban walls in this country: thin, flimsy, easy to put a hole through. There was no paint and Kovac guessed from the texture that he was dealing with some kind of compressed, composite wood. But could he pass through it at a run?

No.

The bathroom window was out, too. Too small, and too loud even if he could somehow squeeze through.

He kept walking, a whole lot less impressed with his plan now that it involved the snack bar's front door.

CHAPTER 6

The three thugs were still lying dead in the alley. The building didn't have windows facing the street, so Kovac was able to step around front undetected. The screaming inside had stopped, which unnerved him. At least with the screaming, he had known what was what.

There was a faint chance Masuda had made a run for it, but that felt unlikely. Kovac's money was now firmly on the old crime boss staying put and waiting for reinforcements.

He wished he had more to work with. Smoking Masuda out would be the safest course. He even considered it now. There was a convenience store not too far away. He would select a bottle of vodka that was big but with glass that wasn't too heavy. Enough weight to throw, not so much weight it would fail to shatter. He would empty about a quarter of the vodka, soaking a handkerchief in the processes and stuffing it into the bottle. Definitely a handkerchief, he thought, because he knew from bitter experience paper towel disintegrated. Shake it a few times, draw the handkerchief out again, and then *tsst-tsst* with the lighter. Put that through the bathroom window round back and all he would need to do was wait here with his knife.

He was sorely tempted. He always liked the whoosh of alcohol vaporizing. But if Masuda had called on reinforcements, Kovac simply didn't have the time.

Knife at the ready, he approached the front door. Sometimes there wasn't a safe way to do things. Sometimes the job was just a matter of finding the courage. Anyone who said a soldier could eliminate all risk was full of shit. In the SEAL teams of Kovac's youth, there had always been doors to kick in and rarely a perfect picture of what lay behind.

He aimed with his foot. One, two and –

Vehicles.

CHAPTER 7

Kovac didn't have much time to find cover. But he managed to cross the alley. He did it a moment before three Mercedes-Benzes rolled into view.

There was no way to see inside. Black cars, black windows. Three identical S-Classes.

He was back standing sideways, back wedged between two buildings again, invisible in the gloom.

The cars crawled their way cautiously along the alley, speeding up when they spotted the snack bar.

Kovac had missed his chance.

He watched the cars stop at the three corpses, twelve guys piling out. These replacements looked more or less exactly like the ones he'd killed, like maybe there was a factory pumping these guys out in batches.

The drivers were still in the vehicles, which meant they had been packed in five to a car.

Cozy, Kovac thought. He imagined them all jamming in, shunting the newest recruits to the middle, rear seat.

Five or six of the new thugs wasted time confirming that their dead buddies were dead. A few others stood around shouting in panicky, aggressive Japanese. Two more went round the back of the snack bar, and one free-thinker headed off down the street.

Only one man thought to open the front door to the snack

bar and go inside.

Ten seconds passed.

Then this lone smart guy emerged with Masuda.

All the other goons immediately pulled together to escort Masuda to the nearest car. Some brandished knives, two had pistols. They protected their boss like he was a U.S. President under fire, draping themselves over him, scanning for threats.

Kovac watched as they loaded the three dead bodies into the Merc's trunks, one per Merc. He was memorizing faces but also fighting down a new unease. The girl hadn't come out.

There was another problem, too – something Kovac couldn't explain. There was an extra guy. Everyone was back in the vehicles, along with Masuda. Kovac had counted them as they got in. All seats were taken. But there were still two goons in the street.

It didn't add up.

One guy left made sense. The guy who had headed off down the street at the beginning of all this, presumably to secure some kind of perimeter. He had now lost his seat to Masuda, and fair enough. Masuda was the boss. *But two goons left to walk home…?* Where had the second one come from?

Kovac waited for the Mercs to leave, at which time the two remaining men went into the snack bar.

'Shit,' he said under his breath, readying himself to cross the street.

But in the end, he didn't need to cross the street. Or even give up his cover. Before he could move, the two men emerged again – now with the girl. One had her by the wrist, a tight grip, like he expected her to resist.

She wasn't resisting, though. She was coughing and stumbling, but she looked all too happy to be led. She paused, but only to kick off her high-heels, and suddenly her gait was right again. Fast and fluid and – Kovac had to admit it – sexy as all get out.

He scrubbed this last thought from his mind. She was a kid practically, and she wasn't clear of this yet. Not by half.

He figured they either planned to rape her or kill her. Or both. If they had no interest in her, they would've left her in the bar and walked away. If it was a simple eviction, they could've dumped her in the alley now. But they weren't doing either of these things.

They were leading her somewhere, away from a property that was owned and operated by their boss.

Maybe the girl came to the same conclusion because Kovac saw her suddenly slip free and run.

Scream, he thought. For God's sake, *scream*.

CHAPTER 8

She didn't scream. It was just the sound of her bare feet slapping cold blacktop.

She made other errors, too. She didn't run towards the nearby commercial district, which would be humming even at this late hour. She ran away from it: down a series of narrow streets with near-identical, modern two-story homes. At this point, Kovac still assumed she'd think her way out of her predicament. He assumed she would stop at any one of these countless houses, all with lights on and cars in garages, all with front doors she could easily have knocked on. She needed a witness, someone to usher her inside, or even just to stand with her under a porch light. But she didn't seek help. She went on inexplicably running, seemingly set on the idea of escape.

Kovac followed the men as they followed the girl. Now and then the men jogged, but mostly they kept to a fast walk. The girl had sprinted at first, but now she was conserving energy, too. She was glancing back at the men, matching her pace to theirs as they did the same. She was tired. She was half-jogging, stumbling, sometimes hopping when she stepped on rocks or other unpleasant objects.

Kovac felt sorry for her. She would be terrified. She had reached a park that was a perfect spot for a murder. It was on a slope, between densely populated suburban blocks. There wasn't any play equipment, save for a long metal slide built into the slope itself. The park looked like it had been set up in a rush: a few benches for adults to sit on and the slide to keep children occupied for ten minutes. The area had big trees with canopies, and because of this it was more dirt than grass. At this hour, it was black and spooky, and completely deserted.

The girl ran down the slide. The men went either side of it. They began to speed up and close in, twigs snapping loudly under their boots. They were looking to run her down before she made it out of the park. Kovac followed them, albeit at a safe distance. He had studied this entire area when planning for Yamada's bath, and he knew the girl was heading towards a river. She didn't know it, but if she made it through this park the river would create a dead end. When she reached it, she'd be out in the open. There was a walking path, but otherwise it was just long dead grass and distant bridges.

Things sped up and Kovac realized all his thinking was academic. The girl wasn't going to make it out of the park. The men had suddenly started sprinting at her, and she had been slow to detect it. She was picking up speed too, but not enough of it. And she had the disadvantage of bare feet. They were going to get her.

Kovac ran through his options and decided to reveal himself. He stopped, pulled out his phone, and took a photo.

The flash lit up the park. Or at least, Kovac assumed it did. He shut his eyes when taking the shot to preserve his night vision. When he opened them again, the two men had come to a stop. They had turned, confused. They were squinting back up the hill towards him.

Thinking of police, Kovac hoped. Or of their dead buddies in the alley back at the snack bar. Either would do.

Kovac closed his eyes and took another photo, and this time when he opened them again both men had their arms up, shielding their faces.

Without revealing his identity, he was now the witness the girl needed. To the men, he was just a light in the trees, a flash in the dark, a shadowy presence where they had assumed there was nothing. He was an unknown.

He let them think. He let them imagine. The more they thought and imagined, the more dangerous he would seem. Unknowns bred anxiety. It was human nature.

The men decided to cut and run. They gave the girl a wide berth. She was standing in the street at the bottom of the park now, and both men raised their hands in a show of harmlessness.

Almost contrition, Kovac thought with satisfaction.

He watched them step into the street and disappear.

The girl watched them too, confused.

She looked back up the hill towards him, into the darkness of the park.

Kovac gave it a moment. Then he said: 'I'm a friend.'

CHAPTER 9

She was standing frozen at the street's edge. He walked down to her, emerging out of the gloom. 'What's your name?'

She didn't answer. She was staring at his empty hands, which still had dried blood on them. He reached for her hand. 'You can trust me.'

She nodded.

But she didn't trust him. He could see it in her eyes. He was the drunk guy from the bar. Three goons had gone after him and she had perhaps heard what happened to them.

She took a few steps back, glancing at the street.

'You need to follow me. We can talk about this after, but right –'

She looked on past the houses, towards the river.

Kovac knew what was coming. He could see it in her eyes when she looked back at him one last time. Flighty. She'd already made up her mind.

She ran.

But not towards the river.

She went left.

The same direction the Yakuza thugs had gone.

This surprised Kovac. So much so, he gave her some latitude, and in time she once again fell to a jog and finally a walk.

They were back to cat and mouse.

Same game, new players.

Or maybe same players, new order. It was possible the men had looped around and were now tailing Kovac. He checked behind him. Checked left and right. All clear.

He followed the girl at a distance, enough distance to give her some sense of control. Then he decided to drop back and give her the illusion he had given up on her. There would be plenty of time to question her but only one chance to follow like this and see where she took him. They passed more houses. More cars in garages, more pot plants, more empty clotheslines. The streets smelled faintly of shit.

She had stayed when all the other women in the bar headed out into the night. Why? And now it felt like Masuda had ordered her death. Again, why? Kovac couldn't afford to ignore the possibility she was caught up in this and no innocent at all.

But within ten blocks, it was clear to him this girl had nowhere to go. She was moving on instinct, and her instincts were still all messed up by fear. She was lost, alone, scared.

Kovac had questions, but he wanted her to feel safe. He decided not to approach until there were other people around, and he was relieved when she eventually wised up and gravitated to the busiest street in the area.

In the end, busier than he wanted. The road was six lanes wide, the buildings all tall and concrete. Bright signs ran up the sides of each, like cascading neon ladders. Even at this late hour, it was crowded.

Kovac watched pedestrians mass at a giant intersection, then cross all at once. All except for the girl.

She was clearly in shock now, standing numbly as all this life swirled around her. People noticed her, her bare feet, but they pretended not to see. A foreign girl this beautiful, standing barefoot, it wasn't an everyday thing. Possibly not an entirely nice thing, either, not at this hour. Everyone left her alone.

Except Kovac.

He approached slowly, and he was careful to speak so as not to startle her. 'How are the feet? Cold?'

He had found a faucet in all his walking and cleaned himself up as best he could. His knife was safely out of sight too.

'Cold?' he asked again. A more general question this time.

She looked at him suspiciously. Or maybe she found the question redundant. The night air was so cold snow felt possible.

She turned and reversed away from him, until one bare foot dropped down a few inches, onto a metal manhole cover. She winced, raised it an inch, glanced behind her, then remained like this for a moment. Kovac thought she was going to run again, as if maybe this was going to go on all night. But she surprised him and abruptly sat, folding her knees up to her chin to keep her feet off the cold metal of the manhole cover.

She started crying.

Her feet must have been throbbing from the cold. Or maybe they were so numb now she hardly felt them. Kovac wished he could trust her enough to offer her his shoes and jacket. But he needed his shoes, and his jacket had his knife, succinylcholine, four phones and an earpiece stashed in its various pockets.

He checked his surroundings and reassured a few people that the girl was fine, that she was with him. Then he sat on the curb beside her, watching one swam of pedestrians after another cross the vast kaleidoscopic street.

'Let's find somewhere warm,' he said. 'We can talk.'

She ignored the offer.

He waited a moment in case she changed her mind. When she didn't, he said: 'Before I showed up, did anyone visit that snack bar you were in?'

She glanced at him but didn't speak.

He waited.

Nothing.

He was going about this all wrong. He rewound and slowed down. 'What's your name?' he asked.

'You first.' She had some kind of European accent. German maybe.

He shook his head. 'No.'

She almost laughed at this, a tiny snort amidst the tears. 'I'm Anna,' she said.

'Nice to meet you, Anna. Before I showed up, did anyone visit that bar? Anyone out of the ordinary?'

'No.'

'No one?'

'It was earlier. At a different place.'

The reply caught him off guard. 'What? Where?'

'Masuda's place.'

'Why were you at Masuda's place?'

She pursed her lips as if she resented the question. 'His bedroom.'

It took Kovac a moment to realize what she meant. She was studying his eyes, perhaps expecting judgment.

'Oh.' He didn't care about her profession. 'Okay. What else can you tell me? Male? Female? Foreign? What was said? Any details you can remember, Anna.'

She went on studying his face. And when she next spoke, it was in a whisper. 'Are you John Kovac?'

CHAPTER 10

The two men from the park called it in, and Ken Masuda took the call while instructing his driver to speed up.

'Understood.' Masuda hung up.

The assassin Sukhomlinov was sitting beside him. He had slipped in with Masuda's men during the rescue, leaving two men to deal with the girl. The same two who had now called Masuda to confess failure.

Masuda gave his driver directions.

'What's happening?' Sukhomlinov asked in English.

For a moment Masuda didn't answer. They were passing through a section of the city he always enjoyed. The street had its share of neon signs but also had rows of trees planted at even intervals. Masuda didn't know what type of trees – maples maybe – but they were all young, and all without leaves this time of year. White lights had been strung up, trunk to tip, vertically. They gave the trees the look of white flames, one after the next.

'What's happening?' Sukhomlinov asked again, this time switching to Japanese.

His Japanese was good. No doubt it was his Asian heritage. As far as Masuda had been able to determine, Sukhomlinov's father was Russian, his mother Cantonese. The man's almost prim British accent was from an International School in Hong Kong, and Masuda envied it. He had battled half his life just to learn passable English. 'He's found a way into my house,'

Masuda said.

'How?'

'A girl, an Austrian girl. Kovac's sitting with her right now – in the street. They're talking.'

'Why would he do that?'

'She overheard our conversation. She was with me when we were planning. She heard my side of that phone call. She's meant to be dead.'

'So why isn't she?'

'My men failed me.' Masuda studied Sukhomlinov in the dim light and saw a slight frown form on his face. No doubt he was confused at being cut out of things back at the bar. But too bad, Masuda had wanted a shot at Kovac himself.

'Does the girl speak Japanese?'

'Some,' Masuda said. 'Possibly enough to understand the gist of our conversation. And I said his name. John Kovac. She heard his name.'

Masuda's phone rang again. He took the call and listened. Hanging up, he said: 'They've gone to the train station. They're hoping to ambush me.'

'How do you know?'

Masuda ignored this. 'But to do that they need to exit the train system, which means we can ambush them first. There are three train stations within walking distance of my house, one closer than the other two. They'll likely exit there. You can intercept.'

'How does he have access to your house?'

'The girl, I gave her access.'

Masuda had numerous houses dotted across Tokyo. He wasn't referring to the post-modern palace and adjoining underground bunker which housed his wife and children, nor to the equally fortified penthouse apartment which housed his retired father. He was referring to a plush but nondescript house that functioned as a bachelor pad. This house had 24-hour guards, so access was never really access. In this case, it was just a door code.

Even so, he regretted giving access to a whore. And he particularly regretted talking frankly around her. That was why she needed to die.

Masuda straightened out his purple tie as the car turned left, into a quieter road with ramen noodle shops and small bars. The bars steadily became seedier, until the car stopped outside a traditional building with two old-fashioned lanterns.

'And if you're wrong about all this?' Sukhomlinov asked. 'If they're not attacking your house, if they go somewhere else?'

'Leave the worrying to me. Ambush him tonight.'

'Masuda-san, with all due respect – he'll be expecting it.'

'On the contrary…' Masuda moved to get out of the car.

'I'll need a rifle. Ammunition, too.'

'It's being arranged. Finish them both tonight, Sukhomlinov, and I'll forgive you for killing Yamada. I'll also forgive the fact you didn't come to my aid when I was trapped in that bar.'

'I was hunting Kovac. My decisions were based on your –'

'Kill Kovac tonight, and it's all forgiven.'

Masuda got out of the car. His men immediately flanked him on all sides. He stepped straight into another, near-identical vehicle, one heading in the opposite direction. He was headed back to the trees he liked, and from there up into the mountains. He needed to meet with a man whose power far exceeded his own, a man so terrifying many believed him to be a myth.

If only he were, Masuda thought, regretting his deal with the devil. *If only he were…*

CHAPTER 11

While flagging a cab and directing it to the nearest train station, Anna had told Kovac about Masuda's phone call, during which Masuda had said Kovac's name.

Kovac had sat in the back seat with her, listening. She had sat with her forehead to the window, chewing at a thumbnail, speaking in a monotone. He had studied her reflection in his window. *A girl in genuine distress*, he had eventually decided.

Now, they were entering the train station.

Anna bought train tickets for them both. They were the size of postage stamps and magnetic on the back. They came out of giant machines built into the station wall. Kovac followed her instructions at the ticket gates, because he was new to public transport. He hadn't been on a train once since landing in Japan. This trip so far had been sleek black cabs, start to finish.

'Wait here,' he said, as soon as they were on into the train station proper. He went into a drab, overly functional restroom and cleaned off the remaining flecks of blood, rearranging clothing and covering up the stains. He was grateful for his dark jacket but would need to shop for new clothes at some point. Daylight would be revealing.

'He'll kill me,' Anna said when he returned.

'Who, Masuda? You don't know that.'

'I do. And he said he was planning to kill you, too. As a favor to some other guy, some guy up in the mountains. I heard it, Kovac. We both know what sort of man he is. He won't just forget about me. But you can kill him first. You can save both of us.'

'You prepared this little speech?'

'Kind of.'

'I never said I was John Kovac – or a hero.'

'You killed his men. I saw what you did. Masuda made me look, he made me check. You stabbed them.'

'That wasn't me.'

'I can get you into his house, past his alarm. I've thought about this. Every way. And this is the only way I survive.'

Kovac led her down an out-of-service escalator to the platform. 'Tell me about Masuda's place. You can get me inside how?'

'He gave me the code. He has guards, but they're idiots. They're bored and always horny. I can distract them, trust me. They won't even know you're there. I'll leave, and you stay. You hide in the bedroom. They'll relax again and I'll arrange to meet Masuda like normal.'

Kovac dismissed the plan immediately. 'Have you thought this through?' he asked.

'Yes.'

'Why do you think Masuda sent those two thugs after you?'

'To kill me.'

'So even if his guards do let us in, what do you think Masuda's going to do when you call and invite him to his own house?'

He saw her face fall at this obvious flaw in her thinking. She stepped from the last step of the escalator and joined him on the platform.

She said: 'So what do we do?'

'What's the code, Anna?'

'No.' She glanced at him suspiciously.

'No?'

'You have to promise to kill him. Don't cut me loose, Kovac.'

Kovac searched the platform for threats, left and right. Then the train line itself. All the signal lights were set to red, glowing bright in the dark. 'As I said, you haven't thought this through. I'm sorry but we do this my way, Anna, or not at all.'

'And what way is that?'

'You show me where Masuda's house is, give me the code and disappear.'

'You'll kill him?'

'I haven't promised you a thing and I won't. So quit asking.'

They both stood in silence after that. They endured a long wait for the first a.m. train, and when it arrived they took it three stops, changed trains, waited again, then rode the new train for another five stops. More staring out windows, more studying reflections. Anna was chattering from the cold and looked utterly morose. Kovac held off talking until they were nearing the final stop. When he did speak, he kept it general. There were other early-bird passengers now, listening to every word he said: 'Where are you from, Anna?'

'Austria.'

'Where in Austria?'

'Graz.'

'And you came here because...?'

'I was going to teach English.'

'What happened to that plan?'

'I'm fluent, but Japanese people want a real accent.' She was warming her bare feet against the carriage heater, faded pink polish on the toenails. If there had been socks at any point, they were long gone.

'What's a real accent?'

'American, British – Australian even. Not Austrian.'

'So what, you started working for Masuda?'

'No. Russians first – through a friend of mine, a girl who was working for them. They introduced me to Masuda.'

The train began to slow. She twisted in her seat and put her head to the window, looking on up the line. She seemed relieved to be done with the topic.

'This is our stop?' Kovac asked.

'Yeah. He lives near here.'

They got off the train, leaving behind the faint smell of cleaning products. The freezing Tokyo air hit them hard, especially Anna.

Anna had given Kovac two tickets and he needed both to exit the station. He slotted them through the machine one atop the other, like Anna had shown him to do. There was a beep and little gates opened.

'You hungry?' he asked.

'Yeah. You?'

He nodded.

'The chain restaurants and cafes are all shut at this hour,' Anna explained. 'But we can get supplies over there.' They had exited the station but not the building it was housed in. Anna pointed across a wide expanse of tiles to a convenience store. 'It's all that's open this late.'

Kovac didn't like the store. It was narrow and long and filled with shelves that ran high. Just the one entry and exit, he noted. A real hole-in-the-wall, with countless blind spots. 'You go in,' he said. 'I'll stay out here.'

The other passengers had already vanished. At this early hour, it was now just the two of them.

Kovac didn't know if Anna had money on her or not. He presumed no. He gave her 10,000 yen. 'Get whatever you want, and I'll have anything with meat in it. To go. All of it to go. They have clothing of any kind in there?'

She took the money. 'Underwear maybe. Socks. Stuff like that.'

'Get whatever you can.' He gave her another 10,000 yen. 'You're going to get frostbite otherwise.'

She was already subtly stepping from one foot to the other on the cold tiles, like a stork. She didn't argue. 'Anything else?'

'Yeah. A map. Any map covering this area.' He held up the two train tickets. 'Do I need these still, or are we done with trains?'

'We still going to Masuda's place?'

'Not in the way you're hoping, but yeah.'

'Then we're done with trains. We walk from here.'

Kovac looked around for a trash can but there wasn't one. He pocketed both tickets.

'I'll meet you back here then?' Anna asked, sounding like she expected him to walk away.

'I'll wait over there.' Kovac pointed towards the building's west wall, which was transparent. It was made of glass or heavy-duty plastic, and it would give him a good view of the building's immediate surroundings. 'I have a phone call to make.'

CHAPTER 12

Anna went into the store, glancing back every few seconds, shivering again. Kovac wandered until he was well clear of her. In his down jacket pockets, he searched for the familiar lump of his earpiece. He put it in and tapped once for an encrypted call to Australia.

It rang three times. He heard Bishop's deep, calming voice. 'You at the airport?'

'No. Wake King up.'

'At this hour?'

'Yeah. We're compromised.'

There was a pause. Kovac wasn't surprised. There had been problems before but nothing like this. Not in ten years.

'You need anything?' Bishop asked.

'A rucksack should cover it. I'm doing reconnaissance tonight because I've got more questions than answers right now.'

'I'll bring it in person.'

'Thanks. And watch your back.' Kovac hung up.

Standing here, he was on the second floor of the building that housed the train station. He estimated he was a little past the middle of the building. The open expanse of tile was a kind of atrium, with see-through external walls and two staircases leading down to the street outside. Kovac imagined it from the air. The staircases came out from the building but then ran parallel with it, like cactus branches. One staircase ran down to the street on the east side, the other ran down to the street on the west side. He was standing at the west side of the atrium now, at the top of the west staircase.

He heard a train pass underneath. The building shook slightly. He studied the staircase. It was wide – almost as wide as a tennis court. Fifty steps top to bottom, he guessed.

He could see west from here because of the transparent wall. There was a U-shaped road outside, with a few hotels and a McDonald's, and a large Isetan department store. The middle of the U was open and empty. All floodlit parking lots.

At this hour, there was hardly anyone around. But it clearly got busy during the day. The width of the staircase and size of the department store testified to that. The building he was in was huge, too.

Kovac noticed a few flakes of snow outside. Light for now but looking like it could get heavier.

His eyes moved across the parking lot, towards the largest of the hotels.

Twelve levels, he noted absently, the highest vantage point he could find.

How the fuck had he ended up here? And with a girl who knew his name, no less. He needed answers. He needed to search the three Japanese phones. But they would be in Japanese and require translating.

He would give them to Bishop. But for now all he had was Anna. Anna, and a door code she was too smart to hand over.

It wasn't enough. Not by half.

He was slipping the earpiece back into his pocket when he heard Anna return. She was padding across the cold station tiles, still barefoot by the sound of it. He turned and saw that she was carrying two plastic shopping bags, her thin, goose-bumped arms as taught as ropes. No jacket, no shoes. And no use to him at all beyond the code. 'You get a map?' he asked.

'Yeah. And they had these.' She dropped one of the plastic shopping bags to free up a hand, then thrust this free hand into the other bag. She threw him a couple of plastic packets shaped like tiny pillows, before sitting down on the station tiles. She tore a third plastic packet open – for herself.

Kovac watched her pull out black socks. When she put them on, they only just reached her ankle. They didn't look much thicker than stockings.

He imagined her sitting on Masuda's bed – without the dress.

He pushed the thought out of his mind and studied the two packets she'd thrown him. They were long-sleeved thermal singlets. L-size, both navy blue. A smiling Japanese model on a single sheet of cardboard inside.

Kovac ripped open the first bag with his teeth, then the other. He pulled off his jacket and two T-shirts. He ignored Anna's sidelong glance at his lean, tattooed torso and slipped into both the thermals. They scratched and he located tags and yanked them free, adding them to the train tickets for later disposal.

He put his T-shirts on again, over the thermals now. He was colder, not warmer. 'And the map?' he asked, threading one arm and then the other back into his down jacket.

She nodded to the other plastic bag, which smelled as if it was filled with recently-microwaved carbohydrates. Carbs and cheese. 'In there,' she said. 'What's it for?'

'I'm putting you up in a hotel.' He pointed out across the parking lot. 'That one over there. You can mark out where I have to go on the map and give me the door code. You don't have a jacket. And those socks aren't shoes. Without shoes, you'll only slow me down. In the morning, get on a plane or a bullet train, I don't care which, and get out of Tokyo. Cash, no cards.'

He dropped more cash on the tiles in front of her. Then he located the small station map in the shopping bag. He used it to get his bearings while mindlessly tearing open and devouring some kind of hot cheese and ham wrap. It wasn't what he had meant when he said meat. He had been hoping for a little more protein than a single slice of ham. But it was warm and calorie-dense. It would do for now.

He had been mentally tracking his location as they moved through the city. With the map, he narrowed it down even further. His phone was secure, even for GPS. But with everything that was happening, he wouldn't use it now unless he had to. 'Show me where Masuda's place is on this map. And describe it.'

Anna did, standing and marking it with a fingernail. But she was pouting, clearly angry. The money was still on the tiles, untouched.

'I'm coming with you,' she said.

A red flag, Kovac thought to himself. What girl in Anna's situation wouldn't take the hotel room?

He tried one last time to talk sense into her. 'You'll get about ten steps before your new socks there are soaked through, and ten steps after that you'll lose all feeling in your toes again. You'll be hopping from foot to foot like you've been doing all night and –' He half-turned to gesture towards the snow outside but saw a flash from the top of the hotel, which was almost out of view.

He felt his legs give out as he hit the tiles in front of Anna, and there was a thwack at the same instant, the sound of something passing a few feet overhead at an impossible speed. Kovac didn't need to look at the station windows to know there was a hole in one panel. He knew all these sounds, knew them from his training and years on the job. He knew them the way most people knew the sound of photocopiers and keyboards.

Sniper.

CHAPTER 13

Kovac was at a huge disadvantage. He knew sniper rifles. He had used all kinds over the years, and from all heights. This setup – like most involving an ambush with a high-powered rifle – favored the sniper.

For one thing, the wall on this building was transparent.

Adding to that, the hotel was tall without being too tall: the sniper had a good angle of attack and would be able to see a lot of the atrium.

Last but not least, the tiles in this atrium were white and endless, with banks of fluorescent lighting overhead.

About the only thing working in Kovac's favor was the fact he was already moving. He had been since the moment he dropped.

His only option was the convenience store. If they could get a little closer to the wall which housed its doors, the sniper would lose his line of sight.

There was another shot.

Kovac didn't see this one. He just heard the thwack as it punched a hole in the station's west wall. The bullet had passed overhead before he could think, ripping the air open and smashing into something over near the east wall.

The sniper was good.

But Kovac had a chance if –

Another shot.

This time Kovac felt the gust of air on his face. His heart skipped in a frenzy of panic. He was on his side now, his limbs flailing, his free hand seeking any purchase. He grabbed Anna by one arm, by her wrist, her floppy hand acting like a knot in a rope. He pulled at her but she was a dead weight.

He didn't let go. He screamed at her to follow him, and eventually she did.

If there had been a fourth shot during all his shouting, Kovac hadn't heard it. 'You hit?' he asked, as soon as they reached the relative safety of the convenience store.

'What?'

The convenience door tried to open, striking Kovac. He shoved it off with the base of one hand, his mind a million miles ahead. He hadn't thought about anything up until now. He had more felt it, somehow comprehended it all instantaneously and entirely on instinct. But now he needed to plan.

Anna cut through his first attempt to puzzle a way out of their predicament. She was confused, beginning to panic. 'What's happening?'

She still didn't understand they were being shot at. Which meant Kovac had just saved her life. She would presumably have stayed where he first pulled her down, and two or three seconds of staring at him open-mouthed would have been a death sentence. He was surprised he'd done it. It had lowered his chances of survival.

The shooting stopped now that the sniper couldn't see them. Luck was back on Kovac's side and all that mattered was capitalizing, but he couldn't do that with Anna in tow. 'I'm going to give you a phone number. Ready?'

Anna nodded dazedly.

He said the number as slowly and clearly as he could. She shook her head, frowning.

'*Focus*, Anna.' He started again. This time he gave it to her as four larger numbers. Less demand on her short-term memory that way.

She repeated it back. It was halting but she had it. 'Good. Again. Say it to me again.'

She repeated it.

'Now, stay in this convenience store. Get them to call the police and report a shooting, and find a security camera. Stand right in the center of its frame. Don't move until police arrive.'

'Where are you going?'

'Did you hear me?'

'Yes. Stay here, find a camera.'

'Do whatever the police say, but tell them nothing.'

'Are we being shot at?' She nodded like she was deciding yes, that's exactly what this was. Her eyes darted around, looking in all the wrong places.

'You have no ID on you, right?' The dress was so sheer Kovac knew the answer before she even gave it.

'It's back at the bar. All my things were –'

'Good.'

She spotted the holes in the transparent wall now. 'Oh shit.'

'The number again, Anna.' She hesitated but managed to recall it. 'Keep saying it. In your head, over and over.'

She looked at him, trying to get hold of his arm. But Kovac was already up and moving. 'And you?' she called after him.

He ignored her. The hotel was twelve levels. The sniper wouldn't use an elevator for fear of ending up trapped. That meant Kovac could flip this situation providing he moved fast enough. He was facing perhaps five-hundred yards. The shooter was facing a few hundred stairs. Two yards to a single stair was a fair race, or closer to fair anyway.

Kovac had a few other things working in his favor now, starting with the east staircase. It mirrored the west staircase but would leave him on the east side of the station, putting the hulking building between him and the shooter. He was back to working alone again now too, back to his usual speed.

He got to the top of the east staircase without hearing another shot. He was able to run down it with the entire building acting as cover. He took the stairs two at a time, then ran along behind.

At first, the building that housed the station was enormous, comforting even. But it quickly shrunk and petered out.

Not ideal. Kovac knew what this meant.

Sure enough, he soon found himself at the edge of an exposed level crossing, coming to a stop like he was on a cliff edge. He hugged the last of the cover available to him – a small signal booth.

The boom gates were up. No one around. Just him and two sets of gleaming tracks, all buffed to a perfect shine by millions of train wheels and a little snow.

He stayed like this for half a second, breathing hard, assessing.

No way to cross safely, he realized. He'd be directly visible to the hotel.

Was the sniper still up top, eye to a scope, staring at the same four tracks?

Maybe.

And there were a lot of other maybes, too. Type of rifle, type of cartridge, type of bullet. Probably the only thing Kovac could be sure of was the fact the projectile would take less than a second to get from the hotel to the tracks, to him. He wasn't going to outrun it. If he got to the other side, it'd be down to dumb luck, and dumb luck was a shitty plan.

Kovac took a slow, deep breath. And threw himself forward.

CHAPTER 14

No gunshot.

Which meant Kovac's sniper was likely on the move.

Kovac kept sprinting. He cleared the southern end of the building that housed the station, crossing the tracks and making directly for the cover of the Isetan department store. He was now back on the west side, on the hotel side. He was completely exposed.

His mind was working overtime, calculating lines of fire and angles of approach, but also processing the bigger question: how had the sniper managed to take up position? It was impressive, given Kovac himself hadn't known what train station he was going to exit at. He had left that to Anna.

His feet echoed out across the deserted parking lot to his left as he continued sprinting directly towards the hotel. He was targeting a giant Christmas tree out front of the department store, and he maintained this approach for as long as he dared before snapping right.

As he ran, the mess of thoughts in his mind coalesced into a list of possibilities. Three in all.

One, Anna wasn't an ally.

Two, he was being tracked.

Three, the sniper had simply guessed.

He reached cover again, out of view of the hotel as he circled behind the hulking Isetan department store. The store didn't have a parking lot back here. The parking lot was out front. Here, it was just a narrow street with countless small houses. They were all crammed into tiny blocks of various shapes, other streets joining at diagonals.

At this early hour of the morning, it was dark and silent. Kovac slowed a little, almost back to a jog, reducing the sound of his footfall. Scanning, always scanning. The road wasn't much wider than a car, with a large recycling depot crowding it yet further. He was breathing hard now, still working the problem as he closed the distance between himself and the hotel.

He could eliminate the second possibility. They weren't tracking him electronically. He made it a habit to check his luggage and clothing for devices and his phone ran on a bespoke, locked-down version of Android. Arriving in Japan, he had purchased three SIM cards from the one dispenser spiral at a randomly chosen airport vending machine. He had only kept and activated the third card. The three phones he had stolen were turned off, and since then he hadn't acquired anything new.

He spotted a loping stray dog.

No other movement.

He pressed on, his mind looping back to the first possibility. Anna. Anna might have been working for the yakuza, but he doubted this attack was the yakuza. A sniper attack like this was not in their history and not at all their style.

It was however *his* style.

Which meant what? The sniper was tracking Anna?

He doubted that, too. She wasn't carrying anything and a device in the fabric of her dress seemed unlikely.

He struck "tracking" and "Anna" off his list of three. Occam's razor had its risks, but it was all he had right now.

He reached the hotel end of the long department store and paused.

Same dilemma as at the level crossing. It was open pavement from here to the hotel. If the sniper hadn't made for the stairs already, he'd be expecting Kovac. No other way, and no cover.

Kovac was down to his third and last possibility. The sniper had guessed. He had seen Kovac's choice of train line and knew about Masuda's residence. He had recognized the train line as passing through this area, where Masuda maintained a house, and he perhaps even knew Anna had a house code. He had predicted Anna's ambush and countered with an ambush of his own.

All of which had left Kovac standing here.

Kovac had walked straight into the trap.

He didn't need to cross this final exposed stretch. To turn the tables once more, all Kovac needed was a photograph of the sniper's face. One picture, before this man melted back into the larger city. The sniper had possibly vanished already, but Kovac didn't think so. He hadn't heard anything to suggest that. No doors opening or snapping shut again, no vehicles.

One photograph, he thought, to open this thing up and give him a lead.

He took out his phone and double-checked the flash was disabled on the camera. It was. He activated the inbuilt zoom but heard vehicles.

He felt a stab of fear and spun back, hugging the wall before mentally resetting. He slowed his breathing, controlling his adrenaline and channeling it into excitement. It was a primal thing, adrenaline. It could swing either way, paralyzing him or bestowing almost superhuman speed and focus.

One Mercedes S-Class, coming straight at him from behind, upsetting the stray dog and causing it to drop its tail and vanish. Another coming from out front, out near the hotel, this one rolling so slow Kovac could hear the weight in the rubber tires.

A Goddamned pincer attack.

CHAPTER 15

Kovac had to find some way into the department store. There was no way to keep line of sight with the hotel without also revealing himself to the yakuza goons. They would see him any second now.

But then the car coming from behind turned, rolling into one of the diagonal roads. It headed away from him, still patrolling.

Kovac kept hold of his phone and refocused on the hotel. He watched the other S-Class stop, the one directly out front. A rear door opened but no one got out. For a long moment, nothing happened.

Kovac checked his six again. Checked every hour on the imaginary clock, and then checked overhead, too. Nothing, no cars, no drones, just low cloud and light snow.

The front door to the hotel opened. A man came out, moving fast, carrying a bag – the sort of bag Kovac would choose if he were lugging a sniper rifle around. The man was Asian. Or half Asian at least. Kovac zoomed in and took a series of photos as this man got into the waiting Mercedes. Then Kovac pocketed his phone, turned and retraced his steps, walking with his hands in his jacket pockets and his head down.

He heard the S-Classes disappear, then heard new vehicles: cheaper engines now, less heavy on the wheels. He paused at the other end of the department store, back with a view of the level crossing. He saw two police cars. They pulled up in front of the train station, their lights swirling but no sirens.

Kovac wasn't going to get back to Anna ahead of the police, and he was suddenly tired and cold. As he had expected would happen, the girl would likely be taken in for questioning. That meant he had two choices: surveillance of Masuda's place, or retreat. He was leaning towards retreat. It would give him a chance to recharge and rethink.

And really, what did he stand to lose? Masuda wouldn't use the house now; he knew it was compromised.

Kovac watched the officers make their way into the train station. He watched them appear at the west wall and examine the bullet holes. They were trying to puzzle out what kind of weapon would do it, both frowning in a collective failure of imagination.

Had the S-Classes brought the sniper to this station ahead of him? That was Kovac's best guess. The yakuza had enabled the sniper – whoever he was and whoever he worked for – to get out ahead of Kovac's train. But Masuda wasn't Kovac's real enemy. He was increasingly certain of that.

Kovac peeled away from the department store, heading away from the train station. He switched his phone to an emergency-secure mode which would lock out his handler, Bishop, and by extension, King. He'd still be able to use the device, and they'd still be able to contact him on it, but he had paused their backend access. It was a feature Bishop had insisted on in case Australia was ever compromised. Kovac had always known it was available to him, but he had never truly believed he would need it. Activating it now was an oddly upsetting move. He felt alone, betrayed, cut loose. It was perhaps the first time he'd felt this way since his early twenties, and though he knew betrayal was unlikely, logic didn't help with the resentment. He especially didn't like the flexibility the risk of betrayal now ruled out. He had to treat the entire world as potentially hostile.

He walked through snow-muted suburban streets for

twenty minutes, keeping alert and keeping to shadows. He bought hot meat buns and potato fries at a convenience store and ate as he walked before dumping all the garbage in a trash can at yet another convenience store. At this second store, he bought a sports drink.

He finally located a love hotel that was open and willing to give him a room for a few hours. There was no one manning the reception, which suited Kovac just fine. He secured the key with cash from a vending machine.

As he navigated a drab corridor to his room, he thought about Anna. She might cave under questioning. But if that happened, he would know. The call would come from the police instead of Anna. Kovac didn't feel this was likely. He had a feeling Anna would do exactly as he had instructed, and if she didn't too bad. It was out of his control now.

The room was less garish than he had expected, all in black and muted golds. It had a full Jacuzzi bathtub and shower, and a large-screen TV with video on demand. There was also a kettle and what looked to be a king-sized bed.

Kovac locked himself inside, using the emergency escape information on the back of the door to memorize the building's exact layout along with all its exits. Then he showered, making use of the body soap and razors. There were free condoms, stacked in a small box next to the faucet, but sadly he had no use for those.

He managed to get more blood out of his clothes before hanging them up to dry. He cleaned his knife thoroughly, then exited the bathroom and put on underwear. He lay down on the bed and used his phone to send the photos of the shooter to Bishop in Australia. The screen flashed "sent".

Kovac was in two minds: simply lock his phone, or switch it off? It was a question of trust. Did he trust Bishop's emergency-secure mode?

On balance, yes. Some of the resentment had faded. He was thinking more clearly after a shower.

And anyway, he was waiting on a call from Anna. A call that could come at any time.

He set the phone up to recharge, locked it, then tried for darkness. Dimming the lights was easy but switching them off seemed impossible. He did battle with a giant console, unable to read a single word on it. The lights in the Jacuzzi were the hardest to extinguish, but when he finally got those, the resulting darkness was absolute. The room had no windows.

He set his alarm. He had the room for three hours, so he set the alarm for two.

He was asleep in mere seconds.

CHAPTER 16

Megan Curzon – the Chief Executive and public face of Curzon International – detected the subtle change in cabin pressure. She knew what it meant; her Gulfstream G600 had begun its descent down into Alice Springs.

She was returning home to Australia after two days of back-to-back meetings in Manhattan. Of her small cabal of staff, she was the only one not currently absorbed in work, the only one not staring at a screen. She was doing her seated leg stretches instead, while looking out past the jet's wingtip. Out over the red-brown expanse of central Australia.

It was a bright, clear morning. The red-brown desert below was streaked with mountain ranges and vegetation, which from this height resembled inky rivers and lakes. She could see the curve of the earth from up here, the red-brown gradually shifting to blue at the horizon, then a band of fluorescent blue as the desert gave out to a dazzling, a.m. sky.

She was trying to meditate, to be present in the moment by listening to an audio recording of a favorite gorge and small waterfall on the family cattle station. Stress gave her psoriasis, and this was her therapist's idea for keeping it at bay.

But her mind was stuck in Manhattan. It kept running back to the hiss of buses, to car horns, sirens and helicopters.

She slipped off the noise-canceling headphones, relieved to feel the pressure lift from around her ears. She put her head back and closed her eyes. She reminded herself it always happened like this. It always took her a while to decompress.

She had to be kind to herself. She was jetlagged, and this was no ordinary flight. She had learned things about her family during this flight, dark secrets she would never have believed had she seen them in the tabloids.

She went on rolling her feet in slow circles, wondering how she maintained this schedule. Her body and mind circumnavigated the world, but rarely in tandem anymore. She felt like she spent half her life in this jet, unable to sleep.

For what?

Up until this flight, she had believed Curzon operated strictly within the confines of American and international law. She had told herself the company improved the lives of people around the world.

Not anymore.

She paused her foot exercises for a little turbulence and rode the rollercoaster, a sensation she had taught herself to enjoy. She thought about her twin brother, Daniel, who traveled almost as much as she did but who seemed to pull energy from the lifestyle. Did he ever wonder at the costs to his health, or what it was all for? He had been privy to the secrets she had just discovered for years already. Had they changed him?

Daniel was a member of the company's six-person Executive Leadership Team, under the appropriately vague title of General Counsel. He would be arriving at the homestead today, too – an hour after Megan. Megan's father, Chairman of the company for more than thirty years, would be there to meet both of them. So would Megan's baby step-sister, Charlotte – or Lottie as she liked to be called.

Maybe that's what it was all for. Lottie.

Megan couldn't wait to hug Lottie, though she knew the reunion would be tainted.

Everything was tainted now.

She dropped her feet down, put the headphones back on and chose something that better reflected her growing fury, if not her age. Metallica. She played it loud and left it on as she returned to working on her laptop. She started re-reading the encrypted attachments her father had sent through just before she departed New York.

John Kovac.

She had no idea a John Kovac existed until this flight. And yet here he was, in these encrypted documents, threaded through every facet of her history, every facet of her life. She wasn't related to him by blood, had never met him, but she felt as if her father had just announced a hitherto unknown sibling.

Only, it was worse than that. *So much worse*. Her father had revealed a hitherto unknown assassin.

Megan double-clicked the first file, which gave a summary of Kovac's childhood. Born in America, he had lost both parents. After that, he had drifted through a string of family member's homes, before falling into a gang. He had sisters but it didn't say if he was still in touch with them. Megan got the impression no, given Kovac was on record showing psychopathic tendencies before he was even a teenager.

According to his file, that was exactly what had appealed to Bishop. The fact Kovac had turned criminal all on his own, teaching himself to kill. That, and his ability to control his emotions and decisions, exerting maximum influence on others.

She returned to his IQ tests and marveled. The man didn't have a photographic memory, but it was as close as she had ever seen.

Like an evil kid savant, she thought, before muttering: 'And we brought him in-house.'

She read on. This was her second time through, and this time she was looking for anything that jarred.

Curzon International had raised Kovac in secret, educating and training him. He had been Bishop's idea and, seemingly, his pet project. Via Bishop, the company had enhanced all the tendencies that made Kovac a monster in the first place. The document referred to Kovac as Kovac right throughout, but

Megan saw it wasn't his real name. His real name had been erased at some point, along with all photographs.

There was a gap between Kovac's eighteenth birthday and his first mission for the company – which had been in Tanzania. Seven years or so, as if an entire file was missing. It looked as if Kovac's life had been scrubbed clean during this time. The Tanzania file had a reference to tattoo removal, but Megan knew it likely went deeper. In this digital age, there would've been facial surgery, record hacking, bribes. The list of tools at Curzon's disposal was nothing if not extensive.

As best she could see, the result was a ghost, a man living beyond the confines of society. *Of all societies.*

She ran through the mission files one by one, looking for a photo of Kovac, but there wasn't a single image. There were only photographs of his victims, which extended to women but mercifully not children.

She shut everything and looked out the window again. She didn't understand how it was possible. How could her father, a principled, law-abiding man, sign off on a program like this? And what were they all now, if not just another crime family?

She closed her dry, sore eyes, and returned her attention to the turbulence. She couldn't sleep, but she could pretend to sleep. She had long ago learned it was the next best thing, and worth the effort. She listened to Metallica and rode the humps and dips down into the airport in Alice, only opening her eyes when she felt the abrupt jolt of the tarmac.

By the time the jet rolled to a stop, she was feeling slightly better. Not okay, but ready for the looming meeting.

She transferred to a helicopter for the flight out to Pemberton Downs cattle station and resumed working. The meeting would start formally, with personal assistants and video links to other members of the Exec and Business Leadership Team in Sydney. But it wouldn't stay on the record long. Not today. Except for Bishop, anyone who wasn't family would be asked to exit. And after that, her father would shift register. There was a severe reprimand coming, one that couldn't be delivered by the Chairman of the company, only by a father. Only by King.

That would be Megan's chance. She needed the missing file, the missing seven years of Kovac's life. And she needed a photograph.

CHAPTER 17

The call came ten minutes before Kovac's alarm went off.

It was a woman, but not Anna.

A British accent.

'Mr. Kovac?' she asked.

Kovac said nothing.

'Mr. Kovac? Mr. Kovac, I have Anna.'

She had used his name three times in three seconds, like she wanted it on the record, like maybe she was recording this call. 'And?'

'She'd like us to meet.'

The woman gave him an address and a time. He confirmed he'd heard both correctly then hung up. Kovac didn't generally need to repeat things twice to remember them but these were Japanese words, a jumble of hard sounds and soft vowels alternating one-two, one-two. He ran them through his mind three times until sure they would stick.

He had received an encrypted message while asleep. It was from his handler, Bishop. Equipment had been arranged. He could collect it later in the day. Another address, more hard sounds and soft vowels. He memorized this string too.

Bishop was "working on getting an ID from the photos".

Kovac checked out and returned to the busy intersection where he had sat with Anna the previous evening. He watched trains snake in and out of an overhead station as the sun took on all the neon at once and won. Dawn. Cars turned from impressive glowing bread-loaves into dull metal boxes throwing up brown slush. It reminded him of Vegas, another city that always looked bleak and small after a long night of neon.

The address the woman on the phone had given him was for a Doutor chain coffee shop. Kovac took up position in a department store opposite. He chose a window seat in a bakery with a French name. The table was wonky and cheap. He chocked it with a few napkins then ordered a pastry.

He ate as slowly as he could, watching the Doutor chain coffee shop for half an hour. Eventually Anna showed up with a woman who looked to be in her early thirties. The woman was wearing a suit. She was pretty, with dark hair that fell to her shoulders. Anna finally had some real clothes on, too. Her hair was still damp, like she'd just had a shower and cleaned up.

Kovac watched them both take a seat. Then he rang the number that had called him. He watched the woman with dark hair fish out her phone from a purse hung over her chair. He couldn't see what color purse. He couldn't see much more than silhouettes now. The reflection on the store's windows was getting worse as the morning sun strengthened. He saw her put the phone to her ear. 'Hello?' she said.

'Okay,' he said into his phone. 'I'll bite. Who are you?'

'You're not going to show your face?' Her voice oozed contempt.

To Kovac's way of thinking, it felt a little too early in the call for contempt. But it was the same voice as earlier in the day, with the same British accent.

'I'm India Bennett,' she said.

'Ms. Bennett.'

'Is this John Kovac?'

'Let's call me a friend of Anna's.'

Bennett scoffed. 'I work for Resolute, Mr. Kovac. Tokyo branch. Have you heard of us?'

'Nope.'

'We look out for young women who have been dragged into sexually exploitative situations by assholes exactly like you.'

Kovac understood. The police had palmed Anna off to this woman, and she was better at extracting information than they were. She had his name and number but nothing more than that – not if she thought he was Anna's pimp. He decided to let the misunderstanding run. It gave him a neat role in all this.

'Are you still there, Mr. Kovac?'

'Why wouldn't I be?'

'Most hang up at this point.'

He watched her brush something from her suit pants, even as she grabbed the attention of what might have been a passing waiter. Or waitress. It was too hard to tell that deep into the store.

He saw Anna order something too, but the phone didn't give him much of that. She was lost to the general din of the place with its elevator music and hissing, grinding machines.

None of the charm of his faux patisserie, he thought.

'Anna doesn't work for you anymore, Mr. Kovac. Not in any capacity. Do you understand what I'm telling you?' Bennett's voice was cold and confident, but the words sounded scripted. 'If you go anywhere near her, Resolute can ensure you face police prosecution and legal action.'

Kovac doubted the strength of this threat. There was no way the Russians or even the yakuza surrendered girls this easily. Presumably, they hung up because they couldn't be bothered arguing. No moral high-ground for pimps to enjoy here, and all in English no less. Tiring all round.

He wondered how it normally played out. They probably waited for Resolute to run the girls through some kind of rehabilitation program then collected them again afterward with the trusted old mix of promises and threats. It was a process Kovac could see repeating itself a few times a year, with the police happy to palm responsibility off to Bennett, and Bennett not able to do anything much at all except this phone call.

'I need her back,' he said simply.

'She's not yours, you piece of shit. She might be scared of you, but I'm not. There's a reason you're calling and not showing your face. You –'

'Stop.'

The calm command had the desired effect. Bennett shut up. Kovac could see her mouth open. A silhouette of her jaw, hanging there in surprise. A waitress set down coffees and food.

'Ms. Bennett, was it? Now here's what's going to happen, Ms. Bennett. You're going to keep quiet, eat your croissant, drink your coffee and get the check. Then you're going to stand up, walk out into the street, turn left or right – I don't care which – and disappear. I never want to see you anywhere near Anna again. I so much as get a hint you're messing around in my business, I'll kill you.' He didn't elaborate. He just let the threat hang.

He could see Bennett thinking. She shut her mouth. She turned her coffee cup ninety degrees. She tapped the cup's handle a few times. And then she did something Kovac didn't expect. She smiled. 'Go fuck yourself,' she said.

CHAPTER 18

The helicopter transfer took close on an hour.

As always the last of it gave Megan a phenomenal view of the 3,300 square miles of open plains, floodplains and wooded sandhills that made up Pemberton Downs. The property carried about 38,000 head of cattle, including 20,000 Brahman breeders. It had been in Megan's family since 1877, the date of the first base camp near the present site of the homestead. It was the foundation of what had, over time, become Curzon International.

It was also where her father now chose to spend the majority of his time.

They landed behind the sprawling sandstone building, on a swathe of lush green lawn, just beyond the palms and tennis court. The homestead had been meticulously renovated over a three-year span by Megan's step-mother, resulting in a stylish blend of classic grandeur and contemporary living. It was an imposing home, framed by historic stone fencing, and Megan loved it: both the building and its hundred-year-old grounds.

Especially the grounds.

She scanned them now. They sat as a patch of vibrant fertility in the vast red desert, and she could see why her father, Luther Curzon, rarely bothered to leave anymore. Located right in the heart of Australia, Pemberton offered complete privacy and seclusion.

Luther had cancer. He had been given a year to live five years ago, and it had marked an end to his globetrotting days. He now rightly saw international travel as a waste of the years he had left. He was perfectly content here in central Australia. It was where he had grown up, and where Megan and her brother had grown up, too. The family company had started in agriculture here, then moved into mining as Curzon Prospecting, before branching out into countless other pursuits worldwide.

Megan's father wasn't a figurehead Chairman, despite his illness. He still made every important decision within the company, and Megan never let herself forget it. She had made the mistake of often questioning her father's judgment when starting in the Business Leadership Team as CEO of Curzon's global packaging operations. But she could count on one hand the number of times she had been right and her father wrong. At 72, he was still at the absolute top of his game, always quietly and graciously showing her how it was done.

She crossed the lawn and sweeping verandah, entering through doors that were open almost year-round. She breathed in what smelled like fresh scones and took in the soaring ornate ceilings and exquisite cedar detailing. While here, she would stay in one of the three inbuilt guesthouses with her own bedroom and gym, looking out over the endless expanse of the station.

Unpleasant as the cause of this visit was, she would be devastated when it came time to leave.

Megan's step-mother, Carmen, was the first to greet her, having been alerted by the sound of the helicopter. Her breath smelled of tobacco smoke as she kissed Megan on the cheek. Their relationship was occasionally strained but had deepened in recent years. There was mutual respect between them and a common interest in Lottie, who now came bounding out of a nearby hallway. 'Oh my *God*!' Lottie pushed her mother aside and gave Megan an enormous hug, eventually jumping up and wrapping lithe, eleven-year-old legs around her.

Eleven, going on sixteen, Megan thought.

'No one even told me you were coming! What the heck,

Meg?'

She screamed it all, her voice so loud and high, it distorted Megan's already flight-clogged hearing.

Lottie was the only person Megan ever let call her Meg.

The same glowing skin, Megan thought, the same perfectly straight red hair, the same dire need for braces. She was relieved nothing had changed with Lottie.

'Your brother's here, too,' said Carmen.

'Already?'

'He arrived late last night. He looks, ahm...'

'Last night?'

'Yes. Is everything okay?'

Megan kept her tone breezy. 'Of course. Just the usual organized chaos.'

She refocused on Lottie. 'Do I get to beat you in straight sets again later this afternoon? Or have you been practicing your serve, like we agreed?'

Lottie grinned and gave a coy shrug, her eyes going to the corner of the room.

Megan turned. Her father had appeared at the door. 'Welcome home,' he said.

He looked ill. He always did these days, but this was far worse than Megan had expected. There was a new stiffness and frailty, and a faintly yellow tinge to his speckled, sun-damaged skin.

'I'm afraid we had to start early. You'd best join us. Carmen, can you and Lottie take Megan's things through to her room when the pilot brings them in? Anyone else fly out with you, Megan?'

'No, my staff all stayed back in Alice.'

'Good.' He gestured for her to follow him through the endless house to the boardroom. There was no hug, no hello, nothing beyond the perfunctory "welcome home".

Megan knew what this meant. It was all far worse than she had dared to imagine. The entire company was under threat, and the next few days would be a test like none she had experienced so far.

She gave Carmen a reassuring smile and Lottie a last hug, then followed her father. She was just glad Luther was well enough to help her with this. She wasn't ready to take on Daniel alone. Daniel was a younger sibling, if only by a few minutes, and as such he always had something to prove. He never listened to Megan and probably never would. He was also a sarcastic hothead who didn't ever stop to wonder if maybe, just maybe, he was wrong. Only her father could help Daniel see sense. But even Luther seemed different to her now: less perfect than she had allowed herself to believe, and somehow more callous.

She realized it was the files from the plane.

They had changed everything, and it was beginning to feel like the men in her family had put the entire company on a path to ruin.

CHAPTER 19

Bennett finished her croissant and coffee. But she didn't pay the bill, and she didn't stand and leave. Which Kovac found both impressive and irritating.

He risked a quick Google search. Bennett was all over the Internet, most of it her own doing, so it didn't take him long to put together a basic bio. Born in the English Midlands to a British mother and African American father, she looked to have enjoyed a moneyed childhood, most of it coming from the mother's side. There was a long stint in Japan while her father was stationed in Okinawa, and there were boarding schools in other parts of Asia, too. There were photos of a teenaged Bennett in European-looking bars with equally young women, all with cocktails and smiles. And there was a reference or two to Oxford. Maybe that's where the shots with the cocktails had been taken, Kovac thought.

If so, it was the end of Bennett's partying phase. Based on her more recent tweets, she was all business. She was committed to Resolute and made it sound like the organization had offices right throughout Asia. Kovac didn't buy it. He dug a little deeper and decided it was all just Bennett. Employee Number One – of one.

Bennett and Anna remained where they were, forcing a strange Mexican standoff.

Kovac waited, gradually losing hope. 'Shit,' he muttered, realizing he was going to have to get up and go down there.

He didn't trust Anna any more than he had yesterday. But

she was a lead. Aside from the photos he'd sent through to Bishop, his only lead. And yes, unprofessional though it was, he was also here to make sure Masuda's goons didn't hurt her.

While he waited on Bennett, Kovac Googled Anna. He added details to her first name in the hope of a hit. Nothing came up. He tried the snack bar from the previous evening, hoping to get something on her that way. Another bust, though the bar itself popped up. It featured in an article released earlier in the morning. The bar was linked to a murder. A low-ranking yakuza pimp had been drowned in his bathtub.

Yamada.

There was a police officer quoted, saying the two locations were linked. Which seemed like lazy policing, really, save for the fact it was correct. Kovac knew it was correct because the bathtub was his plan.

He hadn't told anyone his plan, save for Bishop. Bishop, who now could not put a name to the Asian face Kovac had emailed through before getting some sleep.

Kovac felt a tingling in his neck, which spread across the tensed muscles of his back as he hunched over his phone. *What the hell was this?*

Someone had completed the job for him?

Why?

He went to stand but realized a black S-Class had appeared outside the coffee shop. He paused, watching.

This time, only two yakuza punks stepped out. Kovac recognized one from the previous evening but not the other. There were no available parking spaces and the flow of traffic was putting pressure on the yakuza driver. This third guy had his hazard lights on but the vehicles behind him wanted him to move. He held out for a few seconds, giving the goons instructions via the passenger side window. Then he seemed to decide he didn't want a scene. He wound up the passenger window, pulled out to the center of the road, and drove on.

The two goons rolled their heads and cracked their knuckles and entered the coffee shop. Kovac knew what that meant. He stood and paid and left the fake French bakery. He took an escalator down to the street, crossed the road, and entered the Doutor chain coffee shop.

The scene that greeted him was unexpected.

The two men had presumably been planning to work quietly and in unison, but they had underestimated Bennett. In the time it took Kovac to get to the cafe, Bennett appeared to have maced the first guy and was now resisting the second with nothing more than a fork. This might have been an effective strategy had the fork been metal, but it wasn't. It was plastic. Bennett had gone disposable.

Still, Kovac thought, credit where credit was due. The second man's face looked like he had done battle with a stray cat and the fork was already missing three of its four plastic teeth. With the remaining plastic tooth, Bennett seemed to be going for nothing less than an eardrum.

Both men were armed with pistols, but they were still inexplicably trying to do this quietly. Neither had pulled a gun. Both weapons were holstered beneath flailing black suit jackets.

It was an easy lift. The closest man to Kovac was already half-blind from Bennett's mace, and Kovac got to him just as he grabbed Anna and started leading her out of the coffee shop. Kovac doubted the man even saw him before surrendering his weapon – a big old Colt 1911, safety on.

It should have been as simple as putting the muzzle up under this first guy's chin and pulling the trigger. But there were probably cameras by now. If not in the store, then in citizens' hands.

That called for subtlety.

So Kovac head-butted the guy instead, hard and straight, sending him down and clearing the way to advance on the second goon.

The second goon had made real progress. He had managed to snap the plastic fork in two and also break a couple of Bennett's fingers. He was trying to bear-hug her into submission but was howling every bit as loudly as she was.

This second goon was fat, which meant heavy. Perhaps 250 pounds, distributed across two knees, 125 pounds each. Given the fact he was trying to hurl Bennett towards the front of the store, it was more like 200 on one, fifty on the other. Kovac chose the knee carrying all the weight and drove his heel hard down into the front side, feeling tendons snap and muscle tear and bone jag free. The leg buckled and the man swiveled, screaming. He landed on his good knee before toppling. All that weight coming into play again, catching up, pulling him over the way statues topple. Then a lot more screaming, and a lot more rolling in pain, hands gripping just above the knee, the ruined leg pointing into the air, but with the angles all wrong.

Kovac stomped on his neck and grabbed the gun, all in one simple movement like he was starting a lawnmower. It was another 1911, leaving him with one in each hand. He emptied one gun and passed it to Bennett, pocketing the ammunition. Then he went for the two phones, appropriating fingertips to remove the security and bringing his collection to a total of five.

He pocketed these, before scanning the shop. No one filming him, no one spoiling to join in the fight. Just a lot of customers cowering. The situation was under control, save for the S-Class, which would be back any second.

CHAPTER 20

Except it didn't come back.

Kovac waited a few seconds, before deciding it was waiting on him.

He guided Anna and Bennett out of the coffee shop, and sure enough there it was – just up the street, facing away from them, its bright orange hazard lights on.

Cars were going around it now, and Kovac could hear bass thudding inside. 'Keep close, okay,' he said to Anna and Bennett.

He stuck to the sidewalk until he reached the rear of the car. Then he slipped around it and came at the driver's side door from behind, his Colt 1911 raised and ready. The driver was focused on his phone, checking a map.

Kovac had two options. Shoot the man before he even realized he was there or use manners. He opted for manners.

He tapped politely – subtly – with the muzzle of the gun on the glass of the driver's side window. No need to make a fuss, this tapping said. Let's do this quietly.

Kovac couldn't see much inside beyond the glare of a phone's gazillion-pixel screen. But that gave him the dim outline of the driver's fingers and head. The man wasn't armed.

Another feature appeared as the man swiveled and attempted to examine Kovac – a big flat nose.

The driver's eyes came to rest on the muzzle of the Colt 1911.

Kovac flicked it an inch towards the street, signaling for the man to step out of the car.

He shook his head and refused. He locked the doors.

Kovac gave him some time to think.

He did. He thought about glass and bullets and obviously concluded the glass between him and Kovac's gun wasn't guaranteed to stop a .45 caliber round traveling at 800-plus feet a second.

He unlocked the car and got out.

Kovac frisked him, then gestured for him to keep moving: out towards the center of the road, out into traffic. The man did as ordered and stopped in the middle of the road, halting traffic again, but with less nonchalance now. He had his hands up, his eyes dancing around in a futile search for help. Like maybe this was the one part of the city where citizens made a habit of helping gangsters.

'Keys,' Kovac said.

'I have child. Two.'

Kovac pointed inside the car and enunciated the word. '*Key*.'

The man frowned, lowering himself down onto his knees. 'Please. I have child. Two childs.'

Kovac was getting impatient now. He mimed pressing a button with his thumb: 'Beep beep – open.'

Comprehension spread over the man's face. 'In,' he said.

'Inside? The keys are in the car already?'

The man nodded, now with real enthusiasm. He wanted Kovac gone.

Kovac took a closer look. Sure enough, there was a key fob lying on the passenger seat, black on black.

Kovac threw all his gangster phones onto the same seat and checked for Bennett and Anna. They hadn't followed.

They were standing outside the coffee shop. Anna comforting Bennett, who was holding her broken hand like it was a tiny delicate bird.

'Time to go,' Kovac shouted.

They hesitated and exchanged a few words. Kovac could guess the gist. Anna asking Bennett if she thought it was safe and Bennett saying she didn't think so, maybe they should wait for the police. Then Anna again, explaining Kovac wasn't a pimp; that actually, he'd helped her once already.

They finally started forward, clinging to one another, cradling Bennett's damaged hand, moving unsteadily. There was no one between them and the car. Everyone who had been close enough to see the gun had stepped clear long ago. Presumably phone calls had gone out to police, which would mean journalists. The whole circus would soon descend on this location, and the search would begin for a white madman in a Mercedes S-Class. Two female hostages.

Kovac helped Bennett and Anna into the back seat. The gangster in the street didn't move. Maybe he was listening to the yakuza thug back in the coffee shop scream and sob. Maybe he was wondering why the first guy was so quiet. Kovac darted out to him. One more phone, walking the guy through the steps to remove the security, like a grandkid with a confused grandparent.

Then he doubled back and got into the driver's seat. He tossed gangster phone number six onto the passenger seat and pulled the door shut with a thunk. He was armed and seated in a luxury car, with a near-full tank of gas.

Happy days, he thought, save for the fact he was now on the lam.

CHAPTER 21

The boardroom had cleared out. It was now just Megan Curzon and her brother sitting on either side of a cedar conference table, with her father at the head of this table. Bishop was on speakerphone via a black, UFO-like device. The connection wasn't the best because he was already forty-thousand feet up, en route to Japan.

Daniel said: 'I don't know anything about this.'

Bishop's voice exploded through the speakerphone. 'Bullshit!'

Daniel took off his black reading glasses. He used his tent-like shirt to clean the lenses, then tossed the glasses onto the table. He was sweating, and he appeared to have put on yet more weight. Megan guessed he was now up around 230 or even 240 pounds, heavy for his five-seven frame. She wasn't as tall – five four with good shoes – but she was almost half his weight at 123 pounds. His neck was a frog chin, running uninterrupted down into the open collar of his shirt, whereas she felt her chin was too pointy. At age 29, soon to be thirty, it was hard some days to accept they were twins. Even the difference in hair color was stark: his blond, hers red like Lottie's. About the only thing they seemed to share these days was a pale complexion.

Lucky you found a wife before the weight really piled on, she thought, with a malice she didn't like to indulge.

She decided to start subtly digging for the missing seven years of Kovac's life. She cleared her throat. 'As I understand it, from my reading on the way in, Kovac's a long-term investment for us? We cultivated him as an asset so we wouldn't have to look for…' She wondered what the right term was. Linguistically, this was new terrain for her. She decided just to call a spade a spade. '… assassins.'

'Talent,' said Bishop via the speakerphone. 'So we wouldn't have to look for outside talent.'

'So why would Daniel or anyone in this family compromise that? And let's all go easy on the accusations, shall we? Let's keep it productive.'

As soon as she heard herself say this, she realized she was on her way to hijacking the meeting. She was so used to being in charge of meetings these days, it was habit. She glanced at her father, who remained silent. He was a small man, made even smaller by disease. But he still held himself with a relaxed authority – an authority Megan had never quite been able to match. He was well back in his chair, one leg over the other, the fingertips of his right hand drumming silently on the table.

'Couldn't agree more.' Daniel dragged a notepad towards him. It had been left behind by one of the evicted personal assistants. He picked up a pen and started doodling, just like he did in ordinary meetings.

Megan waited to see if anyone would speak. No one did.

She gave them all another five seconds.

Nothing.

'Granted, I'm still playing catch up, but am I right in understanding Kovac's –'

Bishop cut over her. 'Until today, there were only three people who knew about Kovac. Me, you and your father.'

Megan realized he was cutting to the chase, addressing Daniel.

'Kovac's like my own son was to me, Daniel. You get that? Can you comprehend that? Can you understand there's a relationship there?'

Daniel leaned in. 'Like I said, I don't know anything about this. But I can't say I'm surprised. Kovac's a nuclear bomb, Bishop. You're just too blind to see it.'

Bishop, normally a reserved man, raised his voice yet more. 'I completely agree. Because if he believes this was in-house, he'll come for us. He'll come for all of us, and he'll keep coming until we're six foot under. He knows every move we're going to make before we even consider it. You think he doesn't know where we all are right now?'

'Because you handed him our security protocols,' said Daniel with a smirk.

'Because he *is* our security protocols, you fat fuck.'

Megan had never heard Bishop talk like this to Daniel. Or to anyone. She had known this meeting would get heated, but this was extreme. Bishop was dredging up a lot with his choice of words, and there was every chance he was doing it deliberately.

Bishop had trained Daniel and Megan. Megan's association with him ran back almost as far as Kovac's, despite her never having met Kovac. She and her brother had spent summers with Bishop and his son at the farm. "Self-Defense Camp", as her father had called it. These stints had been amongst the most grueling stretches of Megan's early life. 5:00 a.m. starts, two classes for theory and three physical sessions a day, all under Bishop's expert tutelage. The first time she'd been sent down to the farm, she'd been six years old. She had been out of shape, a girl with a penchant for sitting around eating and chatting on the phone with friends. Bishop had been exactly the bucket of ice-cold water she had needed, though it would be another twelve years before she fully accepted that as fact and appreciated the confidence and discipline he'd instilled in her. She had often been a complete bitch to the hulking, macho ex-SEAL. She had loathed everything about him and had let it be known at every opportunity. Daniel, on the other hand, had been in awe.

With the onset of adulthood, everything had flipped.

Her father said: 'Do you have evidence, Bishop? Because if not, I suggest you cool it.'

Daniel put the pen down. 'Thank you,' he said, with a hint of surprise.

Megan could practically hear Bishop grinding his teeth at the other end of the line, forcing himself to keep quiet. She wasn't much better. She was trying not to wince. Long experience had taught her when her brother was bluffing, when he was outright lying. And he was doing both right now.

Her father said: 'Work through it chronologically for me, Daniel.'

Daniel picked up his glasses again. He swirled them in his hands and stared at the ceiling, feigning exasperation but overdoing it. Megan could see her brother was on the ropes. This was more like a trial now. And unless he could find some way to clear his name in the next few minutes, he would cease to have any major role in Curzon International.

Daniel started speaking in a weary monotone, still staring at the ceiling, like this was now all a chore. 'I've utilized Kovac within the parameters established three years ago. I've had him investigate fraud, I've had him look into an employee we suspected of industrial espionage, and I've had him deliver an anonymous beating to a man threatening to drag me through the courts. All disclosed. All approved. No wet work.'

Her father remained silent.

Megan shifted her gaze to the speakerphone at the center of the conference table. But there was just soft static, static which quickly began to feel like a rebuke.

Why had all this been kept from her? Why was it *still* being kept from her?

She tried to tamper down a sickening sense of rejection and pull her thoughts into shape. She said: 'So let me see if I have this straight. Kovac's compromised, and if he's right about that, it has to be someone in this room – someone other than me. Oh, and he can kill us. That it, or is there more? Do we have a secret love of the KKK or a dungeon full of kidnapped girls I don't know about, or does this stop at cold-blooded murder?'

She had not meant to sound nearly so glib.

She saw her father recoil in the silence that followed, as if stung by her words at some profound level. He finally said in a whisper: 'Can we have the room, Megan?'

She looked at him in disbelief. '*Excuse me*?'

'You heard me.'

She stood abruptly, pushing back her chair so hard it hit the wall. Her eyes were locked onto her father's. They looked old and watery. Sad, too. 'I don't understand.'

'You can be of assistance later, believe me.' He gestured to the door, clearly upset but still somehow managing to convey his love for her, his compassion.

She softened her tone, feeling the first tinge of embarrassment. She was the only female in the room. Family or no, she had to fight against the unspoken belief she would forever be vulnerable to idealism, to sentimentality.

To emotional outbursts exactly like this one.

Or did it go deeper than that?

Yes. Patterns in families were set early on: roles, expectations. She glanced at her brother, but he couldn't hold her eye.

She had been excluded because no one here believed she had the stomach for Kovac.

She didn't leave. Not right away. Instead, incensed again, she poured herself a coffee and crossed to the boardroom's floor-to-ceiling windows. She looked out beyond the stone fence, out into the desert. Her ears were ringing slightly from the stress of it all. If Kovac was right, someone in this room was actively working against the company, against her family.

She took a sip of coffee and finally began to think rationally. Staying in this room was not the right move. No one was going to say another word until she left, and right now she didn't even know what she didn't know. She needed time. She needed information. And most of all, she needed a plan.

She took another sip, then put the coffee down on the table. 'I need a workout anyway,' she said, 'I'm jet-lagged. Bishop, send additional security to us here at Pemberton. That's all I have to say on this. Fix it.'

It wasn't much of a recovery, but it wasn't going to be improved by more words.

She walked out of the conference room, and as the door clicked shut behind her she heard her father's voice: soft, but suddenly focused. 'Okay,' he said. 'Next moves. Bishop, how long until you can hand over the rucksack?'

CHAPTER 22

Kovac scanned for underground parking lots and rolled into the first he saw. He jabbed the ticket machine like he was giving it a warning and it spat out a ticket in alarm. He spiraled down through the levels. Each corner with a little more speed and confidence, like it could never be him who tore great chunks out of the pylons and walls. He parked with less than an inch between the front bumper and water-stained concrete. Three heads lolled forward.

He shut the engine off, and for a second they all sat listening to it tick.

Kovac removed all the bullets from both pistols and pocketed them. Then he slipped both guns out of view, under the passenger seat with all the phones he'd collected. He got out of the car but paused, one forearm to the open door. He stooped momentarily to look back into the rear seat. Both women were sitting straight-backed, seatbelts on. 'Don't touch anything,' he said, 'and wait here.'

Bennett asked: 'And if we run?'

'Then you run. You're free to go whenever you want, but if you're sticking with me, you do what I say.'

'Starting with staying here and not touching anything?'

'Starting with that. Your phone off, like I asked?'

Bennett nodded, still cradling her broken fingers.

Anna reiterated that she didn't have a phone.

Kovac shut the door, which sounded a lot heavier than it was down here thanks to the echo. He used the key fob to lock the vehicle. Another echo, bouncing off a low ceiling. Every surface flashed orange.

He set off on foot for a store, retracing the winding racetrack back up to natural light. His jacket pockets sounded like they were full of marbles – all the bullets – but mercifully he was back to carrying just one phone now. His own.

He checked it as soon as he was back above ground.

Still no reply from Bishop.

He needed a hardware store, but as ever there were only convenience stores. Thankfully they had more than their American counterparts. He found one which carried a first aid kit and a few basic tools. He bought what he needed along with painkillers and ice, then carried everything back to the parking lot.

Round and round, down and down.

At the car, he got on his haunches. He used flimsy cutters, screws and rapid-set glue to swap the Mercedes' license plates with a nearby vehicle from a different prefecture. Then he unlocked the car and slid back into the driver's seat. He was breathing somewhat hard by this point.

The car smelled like pine, some kind of freshener. He wondered if either Bennett or Anna had given something a squirt while waiting for him to return.

They were still in the back, but with their seatbelts off now. Bennett was clearly in a lot of pain. 'Okay, let me see that,' Kovac said. He opened the first aid kit and dumped the contents onto the passenger seat along with his knife. Then he used the first aid kit to create a basic splint. He wrapped the ice in bandaging and strapped that to the splint, too. A hospital would have done a better job, one that didn't melt and drip quite so much. But a hospital would also have involved police.

Kovac had no interest in explaining anything to the police right now. They would have their version of what had occurred at the coffee shop and that was fine with him. Life was all opinion, after all.

The interior of the car was cold. He had been sweating slightly after swapping the plates, and a shiver ran through him now as he rapidly cooled. He started the engine and turned up the heaters.

The three of them sat warming up. With Bennett patched up, Kovac took a look at the phones he had collected. He examined them in the order he had appropriated them. The first three from the snack bar were all in Japanese. So were the next two, from the cafe. He dared to hope the last would be different, but it wasn't. More squiggles.

He started back with the first phone. He scrolled through the five most recent conversations. Nothing but Japanese text. Same for the next four. Not even an emoji. Then he hit something different. The third conversation from the top in the last phone broke the pattern. This was the phone from the driver, the guy Kovac had left standing out in the street less than an hour ago: the same one who had been distressed and intent on giving Kovac his family history. The third conversation down in his phone contained a video.

There was nothing else in it. Someone – an overseas number – had sent him a short 33-second clip, no text, no reply.

Kovac pressed play.

The video started innocently enough. A profile shot of a young girl: Asian, maybe twelve years old. The shot was gloomy. Then a light clicked on and Kovac saw this girl was sweating. She started blinking, turning her head away from the new source of light, wincing.

The cameraman took a few steps back and panned down. The girl was one of many. They were all naked save for underpants, and one had a bad wound in her forearm. Another appeared to have wet herself.

The cameraman zoomed in on one girl's face and Kovac could see her heart. A flutter in the damp skin between thin ribs.

'Jesus,' he said under his breath.

He sensed movement behind him. Bennett coming forward to see what the noise was. He paused the video and caught her eye. She sat back again.

He turned the sound down to nothing with a button on the side of the phone and watched through to the end, which was another ten seconds or so. He counted nine girls in all.

Excruciating to watch.

He had seen a lot in his career, but this was up there with the very worst. It was the girls' faces, the abject misery and complete absence of hope in their eyes. Whoever had made this and sent it was a monster.

Kovac also noted the details most people would miss. Metal walls, metal girders under a metal roof, two circular windows, and the sound of birds just before the light was switched on.

They were on a boat.

He shut the phone off and sat trying to understand what he had just seen. His mind went to the man in the street, the man he had taken this phone from. Kovac had misunderstood. He had assumed the man was saying "don't shoot me, I have a family to support". And in a way, he was. But maybe not in the way Kovac thought. Maybe it was more like "if I don't do what I'm told, this is what will happen to my daughter".

Kovac had heard of cartels using their crimes to simultaneously strike fear into the hearts of their rank and file. It was an effective way to squeeze even more mileage out of the crime.

'What was that?' Bennett asked from the back seat.

'I don't know. It was the phone from the guy who was driving this car. A threat maybe.' He looked at her in the rear-view. She was definitely out of her twenties but had a tan face with alluring hazel eyes. He was surprised by her. For all the peppiness, all the fiery red lipstick and apparent cuteness, she hadn't run, and she hadn't complained once as he worked on her broken hand. She was a hell of a lot tougher than she looked.

He wondered how much Anna had told Bennett while he was off getting supplies.

Probably everything.

He said: 'So you decided to stay.' He nodded to Anna. 'You tell Bennett I'm not your pimp yet?'

Bennett nodded. 'She told me back at the coffee shop before those men came in.'

Kovac waited for his apology.

No apology was forthcoming.

Bennett said: 'We need to go to the police.'

Kovac shot her a look via the rear-view. 'Oh yeah? And how does that play out, in your experience?'

'How does it play out? Well, police don't commit murder, for one.' Bennett's eyes broke contact with Kovac's and drifted out across the underground parking lot, like she was half expecting an ambush. 'Anna told me about last night at the snack bar.'

Kovac had been scanning since returning. There was no ambush coming.

'You a gangster?' Bennett asked.

'Nope.'

She looked back at him. 'Then the police will understand.

The same in the cafe. Anna will corroborate your story, so will I. Self-defense.'

'A kind offer. But I don't think you scare that easy. An hour ago, I threatened your life. Most people in that situation get up and walk away. You didn't. Why not?'

'Anna needed my help.'

'Anna still needs your help. The man she was...' Kovac searched for a gentle word. '...*involved* with –'

'Masuda,' Bennett said, nodding.

'You're familiar with him then?'

'Yes.'

'Masuda will finish what he started. Now that he's tried to kill Anna once, she's a loose end. Anna knows it. You know it.'

Bennett put a reassuring hand to Anna's shoulder, the gentlest of touches. 'It's not that simple, Anna. We're innocents in this. The police –'

'I'll take my chances with Kovac,' Anna said, cutting her off.

Everyone was silent for a moment.

Finally Bennett said: 'What's in this for you, Kovac – if Kovac is your name? Why do you care what happens to Anna? You didn't say what exactly you do for a living, either. Or why you're afraid of the police.'

Kovac shook his head, smiling. 'Believe me, I'm not scared of the police.'

'Then what? Why help?'

He shrugged. 'There's a third party involved, someone who seems interested in hurting me. I don't know who yet. But Anna can help me find out. I tidy it up and get back to my life. Both of you get back to yours. Win-win.'

Bennett winced, having accidentally moved her strapped hand. 'This is insane,' she said as the pain settled. 'Completely insane.'

'But you're thinking about it.'

She scanned the parking lot again. 'Let's say I am. Let's say for a minute I agree to hold off on police. What would our next move be here, hypothetically?'

'I heard you swapping the plates on this car,' Anna said. 'I assume we're not ditching it. We're driving somewhere?'

Kovac adjusted the rear-view mirror, so he didn't have to strain his neck to see Bennett frowning. He gave it to both of them straight: 'We're driving somewhere, yes – to get weapons.'

'Shit.' Bennett dropped her head back and focused on the car's ceiling. She clucked her tongue a few times. 'I saw that video.'

'And?'

'Who are those girls? Who are the people doing that to them? Not even the Yakuza would do that.'

'I don't know yet.'

'But when you find out?'

'Honestly? I'll probably kill them.'

'Good,' Anna said softly.

Bennett didn't get out of the car, so Kovac decided to push for a commitment: 'You know the police won't do anything, Bennett. Maybe they can't, maybe they just don't want to, but it's all the same. Anna dies. Those girls die. If you want to help Anna, now's your chance. I know what I'm doing, and I could use your help.'

He waited. In truth, he couldn't use her help. But it was much simpler to keep her close right now.

Bennett studied her broken fingers for a few seconds, then nodded. 'Okay,' she said. 'Fuck it. Why not? I'm sick of seeing this stuff and not being able to do anything about it. I'll help – up to a point.'

'Okay. Good call.' Kovac straightened back up and started the engine. 'In that case, two things to keep in mind. One, I'm in charge.'

'And two?' Anna asked.

He put his seatbelt back on, along with the yakuza driver's sunglasses. 'Two, when this is done and we've all gone our separate ways, it never happened.' He started reversing the car out. 'You never met me.'

CHAPTER 23

Megan finished a brutal 45-minute HIIT session on the treadmill. She stepped off the belt, feeling better. As she toweled off, she ran over the meeting again. She tried to order it, but it came in snippets, in tiny grabs. She hadn't handled it well. That was the simple truth of it. She hadn't been the calmest person in the room. Her father had claimed that title today – with her brother as a close runner up. She could understand why Bishop hadn't kept his cool, but what was her excuse? Wasn't this why she meditated at night? Wasn't this why she routinely stepped behind the waterfall, dispassionately observing the torrent of her thoughts? *How had all those hours coming back to her breathing helped her today?*

She didn't bother with a shower. She didn't bother contacting the kitchen for food, either. She had a glass of white wine then made cup noodles and sat at her desk. She opened her laptop, kicking off her running shoes and dragging each sock off with the opposing toe.

While she waited for the noodles to soften, she activated the company VPN and logged into the network at Curzon's head office in Sydney. She opened the program which tracked and reported on employee expenses. She had complete access and her login allowed her to run back through her brother's travel history and expenses. It was as predictable as it was exorbitant. There were countless charges which could only have been for his wife, who no longer seemed to spend any time with him. Costs for a nanny, for their three-year-old. The private jet. Hotel rooms. Renovations.

Daniel's salary was absurdly inflated as it was, but it didn't look like he was using it at all. Every significant personal cost was coming out of company coffers. It would catch up with him, and Megan would let it. It would embarrass the family when shareholders caught wind of his flagrant theft, but choices had consequences. Her father had taught them both that from day one.

The one good thing about Daniel's stealing was that it left Megan with a near-forensic picture of her brother's movements the past few years.

She video called her personal assistant – a young man named Nixon Hsu – who was back in Alice Springs. He was in a serviced apartment maintained by Curzon. She found him working in the complex's austere office, making use of the photocopying and printing facilities. 'What are you doing right now?' she asked when he accepted the call.

'Working on your press conference for Berlin next week. I should have a draft of the statement –'

'Cancel it. Cancel everything I have for the next two weeks and clear my calendar.'

'*Everything*? That's ah –'

'Everything. And I need to put you on something else.'

There was caution in his voice. 'Okay.'

Megan had good software at her disposal. She didn't need to trawl through the data. She was able to arrange it. She shared her screen so Hsu could watch. Then, dragging steaming noodles from the cup to her mouth with a plastic fork, she began clicking. She focused on Daniel's travel. 'What doesn't fit here?'

'Macau,' Hsu said.

'Exactly. It all makes sense, save for Macau. Curzon does no significant business in China.'

Megan knew plenty about Macau. It was in the western Pearl River Delta and was a former colony of the Portuguese Empire. It had been leased out to the Portuguese as a trading post by the Ming Dynasty, and it remained a special administrative region of the People's Republic of China. It was one of the most densely populated patches of land on the planet, and the one place she used more than any other to blow off steam.

'You go there plenty,' said Hsu.

'That's different. We both know why I go there. Why's Daniel going there? He can't play snap, let alone poker.'

They continued trawling through the data. When done with the noodles, Megan held out the empty cup and dropped it in a wastebasket without taking her eyes off the screen. 'Looks like some touristy charges to his company credit card at Cheoc Van. And restaurant charges at La Gondola, McDonald's and Hard Rock Cafe.'

It was all mundane. What caught her eye was further down. A visit to a tattoo parlor she knew, and three visits to a Brazilian beauty parlor called Waxworks. Both were fronts for regular, high-stakes poker games. Games she had taken part in.

'He's digging up dirt on me,' she said, draining the last of the wine.

'How do you know?'

The video glitched. Megan wasn't surprised. Due to its remote location, Pemberton was connected to the outside world with a dedicated, encrypted satellite link. For most things, there was a lag, and it often dropped out for hours or even days at a time. The property always struggled with high-def video. She waited on the frozen image of Hsu, making a mental note to fly in some computer nerds. She needed to sort out Pemberton's desert comms once and for all. It wasn't a question of cost. It was her father not caring for computers and secretly enjoying the isolation.

Hsu's video cut to black, then returned. He was saying: 'Megan? You there?'

'I'm sending you my brother's spending history. Look into the Macau charges for me. I'm seeing seven visits in the past year alone. That's as far back as I've gone, but there may be more. Focus on the most recent first and work back from there. Compare his trips there to mine.' She clicked send on an export of the relevant data. 'Get the email?' she asked.

'Yep. When do you need this?'

'As soon as you have something. Anything. After you've cleared my calendar, it's the priority, Nix. And don't discuss this with anyone.'

He raised his eyebrows at this new workload but didn't grumble. 'Understood.'

She ended the video call and sat for a moment, wondering if she was foolish to bring Nix into this. *But what choice did she have?* The wine, noodles and jetlag were already taking a toll, and if she fought it her productivity was going to plummet. Better to get to bed in the next half hour, then come at it fresh when she woke in the middle of the night. Hopefully Nix would have something concrete by then, and hopefully she could find enough leverage to get her seat in the conference room back.

She stood and stretched. She thought about Kovac. She wondered where he was right now, what he was working on. And, more to the point, who he was working for.

CHAPTER 24

The equipment was waiting for Kovac in one of a dozen nondescript buildings in Takumimachi-Dori, Kofu. Kovac hadn't seen the Bombardier Global 8000 private jet land, nor had he seen its pilots. But its sole passenger was now striding towards him.

The man was his handler, Bishop. Bishop was turning 50 later in the year but he still looked like an action figurine. Anyone drawing him would've started with the general shape of a kite stood upright on its tail, then filled in details from there. It was the man's chest. It was enormous.

He approached Kovac with his hulking forearms set out a little from his torso: one giant bear paw of a hand gripping a rucksack, the other offering a handshake. Bishop was a gym rat. He weighed in at a lean 230 pounds, hardly any gut around the middle of his navy-blue polo shirt. He walked with his spine ramrod straight and his shoulders back, like he was heading into a fight. The only part of him that ever deviated from vertical was his shaved head: always slightly forward and down, but with the eyes up, scanning, calculating. It was his default setting. "Aggressive defensive", he only half-jokingly called it.

The handshake became a loose hug. Bishop was the closest thing Kovac had to a father. It was Bishop who had recruited Kovac at age fourteen in New York; Bishop who had smuggled him into Australia and overseen his training at the farm; and Bishop who had paved his way back to the U.S. and into the

SEALs.

Kovac handed him the six phones: all stacked and making a small metal and glass brick. 'I'll need a network of known contacts. There are plenty of photos and videos on these devices, along with email and texts. Get whatever you can.'

'Lock screens?' Bishop asked.

'Deactivated.'

'Like their owners, I presume.' As ever, there was no smile. Bishop's face didn't do much in the way of expressions. The eyebrows were fixed in a permanent, furrowed scowl. It wasn't personal. It was just Bishop. Like the rest of him, his face didn't waste energy on niceties.

As a teenager, Kovac had always assumed this was a SEAL thing. But it wasn't. Bishop's stateside SEAL contacts had turned out to be a diverse bunch, with wildly differing personalities. They had been consistent only in their willingness to offer Kovac whatever support he needed to find his way to Great Lakes, Illinois, and from there to Coronado.

Kovac hadn't let Bishop down. With his trident in place, he had served with distinction as a Navy SEAL right through to the day Bishop staged his death in a recreational diving accident in a remote corner of Africa.

As far as the U.S. government knew, that was the end of the kid from New York who had lost his parents and fallen into a gang before turning his life around. It was also the day Kovac received his new name and life. He had never thought of himself as anyone but John Kovac since, and he immediately set to work paying off debts. Not to Bishop this time, nor to the U.S., but to Curzon International.

To King.

Bishop pocketed the phones and handed Kovac the rucksack. 'Equipment.'

Just as Kovac had never let Bishop down, Bishop had never cut Kovac loose.

Kovac took the bag. It was heavy, which was good. He felt familiar gratitude. There had been times in his training when he'd wanted to kill Bishop – plenty of them – but he had long ago accepted the fact Bishop had his back. 'Sorry you had to accompany it,' he said.

'Wouldn't have it any other way.'

Kovac noted the sincerity in the words, and not for the first time he marveled at the path his life had taken. At age eleven – after a brutal twenty-second initiation beating in a park – Kovac had won access to the little-known New York gang, Catelo. His entire life up to that point had been a small, poverty-stricken tragedy. His mother and father had died of cancer and suicide respectively. His sisters had gone into foster homes. And he had moved through begrudging aunts for three long years until there were no more aunts.

Then Catelo. He had managed to stifle all outward signs of pain during that initiation beating. He had kept quiet as boys kicked and punched, and those same boys had soon become the family Kovac craved.

He should have been in prison by now. *Either that or dead.*

Instead, he was standing here.

'What did King say?' Kovac asked, pushing thoughts of Catelo aside.

'He's not happy.'

'With me?'

'With any of this.'

'Someone inside Curzon had access to our plans, Bishop – possibly even our comms.'

Bishop just sniffed, as if he wanted to keep an open mind on this point.

'They were waiting for me. It was an ambush. Then someone finished the job, exactly like you and I planned it. They killed Yamada in his bathtub, Bishop.'

Saying all this, Kovac instinctively checked his six. The building Bishop had chosen for this meet was some kind of warehouse. The place had an olive-green floor with yellow lines painted on it, every scuff and scratch illuminated by banks of stark fluorescent lighting. It had a lot of cardboard boxes, all taped up tight and addressed, having arrived from somewhere and now ready to go somewhere else. The only noise was a big humming heater with rattling vents.

No doubt the Japanese workers who usually spent their nine to five here had taken payment to go kill a few hours someplace else. Kovac didn't know how Curzon had its corporate hooks in this warehouse, but there weren't many locations where Bishop couldn't commandeer a building.

He wondered how long Bishop had been here. And why this town? It was obviously close to an airport of some kind. 'Anything off about your flight in?'

'Just the usual. Two immigration officials at the stairs, bowing a lot, doing a quick passport check. They didn't so much as eye the rucksack.'

'So we still have our old agreements.' Kovac wasn't surprised. Curzon paid to avoid scrutiny and bureaucracy. It was the same everywhere in the world. Private jets carried weapons, drugs, girls and more. Only a fraction of it was ever detected, and when checks did happen it was profiling at its finest. Legitimately rich individuals like King were left alone. Customs went after kingpins.

Bishop said: 'I've got to ask, Kovac, what's with the girls out in your car?'

Kovac smiled. He wasn't surprised Bishop had clocked this, or that he was questioning the wisdom of it. 'They're involved in this. I'm just not sure how yet.'

'Bullshit.'

'It's not like that, Bishop.'

'Pretty sure you said the same thing at the farm – the day you first saw Megan Curzon.'

The comment took Kovac back. A long, cedar-lined driveway flashed in his mind, a vineyard, a creek. He would never forget arriving at the farm that first day, the intensity of the Australian sun. It was the year Bishop broke him, the beginning of the long and painful rebuild.

Kovac did the math. 21 years together, though it should've been more. Bishop had been slow getting to him. By the time Bishop had taken an interest, Kovac had been going on six-foot-tall. He had done his time delivering the initiation beatings and had risen yet higher in Catelo. He had been merciless in that last year in the gang. He had instigated a program of knifings to win new turf, and he had figured out when factory workers received their pay, developing a range of lures that led to stickups. He had brought in money, and money had changed the gang. It had won Catelo guns and girls. There had been parties, drugs, mistakes.

Just as he always did, Kovac reminded himself that it could never have gone any other way. His rise within Catelo was exactly what had drawn Bishop to him, along with his willingness to kill. If anyone so much as looked at Kovac the wrong way, he put them in a hospital or worse. It was part of his DNA, the one thing about him that had never changed.

It was also the reason he was carrying both the Colt 1911s. He had loaded both in the Merc before coming in.

Somewhere, a long way back in the building, Kovac heard a roller door go up. Bishop took out a Glock, and Kovac held his eye a moment, looking for any tell.

An ambush? Kovac had studied his competition. He knew his

value, and he knew King had achieved the impossible. Even with adequate pay, professional killers sometimes got greedy. Either that or they gave into fear and turned rat. There were a million ways it could go wrong, but not for King. Where others in King's position struggled with multiple contracts spread across multiple, unreliable contractors, King had Kovac.

Even so... Curzon was a business. And King was a businessman. Viewed this way, without sentimentality, Kovac was a simple asset. And not the type which improved with age. He was the sort which slowly accrued wear and tear, along with secrets.

'We expecting anyone?' he asked.

Bishop held his eye but said nothing.

CHAPTER 25

Kovac realized it was just Bennett – Bennett with Anna in tow. He could tell from their hushed voices and footfall.

He loosened his grip on the 1911.

Bishop put his Glock back in its concealed holster.

Kovac said: 'If you can't explain what's going wrong at your end, can you at least tell me what I'm up against here?'

Bishop nodded. 'The Asian man in the photos you sent is called Sukhomlinov. A Russian father, a Chinese mother, raised British with an accent like Prince Charles. But loyal now to who- or God-only-knows what. Our Australian Federal Police contact said he's on their radar in connection with a drug cartel called The Association.'

'Sounds like something out of a Bond movie,' Kovac said skeptically.

'Less Bond, more an amalgamation of nationalities and interests looking for a suitably bland name, something racially non-specific.'

'He's in my line of work, presumably, given he took a shot at me?'

'You sent the photo, I sent it on, and that's what our AFP friend sent back. No details beyond a surname. If you say he's in your line of work, I believe you. But we don't know that as fact.'

Both women had to call out to triangulate Kovac. He yelled

back through the walls of boxes: 'This side.' Then, lowering his voice, he muttered: 'None of this makes sense, Bishop.'

'There's more. The Association's headed by a guy called Peng Biao. That's why I arranged to meet here. When in Japan, Peng has a place up in the mountains.' Bishop handed him an address, along with an encrypted flash drive. 'You're already en route.'

Kovac recalled what Anna had told him. She had said Masuda was planning to kill him, as a favor to some guy up in the mountains. 'And we have Peng in Japan right now?'

'Possibly.'

'Defenses?'

'It's not like you'd expect. It's small, low key. An apartment in a building we think he indirectly owns and maybe even built. The rest is on that flash drive.'

'What about Masuda?' Kovac asked. 'He connected to Peng that we know of?'

'Masuda's headed for the same town.'

'What, right now?'

'Right now.'

Kovac thought for a moment, realizing he was missing a large piece of the puzzle. 'You and King put me on Masuda, on Yamada – why?'

'Masuda owed us money. He wasn't paying, and he started making threats.'

'What kind of threats?'

'Against Daniel. Recently, the threats became more specific, more alarming. So we decided to send a message.'

'*Daniel*?' Kovac hadn't expected this. Daniel was King's only son. A threat against Daniel was tantamount to a declaration of war. 'Masuda doesn't have the resources to go to war with

Curzon.' But as soon as he said it, Kovac realized his mistake.

'You're Curzon's reaction to all serious threats,' Bishop said, 'and from what you've told me, Masuda was ready for you, right? Far from being a surprise, you were lured into a trap.'

'They're aligned? Peng's backing Masuda in a play against Curzon?'

'It's possible.'

'And they have someone in the highest levels of Curzon helping them?'

'Less likely,' Bishop said, 'but for now we have to assume that's possible too, yeah.'

Bennett and Anna rounded the corner and saw Bishop. Both stopped dead, like children encountering some hulking, mythical beast.

'I know,' Kovac said. 'He has that effect on people, but he's on our side. Anna and India, meet Bishop. Bishop, Anna and India.'

'Pleasure,' said Bishop without any apparent pleasure.

'I thought I told you two to wait for me in the car,' Kovac said.

'We weren't sure you were coming back,' said Anna.

Bennett cut over her: 'What's the secret meeting all about?'

'Meeting's over,' Kovac said.

'I didn't ask if it was over, Kovac, I asked what it was about.'

'Business. I work with Bishop, that's all.'

'Doing what?'

To Kovac's surprise, he found himself tempted to give her a straight answer. He was tempted to explain that King and Bishop had seen a need for someone exactly like him long ago. In-house. A problem-solving department of one.

But he just said: 'Business.'

Bennett folded her arms. 'Yeah? What's in the rucksack?'

'Gear.'

'Drugs?' Anna frowned.

'Not that sort of gear,' said Bennett. 'Guns, right Kovac? That's your business? You're a weapons dealer?'

Kovac turned back to Bishop. 'You arrange a vehicle? The higher up into the mountains we go, the more that Merc is going to turn heads.'

Bishop handed him a single key. 'A block from here. An old delivery van. Pale blue.'

Kovac took the key and pulled the rucksack up a little on his shoulder. He shook Bishop's hand again. 'Take care.'

'You too. I'll be in touch.'

Kovac started back towards the women but heard Bishop call out. 'Kovac.'

He turned. 'Yeah?'

'You want my help?'

'That's not how this works, Bishop, and you know it.'

'Normally, sure. But we don't know much about this guy, just an address. It doesn't sit well with me. Maybe this time we –'

'I'll be in touch as soon as I have him.'

CHAPTER 26

The van was old. Just a radio for entertainment, which mixed music Kovac had never heard with words he didn't understand. The heater made a lot of noise but wasn't any sort of a match for the weather outside, which steadily deteriorated as they gained altitude.

They stopped at one of the larger towns en route – Ueda – and bought food and warm-weather gear. Kovac paid in cash for everything. He had just under a million yen on him. Or at least, he had been carrying just under a million when he first landed in Japan. That was the limit before he had to declare it. He wasn't sure how much he had on him now but the wad in the envelope in the inner pocket of his jacket still felt reassuringly thick, and all of it 10,000-yen notes.

While Bennett and Anna went in search of ramen noodles, Kovac bought twelve chicken nuggets and a coffee from a McDonald's. He sat and plugged the flash drive into his phone. It used a plug size that was custom made for Bishop, and which no one else in the world had access to. He unlocked the encryption, then worked his way through the contents while chewing absently on chicken nuggets. He read up on Peng, learning about his organization and his extensive medical history, and he was on a second read through by the time Bennett and Anna returned.

They drove for another hour and a half and parked near the address Bishop had given Kovac. By this time, it was close on dark.

The three of them got out of the van.

The town seemed to be in a long valley, wedged between two opposing sets of foothills. The main road ran down the center of this valley, small buildings and rice paddies on either side of it until the land became too steep and densely forested.

Silent, Kovac thought. *Too silent.*

It was as if someone had pressed mute on the entire town.

He hoped it was just the snow, which was nothing like the snow in Tokyo. There were big fat flakes here, all coming in at a steep diagonal: so many, the ground and sky were both a solid white.

The address Bishop had given him for Peng Biao was a few hundred yards out in front of them, currently obscured from view by a junior high school gym. Kovac pulled his jacket hood up and zipped the front, covering his face up to the nose. He did a quick, surreptitious reconnaissance walk while Bennett and Anna waited at the van. He quickly located the apartment building. It was a new complex, overlooking the junior high school. He counted eight apartments in all. Four downstairs, four upstairs. They all had front balconies, and there were stairs at either end at the rear. The building appeared to sit atop its own underground parking lot.

Kovac circled it again, keeping his distance and keeping his head down. Behind the complex, there were a few blocks of houses. Then it was the foothills and forest – a wall of cold white trees.

He noticed the houses looked older and more traditional the higher up and closer to this treeline they got.

He returned to the van.

Anna and Bennett had got back into it.

He got back in, too.

Anna said: ‘I need to buy something – from over there.’ She

pointed to a convenience store off to the right of the school, like a dull lamp in the falling snow.

'We need to find accommodation first.'

'It's fine, I still have the money you gave me. It'll only take a few sec –'

'Not yet,' Kovac said.

She did a double-take, like she resented him giving orders. 'Kovac, there's no one around.'

He ignored her, trying to warm up, watching the edge of the forest send down a million tiny ice spears.

No one around.

At one level, she was right.

The town was deserted.

But Anna didn't know about Peng.

He blew warm breath through a new pair of gloves he had bought at Ueda, eventually noticing they still had the tag hanging from them. Everything in this country seemed to have a tag, and still no trash cans. He read the English words. "Wool-like with bio-lining".

Whatever that meant.

He added the tag to his Japan junk pocket, along with the train tickets and tags for his thermals.

Kovac waited for darkness, then forced himself out of the van again. He grabbed his rucksack. 'Okay, c'mon. Time to find someplace we can stay the night.'

He led Anna and Bennett towards the foothills, giving the target apartment the same wide berth as before. They walked up through dark winding streets to the last of the houses, where the foothills and forest started.

The streets here were steep and slippery: so steep, the sidewalk had stairs in a few spots. Kovac smelled cooking.

Fried meat of some kind, with a sweet and salty sauce. He traversed until he came to an area where he couldn't smell food, where all the lights were off.

'What are we doing up here?' Bennett whispered. 'There aren't any hotels here.'

Like Anna, she was hugging herself and shivering against the cold.

They had gained enough altitude from this short walk to be looking down on the target apartment building. Kovac could see the roof from street level here, which was what he wanted. He picked a tall house that was rundown and dark and knocked on the door.

No answer.

He knocked again to make sure.

The houses on either side were dark and cold-looking, too. No lights blinked on.

'Wait here for a second,' he said to Anna and Bennett.

He went around the back. The place he had chosen had a rear door and, beside that, a little golf cart. Except it was too fat for golf. His guess was a little cart to assist someone with shopping, someone who didn't have a car maybe.

He tested it.

One wheel rolled fine, but the other was seized up, meaning the cart turned in tight little circles. He knocked again – on the rear door now.

Still no answer, no movement inside.

No lights snapping on, either.

All as expected, Kovac thought. The house was old, with a shopping cart for an old person who had lost their car license. And one wheel on that seized up from a lack of use. His money was on this house having seen its last generation.

And probably a long time ago, too. From what he'd researched before flying in, and from what he'd seen of Japanese architecture since, this wasn't a population that embraced old houses. The owner's children were probably down in town, enjoying central heating. Or more likely down in Tokyo, enjoying heat that turned on when they clapped their hands.

The rear door was even flimsier than the front door, which made sense. Japan had one of the lowest crime rates in the world. Why put a good rear door and lock on an unused house in a town with zero crime?

Kovac did a final quick search for a key but didn't find one. He took aim, and a single well-placed kick unlocked the door for him. He didn't even need to put much effort into it. The door flung back, brittle wood splintering.

Somewhere off in the distance a dog started barking. But that was it for neighborhood watch.

Bennett came round at the noise and he led her inside. 'Where's Anna?' he asked.

'She went down to get something from the store.'

'I told you both to wait.'

'Don't worry, I gave her my phone.'

'She switched your phone on?'

'No. We're not idiots, Kovac. I told her to keep it off unless she ran into trouble.'

Kovac didn't like it. Anna was too keen to go shopping, especially given the stop at Ueda on the way up. But he couldn't do anything about it right now and he didn't feel like discussing it with Bennett.

Inside, the house was cold and dark, yet somehow musty, too – like it was full of air trapped back in summer, and now run through with frozen mold.

He blew warm air into his gloves, irritated by Anna's blatant insubordination. 'Upstairs,' he muttered.

CHAPTER 27

But Bennett didn't lead him up the stairs. Instead, Kovac could see her shadowy form palming the wall, like someone washing a car.

Looking for a light switch, he realized.

'No,' he said. 'Leave the lights off. Leave everything off. Find blankets and bedding. We'll spend tonight upstairs.'

'That a line that normally works for you, Kovac?'

'You know what I mean.'

Bennett shrugged and picked up a bottle with her good hand. She struggled to open it.

'What's that?' he asked.

She sniffed. 'Alcohol of some kind.'

'Ditch it.'

He made his way up the old staircase and went to work sorting through the equipment in the rucksack. He did the best he could in the dark. Bennett arrived a few minutes later and he could sense her watching him, taking angry gulps from the bottle. 'Do you even know what that is?' he asked.

'Rice wine, I think. It's drinkable. Want some?'

'No. I said ditch it. We'll take shifts tonight.'

'Shifts?'

'That's right. Shifts. I need sleep, too.'

'This how you live, Kovac?'

He ignored the question. He was waiting for Anna to return. If she'd gone to the store, she should be back in a few minutes. Anything more than that and –

'And you're okay with that?'

'With what?' He looked up, trying to see Bennett in the dark, trying to remember her question. She was low on his priority list right now.

Another gulp, swigging it from the bottle's neck. 'It must be nice,' she said.

'What must be nice?'

'Doing what you do.'

'How do you figure?' He kept working his way through the rucksack, tossing the bug-out survival items off to one side. He paused when he found what he was after. Night vision. Not pano, just dual. But more than adequate for tonight's purposes.

This whole bag had been pulled together with the same mentality. *Adequate.* Nothing military-grade, everything civilian, so he could pass it off as survival and hunting gear. Maybe to the Japanese there wasn't much difference between a guy wandering around with an AR-15 instead of an M4, but in plenty of other places there was, and Kovac packed for all environments.

The night vision was top quality: Gen 3, white phosphor. He took out a black ballistic helmet that was upside down in the bottom of the rucksack. He removed the ballistic goggles and other items stuffed into it. Then he clipped the night vision to the helmet's mount. He attached the battery to the back of the helmet as a counterweight. He'd done long stretches in this gear without tension headaches and knew he'd be able to trust it tonight.

He put the helmet on and adjusted, eye by eye, until Bennett was in focus. It was so dark up here Bennett didn't even seem to realize he had gear on. But with the IR illuminator on her face, he could see her with ghostly blue precision.

‘I waste half my life on self-defense courses for women, and I’ll probably never use any of it. But you…’

‘What about me?’

‘You *do* something.’

She was staring at what she thought was him, but was actually just a sliding door with a mountain scene painted on it. He said nothing. He was still thinking about Anna, about all the things he didn’t want to think about.

If Peng had her, would he kill her?

Probably.

If not, would he move her?

Probably. Kovac couldn’t say where for sure but the forest would be logical.

And then he’d kill her. If he hadn’t already.

Or maybe Masuda had her.

If so, it was the same equation.

The only way Kovac could see her surviving the night was if either man decided to use her as bait.

‘Anna told me.’

‘Anna told you what?’

Bennett had put the bottle down and was cradling her damaged fingers. ‘What you did to those guys at the snack bar. Back in Tokyo.’

‘She exaggerates, you know that.’

‘I don’t know that. If anything she seems to understate. Very German.’

‘Austrian.’ Kovac made his way to the front of the room. He edged back a curtain. He adjusted the lenses again – long-range focus now – and scanned for Anna. He did it while running through a checklist in his head: things besides Anna which could get him killed.

There was no sign of her.

Of anyone.

It was too cold even for stray animals tonight.

Bennett was still talking. 'There have been so many men in this work I do with Resolute, men like Masuda who... *just complete animals*, Kovac.'

He could feel her waiting. He was meant to seek clarification about what she wanted to do to these animals. He didn't.

He wondered if the alcohol was already having an effect.

She eventually continued. 'I don't even know why I'm here. This isn't me. This is... I don't even know what the fuck I'm doing. What are we doing, Kovac? Am I even allowed to leave?'

She was suddenly depressing company.

He saw her blue hand come out for the bottle, saw her take a swig.

'I said go easy on the alcohol.'

'Why?'

'My rules, remember.'

He needed to get moving.

The AR-15 was collapsible. He put it together, then put on his belt. He checked his magazines and slid one into the AR-15 and the other two into mag pouches. He slung the rifle over his body by its strap and loaded an HK45 pistol, slotting it into a mid-ride holster.

'That sounds like a lot of guns.'

'Just two actually.'

He removed whatever he could from the rucksack, wanting it as light as possible, then slung it over one shoulder. He made sure to keep his knife and all the ammunition for the big old 1911s. He didn't want any of that lying around with Bennett drinking like she was.

Good to go.

Or good enough. His rucksacks never ended up containing everything he needed, and every rucksack also ended up with items that felt ridiculous. In this rucksack, the odd item out was a mini scuba tank the size of a drink bottle. Not much use for that up here in Nagano. But he couldn't pack for all missions, and so long as the rucksack had a rifle – which this one did – he was happy.

'You're leaving? You don't need to leave.'

He kept her blurry in the lenses. He'd be outside in a few seconds, where the long-range focus would be ideal. 'I need to find Anna.'

'No, you don't. She'll be back.'

'How do you know?'

'She told me what she needed, Kovac – from the store. Tampons. She's young, that's all. She's embarrassed to say that to a man.' Bennett flapped a hand towards him. 'But that's all it is. Tampons.' She hiccupped softly, more a burp really. 'She'll be back. She'll be back in a few minutes. You'll see.'

'Why didn't she get them when we got food on the drive up?'

Bennett pointed at him, as if he were explanation enough.

'I'll be back in an hour,' he said. 'Sober up.'

'It's a good painkiller – for my fingers.'

'Even so.'

'And if you're not back?'

He paused. He needed to scare a little sense into her: some adrenaline to counter the rice wine and self-pity. 'If I'm not back in an hour, get out of this town. Then get out of this country.'

But she didn't seem to hear him. She was looking around like she'd lost a set of car keys. 'What do I do for heat?'

'Find more clothes. Put them on. Don't turn anything on, no lights, no wall sockets, nothing.'

He snatched the wine or whatever it was from her, ignoring her protest, and headed downstairs. He emptied it into the sink and quietly lowered the bottle to the floor. Then he moved to the rear door and gave himself a final once over. He was fully rugged up in his black down jacket with his wool-like gloves on.

Rucksack on his back, AR-15 in hand.

He was angry. But he needed to control that. He needed to think straight and get a better feel for this town while he had the chance. He had a sense it would end up a battleground, and that was fine by him so long as he knew the terrain better than anyone else. He was confident he would have the drop on Masuda, but Peng? Peng was a local with extensive resources, who was possibly already exerting an influence over Kovac's decisions.

Still, Kovac didn't have a choice. He needed intel. Both on the layout of this town, and on Anna. And he wasn't going to get that drinking rice wine with Bennett.

Grumbling about women, he let himself out into freezing night air.

CHAPTER 28

The helmet, night vision goggles, pistol and rifle meant Kovac couldn't just amble down to the main road. So he went up into the foothills and trees.

The snow was deep, but he'd invested in a pair of Japanese hiking boots when purchasing extra winter gear earlier in the day. Boots were something he had never thought to include in his rucksack. He had always assumed he'd be able to buy boots, but he hadn't considered Asian sizing. The store had only carried one type of boot large enough to fit him, and even then it had been a half size too small. His feet started to hurt almost from the outset, but at least they were dry. He told himself the boots would stretch.

He followed the edge of the town, keeping to the demarcation line where town met forest. There was no path he could see, but he suspected he was on one. Trees had been cleared. Undergrowth, too. There was a nice channel of undisturbed snow.

He paused even thirty feet or so, listening, scanning his surroundings and considering his vulnerabilities. He was much higher than the main road, which was well lit, and with the night vision he had a good view of the town.

It filled the contours of the valley below. The town's perimeter, he realized, was shaped more like a pear than a surfboard, with him at the fat end. He looked for Anna but there wasn't anyone. Just a few cars and vans coming down the main road, the vans shaped like little bread-loaves with headlights.

He resumed trudging through snow, and after about fifteen minutes he still hadn't seen any trace of Anna. He began to think about starting back. His feet were sore. He could feel blisters starting.

But then something caught his eye. It was at the far end of town, at the narrow end of the pear. There was a small train station, with a lone figure standing on the platform.

Female. Thin. And definitely cold.

He figured it had to be Anna. Locals wouldn't stand out in night snow waiting for a train. They'd check the schedule and roll up in one of the warm bread-loaf vans. Right on the dot. Warm van to warm train, with only the shortest possible exposure to mother nature.

Anna – if it really was Anna – looked like bait. That was his first thought. To get to her, he needed to get right to the end of town. Though if she was bait, why put her all the way down there? Positioned where she was, he could get most of the way to her while staying up in the trees, only dropping down at the last second. That meant he could keep the helmet, night vision and AR-15. He could stick to the trees and arrive dressed to kill.

If it was him, he would've put Anna back in the center of town. More chance of her being spotted there, less chance of a stealthy, armed rescue.

Which meant what?

She was leaving town of her own volition?

Kovac doubted it. She had taken orders from him in Tokyo. Why not here, too? He didn't buy that she had snuck out for tampons. Maybe she had told Bennett that, but it sounded like a lie crafted for Bennett. It played on Bennett's biases, not his.

He watched the female figure on the platform pace back and forth. Watched her lean back against a fence. Watched her pace some more.

Bored or nervous or both, he thought.

He moved a lens out to check his watch. He had burned up twenty minutes and had forty left before Bennett got out of town – assuming she had even heard his instructions.

He returned the night vision lens to position.

He had time, and it was worth the effort. If someone was manipulating Anna now, she was Kovac's link to that someone. She could well lead him to Peng, or just as easily, to Masuda. She might even reveal Kovac's sniper, Sukhomlinov. The exposed platform made more sense when viewed through the eyes of a sniper.

Kovac rolled the tension out of his neck, then refocused on the platform. He realized he was conflicted. He had two goals – dangling Anna to see what came out of the woodwork, and protecting Anna. They weren't necessarily compatible.

He started the exaggerated, loping walk through snow and trees again, his blisters getting on his nerves. Slowly, painfully, he came up level with the station, but remained invisible in the trees. The girl never moved from the platform. No one came near her. It was just her, standing in front of a signal box the whole time.

He positioned himself behind an especially large tree. He pulled one night vision lens aside again and took out his phone. He switched it on under cover of his jacket, the screen's light on its lowest setting.

If she was bait to smoke him out, they would've made her turn Bennett's phone on. Even if she was leaving by choice, she would've turned it on to check train times.

He located Bennett's number in his incoming calls and rang it. Then he switched the screen off and brought the phone up to his ear. He was back in perfect blackness and he moved out from behind the tree again.

Sure enough, it rang. And sure enough, the blue figure down on the platform fished around in a pocket and pulled out something bright and rectangular.

Anna.

Kovac was making do with one night vision lens now, keeping his other eye shut. But one was plenty, and he could see the basic shape of her face as she put the phone to her ear. 'Hello?'

'It's me,' he said.

'What do you want?'

'Bennett said you're getting supplies?'

She circled a toe in the snow in front of her. 'Yeah.'

'What's the delay?'

She looked up, checked around her. 'Where are you?' she asked.

'Just some place we found.'

'The one you made me wait at with Bennett?'

She was fishing.

'No. We chose a different one, down in town.'

She turned away from him, scanning a small parking lot behind her. 'Okay,' she said. 'I'll be back soon.'

'How soon?'

'Soon.'

There was a long pause. Then she surprised him. 'What do you want, Kovac?'

He was thrown by the question. She hadn't asked it in a way that made him think she was after a shopping list. More like, what did he want from tonight, from her? 'Are you really coming back?' he asked, answering her question with one of his own.

He saw her lean out and check the line of the tracks: 'Maybe I'm safer on my own.'

'So you're not coming back?'

No reply.

'How do you figure you're safer alone, Anna?'

'You're using me.'

He didn't argue this point. From a certain perspective, she was right. She was a smart girl. 'So what's the plan? You go where?'

'I don't know.'

'Which direction, do you even know that much?'

'No.'

'And after you arrive, what then?'

'I have your money.'

'That won't last long.'

'I'll make it last. I'm good at that.'

'I'm keeping you close to keep you safe, Anna.'

'Liar.' He heard tears in her words. 'I just want you all to leave me alone. Can you do that? Can you please just let me go?'

She hung up. He saw her do it, then he heard it through the phone.

He had been right. He couldn't have it both ways. He was going to have to choose. Either Anna was bait, or he protected her. But he couldn't do both at once.

It was an easy decision.

Kovac chose bait.

CHAPTER 29

Megan Curzon took a seat at her favorite table on the homestead's veranda and looked out towards the desert, taking in the last of a magnificent sunset. There were clouds tonight, grey-blue and diffuse, reminding her of waves photographed from underwater.

She sensed something at her fingertips and looked down to find Mollie, her step-mother's new dog. Mollie was still just a puppy. An Australian Kelpie, she was stubborn and proving a hard pup to train.

She was licking at Megan's hand, and Megan gave her a gentle tap on the nose. 'No.'

'I'm sorry about the meeting.'

Megan turned to see her father. He was holding an envelope in one hand, using it to fan his face against the late evening heat.

He sat down opposite her and put the envelope on the table in front of him.

'Why tell me about John Kovac if you're not going to let me sit in on meetings? I've canceled Berlin, I've canceled everything I have for the next two weeks to be here, and you're shutting me out.'

Her father nodded, as if he had expected this. He placed one bony leg over the other, so stiff he needed both hands to help position it. He smoothed out his slacks and studied the same clouds Megan had just admired. 'You feel I'm preferencing your brother?'

'It's hard not to think so, yeah.'

'Your brother's a fool, Megan. Which would be tolerable if he were an ethical fool. But we both know he isn't.'

She recoiled slightly. She had long suspected her father felt this way, but he had always gone to great lengths to treat them equally. She had certainly never heard him badmouth Daniel before.

He continued: 'I asked you to leave the meeting because I wanted to speak with you one-on-one – before you heard anything more. I have some explaining to do. I thought maybe I could do that in the meeting, keeping everything transparent. But the way it went, well, I saw it had to be like this.'

She shifted nervously.

Her father dropped his gaze from the clouds to the vast, desolate paddocks laying in half-darkness out beyond the lawn. 'Have you ever heard of a God Committee, Megan?'

'No.' Megan felt her insides go cold. *Was he really going to try and rationalize all this, justify it to himself in front of her?*

'The first God Committee had a handful of members coming from various professions. To this day, we don't know their names. We know them only by their work. This was in Seattle in the early sixties. They met because a university professor had invented artificial dialysis. It was one of those game-changers that come along every so often. People with a month or less to live no longer needed to die.' He glanced at her, emphasizing his words. 'But there was a problem. At that time, more than 100,000 Americans were dying of end-stage kidney disease. *Thousands* of viable candidates, and the program could only take ten. Who lives?'

'The God Committee was set up to decide?'

'Yes.'

'And did they?'

'Yes. Aside from certain practicalities like age and distance from the hospital, they were instructed to decide based entirely on their own conscience. That's all they had to work with. Their conscience. The ten they selected lived, the remainder died.'

'Why are you telling me this?'

'Because it's the job. It's my job. And I've just signed legal documents which state that, in the event of my death or incapacitation, it's to become your job.'

'Mine exclusively?' Megan blinked in surprise. Just as her father had always sought to be even-handed with his children, he had also avoided any serious discussion of succession.

Megan felt Mollie's wet tongue on her fingers again, but she was now too preoccupied to tap the animal away.

'I need you to understand,' her father said, 'that you'll be a God Committee of one, unable to consult with anyone but Bishop, and guided entirely by your own conscience. That's why it has to be you. You're brother's a thief. He's self-serving. But you…' His voice trailed off.

'What about me?'

'Well, sad to say, you're just like me.' He gave her a small smile and shook his head. He unfolded his legs and leaned forward, reaching for her hands. He gripped them with a quiet desperation she wasn't used to.

'Your sister was the same. The three of us, we live for others.'

'Lived,' Megan corrected reflexively.

He released her hands and sat back again. 'Yes.'

He raised his face to the sky again, but closed his eyes this time. 'How much do you know about Katie?'

Megan had never heard anyone call her sister "Katie". It had always been Kat.

'Not a lot. Just what you've said. Mum doesn't speak about her.'

Her father nodded. He opened his eyes again. 'Your mother and I married young.'

'I know.'

'Very young. We had Katie almost right away. I was 42 when she died. Had she lived, you wouldn't exist. Your mother and I had no plans for more children. It took that tragedy, and a long battle with IVF.'

'I know that, too.'

Megan was having trouble seeing how this related to John Kovac, but she had long ago learned to be patient with her father. He had a habit of circling a topic, gathering stands he would eventually weave together given enough time.

'Your sister started to come apart in her second year of university. Until then, she had been driven by success, by winning. She viewed life through the lens of more. Not possessions, as some do. Not more wealth. She had been born into money and knew its limits as only the rich do. No, your sister was bent on testing herself, her stamina, her capacity for suffering. She wanted more pain. She thought if she could starve herself enough, run far enough, study enough, well then maybe one day it *would actually be enough*. I didn't detect it until I got a phone call telling me she had collapsed in the middle of the night, halfway through an ultramarathon. I didn't even know what that was until I flew out there. I thought it would be dehydration or some kind of injury. It wasn't. It was mental. She told me she had forgotten why she was running, and without that, she had nothing. She was sobbing.'

'What did you say?'

'Nothing helpful, I don't think. Even months after the fact, I put it down to exhaustion. She had run thirty-something miles. She was skeletal. I failed to spot it, her compulsion to test limits, like a drug. And with every limit she reached, she had no choice but to locate another. To chase that hit again, thinking maybe, just maybe, *this time*...'

'I'm not like that.'

'You have the same drive, the same tendencies. But I was ready for it with you.'

'You think *you're* the reason?'

'Hear me out. Your sister slipped into a long depression. She dropped out of university and began to travel.' He paused as if recalling, as if amazed he hadn't been able to change the trajectory of it. 'We offered her money, but she wouldn't take it, of course. The search for suffering and pain returned, but without any pleasure now. It was hostels, camping, scraping an income in dangerous undocumented jobs in Europe, Africa, South America.' His voice wavered slightly as he said these last two words.

Megan knew why. Kat had died in Mexico.

Her father called Mollie to him, locking her head gently between his knees and petting her as he went on speaking. 'She always wanted to help others, but she got in her own way. She had been studying nursing before dropping out, and in San Fernando she had a win. She found work in a public hospital there. In one letter to me, she described making a uterine incision, extracting the fetal arms, then grasping the baby's feet. She pulled that baby out of the womb upside down, delivering him. She said she was happy. For the first time in as long as she could remember. The woman had been helpless, an immigrant from Venezuela. She would've died without Katie, the baby too. She found her calling.'

'And then she got sick?'

'No.' His voice changed, tightening suddenly. 'That's what we've always told you, but the truth is uglier. She was murdered.'

Megan tilted her head, feeling a sting of resentment at this. She had read the rumours about her sister on the internet but there were so many. She had opted to believe the family's official version of events. Illness. 'Why would you both lie about something like that?'

'That's what I'm explaining.' He let the dog free, finally holding Megan's eye.

Megan stared straight back, blinking, her heart rate suddenly up, her neck and throat tight. She was angry. She swallowed hard and fought down the urge to reprimand. 'Okay,' she said. 'Explain.'

'She must have told someone her name, and someone else must have connected that name back to Curzon International, to money. She met a young man, she fell in love, and...'

Her father's eyes moistened.

'And?'

'He took her on a date, a second date, a third. At an intersection, he got out of the pickup truck, leaving her alone on the bench seat. Two other men – two strangers – got in. They pushed Katie to the middle of the seat, and they drove her somewhere.'

'Where?'

'We never did find out where, but we received eight ransom demands in all. The first few felt legitimate. We paid them. Then, as the story of the abduction of a wealthy Australian girl spread, we got more demands, asking for less. A lot less. They felt opportunistic, but we paid them, too. I stood in a park on dusk, surrounded by dirt roads full of deep puddles, waiting for a rendezvous that never eventuated. I stood out on a track in a stretch of scrub. Same again. I tried everything in my power to get her back – I berated police, I offered rewards – and it wasn't enough.'

He pushed the envelope across the table. 'I was already a millionaire then – more times over than I cared to count. And I was powerless to get back the one thing that mattered to me most. I had been beaten by a cartel. Not even that. By amateurs. The few men they eventually linked to the crime were street vendors, selling watches and flowers and the like. They'd turned to crime out of unhappiness with their lot, greed. They probably killed her by mistake. Like I said, amateurs.'

Megan said nothing, but she now understood how the threads of this conversation would come together.

Her father said: 'That's when I realized I needed John Kovac. I began my search. Two years later, you and Daniel were born, which made me even more determined to get it right. And six years after that, I finally found him.'

Megan opened the envelope, expecting it to contain the missing information on John Kovac. It didn't. There was just a single photo in it – a photo of a South American man. His arms were tied behind his back with rope, but he was hanging from a roof beam by the wrists. Both shoulders looked to be dislocated, and he had been savagely beaten. 'Who is this?' she asked.

'The man who organized Katie's kidnapping. That photo was taken when you were seventeen.'

'Seventeen? That's...'

'Almost twenty years after Katie was killed, yes. Mine was a patient revenge, but that's not the point.'

'What's the point?'

'You need John Kovac.'

CHAPTER 30

They were silent for a long time.

Finally Megan said: 'But why the torture?'

'To extract the names of all involved.'

'And what, now they're all dead, too?'

'No. Only the man you're looking at, whose idea it was to take my daughter from me. The remaining seven – including the man who seduced Katie – live with varying degrees of permanent, inescapable pain.'

'Pain inflicted by John Kovac?'

'At my discretion, depending on their degree of involvement, yes.' He stood, his body stiff and uncooperative, the fingertips of one hand on the table to keep him stable.

'Your God Committee of one,' Megan said under her breath, before turning the photo over. There was a phone number on the back. She began to ask about it, but her father spoke over her:

'This company has things other people want, and many of those people operate outside the law. We're multi-national, so we're constantly under attack somewhere. Eventually, you'll need to accept that and face the responsibility. You'll come to see that – no matter how you attempt to frame it, how you attempt to rationalize it – it's never more complex than the needs of the company against your own conscience.'

'How do I know when I've made the right decision, the

proportional decision?'

'You don't. The best I've managed is simply to feel it, to be at peace with it. And that's why it can't be Daniel. That's why it has to be you.'

He started back towards the house.

Megan called out after him: 'I have my secrets. I'm not some perfect –'

He paused. 'The poker in Macau?' Without turning, he let out a small snort. 'I have two children, Megan. One comes to me with damning evidence of a twin sibling's compulsive gambling. The other says she's not perfect. Which would you choose?'

He started walking again.

'Wait.'

He didn't stop but half turned this time.

Megan was about to tell him that she wasn't ready, that she didn't want to make life and death decisions, or be the one who potentially lost control of a corporate empire. But at the last second, she realized she had no choice. She had no choice precisely because her father had no choice. 'In the meeting,' she said, trying to process the enormity of all she had just learned, 'what ahm…'

'What did you miss after you left? When you've collected your thoughts, call that phone number on the back of the photograph.'

Megan watched him head inside. She sat for a moment, but the thirst for more information overran any attempt to reflect. She took out her phone and dialed the number, and found it connected her to Bishop in Japan.

'He's spoken with you?' Bishop asked.

'Yes.'

'Okay. Welcome, I guess.'

Bishop proceeded to give her the basics on a man called Peng Biao, a Swedish national with a Chinese passport. 'Most of what we have comes from the Australian Federal Police. I've passed the same report on to Kovac. Peng formed a cartel from an alliance of five Asian triad groups, which he calls "The Association".'

Megan had more questions about Kovac but knew Bishop expected her to get her head in the current game. 'Sounds like something from a movie,' she said, trying to focus.

'I'm aware.'

Megan heard him get into a vehicle, while he explained that most of The Association's money came from funneling tons of heroin, methamphetamine and ketamine to wealthy nations. 'Japan's one, and our AFP contact specifically links Peng to Ken Masuda's yakuza clan.'

Megan already knew of Masuda. He was a degenerate gambler who shared her taste for high stakes poker but without the skill. He had caused her headaches in the past, and Megan wasn't surprised to learn he was indirectly involved in meth. He was a lowlife.

'What's this amalgamated cartel worth?' she asked, as Mollie lay down to sleep, her mouth on her paws.

'The United Nations Office on Drugs and Crime put The Association's meth revenue last year at a little over eight billion.'

'You mean eight million?'

'I mean eight billion.'

'That's serious money, Bishop. The whole of Curzon International brought in 10.4 billion last year. That's comparable in scale.'

'The Association dominates the wholesale meth market, so

much so it's started using legitimate companies, hiding its drugs in their products. In tea, for example. Where those companies complain, there are repercussions.'

'Can't we just give the AFP what they need to take it down?'

'Given the scale of its operations, it's infiltrated law enforcement. And it can afford to endure endless drug busts while still making good profits. Its margins are sensational. Added to that – or perhaps because of it – it's growing. Twofold growth over the previous five years, set for threefold growth in the coming five.'

'Jesus. If it were legit, I'd be looking to buy it.'

'Peng wouldn't sell. This is all personal with him. His life has been anything but straight-forward.'

She was still thinking about Kovac. She forced herself to focus on what Bishop was telling her. 'How so?'

She heard an engine start and Bishop's voice changed as he swapped across to the car's internal speakerphone.

'In his twenties, Peng suffered acute septic shock. An infection entered his bloodstream, unleashing an inflammatory storm. His body started to shut down and his limbs went first. At the ER, he was blasted with antibiotics and fluids and put into an induced coma. But when he woke on a ventilator, he found his arms and legs necrotic.'

'As in… dead?'

'As in black and dead, yeah. The arms were removed up to the elbows, the legs up to the knees.'

She heard a turn signal ticking.

'For years, Peng made do with split hooks for hands. This was back when he was just getting started. He took up software programming and hook-handedly created an online start-up selling millions in painkillers to American customers.'

'Almost admirable.'

'The hook-handed typing and determination, sure. But not his contribution to society. He was one of the original contributors to America's painkiller epidemic, and he leveraged that to launch The Association.'

Megan's phone buzzed. She pulled it away from her ear and saw a message from Nixon Hsu. It read: "found nothing more, sorry".

She texted: "figured out Macau, look wider".

When she returned the phone to her ear, Bishop was still talking in his deep, gruff monotone. '– to the rise of vascularized composite-tissue allotransplantation, all of which meant hand transplants.'

'The rise of what?'

'Never mind. Point is, Peng had hand transplants.'

'When?'

'Age 41. He worked for three years to grow connective tissue down into the new hands and retrain them, and before long he was opening doors, driving a car, even lifting light weights.'

'Given what he managed with hook hands, I'm guessing this wasn't good for the world?'

'It certainly didn't put him back on the straight and narrow. He doubled down on drugs. Thing is, the hands didn't take. By 52, his hospital records suggest complications. Stage 3b chronic kidney disease, for one, presumably due to the immunosuppressants. He altered his medication, but he got sicker. He got a re-amputation.'

'That can't have been an easy choice.'

'Before you feel too sorry for him, we think he uses a body double – and the guy they found for that role gave up four perfectly good limbs to take the job.'

'Jesus. What a monster.' Mollie had given up on sleeping. Megan sensed licking at the tips of her fingers again, and this time let it go. She had a new appreciation for the sensations in her hands. 'Tell me about their logistics.'

Bishop didn't miss a beat. 'The meth is mass-produced in super-labs in Myanmar's Shan State. From there, it runs through Hong Kong, Macau, Taiwan, Malaysia, Myanmar, Vietnam and mainland China.'

'And from China out to the rest of the world.'

'Exactly.'

Megan had known Bishop was unmatched physically, but she was getting her first taste of his aptitude for detail and it was impressive. 'So what do they want from us?'

'Access to our international distribution networks. They consider Curzon a soft target. They have the yakuza, after all, they have bikers, and they have ethnic Chinese gangs across Southeast Asia. They think they have a monopoly on violence.'

'But we have Kovac.'

'He's just one man, Megan.'

'Trained by you.'

'And I'm just one man. Kovac's going after Peng as we speak but... look, here's the truth of it – he's outmatched.'

Megan was reaching sideways and stretching for a tennis ball, planning to get Mollie up and moving. She was wondering how to ask Bishop about Kovac's missing years when she heard a helicopter.

She froze, listening for a moment.

Finally, she said: 'You arranged extra security, right? For this place?'

'Yeah.'

'Arriving by air?'

'Helicopter. Why?'

'They're here. I'll call you back in ten.' She hung up.

CHAPTER 31

Megan stood and walked out to the middle of the lawn. She turned on the spot, trying to triangulate the rotor and engine noise. The sun was almost gone and she couldn't see anything. She kept turning, confused.

She realized it was more than one helicopter. And they were coming from different directions. Sizeable machines, too. These weren't the little bubble choppers Pemberton Downs used for cattle work, nor even the chopper she had come in on. Bishop had gone all out.

Megan started to get an uneasy feeling in the pit of her stomach. She immediately phoned her father, the call running through satellites, just as everything at Pemberton did. He picked up on the first ring. 'I hear them. Is Lottie with you?'

'No.'

'I'm with Carmen, Lottie's not with us. We'll find her now. Get Daniel, and get inside.'

'You think this is hostile?'

'I don't know what it is.'

Megan hung up and phoned Daniel but there was no answer. *Pick up the phone you moron.*

The incoming choppers were getting loud now. She hung up and immediately received a call from her father. She answered, still scanning the sky: 'Yeah?'

'We just found a note in the kitchen. Daniel left almost

two hours ago. He's out riding with Lottie, they're planning to camp out.'

'Oh no.' Megan spotted what might have been a helicopter. She narrowed her eyes, squinting into the gloom as her mind ran the options. She knew exactly where Daniel and Lottie would go if they were on horseback and planning to camp. McCartney Gorge. Lottie loved to swim in the waterhole, which was freezing year-round and a perfect way to find relief from the summer heat. She also loved searching for lizards in the rocks and gum trees, and climbing on the old pioneer cattle yards. The family had installed kitchen facilities and a decent restroom there, which made it an easy choice for an impromptu night under the stars.

But it was a communication dead zone and a fifteen-minute drive.

As much as she wanted to, Megan couldn't do it. She would only send up a plume of red, desert dust. Even at this late hour, the helicopters would see it and one would certainly follow. If they were hostile, she would lead them straight to the gorge, a gorge they would otherwise ignore.

She considered going on horseback, but again it wasn't worth the risk. Whoever was coming, they didn't know of the gorge. She had to hold her nerve and trust in that.

She ran back towards the homestead, phoning her father again as she crossed the veranda and now dragging Mollie by the collar. 'They're probably at the gorge, but I can't get to them.'

'You're right, you can't. Get inside now. We'll hold the core for you, and then –'

The call cut out.

She tried again, but her phone no longer had any kind of signal.

She stared at the device in disbelief, thinking about what

her father had just said. She knew he was just trying to make her feel better. Once they locked down, there was nothing they could do for Daniel or Lottie. The core her father had referred to was an inner section of the homestead: a 3,700-square-foot, steel-reinforced concrete nucleus with biometric recognition. It had been part of the renovation, and all bedrooms were now located within its confines – even the guest rooms.

Megan picked up Mollie. The helicopters were arriving. She could hear them beginning to circle and could see them blowing up dust and leaves outside. She had never seen machines like them before.

She made her way straight through into the core, where she released Mollie again.

For a visitor, the only clue this core existed was in the weight of certain internal doors. The biometrics were all integrated into the house, which was constantly collecting facial, voice and behavioral data to maintain a 24/7 keyless system.

It didn't stop there. Given the remoteness of the homestead, the company that installed the core had insisted on a host of anti-siege measures. Generators, air scrubbers, food and water stores... the list went on. Megan had always felt it was overkill but had gone along with it because it reassured her father and step-mother and enabled the family to keep the house open year-round. It gave the place the relaxed outback feel of a century ago.

Now, however, it felt like the life-support system it was, and she was going to need to lock everything down with Daniel and Lottie trapped outside.

Never in a million years had Megan expected things to play out like this. She felt like a coward.

She found her father and step-mother reassuring Curzon staff that everything would be fine. As soon as he spotted her, Megan's father took her aside and led her down into the wine cellar, which contained the disguised entrance to a small passageway. This in turn led to a steel hatch and ladder down into a panic bunker with food, water, a toilet, a gun safe and monitors.

'The core sealed?' she asked, following him down this ladder.

Her father moved slowly, struggling with the rungs. Once down into the bunker, he checked a computer monitor, driving a mouse and clicking frantically. 'Three more seconds,' he said. He held up fingers, counting down. As the last finger dropped, the computer informed them both in a cool, robotic tone that they were fully protected from external threats.

'Let's hope so,' her father muttered. 'We've lost our satellite link and they've cut the old copper landline. We can no longer call for help.'

Megan realized she hadn't alerted Bishop. She silently cursed her stupidity but tried to push it out of mind. Catastrophic as the error was, what was done was done. She had to stay in the present.

She focused on the computer monitors. She counted three Bell helicopters. They had landed on the north, east and west sides of the homestead respectively, and she watched as soldiers exited all three: all men by the look of them, all in high-quality tactical gear, and all with assault rifles. 'No insignia,' she said.

Her father nodded. 'Mercenaries.'

'You think they know about the core?'

He shrugged. 'Contractors and household staff all signed NDAs. Our name was never on any of the legal documents or building plans submitted and I kept the security overlay separate from the architectural drawings, but…'

'But?'

'These guys don't look like amateurs. And if they can hijack our comms, they –'

'– heard us talk about Lottie?'

Her father's shoulders dropped. '*Shit.*' He dropped down onto an office chair, rubbing at white stubble. 'Peng,' he said softly.

Megan nodded. 'Bishop brought me up to speed on him. Sounds about right. This is way beyond Masuda.'

They watched as the mercenaries cleared the homestead's open, outer rooms one by one without need for flashbangs or gunfire. Unopposed, they quickly reached the core. They tried the doors and, finding them locked, made their way around the core's perimeter. There was a lot of hand gesturing and talk in what sounded like Chinese, a lot of testing. Within two minutes, they seemed to know exactly what they were dealing with – an internal section of the house that looked like all others but was in fact a fortress.

Three of the mercenaries headed back to the helicopter, moving slowly now, looking relaxed. They returned with explosives and started rigging up charges on the core's concrete walls.

'They were expecting this,' her father said. 'I doubt they'll be able to blow a hole in the core but we need to bring everyone down into this panic bunker and seal it off. He got up out of the chair and moved to climb the ladder.

'Wait,' Megan said. 'Look.'

He returned to the monitors. 'What?'

She pointed. 'They're packing up.'

They watched the mercenaries retreat to the helicopters. Two remained at the homestead, rotors winding down, but one did the opposite. It powered up and took off.

Megan felt sick to the stomach. As expected, the airborne

helicopter set out in the direction of the gorge.

CHAPTER 32

Kovac pulled the second night vision lens back down into position.

He shifted his gaze from the station platform to a business hotel at the far end of town.

He hadn't seen this building until he started thinking about sniper perches. It sat out on its own: brown brick, a perfect rectangle, higher not wider. It was a lot taller than anything around it.

He counted five levels, the curtains open on all rooms except three. Two of the rooms with closed curtains were together, one separate. The separate one was higher. It was on the topmost level, Level 5.

The hotel had a small parking lot, just like the train station. But unlike the station, this parking lot had vehicles. Three in all. It wasn't possible to see every aspect of every vehicle because of a small brick wall running around the perimeter. But Kovac suspected he was looking at two bread-loaves and one Mercedes. All in matching black, all with the same dark tint on the windows. Maybe an S-Class, maybe not. He couldn't say for sure. It was too hard to see from this far out, even with the night vision.

Two roads were connecting the parking lot at the hotel to the train station. The main road that ran through town, then a winding side road.

One route fast, one slow and discreet, Kovac thought.

He watched as Anna, still on the station platform, dialed a number into her phone and placed a call. He shifted his attention to the business hotel, and sure enough, the edges of one set of closed curtains lit up slightly. One of the two rooms on Level 2. The curtain moved – like someone was peeking out.

Anna hung up.

The curtain dropped back into place, and the room at the business hotel went dark for a moment. Then it lit up again, like whoever was in there was making a call of their own.

The room next to it lit up.

Kovac had no evidence, but he could imagine the words passing between these three points in space. First, he imagined Anna's voice. "He rang me". Then the man in the first of the two hotel rooms saying, "stay where you are, text us if he shows up". And then the call to the room next door. "He's coming".

If Kovac was right, the hotel was full of hostiles. And if it was the yakuza, they were probably all about to pile down into vehicles for the hustle across to the station. That, after all, seemed to be their modus operandi: overreact at any cost.

But how had Masuda dragged Anna into this? When and where?

Kovac figured it had to have been on the drive up, while he was reading the file on Peng. Either that or tonight in the convenience store. Maybe Anna really had set out to buy supplies, only to have Masuda corner her in the store.

Whichever it was, Kovac was feeling all caught up now. He had an A point with Anna and a B point with bad guys.

He refocused on the hotel. Short of a guy with hook hands showing up, he figured he was dealing with Masuda. And he knew closed curtains meant occupied. He knew this because he could see into the rooms with open curtains, and they were all perfect copies of one another. Like the same maid had prepared them. The curtains were small and light, and all pinned back the exact same way. The beds had the exact same folds. Even the little signs by the TVs were at the exact same angle on the exact same cabinets. The maid was a creature of habit. She left the curtains open when she was done cleaning. It took guests to close them.

There was one detail Kovac still didn't understand, though. The hotel wasn't fully occupied. It wasn't even close to fully occupied. So why was one room taken all the way up on the top level?

He studied the unoccupied rooms again. They were all the same, right the way up the building. It wasn't like they got nicer the higher up a person went. There was no sprawling penthouse up top, that was for sure. This was a business hotel, utilitarian to a fault. It didn't matter what floor you were on, you got the exact same room prepared by the exact same maid.

The only real difference was the view, and the view was of the station.

The sniper, Sukhomlinov?

A curtain edged back in the top room and the window opened, albeit just a crack. Meanwhile, down below, men piled out of the hotel's entrance and made straight for the vans. It was the yakuza, as Kovac had assumed. They were the usual motley assortment, with their slicked hair and V-neck T-shirts, and their tattoos and suit jackets. All from Masuda's goon factory.

Kovac refocused on the topmost room. A hand appeared, a cigarette between the fingers.

For Kovac, the lit end was like a penlight.

Either Peng, Masuda or the sniper, he thought. At the very least though, a VIP along for the ride up into the mountains. A VIP now looking to deal with the troublesome foreigner.

Engines started in the parking lot and the vans rolled out, one after the other.

Kovac came up off his haunches, feeling the pain from his boots and blisters, and started down the slope.

CHAPTER 33

Looking out over snowy forest, Peng Biao placed the phone call.

As he waited for it to connect, his mind drifted back to his reading the previous night. Peng made it a habit to read regularly and widely. He protected a dedicated block of time from six to eight p.m. each night for books. This reading habit had begun as a search for answers to his own medical challenges, and it had delivered robotic hands and significant progress with his prosthetic legs. So many of the patients he'd met in rehab were content to end their search there. They now devoted their lives to helping others with similar challenges. Peng couldn't understand that. He had solved those problems. He had moved on. His ambitions were far larger, and his reading reflected his broader appetites. It traversed medicine, business, innovation, psychology... He even read biographies and fiction where it helped him understand the mindsets and blind spots of his enemies.

It was Luther Curzon's biography which had first drawn his attention to the opportunities inherent within Curzon International's distribution networks.

'He's here,' Masuda said in English, when the call connected. 'I just sent my men out.'

'Third time lucky then.'

'We won't fail you a third time. We have the girl, Anna. He's coming to save her, just like you said he would.'

'A killer with a conscience.' Peng smiled at the notion. Human incongruities were always as amusing as they were fascinating. 'Ring me when it's done.' He ended the call and placed another, his mind still on his reading. Last night, he had been learning about nanopore sequencing. The technology was complex, but the principle underpinning it was not. The aim was direct analysis of the DNA strand in real time, as the molecule was drawn through a tiny pore suspended in a membrane. The technology used changes in electrical currents to read off the chain of bases. This removed the need for amplification, but also reduced the cost of hardware. The result was quick, cheap sequencing.

His second call – a satellite connection – clicked to life.

'Do you have the homestead?' Daniel Curzon asked. 'You have Pemberton?'

'Yes,' Peng said.

'Did they go into the core?'

'Yes.'

'Without me.' His disgust was palpable, even via this sub-par connection.

No doubt the state-of-the-art equipment Peng was using to block communications out of Pemberton was having an effect on this call, too. He'd been playing with Pemberton's comms for a long time now, increasing efficiency, only to throttle it again, or cut the homestead off completely. The Curzons thought nothing of an outage now. And most important of all, the company was accustomed to losing contact with its Chairman. It would be a long time before the alarm was raised.

'They're putting themselves first, Daniel. They think you don't matter.'

Daniel yelled some friendly instructions to the girl, who Peng knew liked to be called Lottie. He would meet Lottie soon. 'They care about Lottie, though. She's the future, after Megan.

You see how it works now? It's money, Daniel. That's all they can understand. Money, and succession. You can return from the gorge now. You know what to say to them. They'd never come out for you. But they'll come out to save Lottie.'

'And you'll keep your end of the deal?'

'You'll be heading up Curzon International before the year is out, without anyone suspecting you.'

'I don't know. I... What if Lottie isn't enough?'

'You're forgetting Biogen. Lottie threatens succession. Biogen threatens Curzon's money. Luther can't stay put in the face of both. It would obliterate the company, and his legacy.'

'I still think it's too risky, we need more –'

'Daniel, it's too late for second thoughts. This is happening. You have two potential lives stretching out ahead of you. Choose carefully.'

Peng ended the call. His gaze had never left the snowy forest out in front of him. He watched his men working in two teams, deploying anti-personnel mines in the trees. He would likely never need these, but he was nothing if not thorough. Kovac had already managed to get far closer to Peng than he was meant to.

Peng realized it was the mastery over complexity that he most admired in nanopore sequencing – the overwhelming amount of data brought to heel in a simple, logical fashion. That was Daniel. Daniel Curzon was Peng's nanopore sequencer for Curzon International. Cheap, able to be used in real time, and highly effective. Curzon International was larger even than Peng's own organization, The Association. And with so many different business interests it was infinitely more complex. But Peng wanted it. It would be a merger of sorts, providing him the cover and legitimacy he desperately needed. With Curzon's help, he would be able to double or even triple the amount of product he moved each year. He would also be able to move into every drug market on the planet.

The beauty of greed, he thought.

Luther Curzon was dying, and Daniel was stupid but not too stupid to sense the inevitable. The company would end up in the hands of his sister. Peng had played on that fear relentlessly. He had explained that he could put Daniel on top, where he rightfully belonged.

Or, just as easily, he could bring Daniel's years of theft and infidelity into the public realm. He could disgrace him with shareholders and the general public, ending his career and marriage in an eyeblink. Add in concocted claims of sexual abuse of young female staffers, and Daniel would be a pariah.

The seduction of Daniel Curzon had taken place over a long sequence of meetings in Macau, all disguised as Daniel snooping on his sister's gambling habit. Peng had instructed Masuda to run up a debt with Curzon, then to make threats against Daniel. As hoped, Luther Curzon – reacting to these threats – had involved his son in top-level discussions. That, eventually, had been Peng's window into King, Bishop and John Kovac.

Trillions of base pairs, and at last he had found the exact DNA that protected it all.

Peng had often wondered at the company's luck. But attacks in Japan and Australia today would provoke a regime change at Curzon. And with Curzon under his control, Peng would be able to build a monopoly.

He turned away from the trees. Two men had arrived at the door with rifles, looking to set up at the windows. He gestured for them to go ahead.

There was nothing left now but Lottie. Daniel would hand her over as part of their deal, and Peng would run her through the usual trafficking channels. But he would need someone to deliver her. He would need someone to bring her to him up here in the mountains.

He settled on the inept sniper, Sukhomlinov. Sukhomlinov had let him down twice, but Peng would give him one last chance. Masuda would kill Kovac today. Luther and Megan would die today, too. And with Lottie in hand, Peng would lure Bishop.

Almost like CRISPR, he thought. A neat, targeted snip in Curzon International's DNA, with Daniel inserted into the gap.

It truly was amazing what a little ingenuity could achieve.

CHAPTER 34

As Kovac walked, he replayed Anna's words on the phone. "I just want you all to leave me alone." *You all.* Like they were listening. Like she knew they were listening. Like she wanted to warn him.

He certainly hoped so, because his lie about the choice of house was now the only thing protecting Bennett.

He kept moving, coming down out of the trees. There wasn't any way to intercept the vans, even with the heavy snow as cover. He was too slow for them, and he would be outgunned anyway. He needed reinforcements before he worried about the vans.

He crossed the main road where it was dark, just a little out of town. Then he circled back towards the hotel, coming at it from behind and watching the windows for any sign of movement. There was no movement on this rear side, and all windows had curtains open. If there was a sniper, it seemed he was focused on the station.

Kovac climbed the rear fence of the hotel, which was brick up to his chest. It was easy enough to get over, but it took the better part of twenty seconds to do it silently with his rucksack and AR-15. He figured that was perhaps five seconds in a rush – three with adrenaline playing its part. *Quick enough.*

He kept to the wall and made his way along the side of the building, to the parking lot at the front. The parking lot was dark. So was the hotel. He slipped along the front side of the building, gun up, searching for threats. The parking lot was penned in by the fence. There was only one gate, which looked to be permanently retracted. Kovac wouldn't mess with that. Open was good. It could stay as it was.

He flipped up his night vision, which he no longer needed, and slipped into the lobby.

There was a man behind the front desk: young, in his twenties, but with a head of hair that was already well along the Norwood baldness scale. He started hiccupping at the sight of Kovac in his ballistic helmet, with his AR-15 raised.

Kovac cleared the rest of the lobby, then closed in on him, gun up. He said: 'English?' He figured there was a good chance of English, given this man's age and occupation.

The desk clerk raised his hands. 'A little, yes.' He hiccupped again.

'The yakuza rooms. Give me the keys. Three rooms. *Keys.*'

The clerk pointed to a board behind him. All the keys were hanging from it save for three.

'Spares? Extra? More keys?'

'There's a master key,' the clerk said, jutting out one hip to show a wad of keys attached to his uniform with a dog clip. It seemed his English was better than even he had given himself credit for.

'Okay, good. Let's go.'

The man didn't want to come out from behind his desk. 'Speed it up, c'mon.' Kovac signaled with the AR-15, jerking it towards the building's only elevator.

The clerk led him to the elevator: reluctantly now, checking behind as much as he looked ahead.

He pressed the button.

The doors opened.

He led Kovac in.

Kovac said: 'The two rooms that are side by side, what level?'

'Level 2.'

Kovac nodded for the desk clerk to press Level 2. He did.

'What rooms?'

'203 and 204.'

'And the other room, high up – what level?'

'Level 5. 504.'

'They request all three specifically?'

The clerk looked confused.

'Did they ask for those exact numbers?'

The desk clerk still didn't understand.

Kovac took out his phone and showed him the picture of Sukhomlinov. 'Was this guy with them? Japanese speaker, possibly with a British accent.'

'No.'

Kovac described Masuda.

'Yes.' The desk clerk nodded. 'I think so.'

'In the room on Level 5?'

'Yes.'

'Any other guests?'

The desk clerk shook his head. 'Right now, no, it's not so busy.'

He went to press Level 5 as well, but Kovac said: 'No, just Level 2.' Heading straight up to Level 5 was tempting. But Masuda would have subordinates protecting him and he would be in contact with the vans at the station. He could keep Kovac at bay and recall the vans, trapping him.

Ordinarily, Kovac wouldn't have used an elevator. But given the situation, he decided to risk it. The elevator doors shut.

The old elevator made a sharp thump, then started to rattle upwards. Kovac took the chance to lower the AR-15 a little, resting his arms.

Another thump.

The doors opened.

Kovac raised the gun again and signaled for the desk clerk to exit ahead of him. He did.

No dying a hail of gunfire, just an empty hallway.

Kovac followed his human shield out.

There wasn't much in this hallway, save for framed photographs at even intervals between the room doors. They were all scenic nature shots with a Japanese flavor. Kovac grabbed a framed picture of a lily pond and carp from the wall and jammed it in the elevator's doorway, preventing the doors from shutting and locking the elevator on Level 2. 'Okay,' he hissed, 'move.'

He led the desk clerk along the hallway, eventually pausing outside 203.

Not a sound.

He shifted, listening outside 204.

Again, not a sound.

He had been hoping for this. It seemed all the yakuza thugs had headed out, never expecting a visitor while gone. No one had been left in place to guard the rooms on Level 2.

Kovac nodded for the desk clerk to open the door. He put a finger to his lips, signaling "quietly". The desk clerk nodded. He unclipped the keys slowly, as if the slightest jangle, the slightest sound of metal on metal, would trigger some kind of hidden IED.

He unlocked the door, grimacing and turning the key so slowly he looked like he was straining to drive a stubborn screw the last of the way in. When done, he stood back.

Kovac entered.

Slow is smooth and smooth is fast.

He left the lights off. He cleared the bathroom and main room. No one. All empty. There were some personal effects: a suitcase, a few manga comics, tissues, a mask. But no weapons and, more importantly, no yakuza punks pointing guns at him.

He did the same in the next room.

Exactly like the first. Personal effects and nothing else.

He left the lights off in both rooms. He could see without them. And in the second he dropped the rucksack on one of two single beds. He took out a small device with a collection of aerials on top. He put it off to one side, ready to use. Then he took out his phone. He opened a browser and searched for the local Japanese emergency services number, before typing it into the hotel room phone and placing the call. It started ringing.

While he waited, he grabbed a notepad from a bedside table. It had the hotel name and address printed on each sheet, beside the hotel's faux British crest. He could just make it out in the gloom.

The call connected. 'Hi,' he said, 'English please.'

'Yes.'

Impersonating someone on the edge of panic, Kovac gave the hotel name and address. He read it straight from the little note pad. He explained that he'd had an altercation with some men in vans. They looked like gangsters, with tattoos. They'd been drunk. They'd taken an interest in his daughter, and when he told them to back off they'd pulled guns.

The woman on the other end of the call sounded as young as she did incredulous. 'Guns?'

'They have her,' Kovac said.

'Your daughter?'

'Yes. Please, you have to help me. They're still here. They have her in a van in the parking lot. I don't know what they're doing to her, but... *please.*' He gave the hotel address again. 'If they do something to... I... *please*, how long?'

The woman sounded like she was willing to give him the benefit of the doubt now. She asked him to stay calm and stay safe and wait for police, who would arrive soon. She told him not to do anything stupid.

Kovac hung up. He rang Bennett's number and Anna answered on the first ring. 'Tell them I have their boss, Level 5, 504. They can call him, but he won't answer. I flushed his phone. Tell them I'll trade. You for Masuda. You get all that?'

'Yes.' She sounded scared.

'Level 5, 504. Tell them now.'

CHAPTER 35

Kovac listened as Anna told them, then he hung up and returned to the bed. He picked up the device with all the aerials. It looked like a walkie-talkie, but it wasn't. He activated it, jamming the limited range of frequencies Japanese cell phones used. It was a good quality model, and he was confident it would jam every cell phone in the hotel and a little beyond.

'You can lower your hands,' he said to the desk clerk. 'Sit over there. So long as you don't move, you'll be fine. Oh, and get undressed.'

His eyes bulged.

'You heard me, get undressed.'

The desk clerk did it, still hiccupping as he climbed awkwardly out of his uniform.

Kovac moved to the window. He opened the glass pane as far as it would go without disturbing the curtains too much. He couldn't see the train station from this low down, but he had a great view of Masuda's Merc and the hotel parking lot.

He opted to keep the curtains closed and retreated again. He sat on a chair at a tiny desk and ignored his shadowy reflection in a tall mirror mounted on the wall. The room smelled of cigarette smoke.

He flicked through a folder as he waited, scanning the hotel map and ending up on a page detailing the adult channel's offerings.

The desk clerk, now just in his underwear, looked at him with new consternation. 'Underpants?' he asked, his voice trembling and cracking on the word.

'God no,' Kovac said, closing the folder with a snap. 'The Y-fronts stay on, my friend.'

He heard it soon enough – a vehicle approaching. With the window open, it was easy to track it without pulling the curtains. He heard it roll back into the parking lot. Just the one van. Doors opened, doors shut again, one of them a sliding door. The engine cut out.

There were no words exchanged. If one of the gangsters had noticed the newly open window on Level 2, he wasn't speaking up about it. Maybe he was pointing, Kovac thought, but he wouldn't do that for long.

Kovac stood and stabilized himself, AR-15 up and ready. He checked on the desk clerk, who still hadn't moved, then dropped his night vision down again. He opened the curtain with one fluid movement before returning his hand to the gun, and opened fire.

He used IR to target the men below. They were fish in a barrel. The first three he shot and killed, and after that he started shooting to wound. He wanted screaming, he wanted panic and desperate men fighting for survival.

There was no sign of Anna, but Kovac didn't shoot the van just in case she was in it.

When he had emptied a full magazine, having either killed or wounded every visible yakuza member, he pulled back and let the curtain drop shut again. He grabbed a new magazine from its pouch and reloaded without looking down, then flipped up the night vision and stepped further off to one side.

He resumed listening.

It was exactly as he had hoped. Screaming and panic. Desperate, confused men fighting for survival. And all of this layered over new, distant sirens.

Behind him, the desk clerk hiccupped again.

'Hold your breath,' Kovac said distractedly.

'What?'

'Stop breathing.'

Kovac sensed the man raise his hands again.

'Never mind. Put your hands down.'

Kovac listened as the police cars closed in, and smiled when gunfire erupted in the parking lot below. It sounded chaotic, as if it were being directed toward the police. He hung back and listened, but there was no return fire. The police were locals, baffled by the intensity of the fight they'd stumbled into.

Kovac tugged at the curtains, keeping back this time. He immediately took fire, three bullets punching through the light material and making it dance.

He told the desk clerk to take his position and jangle the curtain every so often, and walked to the room next door – a replica of the room he had just left.

He pulled this first room's curtain and pushed the window open in one quick movement. Again, he took fire, but it was wide of the mark now and he saw where it was coming from.

He pulled back, repositioned the night vision, and waited.

Ten seconds.

Twenty.

Thirty.

He went again, pulling his curtain but not shooting this time. He scanned the parking lot. The remaining thugs didn't even look up. They were now either preoccupied with injuries or the police.

The police, Kovac saw, were taking fire from the second van, which was trying to return from the train station. It had found the road blocked by police vehicles.

More police looked to be en route, too. Distant sirens and lights.

Kovac saw men drag Anna from the van in the parking lot below, looking to use her as a human shield. This gave him an all-clear for the second, distant van.

He was momentarily in two minds. If he opened fire from up here again, police might notice. That would make his exit harder. *But Goddamn if it wasn't tempting...*

He waited for another volley of gangster fire, and used it to cover his own shooting. He emptied a magazine into the distant van, watching with satisfaction as it suddenly started reversing. He could imagine the plinking sounds inside, the confusion and abject terror as they realized they were taking fire from somewhere on high. They reversed too fast and went off the road backward, down into a deep rice paddy. The van ended up near-vertical, on its rear doors.

Kovac pulled back, took another magazine from its pouch, and reloaded in a coordinated blur of unthinking arm and hand movements. The spent magazine dropped with a dull thud onto the carpet.

Up with the night vision again, the blue world dropping back into a murky grey. He returned to the first room. 'Time to move,' he said to the desk clerk.

He led him back out into the hallway and marched him to the emergency staircase door. The man was still holding his keys.

'Give me your keys and stay right fucking here. On this exact spot. You got that? If you move, I absolutely *will* kill you. Do you understand what I'm telling you?'

Nodding, the man handed over the keys. Kovac clipped them to his belt, then silently opened the door and entered the building's emergency staircase.

He waited. The staircase smelled strongly of industrial cleaning products. For a long time, the only sound he could hear was the shooting outside, which had become sporadic. It still didn't sound like the police had returned fire. Kovac wondered if they even had guns. Based on his research before flying here, they should all have been carrying .38s.

No door opening overhead, no footsteps.

He wondered if he had been too slow.

One full minute passed.

Two minutes.

Three.

Suddenly, Kovac heard the door on Level 5. There were footsteps in the staircase. They were moving fast, making a lot of noise. Maybe even taking the stairs two at a time.

Masuda and his protection giving up on an unresponsive elevator, Kovac hoped. They were feeling trapped, at risk of arrest. They were looking for a way out, doubtless hoping to make use of the confusion outside for an opportunistic escape.

The stairs were metal and solid. There was no way to see up or down through them. They were narrow, too. Twelve stairs per flight, then a landing and a 180-degree turn into another flight. Then twelve more stairs, another landing, another 180-degree turn – and so on down to reception.

Kovac ambushed Masuda and his three bodyguards as they made the final 180-degree turn into what he was now thinking of as *his* staircase. They came swinging around and he killed two bodyguards and almost killed Masuda too before hooking the shot in a deliberate miss.

One bodyguard remained. He'd been trailing Masuda and he now turned and scrambled back up the stairs, practically crawling until he could get himself upright again. Masuda followed, shouting at him.

Kovac went after them. They tried shooting down, pistol shots bouncing angrily off metal stairs and concrete walls in the enclosed space.

One bullet – or part of a bullet – passed Kovac's ear and made a *tsss* sound, like someone forcing air through their front teeth.

He slapped at his ear, ducking reflexivity, like a man under attack from a mosquito. He retreated five stairs. 'You messed up, Masuda,' he called up.

There was no reply, but the footsteps slowed. Kovac knew Masuda spoke English. It had been in the man's file – the original file he'd been given ahead of the hit on Yamada.

'How many of your guys have I killed now anyway?' Kovac waited, counting to five and then ten in his head. Finally, Masuda's accented voice bounced down the stairwell. 'Kovac?'

He said the "v" like a "b".

Koback.

'You want to get out of this hotel alive, Masuda?'

No answer.

'Because that one guy you've got up there, I'm not sure about him. He seemed a bit... well, shit-scared.'

Still no answer.

'I can get you out of here, Masuda.'

Masuda's voice bounced down again. 'How?'

Kovac was impressed. No "why did you kill my men?". No "I don't trust you". Just a clear-eyed focus on the future. The man wanted out and he was open to ideas. He wasn't a boss for nothing.

'Easy. Kill that bodyguard you've got there, and come down with your hands up.'

'Faku you.'

'Fuck me?'

'Faku you, yes.'

Kovac put his head back against the cold concrete and smiled. 'Okay, Masuda, fuku me. You win.'

CHAPTER 36

Kovac started moving up the stairs again, silently putting distance between himself and the position in time and space where his voice had just been. In Masuda's mind, he'd still be a long way down. Masuda's brain had measured the volume and echo without Masuda even knowing it. And he wouldn't question that information until he heard something new. Either that, or until enough time passed to generate a question: "*I wonder if Kovac's moved?*".

If Kovac was lucky, which he normally was, that wouldn't happen until Masuda's brain gave up puzzling out the deliberately perplexing "you win" and settled on a plan of action. Ten seconds at least.

Kovac stepped soundlessly over the two men he had shot, one dead, one bleeding out onto the metal stairs. He left their pistols where they were and rounded the 180-degree turn with his gun up, but there was no Masuda, no bodyguard. The old boss was doing the same as Kovac – stealthily moving higher.

Kovac started silently up the next twelve steps: gun still up, ready to kill the remaining bodyguard. At the next 180-degree turn, he swung the gun round but overbalanced ever so slightly. It clanged softly against the metal corner, and he heard the two men overhead start running.

Kovac sprinted and caught them bunching at the doorway to Level 5. They weren't coordinating their exit. They were practically working against one another, trying to get through the door at the same time. No one was providing cover, and both were exposed.

Kovac shot the final bodyguard in the chest. 'Offer still stands,' he said to Masuda after the bodyguard went down. 'I need help getting out, you need help getting out, we work this problem together. But if you tell me to go fuck myself again, so help me God, I will put a bullet in your head.' Kovac gestured with his gun for Masuda to come down the stairs.

Masuda hesitated for a moment, looking at the dead man at his feet. Then he complied.

'How?' he asked, coming down the stairs.

'How do we get out? We start with me searching you. Hands up on the wall, high as you can.'

Reaching the landing, Masuda again did as he was told.

Kovac searched him and found a knife and money clip with cash. Nothing else. Masuda hadn't been carrying a gun. The fool had been relying on his bodyguards instead. 'Not so tough without your Fedora and goon squad, are you?' Kovac pocketed the knife and money, putting them with his train tickets and other trash from Tokyo. He noted that the shooting had abruptly stopped outside, which meant either the police or yakuza had prevailed. Kovac hoped it was the police.

'Who gave you my name?' he asked. 'Back in Tokyo, who wanted me dead?'

Masuda said nothing.

'You want out of here, or do I put a bullet in your head right now? Answer the fucking question, Masuda. Who was trying to kill me? Did the order come from you or higher up?'

'Peng Biao.'

'Amputee Peng?'

Masuda nodded.

'What about Yamada? Who killed him? Sukhomlinov?'

Masuda nodded again.

'Who's feeding you this intel?' Kovac forced Masuda back down the stairs, the AR-15 pointed at his back. 'Answer me. Who told you I was coming for Yamada?'

'Peng Biao.'

'Who told Peng?'

Masuda shrugged, cowering now. He paused and slowly turned, hands out. He wasn't smirking or gloating. He was morose, as if he didn't expect to survive the next few seconds.

'*Who*?'

'King.'

Kovac felt a stab of terror. He blinked, stunned by the word. There was no way Masuda could know the codename "King".

And yet there was no doubting what he had just said, either.

Kovac struggled to control his fear, jabbing the muzzle of the gun as close as he dared to Masuda's face. 'Where's Peng Biao?' he asked. 'Where is he *right fucking now*?'

Masuda shrugged.

'*Where*?'

Masuda shook his head. Not as a refusal to cooperate, but in a way that suggested he genuinely didn't know.

'Where's he meeting you next?'

'Tomorrow.'

'Not when, *where*.'

Masuda nodded. 'Fun Manager.'

'Fund Manager? Who's the fund manager?'

The shooting started up again outside – a hollow popping sound, suggesting the police .38s – and Kovac realized he was out of time.

'Okay,' he said, making a snap decision to torture Masuda later, 'you know enough for me to get you out of this building alive. Keep walking down these stairs, get the door – we'll exit at Level 2. No stupid moves or I shoot you. It's that simple.'

Kovac sounded calm, but internally he was reeling. What did he know about King's world really? He'd met the man maybe a handful of times a year. Sure that had taken place over a lot of years, giving the illusion of a long-term relationship – something that went beyond simple business. But it was Bishop he had always trusted with his life, never King.

Had King fucked him? Handed him to Peng?

Yes. He had confirmation now.

And it got worse.

For Peng Biao to know about the hit on Yamada, Kovac was done. He was finished with Curzon, possibly even marked for disposal. He didn't know why Curzon was giving him guns and a file on Peng, and it didn't matter. An enemy of his enemy wasn't his friend.

He was on his own.

His rage boiled over, and he vented it by kicking Masuda as hard as he could in the small of the back. He hadn't planned it, but physics was physics. He sent the old man crashing down into the closed door on Level 2.

It would take some getting used to, and it wasn't something Kovac was able to fully comprehend yet, but from now on he had to consider Curzon and anyone associated with them his enemy.

Including Bishop.

'You didn't see the handle here?' he said, pulling a stunned Masuda up by the hair like a rag doll and slamming him face-first into the door handle.

Once, twice, three times.

Masuda ended up slumped with his back to the door, his legs splayed, barely conscious. Kovac crouched down beside him, still looking to excise his anger. It took all the self-control he had not to spit in Masuda's bloodied face and drive a foot straight into his groin. 'The door handle was for Anna, you piece of shit,' he snarled.

CHAPTER 37

Kovac felt better.

Not a lot better. His world was still collapsing. But at least the rage was under control.

He threw Masuda into the Level 2 hallway, where he lay in a heap, unable to breathe. Masuda stared up with glazed eyes at the young balding man standing over him in his underwear.

It was the desk clerk.

'See what happens to people I don't like,' Kovac said to the clerk, pulling Masuda up again and shoving him forward down the hallway.

The clerk hiccupped.

'The desk clerk's clothes are there,' Kovac said to Masuda as soon as they were back in the room. 'Put them on.'

'Why?' Masuda spluttered the word, his face bleeding. He was struggling to suck in air, as if suffering a heart attack.

'You said you want to get out of this building right? Well, that's what we're doing. And it's not going to happen with you looking like a pimp in your bright purple tie. Get it all off before you get even more blood on it.'

'I don't –'

'You're the desk clerk now.'

Masuda made three attempts to speak. Finally, he managed to get the words out. 'And you? Who are you?'

'A father, desperate to get his daughter back – being led out of the hotel by the helpful desk clerk.'

'Anna is your daughter?' The fear on Masuda's face as he made this connection was priceless.

'No more than you're the desk clerk. But the police think she is.' Kovac deactivated the jammer and slipped it under a bed along with the rest of his gear. He dumped his helmet and night vision in a cupboard and shut the door. Masuda finished pulling the pants up and started on the shirt. It had the faux hotel crest on the front pocket.

'How do you know Peng?' Kovac asked.

'He gives me drugs. Drugs and girls.'

'Where, how?'

'Kanagawa. South of Tokyo. I sell the drugs here in Japan. I make the girls work.'

'Why did you come up here?'

'To find you.'

'To kill me?'

'Yes.'

'That went well for you. On whose orders? King or Peng?'

'Peng. He's my boss. I do what he says.' Masuda finished putting the uniform on. He looked entirely transformed, like he was now on the fast track to an austere retirement.

Kovac transferred the keys as a final touch, clipping them to Masuda's pants. 'Clean up your face in the bathroom and make sure all your tattoos are covered.'

When Masuda was done washing, Kovac led him out into the hallway at gunpoint. 'There are three dead guys in the stairs,' he said to the desk clerk. 'Get one and bring him here. You touch the pistols there, you die. And try not to leave a trail of blood.'

The desk clerk stared at him like he was insane.

'Look, I need a corpse. It can be one from the staircase, or I can use you. You require less dragging.'

The man set off into the staircase.

Waiting for him to return, Kovac said to Masuda: 'There aren't going to be any guns for this next part. So keep in mind, I'm your only way out of this hotel. You attack me, best case scenario you go to jail. More likely, I kill you.'

Masuda nodded.

The desk clerk was taking a while. Kovac led Masuda back to the room and waited there. The desk clerk eventually showed up at the door, out of breath, dragging a corpse. He had stuffed hotel towels up under the dead man's jacket to stop the bleeding and avoid a trail. He dragged him in.

Kovac searched the clerk but the threat had worked. He didn't have a pistol.

'Bit of exercise took care of your hiccups, didn't it,' Kovac said, unloading and wiping down the AR-15. He tossed it over towards the window before swapping to his pistol. 'Now put him over there with the gun, like he was the shooter, and remove those towels. Throw them in the bathtub and pull the shower curtain.'

Again, the desk clerk followed all orders perfectly. He was a good worker.

'Get into the gangster outfit there, purple tie and all. After we're gone, you go to the room on the fifth level. When they search it and find you, you tell them your name is Ken Masuda. Say that for me now.'

'I'm Ken Masuda.'

'And then you refuse to say another word. Not a word. You got it?'

The desk clerk nodded, dressed in Masuda's clothes, then left for the top level, still working on his purple tie.

Kovac wiped down his pistol, unloaded it, and slipped it under the bed. He was sad to be saying goodbye to all his gear. But he had known from the outset it would be the cost of a clean exit with Masuda.

Worth it, he thought. Masuda clearly knew a lot.

'Ready to walk out of here?'

'They will arrest us,' Masuda said.

'That's the plan, yeah.' Kovac gestured for Masuda to lead the way. Unarmed was one thing, but walking with his back to a crime boss wasn't on his bucket list.

He dumped his ammo in the cupboard with the helmet, including the ammo for the 1911s. All he kept was Masuda's knife, which he would ditch in the lobby.

He shut the door again and gave the room one last check.

It would confuse and delay, nothing more. But right now, that was all Kovac needed.

CHAPTER 38

It went beautifully.

There was still a lot of confusion downstairs in the parking lot, even though the police had won the day and Masuda's men were either dead or under arrest. The surviving goons spotted Masuda, but they spotted the hotel uniform, too. They sensed an escape and kept their mouths shut.

A few police officers remained with their pistols trained on the hotel, scanning windows, while others searched Kovac and Masuda for weapons. They found nothing; Kovac had dumped Masuda's little knife on the way out.

No officers entered the hotel.

When Kovac made it clear he was the foreign father who had placed the original emergency call, a female officer returned Anna to Kovac. He gave her an enormous hug. 'Call me daddy,' he whispered, trying not to grin as he said it.

He asked for an officer who spoke English and explained what a support the desk clerk had been throughout his harrowing ordeal. He recounted the way the desk clerk had taken on a few of the gangsters, weathering a beating in an attempt to get his daughter back. He was a hero, no other word for it.

The local officers all bowed and thanked Masuda, and gestured for him to get in a squad car. They tried to guide Kovac and Anna into a separate car, but Kovac was ready for this. 'You know, I'd like to stick with my new friend,' he said.

'He's been amazing, and he speaks English. He can help me understand what's going on.'

There was reluctance. The request provoked a lot of intense conversation and more translation. Kovac could see it travel up the chain of command, to a man in his sixties who gave a curt, distracted nod. He had bigger fish to fry. He was pointing up at the topmost level of the hotel, intent on getting the yakuza boss out.

Clearly, they didn't yet have a photo of Masuda.

Back down the chain of command the answer came, to the same young woman who had returned Anna to Kovac. 'Yes,' she said, pointing to Masuda, who was now in the rear seat of the first vehicle. 'With friend, yes, okay.'

'Yes,' said Kovac under his breath, sliding into the middle seat beside Masuda, 'with friend, okay, off we all go.'

Anna got in after him.

But it wasn't "off we all go". The police shut the car doors for them, and the three of them just sat there, in the back seat, uncomfortable. Police officers came and went. Bad guys were lined up and sorted and photographed. A few officers took photos of corpses, then of casings and finally just of blood. Spoilt for choice, Kovac thought, and not at all used to it.

He worried the police would receive a photo from Tokyo of Masuda. But they didn't, or if they did they didn't make the connection with the desk clerk in the back seat.

Eventually, two police officers got in the car. The young woman got into the front passenger seat and a young man with a short, tubby frame got into the driver's seat. He started the engine and ran the wipers for a bit, clearing snow. He put the heater on and cracked the window ever so slightly to deal with fogging. Then he did exactly what Kovac was praying he would do. He put the car in gear and drove Kovac, Masuda and Anna straight out of the parking lot, through a barricade police had set up.

Kovac said: 'Where are we going?'

The tubby driver said something in Japanese.

Masuda translated: 'Police station.'

The car started back towards town on side roads, snow-filled paddies on either side. Kovac didn't want to hurt the police officers, partly because they had been nothing but friendly and partly because he didn't want the police car veering off into a paddy the way the van had. From the splash of the headlights, it looked like a five-foot drop down into the paddies.

But he didn't want to go to the police station, either.

He didn't have a weapon he could easily access, but there were weapons in the car. Two of them, in the front seats. They belonged to the officers, who had been nothing but friendly. Two Smith and Wesson .38s, if Kovac wasn't mistaken, or some Japanese variant thereof. Both holstered.

He sensed Masuda glance at him as if looking for encouragement or instruction. Kovac didn't move. He was in the middle seat. He could see a long way out in front with the headlights. They were coming up to an intersection, where this road met another road. Also elevated, more rice paddies in every direction. He remembered the layout from his time up in the forest with the night vision. There would be this turn up ahead, then one more stretch of narrow road, and then they'd be back on the main drag that ran through town.

The car was warming up fast, the heater working hard. It smelled like air freshener, faintly floral. Kovac's face was hot, like it was burning up from the inside with fever. He scratched at his scalp, feeling each bump in the road come up through his spine. It wasn't a relaxing ride.

The police radio remained silent, which meant they hadn't yet puzzled out who was in the back seat. But they would.

They drove on.

Exactly 50 kilometers per hour, according to the speedo.

There was an LCD panel on the radio illuminating the woman officer's pistol. But otherwise not much light in the car now that they were out in the paddies.

They slowed for the corner.

They took the turn. Hand over hand on the steering wheel.

Straightening up again.

Accelerating again.

Last stretch of darkness now, then the main road, Kovac thought.

A small section of the roof's upholstery had come loose at some point and, bored, the woman officer started pressing it back into place. She craned her neck and tested the material like she was thinking about how she might repair it later. She certainly wasn't expecting trouble from the back seat.

Masuda glanced at Kovac again.

Kovac said: 'I'm going to vomit.'

CHAPTER 39

There was confusion and questions until Masuda translated, then the car was slowing rapidly and pulling off to the left of the narrow road, Anna getting out and clearing the way for Kovac even before the vehicle came to a complete stop.

Kovac didn't follow. He went for the woman officer's pistol and got it as she moved to launch herself out. She had both hands to her door, her body leaning away from the gun. An easy grab, as these things went.

Kovac aimed at the driver. He ordered the woman officer out, then called for Anna to get in the front seat.

She did, closing the door.

The woman officer was left out on the road.

'Tell him to drive,' Kovac said.

Masuda translated for the driver. It took a while. There was a back and forth, then what sounded like clarification.

The driver eventually shook his head. He had said his bit, seemingly, and he wasn't willing to say a word more.

He wasn't driving, either.

'If it's about his partner, tell him she'll be fine. Tell him to drive.'

Masuda translated again. But he obviously added a little extra again too because the driver unholstered his pistol and handed it backward.

He passed it on the door side, along the side of the car,

directly to Masuda. Out of reach of Kovac.

Kovac went for this new pistol with his free left hand but immediately realized his error. Masuda had reached forward with his right hand. He was going to get the gun in the narrow space between the front seat and the car's chassis, and the front seat was going to protect the exchange and thwart Kovac.

Kovac had miscalculated.

Masuda got hold of the pistol and pointed it at Kovac. There was a single, pressurized pop.

CHAPTER 40

The single gunshot left Kovac's ears ringing and his nostrils filled with the stench of burnt gunpowder.

Masuda bled out fast. Official cause of death: a .38 caliber bullet to the chest.

Kovac was the shooter. He had given up on getting the driver's pistol with his free hand. In the split second available to him, he had jammed the pistol he was already holding into Masuda's ribs. He had not planned to shoot, but Masuda had tried to aim with the driver's gun. Self-defense. Maybe not in a court of law, but close enough here in a police car in the middle of nowhere.

Kovac took Masuda's pistol and phone from him. He had attempted to interrogate Masuda as he bled out, wanting to know more about the fund manager, about tomorrow's meeting, but Masuda had stuck to Japanese. In the end, Kovac hadn't understood a word. Anna said she hadn't caught much either. Apparently, Masuda's Japanese was too guttural and slangy.

The two police officers looked to be in shock. The driver was still in his seat and the woman officer was standing out in the dark. Kovac wasn't surprised to see them both freeze up. They worked in a small town in the safest country in the world, and they had already endured a big night of firsts.

'What did he say to you?' Kovac asked the driver. 'He said I was asking for your gun?'

The driver just held up his hands. If he spoke English he wasn't letting on.

Kovac told Anna to get out of the car. He followed her out. It was freezing and silent save for a strong breeze whipping across the big, snow-filled paddies. Kovac could see it driving up plumes. It had finally stopped snowing, though.

He took the officer's phones, removed the SIMs and switched them both off. He snapped the SIMs, then made the two officers start a long walk out into one of the paddies before ripping out the car's radio.

The snow was deep. Deeper than it looked. The officers had to really raise their knees and trudge.

Kovac knew they would turn around and make their way back to the hotel as soon as he was gone. They would shamefacedly tell their story. But this march would at least slow them down a little, buy him time to maneuver.

The truth was, Kovac was in a world of shit. He had Anna in tow who was slowing him down. He had another woman with broken fingers in a house that wasn't his, also slowing him down. And he had King, who was supposedly protecting him, out to kill him.

Now, as icing on this shit cake, he had just shot a crime boss with two local cops as witnesses.

Masuda alive had been leverage and possibly intel. Masuda dead was just more enemies, in this case the yakuza.

Kovac blew out cold air, completely emptying his lungs, enjoying the fact he could see his white breath even in the dark. It was oddly calming, oddly reaffirming. He wasn't dead yet.

He watched the officers trudging, leaving a deep channel in their wake. He hadn't slept in forever but at least he wasn't making stupid mistakes. He had remembered their phones before sending them on their march.

Anna said: 'You okay?'

'Yeah, why wouldn't I be?'

'Well, you just killed a yakuza boss. And you look...'

He waited.

She shrugged.

'I look what, Anna?'

'Worried.'

'You said it yourself, I just killed a yakuza boss.'

'I was hoping you'd deny it.'

'The killing, or being worried?'

'Being worried.'

'Why?'

She shrugged. 'To reassure me. I haven't seen you worried before, that's all.'

Kovac looked directly up into the night sky, trying to think. The cloud cover had thinned out. He could see stars.

'So what do we do now?' Anna asked. 'Is it over?'

'Switch Bennett's phone off.'

She took it out and switched it off. 'And now?'

'For God's sake,' he muttered.

'I'm serious. What's the plan, Kovac? Are we safe?'

'That's what I'm working on. We...' He shrugged. 'I don't know. We go get Bennett, I guess.'

'You *guess*? And after that?'

He glanced at her. 'Did your parents seem distracted growing up? Never quite listening?'

She frowned as if thinking back. Then she seemed to get what he was driving at. 'I ask a lot of questions and I'm a pest, sure – but you don't answer many.' She wrapped her arms around herself. 'I'm scared, okay. That's all it is.' She was silent for a blissful half second. Then she added: 'Seriously though, what do we do after we get Bennett?'

Kovac didn't know. That was the problem. Normally, this was where he called Bishop. He would hit an impasse and get on the phone and figure it out. Bishop fixed most problems. King and money fixed the rest. Not tonight.

Kovac returned to his thoughts. He tried to prioritize. He decided Masuda wasn't a concern. The police officers would eventually report in, and the news would leak out. Kovac would be hunted by the yakuza, countless goons putting on their warm-weather gear and driving up into the mountains for vengeance. But all that would take time.

Peng and King were the priority. 'Son of a bitch,' he said, more to himself than Anna.

'What? Are we in danger?'

'I think so, yeah.'

'Worse than on the way up here?'

Kovac borrowed a finger to permanently unlock Masuda's phone, then dragged the gangster's corpse clear. 'Can I kick him in the balls?' Anna asked, circling the car and standing over him.

'You don't think maybe you had better opportunities for that?' Kovac rolled him unceremoniously down into the rice paddy. 'Too late now.' He switched Masuda's phone off, then got in the driver's seat and gestured for Anna to get in the car.

'What if we're pulled over?' she asked, glancing back. 'There's blood all over the back seat.'

'The entire local police force is at the hotel. And anyway, we're not taking it far. Just back to the treeline. We'll dump it there, out of sight.'

He started the engine and took out his phone. He saw there were two messages. He'd missed the buzzes in amongst everything.

Both from Bishop: an encrypted text and an encrypted folder.

Kovac skimmed the first text as Anna put her seat belt on. It said the yakuza phones had been analyzed. The results were in the encrypted folder.

Kovac wouldn't be able to trust any of it.

He switched his phone off and pulled the SIM out. He got out of the car again and destroyed the phone with one heel, wincing at the pain from his blisters. He snapped the SIM, then threw it and the ruined phone as far out into the rice paddy as he could manage.

'Feel better?' Anna asked when he got back in and put the car in gear.

'Much.'

CHAPTER 41

Kovac dumped the car and led Anna back along the forest trail. He was back to noticing his blisters again, back to noticing the cold again. He followed his footprints from earlier in the night.

Anna trudged behind, filling in a few blanks. She said Masuda's men had approached her in the convenience store. They had offered her better money if she returned to them and had threatened to kill her if she didn't. They had told her they wanted Kovac.

Kovac noticed the way she glossed over being used as bait and focused on the shootout at the hotel. He found it interesting, hearing it all from her perspective. She told him she had fully expected to die, especially when they dragged her out into the parking lot as a human shield. She talked about how miserable she had been at this thought. The family she wouldn't get to see back home in Austria, the countries she had planned to visit, the family of her own she would never start, children of her own, a whole life. By the time she was done, he sensed she was on the verge of tears. Doubtless, she was still in shock.

'Too soon, not enough time,' he said under his breath.

'What?'

'Too soon, not enough time. It's a lucky person who dies thinking anything else.'

She wanted his version of events. So, in matter-of-fact terms, he gave her a summary of everything he'd done inside the hotel. He spent more time on the hiccupping desk clerk and his Y-fronts than he did on the corpses in the stairwell, trying to keep it light. She laughed at a few points, but when he was done she immediately turned serious again. 'Thanks for Masuda.'

'Literally a pleasure.'

After this, they walked in silence. Kovac remained alert. Masuda was dead but Peng and King remained as real and well-resourced threats. Sukhomlinov was still out here somewhere too, looking for his shot.

Kovac thought about the video of the young, trafficked girls. He thought about the garbled information Masuda had given him before they entered the police car. Something about a fund manager, all of it connected to Peng Biao, and maybe even to King. Something about Kanagawa, too, south of Tokyo.

None of it made much sense.

'How are you doing back there, Anna?'

She laughed. 'I'm almost kind of enjoying this walk. You?'

He grinned. She was a good kid and she deserved better than the shit she'd fallen into down in Tokyo.

He said: 'You know what percentage of this country is mountains and forest?'

'No.'

'Guess.'

'Twenty percent?'

'That's the global average.'

'Ten then.'

'Almost seventy.'

She laughed with surprise.

'I'm serious,' he said.

'How do you know that?'

'I research places – before I visit.'

'For your secret job?'

'For my secret charity work, exactly.'

The old Meiji-era house was dark when they got back, as it was meant to be. Kovac announced their arrival, not that it mattered. Bennett was asleep, having laid out a futon upstairs. She had wrapped herself in multiple layers of clothing and blankets.

So much for getting out of Japan, Kovac thought with a smirk.

Downstairs, he took his boots off. He couldn't see the blisters, but he could feel them. One was still a bubble. The others had all burst and were wet to the touch.

The place smelled different. Like musk now. Almost like Bishop's foul deodorant. He figured it was the new boots.

Kovac laid out a second futon in the kitchen for Anna to use. He told her to get some sleep. 'I'll wake you in a few hours. After that, you and Bennett can keep an eye out while I sleep.'

'You're not going to sleep now?'

'No. Later. I'll take the first watch.'

He moved to the window, edging one curtain back. He stared down at the apartment building Peng Biao supposedly used as cover in Japan. It didn't feel right. It was too bland, too generic. There was more to its crafted disguise, something he was missing.

He turned, sat down and swapped his boots for sneakers. 'Change of plan, you keep an eye out now, then sleep when I get back.'

'You're heading out again?'

'Just for a bit. You can sleep as soon as I'm back, but right now I need you to –'

'But if you don't come back?'

'Then you and Bennett need to get out of Japan.' He nodded upstairs, towards Bennett. 'I told her the same thing, so do it better than that.'

'How?'

His mind was too full of details already. He didn't want to run through a scenario that, in all likelihood, would never eventuate. 'I'll be back in half an hour, probably less,' he said. 'Trust me on that.'

He grabbed one of the Colt 1911s before remembering he had dumped the ammo to get through the police search as he exited the business hotel. 'Shit.'

He threw it aside and picked up the police .38s again. He confirmed both were loaded. He gave one to Anna.

'Is the safety on?' she asked.

'It's been half a century since anyone tried to put a safety on a revolver.'

'So what stops it going off?'

'The trigger.'

She looked like she was holding a tarantula – like she wanted to drop it immediately. 'Don't worry. It's a double-action revolver. With your hand, you'll really need to pull on that trigger to shoot. Just don't let that mess up your aim.'

He tucked his own pistol into his belt at the small of his back and checked it wasn't printing too badly. He hated working without a holster, but stealing the police holsters wouldn't have worked. They didn't allow for concealed carry.

'Who would I be aiming at, though?'

'Bad guys.'

'And how will I know they're bad?'

'They're not me. Don't shoot me.'

Without saying goodbye, he let himself back out into the cold. He walked down the series of roadside staircases to Peng's apartment, which was dark and silent. He circled it.

No one around.

A place Peng used when no one was looking for him, Kovac reasoned. His business-as-usual, Average Joe place. But right now Peng would be taking a very different approach to his security. Less blending in, more hiding behind bodyguards and elaborate electronic systems.

That's what Kovac would do anyway.

He moved round to the rear door, gun still up.

He knocked.

No one came to the door, no one opened it. So, as Bishop had trained him to do, he searched the area. *Never make a scene that could get you killed before checking for a key.* He checked the ledge above the door and checked a few pot-plants. No luck. Then he noticed a small rock garden off to his left. He tried a few of the larger rocks – again without luck – then a few mid-sized ones. Sure enough, one slid up from amongst the others with a plastic pill container glued to the underside. Kovac was able to unscrew the orange container from the white cap glued to the rock. Inside was a key. He tried it, and it unlocked the door.

Kovac cleared the rooms, one corner after another, then flicked the lights on. He was done with stealth. The important thing now was speed. In and out before any of the police over at the business hotel were released to respond.

The apartment smelled a lot better than the house he had chosen for Anna and Bennett. Like someone had cleaned it recently. There was some kind of antiseptic smell. Eucalyptus maybe.

He searched the place systematically.

The kitchen had everything a single man would need. A few plates, a few bowls, chopsticks and a single pot – as if maybe Peng made do with instant noodles when lying low. The food in the cupboards was all packaged, with expiry dates that ran a few years out into the future.

The bathroom was the same. Toothbrush, toothpaste, razor, hand soap. Nothing but essentials.

Kovac moved through into the remaining two rooms. At first, he thought they were unfurnished. But they were tatami, the lack of furniture a deliberate choice. A quick search of the inbuilt wardrobes revealed folded futons, which could be dragged down onto the floor and laid out. Kovac found blankets but no clothing. No suits, jeans, T-shirts, underpants, socks…

He paused, noticing something odd about the back wall of the final wardrobe. There was a door, one that could only have led into the adjacent apartment. He tried the handle. It was flimsy and generic but locked.

He frowned, turning on the spot, thinking this through. The place felt more like a serviced apartment than someone's home away from home. There was absolutely nothing in it that could be classed as personal. And like a serviced apartment or hotel room, it had doors between adjoining suites.

He tried the key in the secret door and it worked. He edged the door open and saw the apartment next door was bare, as if emptied ahead of leasing.

He shut the dividing door and slipped out the rear door again. No neighbors were waiting for him, nor any police officers. Just the same silent, empty streets.

He paused, staring at the entrance to the underground parking lot at the opposite, far end of the building.

Given the lack of response, maybe he had more time than he realized.

He walked to it, counting his steps, and found that it was open to the street. He thought of Bishop's wording: "An apartment in a building we think he indirectly owns and maybe even built". Kovac took out the .38 again and walked down a ramp into the underground parking lot, then started back towards Peng's apartment. There were no cars. Not a single one.

His steps echoed now. Again, he counted them. He came up fifty steps short.

He backtracked and returned to the street, stopping again at the door to Peng's apartment. He could sense people staring at him from nearby buildings now. He saw curtains and heavier drapes drop back into place at the sight of the pistol.

The secret door in the wardrobe was irritating him. Likewise, the lack of cars in the parking lot and the discrepancy between his two step counts. He decided to risk one more search. It was a busy night for the police, after all, and the neighbors were clearly cowered.

He did another sweep of the apartment, then put the pistol back in his belt and focused on the heavy tatami mats. As he had expected based on his step count, one of them had a small finger loop, a tag Kovac could unpick, then untuck. He used it to lift an entire panel of tatami and stepped back.

A high-tech, steel trapdoor.

CHAPTER 42

Peng phoned Masuda to get confirmation of Kovac's death, but the call didn't connect.

The phone was off?

Peng knew what this meant.

He made a few more calls and he was promised answers. He waited impatiently, until finally his phone buzzed. He answered. 'What happened?'

The report was not encouraging. Japanese gangsters found dead at a business hotel, a Japanese man found dead in a rice paddy, a police car missing, and a tall foreigner on the run with a pretty girl.

Peng requested photos of the dead Japanese man and soon received them.

Masuda.

Peng put out orders to check and strengthen all perimeter defenses, then sat down. Staring out over the snowy forest, and hearing the sound of men and dogs below, he knew his next move. He had planned for this. There was a contingency, because that was his nature. Envisage and prepare for failure, never assume success. He'd even discussed it with Masuda. If the hit up here in the mountains failed, it was imperative to lure Kovac away, back down towards the sea. He was too close here.

Peng looked across at the men with rifles. They were lying on tables now, set back from the room's small windows. They were staring through scopes. No doubt they sensed his gaze, but they went on staring, searching for a target.

Fortified as it was, Peng didn't want Kovac coming here. He started planning. He had been intending to use Fun Manager for Bishop anyway; he would now simply swap out Kovac for Bishop, prioritizing Curzon's key hitman.

He could deal with Bishop later.

He wondered if Masuda had played his part to the bitter end? Hopefully the man had kept his honor and told Kovac about Fun Manager, as promised. About King. But even if Masuda had given up Peng's location here in the mountains, the Fun Manager plan could still work. Kovac would default to saving Lottie. He would prioritize her and head for Kanagawa, sparing Peng a pitch battle.

Peng kept thinking. He was down to fine details now.

He would use Sukhomlinov for the Fun Manager hit because there was no time to arrange anyone else. But would Lottie arrive on time?

He decided there were ways around that, too.

It could all still work.

He placed a call to Daniel, using the encrypted comms channel his jammers kept open. 'The plan's changed, Daniel. Add a condition. If they want Lottie back, they hand over Kovac. They deliver him to us tomorrow, Kanagawa.' Peng explained the Fun Manager plan and how Daniel needed to sell it to Luther and Megan. Then he ran through what Megan would need to say to Kovac. Finally, he gave Daniel Masuda's cell phone number. 'Kovac may have ditched his Curzon phone. If so, have Megan try him on this number. I think he's grabbed Masuda's cell. There's no other explanation for it being turned off.'

'Masuda's dead?' Daniel sounded uneasy.

'Play your part, Daniel. Get Lottie in the air, and begin negotiations.'

'Kovac will kill us if this fails.'

'He's one man against our combined strength. It's a delay, Daniel, nothing more. Don't lose your nerve. A few days, and Curzon International will be ours.'

CHAPTER 43

Luther Curzon was woken by Megan gently touching his shoulder. She pointed to one of the monitors in the underground panic bunker. 'It's Daniel,' she said.

Luther had been crammed into the underground bunker all night, watching the monitors with his daughter, wife and all of Pemberton's staff. The helicopter that had gone to the gorge had returned with his son and young daughter, Lottie. He had tried to stay awake, but at some point around 4 a.m. – with nothing happening – he had failed. He was getting old, that was the problem. He was slipping, missing things he would've spotted even just ten years ago. The constant pain of cancer and arthritis didn't help.

On the monitor, Luther saw Daniel standing patiently at one of the core's fortified doorways.

He checked his watch, blinking to wake himself up and fighting down a yawn. He saw it was coming up on sunrise.

Last thing he knew, at 4 a.m., both Daniel and Lottie had been in the stationary helicopter. The two of them had been hostages, hands tied at the wrists. Lottie had been exhausted from crying and continually nodding off only to jolt awake. Now Lottie's helicopter was gone, and Daniel was at the perimeter of the core. Luther knew why.

Negotiations.

He nodded for Megan to turn on the microphone. He cleared his throat, doing his best to project his voice while still sitting on the bunker's concrete floor. 'Are you hurt, Daniel?'

'No.'

'Is Lottie hurt? Have they done anything to her, anything at all?'

'No.'

'Where is she?'

'Unless you come out, they're taking her to Japan.'

'*Japan*? Why Japan? And who's holding you hostage?'

'Peng.'

'Is Peng here in person?'

'No.'

Daniel's hands were free. He was standing with them at his side, staring up at the camera in the top corner of the room. Curiously, no soldiers were guarding him.

'I messed up, dad,' he said.

Luther heard his intestines gurgle. He fought to keep the fear from his eyes, before remembering he didn't need to hide anything. Daniel could hear his voice, but he had no way to see into the panic bunker. 'How so, Daniel?' He had wanted to say "son" but couldn't bring himself to do it.

'Biogen.'

Now there was no hiding the fear. Luther knew of Biogen, of course. It was a large pharmaceutical company that had ended up under the Curzon umbrella as early as 1995. Luther had okayed the deal without fully anticipating the company's outsized risk. Biogen's new and lucrative treatment to relieve debilitating muscle ailments contained trace amounts of botulinum toxin Type-A – a product that could be diverted for weapons production.

Daniel continued: 'I okayed Biogen sales to reputable charity organizations, one of which…' He looked up at the camera and held out his hands. ‘One of which was compromised.’

‘By Peng?’

Daniel nodded. ‘The shipments ended up in Iran.’

‘Jesus,’ Luther said.

‘I didn’t know the charities were operating there.’

Because you probably didn’t even check, Luther thought. He knew his son, and he battled daily not to give in to outright, open contempt. After every opportunity in life, Daniel continued to take shortcuts and half-measures.

Luther knew what Iran meant. Since taking on the burden of Biogen, he had read up extensively on bioweapons development around the world. He was especially familiar with Iran’s program and the country’s continued efforts to circumvent trade embargos. ‘You’re informing me that Curzon’s unwittingly aided Iran’s bioweapon program? We had layers of safeguards in place, Daniel. We met or surpassed all the legal requirements designed to prevent sales to customers with –’

‘The product isn’t with Iran.’

Luther didn’t understand. ‘Why would Iran part with it if it’s –’

‘Money. They were only ever a manufacturer. They had the facilities to turn raw materials into something Peng could deploy, and now he’s using Masuda to set up an attack in Tokyo.’

Luther cocked his head, thinking fast. ‘Masuda was the gangster who wasn’t paying his debts.’

‘There were no debts, dad.’

‘You told me he was threatening you, that –’ Luther cut himself short. He was still groggy and struggling to keep up. With Peng and the entire bunker listening, it was better to say nothing than to babble, to complain.

'I lied about the debt, dad, about the threats. I was acting in the best interests of the company, trying to...' He held out his hands again, a show of innocence that was getting on Luther's nerves. 'I was trying to *fix* things, okay? I wanted to give you plausible deniability.'

The jigsaw slotted together. Luther was in no doubt now. Sending Kovac after Masuda's man, Yamada, had been a mistake. Clearly, it had been a setup, a trap. Luther had been fooled by his own son. He had sent Kovac directly into an ambush, handing him to Masuda and Peng. 'That was Peng's price? Kovac?'

'That's right. I had to make a call. Give Peng Kovac, or sit back and let Peng wipe out half of Tokyo. He had a New York Times journalist primed to run with it. The attack was going to tie directly back to us, to our so-called negligence. I had to protect the company.'

Luther stared at his son on the screen. Slowly, with Megan's help, he stood. Megan stabilized him. He swallowed hard, still staring, half wanting to put a fist through the monitor. But he knew anger would serve no purpose. Nor would reprimands. Not while the fate of his daughter and his life's work still hung in the balance. 'And what's the situation now, Daniel?' he asked. 'Kovac escaped in Tokyo, correct?'

'He did. But we're lucky, Peng's terms haven't changed.'

'*Lucky*?' Luther spat the word. He could see exactly what was in this for Peng. With Kovac gone, nothing protected Curzon. Peng would be able to hold the company's own chemical weapons over it indefinitely, making full use of its distribution chains to run drugs, weapons and God-only-knew what else.

Not that Luther had a choice. He couldn't condemn innocent civilians to death in Tokyo, and even if he did Curzon would never survive the fallout. It would be sued, cut up, siphoned off, until there was nothing left. His life's work would go with it.

A part of him couldn't help but admire the simplicity of it, the chilling effectiveness of Peng's approach. With this plan, Peng had achieved what so many before him had only dreamt of. As King, Luther was now finally in checkmate. There was no move he could make from here that was acceptable to him. All choices were a type of ruin. All that was left to him was the power to choose the least harmful outcome. 'And Lottie?' he asked, his voice cracking on his daughter's name.

'If you give Peng Kovac, he gives you Lottie. He gives you me. He wants me in charge of the company going forward.'

Of course he does, Luther thought bitterly.

He recalled the park in Mexico, the rain, the puddles all around, the sense of helplessness as he wondered which vehicle would stop and deliver Katie back to him. None had.

Could anyone negotiate with terrorists? It had failed last time. What made Peng any different?

Kovac had spared Luther this feeling for so long, he had almost forgotten it. But here it was again. That helpless desperation. He felt his eyes moisten and he fought to keep distress from his voice. 'Then it seems I'll need to contact Kovac. What do I tell him exactly?'

'Not you. Megan. He's more likely to believe her. Megan, I'm going to give you an address – for a landmark. Tell Kovac Lottie's been abducted, but you know where she's headed. Give him the address and tell him it's safe. Safe, and urgent.'

'Is that all?'

'No.' Daniel glanced down at his feet.

'What else?' Megan asked, stepping forward and taking over. Luther saw that her face was wet with tears, too, and he was profoundly grateful for this fact.

'You need to unlock the core,' Daniel said morosely. 'And you need to let these soldiers down into the panic bunker.' He looked up at the camera again. ‘They won’t hurt you,’ he said, ‘you have my word on that.’

Luther noted his son’s tone. There was no conviction in his words. Only resignation.

CHAPTER 44

There was no way to open the trapdoor, but there was a sensor. Which meant a remote. Kovac looked at the door key in his hand. Someone had gone to a lot of trouble with this key, gluing the lid to a rock, possibly even creating the small rock garden to hide it. It felt like the place was designed for communal use, with different people coming and going. And that, to Kovac's mind, suggested he had a good chance of finding a remote hidden somewhere in here.

He searched the apartment and found it on top of the refrigerator. It was one of the first places he looked: out of sight, never really on anyone's mind, but easily accessible.

The remote had a keypad, and having been hidden on top of the refrigerator, the keys had collected a layer of dust. It was heavier on all but four keys.

The numbers that were relatively clear of dust were one, two, three and nine.

Kovac figured it was one of three options.

He tried one, two, three and nine. No dice. He flipped it in his head and tried nine first, then three, two, one. Again, nothing. No lights, no beeping error message, but no sign of anything unlocking, either.

He pointed the remote at the trapdoor a third time and went with the only remaining option that made any sense to him. Nine as his starting point, then one, two, three – in ascending order this time.

Hydraulics kicked in, and the trapdoor began rising all on its own. Kovac stepped back and watched, his pistol at the ready again. The trapdoor looked lighter now, as if maybe it wasn't steel after all.

Anodized aluminum? He wasn't sure, but it wouldn't have surprised him. This was a professional job, beautifully integrated into the room and building as a whole. Most likely a secret addition to the original blueprints. One version for the town planners, another for the builders.

Kovac pointed his pistol down, and when no one fired up at it he risked a quick look. The trapdoor's metal frame capped a concrete shaft, and there was a fixed vertical ladder built into one wall of this shaft.

Perhaps twelve feet deep.

No one appeared at the base of the shaft.

He was certain now. The perfection of the concreting said it all. This had gone in with the original build, giving access to the section of underground parking lot that was walled off. *His missing fifty footsteps.*

He positioned a rolled-up futon mattress across half the shaft's entrance to prevent the trapdoor closing with him still inside, then made his way down the ladder. Fluorescent lights clinked and blinked on automatically.

He stepped cautiously down off the ladder and found himself in a surprisingly cramped space with a low ceiling. Prison cells came off both sides of a corridor. Each cell had three concrete walls and a mesh front with an inbuilt, matching mesh door and padlock. All cells were locked, and all contained identical fire safety sprinklers, beds, basins and toilets. Everything was clean and organized.

Kovac noticed the stench of cleaning products was unmistakable down here. Eucalyptus again.

Behind him, a waterproof keypad on the wall started

flashing. He studied it quickly, hoping some of the keys would have less dust than others. But all of them looked as if they had been wiped clean down here.

Best to leave it alone and get out, he thought.

He took one last look. A dungeon, but perfectly sterile. His best guess was human trafficking. Young girls, maybe, brought into Japan and kept here for as long as it took the world to forget about them. He knew from his work how quickly a missing person dropped down the police priority list, especially if that person was poor and of no interest to the media.

The keypad started beeping and, as much as Kovac wanted to look around, he knew his time was up. He started back up the ladder but the beep turned continuous. He heard the hydraulics again and saw the trapdoor coming down. 'Shit.'

Beneath him, there was a new, heavy dripping. A pump kicked in, and then suddenly Kovac couldn't hear anything but hissing.

Pressurized water, he realized.

He had messed up. The trapdoor hatch hit the futon just as he reached the top of the ladder, but the futon was thin and the hydraulics were more powerful than he had anticipated. They began squashing the futon down. 'Goddamn it.' He struggled against it but couldn't get any real leverage while hanging off the ladder. He pulled his pistol, looking to damage the hydraulics, but they were inbuilt. There was no way to do it without risking a ricochet.

In fact, there was no way to do it at all.

By the time the hydraulics gave up, he was left with a gap not much wider than his arm. He could see into the apartment, but that wasn't going to be of much use to him, not if this dungeon or whatever the hell it was filled with water. Eventually, water would reach the opening and – pushed from below – start flooding over the lip of the concrete shaft into the apartment. It would fill the narrow gap between the shaft and the trapdoor hatch, and he'd be drowned. He would be dead long before anyone detected flooding, too.

Furious with himself, and already doing a mental dance with panic, Kovac tried pushing the trapdoor again. But it had no give whatsoever. The hydraulics had cut out, locking everything firmly in place. Kovac saw it had snared and squashed the futon like a giant rat.

He took out Masuda's phone and switched it on, but it had no signal down here. 'Useless piece of shit,' he said, trying to extend it out over the tatami while still keeping the screen in view. No matter how he twisted his head, he couldn't do it and still type on the screen. It didn't have any signal anyway.

He left the phone on the tatami and made his way back down the ladder. His worst fears were confirmed. Every sprinkler head in every cell was pumping water in a 360-degree fan. He counted eight cells on each side, which gave him sixteen nozzles. He checked the keypad again and decided to give "nine one two three" a go.

He pressed the buttons but it had no effect – not on the trapdoor, nor on the sprinklers.

He tried again.

Still nothing.

He gave it one last go but without any real hope this time.

What did he have to lose?

He tried a few different variations but the keypad soon stopped beeping when he pressed the buttons, as if no longer registering his inputs.

He gave up on it and searched each cell carefully, all the way to the far end cells, but there wasn't anything. Just concrete walls and mesh.

He surveyed the end wall but soon gave up on it. It was solid concrete and no doubt especially thick, given it separated the dungeon from the parking lot. The last thing Peng would've wanted was the muted screams of young girls coming through.

Kovac looked down. He was already standing in an inch of water. He tried to think clearly. He doubted the trapdoor shutting was an elaborate snare for intruders. He doubted there had ever been an intruder until now. *So what was this?* A failsafe – a way of quickly killing girls?

Maybe. Water carried none of the risks to the general public associated with gas. But if this was a failsafe, a way to permanently silence girls ahead of a raid, wouldn't it be set up to dispose of corpses with the same efficiency? Kovac could see narrow drainpipe covers in each cell – all in the same metal as the trapdoor and all currently locked shut. But they would only let water out. He looked around, frustrated and confused. *How did they get the bodies out?*

He couldn't bring himself to believe that happened via Peng's apartment door. Via the street. Peng's name wasn't connected to this place in official documents or financial records, but he came here, and the AFP had linked him to it. He couldn't ever completely distance himself from this apartment building.

Kovac checked each cell with forensic patience, looking for anything that might reveal a secret tunnel. He found nothing grown men could use to drag dead girls out.

There was only the concrete shaft.

Which meant it was his theory that was wrong.

He climbed the ladder and tried pushing on the trapdoor yet again. When in doubt, try brute force.

But it was as unyielding as before. He peered through the narrow gaps on either side, out across tatami. He could see the kitchen. Could almost see the rear door. It was infuriating.

Think, Kovac.

And that was when he finally figured it all out.

CHAPTER 45

It wasn't trafficking. At least, not for sex. It was drugs. The girls were mules. They came here and were supervised as the drugs exited their respective systems. There were no corpses. They walked themselves in and out. And they didn't need to be girls, either. They could be any age, any gender. 'Son of a bitch.'

He took out the phone and pistol and slid them onto the tatami at the edge of the trapdoor. He studied the apartment again and realized it wasn't one apartment. That was why he had found a door inside the closet. The apartments were all linked internally, all down into this one. From the outside, it looked as if families were coming and going, as if the entire building was listed on Airbnb. Inside, all the apartments were empty save for this one. And this one was a factory: carefully extracting value, then flushing and sterilizing whatever remained. A literal rinse and repeat.

Only, he wasn't going to survive his first rinse.

If Kovac was right about what Peng had created here – and Peng probably had buildings like this all over the world, with police either clueless or turning a blind eye – then there was no tunnel, no other way out.

He remained where he was for a moment, trying not to despair, staring through the tantalizing gap under the trapdoor. So close and yet completely inaccessible...

It was going to be a shitty way to die, he concluded. The force of the water from below would fill the gap. He would need to use the .38 to hasten the inevitable.

He made his way down the ladder and sat under the keypad with his wrists on his knees. The water was up to his hips like this. It was ice cold but he didn't care. Maybe it would wake his brain the hell up. *There has to be another way.*

But what way?

He had always known this time would come, past crimes catching up with him. It felt like more than water closing in around him now. It felt methodical, clinical, like a state-sanctioned execution. It was as if all the choices he had ever made were demanding amends, right back to Catelo. *Back to that night. Eventually, his mind always came back to that night, the night Bishop recruited him.*

A sick dread welled inside his stomach and rose into his esophagus, surprising him with its intensity and almost causing him to retch. *He* had chosen this life. He could tell himself he hadn't, but that was a lie. He had chosen it, because there was a part of him that was cold and menacing, a part of him which enjoyed control, craved it.

And now here he was.

Too soon, not enough time.

Perhaps all that remained was doing it well, doing it with a modicum of courage.

He banged the back of his head against the wall at this thought. He had expected an early death, but he hadn't expected it like this. It was almost embarrassing.

He laughed at the stupidity of the thought.

Of course he hadn't expected it like this. If he'd seen this coming, he would've found something stronger than a fucking futon.

As it had been trained to do by Bishop, his mind detected the mental spiral. He stepped one level above his thoughts and forced himself to stand. He needed to get a grip. It was way too soon to be thinking about putting a bullet in his head, even if that was the probable outcome here.

He was alive right now, and what about Anna and Bennett? Like it or not, they were depending on him. If he could get out of here, maybe that was one thing he could do right. He could get them both free and clear, give them the time on this planet they both so desperately craved. Anna had said it herself, Bennett, too. They had hopes, they had plans.

Slowly at first, then with increasing speed, Kovac felt the dread and regret start to recede. He started to think ahead, testing ideas, discarding, searching for new maybes. His old mental models returned, and by the time the water was lapping at his knees he was focused and determined.

He climbed the ladder and tried the phone again, but it still didn't have a signal. He couldn't even get it to deliver a text let alone place a call. He figured the apartment was set up this way, built to resist errant calls and electronic bugs.

He tried yelling for help through the gap, but no one came.

Kovac knew why. It was the same reason no one had come when he let himself in here. Locals didn't want anything to do with this building. It might've looked like an Airbnb, but live opposite it long enough and the façade presumably collapsed. Everyone within one-hundred-yards knew better than to get involved.

He looked at the .38.

CHAPTER 46

Megan wasn't going to delude herself: Peng intended to kill them all. Inheritance by default. That would be the easiest, cleanest way for her brother to take power. Any paperwork drafted under duress would be subject to legal challenge.

She wondered if Peng would find some way to make it look like an accident. A gas leak maybe, or a fire? *Or was he powerful enough to do away with the pretense of tragedy?* He would possibly just fly Daniel out and give him an alibi. With that done, there would be nothing to stop Peng leaving them all as a pile of corpses – a signal to the world that he could reach anyone, anywhere.

For now at least, they were all still alive. It remained a siege, with her turncoat brother as on-site negotiator. Peng seemed reluctant to make a move. He had not blown in the core's concrete walls. Perhaps he feared it wouldn't work. Or perhaps he was smart enough to realize the core wasn't the endgame. He needed the bunker. Without the bunker, there could be no pile of corpses, no inheritance by default.

Megan wanted to brainstorm and plan with her father, but there were too many staff listening, and all of them with far too much at stake. Conversation would only invite opinion, and opinion would cloud her thinking and delay action.

Perhaps following Megan's lead, the staff remained quiet and calm. They were clawing at skin and gnawing at lips and fingernails, flinching at every sound overhead, but so far only Megan's step-mother had succumbed to actual tears.

Megan instructed one of the family's sous-chefs to hand out another round of water-bottles and energy bars from the shelves running along the bunker's east wall. 'We have plenty of food. Everyone eat and keep fluids up.'

A male staff member enquired tactfully about bathroom facilities. Megan pointed to a small corner of the bunker sealed off with painted plywood. It contained an enclosed toilet and shower. 'We're all going to need to take turns using it,' she said. 'So get comfortable with the idea.'

She turned back to her father, whose largely sleepless night had left him in more pain than anyone else down here. She had insisted Luther use the only chair in the bunker, and she hoped it was just pain and embarrassment prompting his dour expression now. She had a feeling it was something more, though. Bishop's reinforcements, most likely.

These scheduled reinforcements – requested by Megan before she left the meeting yesterday and promised for this morning – were now overdue. It was well past dawn and there was no sign of them on the monitors. The mercenaries were still moving about outside with absolute impunity, and Lottie's helicopter was still M.I.A..

Had Bishop's reinforcements been ambushed? They would've had no inkling what they were flying into, because Megan had hung up on Bishop without notifying him of the attack. And if so, how long until they regrouped and tried again? For all Megan knew, they were dead, lost to smoldering helicopter wrecks in the desert because of her stupidity.

She pushed this fear aside and looked up at the reinforced vents and steel hatch overhead. She thought about the bunker's design. It looked like a giant concrete box, no furniture beyond the single desk and chair for the computer. By any standard, it was uncomfortable. It was intended as a final fallback from the larger core, and no one in the Curzon family had ever seriously expected to use it.

This perhaps explained the lack of furniture and cluttered computer wiring, she thought to herself. Everyone had treated it as a pantry for the core upstairs, nothing more.

She needed some way to put pressure back on Peng. Right now, time was on his side. A loss of signal with Pemberton wasn't uncommon, given the closest major Australian city was 600 miles from the homestead. This latest outage would be flagged and tested – and it would eventually prompt a satellite sweep. But from 400 miles up, would anyone in Curzon International understand the severity of the situation on the ground? How would they know to deploy the necessary force?

'The air down here in the bunker, it's on its own independent system, right?' she asked her father.

He jolted slightly at the sound of her voice, which bounced off concrete in the confined space. He looked up at the vents as if straining to comprehend. Then he looked back at her, his old, watery eyes narrowing as his brain went to work. 'Interesting question.' He spun in his chair, which squeaked in protest. He pecked with two fingers at the keyboard. 'The vents and scrubbers down here are connected to... let me see. Five separate intakes in the desert. All disguised and, yes, from what I can see, separate from the core's primary intakes. Why?'

'How much control do we have over temperature down here?'

He jabbed at the keyboard again.

'I'm claustrophobic,' Megan's step-mother said. 'My fear was dying down here. I remember talking with the company that installed this thing. The woman they sent, I was standing down here with her. I told her, I said, that's my nightmare. She had a Ph.D., and she promised me this bunker could withstand just about any external temperature.'

Megan said: 'Your cigarettes still in your office desk?'

'Topmost drawer, yes.' Her step-mother frowned.

'You still have those pocket matches from France?'

'From Denmark, yes. Same drawer. Why?'

'No reason.'

Megan's father was typing again and he hit enter. 'I just moved it up a degree and put it down two. We can set the temperature here to whatever we want.'

'Without altering the core?'

'Without altering the core.'

'What about oxygen?'

'Same. I can alter the percentage of oxygen up or down providing it's within acceptable parameters.'

'Flood the core with it. Is the air down here equipped with a redundancy?'

'No. Well, yes. But that's what I'm using. I've swapped us onto the bunker's own system. By default, the bunker uses the core's vents and air, but –'

'– we're using the redundancy now, to gain independence. Understood.' Megan got up and checked the dates on the two fire extinguishers mounted to the wall. She nodded to the sprinkler nozzles in the ceiling. 'What about those, can you activate the sprinklers here without doing the same in the core?'

'If a fire breaks out here in the bunker?' Her father clucked his tongue. He checked and finally shook his head. 'No. I have a menu option for sprinklers, but it's both. Air I can separate. And drinking water. But not the sprinklers.'

Megan thought for a moment but was interrupted by a young woman of perhaps twenty-five. 'You think they'll set the homestead on fire?' She was one of the employees, but not one Megan saw very often. Megan had forgotten her name.

'No,' she answered distractedly.

She unlocked the gun safe and took out a 9-millimeter Ruger. Of all the weapons Bishop had taught her to use, this had always been her favorite. Which was how it had earned its place here.

She loaded it, then locked the safe again.

She climbed one-handed up the ladder to the bunker's hatch. 'Start a timer,' she said to her father. 'Give me three minutes. After that, you lock down this bunker, no matter what.' She started a timer on her watch, almost dropping the pistol in the process, then spun the handle on the hatch.

'Megan,' her father said. 'Have you thought this through? Do you know what you're doing?'

She shrugged. 'We have to do something, we can't just surrender. Shut off all fire suppression systems in the core. And turn off all internal cameras, too. Give me a one-minute head start, then open the core.' She was forgetting something. She ran through the plan in her mind but was too low on sleep to think clearly. She needed her father's help, his input. Someone to double-check her reasoning. But laying out her intentions would cause panic down here, and that could leave her father facing a mutiny in her absence.

Her father seemed to understand this. He held her eye for a moment and finally gave her a small nod. He turned back, pulling the keyboard even closer.

'I need your word,' she said. 'One minute from now, you open the core. Three minutes from now, you shut it again. Even if I'm not back, you shut this hatch and you lock me out.'

'You're wasting time,' he said, without looking up. 'I understand. *Go*.'

She turned the handle the last of the way on the hatch and pushed it up, climbing back into the corridor that led through to the wine cellar. Pistol up, safety off, she half-jogged to the industrial kitchen the staff used at the far end of the core. It took her less than fifteen seconds to cover the distance. The core was still locked and, as expected, empty and eerily quiet.

She put the pistol down and looked around. This space was almost entirely metal, save for large sections of white tile along various walls. Her mind ran back to the farm, back to Bishop's classroom. She could hear him explaining the most important elements for a successful fire – sufficient fuel and air. She was in the wrong location for fuel, but not for an accelerant.

She searched kitchen cupboards and settled on a cleaning product with ingredients she knew would do the job. She picked up two containers of the product, holding them in one hand, then grabbed her pistol and made her way back through the core again. She stopped at the oldest living room. It had ended up with most of Pemberton's historic furniture after the renovation.

Wrong, she thought.

CHAPTER 47

It was all old furniture, likely stuffed full of animal hair or wool. It would be difficult to ignite and it wouldn't provide a good burn.

She kept moving, settling instead on her step-mother's home office. This room had modern furniture, which meant foam padding, synthetics and cottons. It also had a ceiling fan, which she turned to "High".

Better.

She put the pistol down, then dragged some of the furniture to the drapes. She doused the whole lot, drapes included, with the first batch of cleaning product. Once she got the fire up to the ceiling, the ceiling would spread the fire for her, so she was pleased to see it was wood. As a site for arson, this room would receive Bishop's tick of approval.

She went to the desk and searched it. She found the cigarettes and the book of matches. She snapped a cigarette in half, lit it, took a few drags to get it going strongly, then taped it into the book of matches. She did it with the filter on the match heads and the lit end sticking out one side. It was one of perhaps a dozen rudimentary fuses Bishop had taught her so many years ago.

She heard the core's perimeter doors unlock and open. *Two minutes remaining,* she thought.

She carried her cigarette fuse and a full wastepaper basket across to the sodden furniture and drapes. She upended the paper, using it to keep the fuse and accelerant separate. She would never see it happen, but if all went to plan the cigarette would set off the matches, which would light the contents of the wastepaper basket, and from there *whoosh*. The wood ceiling would catch, and with the fire system off there would be nothing to stop fire spreading within the richly oxygenated core.

Megan put the pistol's safety on and shoved it in her belt. Its handle jammed into her sacroiliac joint as she straightened up with the remaining container of accelerant and she winced.

She strained to undo the lid. Then, leaning forward again, controlling the flow with the cap, she made a trail across the carpet and down a hallway to her step-mother's bedroom.

She doused her step-mother's walk-in closet until she was out of accelerant and tossed the container aside. Her two choices of target had revealed some psychological shit to work through with a shrink, but that could wait. Surviving this self-induced craziness came first.

She took out the pistol and flicked the safety off again. She didn't bother checking her watch. She was good for time and couldn't do anything about it if she wasn't. Checking would only slow her down.

She moved slowly now, deliberately, gun up, clearing each room and hallway one by one. The core was open. It was no longer protecting her. She needed to move back through it, but not so fast she walked into a trap. *Slow is smooth, smooth is fast*, she thought, still channeling Bishop.

No one appeared in her sights, and she was soon back at the wine cellar and striding through to the bunker. She found a Curzon staff member at the hatch. 'Thanks,' she said. 'Get down the ladder. I'll shut it.'

She slipped in, only letting her chest fully relax and expand when she felt the handle lock above her.

She climbed straight down.

'Okay, all cameras in the core back on.' Her father arranged it, and she saw mercenaries moving through the core's newly open doors, weapons raised. They had capitalized faster than she expected. Much faster. She waited until they were all well into the core, then said: 'Good. Lock it down again.'

Her father did. The soldiers all turned, realizing they were trapped. She could see them communicating. They had entered in pairs, utilizing numerous points of entry.

Everyone in the bunker cheered.

To Megan's surprise, they continued pressing slowly inward. Megan had one eye on her step-mother's office and the cigarette fuse. It was too slow. The cigarette was still sending up smoke but precious little of it. She needed the fire to get going before it was found, and before Peng detonated the explosives. She wanted a wind tunnel, but only after she had a fire and plenty of smoke. That was the best way to suffocate Peng's men, while also guaranteeing a conflagration that would eventually be visible from space.

It all came down to simple timing, she saw. And she had the timing wrong.

She kept her eyes fixed on the cigarette – on the faint column of grey-white smoke.

'C'mon,' she said. '*C'mon.*'

She had drawn the mercenaries in to deplete Peng's forces, but now wished she had just lit the fire herself before retreating to the bunker. She had over-complicated things and ignored Bishop's key rule: *keep it simple.*

One mercenary neared the office. He paused, presumably detecting the smell of smoke. He said something into his mic, then resumed his stealthy advance.

He got to the fuse before the matches flared, and he kicked

it clear. Megan swore, only to see the carpet ignite. Flame tore from the room, headed straight for the hallway.

Luther grinned up at her and she squeezed his shoulder. 'Close one, dad,' she said, allowing a small laugh as her step-mother's closet went up in flames an instant later.

'I thought we were done,' Luther said under his breath. 'I really did.'

The mercenaries paused and communicated again. They were good. They didn't panic. They planned. They seemed to settle on a course of action and all started moving with new purpose and speed. 'What are you doing?' Megan asked, directing the words to the monitors. 'What is this?'

Two of them located fire extinguishers and started back towards the closet.

'Oh dear,' Luther said.

Megan threaded her fingers behind her neck, pulling her head down. She couldn't believe her stupidity. She had let them in and given them the time and tools to undo all her work. She turned away from the screens. She couldn't bring herself to watch now.

How had she missed the extinguishers? They had extinguishers down here. She had checked the fucking dates on them! Of course they were upstairs, too.

'What can we do from here?' Luther asked as the two men with extinguishers closed in on her step-mother's room.

'Nothing.'

One arrived ahead of the other and started spraying foam. The other covered him, then saw he was needed, too. He joined the fight.

'Nothing,' her father agreed, falling back in his chair. 'Oh what a curse, we were so close.'

They all watched in horror as the foam began to subdue

the flames. A third mercenary arrived, having located yet another extinguisher. He joined in too, while the remaining mercenaries kept guard.

Megan changed her focus to a different monitor: to the empty stretch of lawn where Lottie's helicopter had been. She pictured her step-sister still sitting in the helicopter, right at its open sliding door, hands and feet bound. Horrible as that image was, it was better than this. Where was Lottie right now? Megan hated not knowing, but Lottie was the one element she had not been able to factor into her plan. Even with an inferno, Megan had known Lottie was lost. She had vanished into an underground network of monsters Megan didn't even want to imagine.

And now the remaining helicopters would stay. They would continue scrambling the homestead's comms and Megan wouldn't be able to raise the alarm. Lottie would become a bargaining chip and eventually die alone in some foreign hellhole. In trying to kill mercenaries, Megan had failed to consider the real priority, the fire. 'I should have just lit it,' she said, returning her attention to the fire. 'Why the hell didn't I just light it? We could've... *the key thing was the fire*.'

'You had no way to know, Megan,' Luther said. 'Light it too fast, and they...' But he couldn't finish. There wasn't a good reason to do what Megan had done. That was painfully clear now. She had tried to accomplish too much, had overcomplicated things, and it had cost them their only chance to get a message out to the world.

The mercenaries were almost done extinguishing the fire. To add insult to injury, they were now safely ensconced inside the core, too. 'We should have kept them out,' she said. 'We should have kept them locked out of the core and lit it, and let the place burn to the ground. That was our only way out.'

She crossed to the wall and sat down on hard concrete. She tried not to cry. She tried to think. What else did she have control over? She thought about cutting the oxygen in the core to nothing. But that was likely impossible, and even if it wasn't it would take too long. Plus, it wouldn't help her send a message. Trapping and suffocating a few mercenaries didn't free her.

How had she not considered that until now?

It was the same with water. She could perhaps flood the core, but that was pointless too. And reckless. They were underneath it.

Between her failure to communicate with Bishop and this latest fiasco, she had doomed them all. Her father had trusted her and she had failed him right when it mattered most. He would have no choice now but to capitulate and betray Kovac. And even that wouldn't guarantee Lottie a twelfth birthday. Peng would double-cross them. Megan knew it.

'Ten minutes,' she whispered, desperately wanting to go back in time. 'That's all I need. Ten minutes back.' She felt the tears but couldn't stop them. 'I could fix it all.' She punched the wall behind her with a bunched fist.

Her father stood and came and sat awkwardly beside her. He wrapped her in a one-armed hug and put his forehead to hers as she began to sob. 'Shhh,' he said, smoothing her hair with his other hand. 'We've lost this battle but not the war. We need to do what they want today. But we're going to get these bastards, Megan.' He kissed her on the head. 'And when we do, you'll be ready. You'll see.'

CHAPTER 48

The water was halfway up the concrete shaft by the time Kovac genuinely considered the practicalities of using the .38. He knew he would need to do it before the gun got wet. He didn't want to risk drowning. He'd seen too many men and women leave this world via that route to choose pointless suffering.

He glanced down at the water. Now that it was in the hatch, it was rising fast. The sound of the sprinklers had changed. They were more like deep underwater jets, more like an enormous spa. They were still going hard though, still forcing water in from below, intent on killing him.

The water rose over his feet.

It was freezing.

Over his knees.

He stared at it, rippling, implacable.

Over his waist.

He tried to shoulder up the hatch one last time, but it wouldn't give. He kept at it, searching for different angles, for anything that might get him more space. But it was useless. The hydraulics had him beat.

Catching his breath, he reached through the hatch, feeling for the .38 on the tatami. He gripped it and brought it back into the concrete shaft. He counted bullets, then fired down into the water until he had just one left. Maybe gunshots would bring someone?

He yelled again. His throat was hoarse and sore from yelling, but he needed help. He screamed, but still no one came.

The water arrived at his ribs.

He put the pistol under his chin and took a deep breath. He tightened his grip on the gun, on the trigger. But he felt his finger go slack. He couldn't do it. And he didn't need to. Not yet. Not quite.

Goddamn it, think.

He slid the gun out onto the tatami again and slammed his upper back into the trapdoor – over and over. He was struggling for breath and his neck and back ached from each bone-crushing collision with metal. His arm and leg muscles throbbed.

He looked down at the water, now licking at his collar bones. 'Okay,' he said to himself, making sure the .38 was within easy reach. When this started, it was going to happen fast.

The water reached his mouth. A few more seconds and that would be it. He twisted his head sideways, into the gap. He gripped the .38, turning it on himself. He shut his eyes, scrunched his face, and willed himself to pull the trigger.

Three.

Two.

Something was different.

He opened his eyes, comprehending what it was. Somewhere deep below him, the nozzles had cut out. The pump was still going, but he couldn't hear the water being forced in. An instant later the pump cut out, too, and he heard the drainpipe covers open with a succession of metallic clanks.

He checked and saw the water had stopped just beneath the lip of the shaft. Sure enough, it was now retreating. He searched the trapdoor frame and found tiny sensors on the underside.

He let out a stunned laugh and dropped the pistol back onto the tatami. He pulled his head out of the gap and came back to straight, stretching his battered neck and spine. He wasn't free. But he wasn't dead.

Progress – of a sort.

It took close to twenty minutes for the water to drain. Kovac watched, following the water down and examining the outlets. He was cold enough now to be shivering but not so cold he was seriously worried about organ temperature. He almost started to feel optimistic.

He watched the last of the water drain out, then turned his attention skyward. Sure enough, just as he had hoped, he heard the hydraulics kick in. He laughed again, almost hysterically now, moving to the shaft and staring up the ladder. He could see the useless futon expanding again, as the trapdoor began to open.

He climbed out as fast as he could and lay on his back for a few seconds, trying to understand it. It was a cycle, like a washing machine? Extract the drugs, clear out all the shit and piss, all evidence gone in one big rinse? He didn't know how the keypad fit in exactly. Perhaps it was sophisticated, programmed to lock down and run a rinse in the case of unauthorized entry. Or more likely, he had just been stupid and triggered something. He didn't care. He was free. And he was alive.

He sat up, dripping wet, grinning and shaking his head. Slowly, unsteadily, he stood up. The apartment was perfectly dry. Which made sense. Whoever designed this would've been under strict instruction to make sure it never flooded the building and street. No drug operation wanted that sort of scrutiny.

'Okay.' Kovac scooped up the .38 along with Masuda's phone. He locked the dungeon and returned the remote to the fridge. Then he tidied the place up and let himself out. He locked the rear door, returning the key to its orange container and the container to the rock. He squatted, put the rock back in the garden, stood straight again, and walked away.

CHAPTER 49

Even though it was light out, Kovac risked a trip to the nearby convenience store. As much as anything else, it was the closest source of heat.

Keeping an eye out for police, he lingered in the heated environment for as long as he dared. He feigned confusion in every aisle, playing for time, for warmth. He picked products up, compared them, put them down.

He ended up buying nine meat buns from a glass oven at the counter, and three cans of equally hot coffee. He warmed up a little more while paying, adding a scarf and gloves to his items. The clerk had no doubt noticed his sodden clothing and uncontrollable shivering, but he followed Kovac's lead. He said nothing.

No one came into the store the whole time Kovac was there. He put the scarf and gloves on and made his way back across the main road. His feet were numb, and his icy sneakers weren't coping well with the snow. But his hands were doing okay in the new gloves, and his vital organs were warming, too. He carried the hot meat buns and coffee under his zipped jacket, wrapped tightly in their plastic bag.

He braved a circuitous route, checking for a tail. But there wasn't anyone. When satisfied he was alone, he circled back to the house with Anna and Bennett in it.

Anna had been no better at fleeing than Bennett. She met him at the rear door, looking groggy and strung out. She was moving with a sleep-deprived jerkiness Kovac hadn't seen in her before. 'You got food,' she said, sounding surprised. 'And you're shivering. You're drenched, Kovac.'

'Yep. Bennett up?'

'She was earlier. But she went back to bed.'

Kovac stayed downstairs, checking outside for any unusual movement.

Still nothing. Or more to the point, no one.

Anna went upstairs. He heard her wake Bennett. He hoped they'd stay up there for a moment because he needed to undress and hang his shirt and pants over a small electric heater.

Not that they could see much in the dark.

He did it as fast as his frozen limbs would allow and switched the heater on. Remarkably, the orange light blinked to life. The place had electricity.

Anna and Bennett came downstairs. Bennett looking groggy in the faint orange glow until she saw Kovac in nothing but his underpants. He was dragging the heater with his clothes on it to the kitchen table to keep warm. He could sense her eyeing his lean, battle-scarred torso as he set about wrapping himself in blankets and sat down to eat.

He arranged a sort of breakfast on the little kitchen table. They sat and in the orange light and ate in silence until Bennett finally asked: 'So what happened? Why did you end up drenched? Snow?'

'Yeah.' He was too tired to explain. He ate four meat buns and drained the coffee from its metal can. The caffeine had no effect.

He told Bennett to wake him if anything felt amiss, then trudged upstairs. He slipped out of the blankets and used the same futon and bedding Bennett had used. It was all still warm and it smelled good. He didn't bother with clothing and was asleep in a matter of seconds – a deep sleep that was mercifully free of dreams. The sort of sleep he only ever got when working.

He was woken by the feel of someone climbing into this quasi bed beside him. A woman. At first, he thought it was Anna. He was confused. He shook his head and mumbled, 'no, use your bed.'

It was bright outside, light streaming in around the edges of the drapes. He opened his eyes and saw it wasn't Anna.

It was Bennett.

She wasn't lying with her back to him. She wasn't lying like she simply wanted to get a little extra sleep, like she was willing to put up with him in the bed. She was lying with her face to his, her breath fresh. Mouthwash or toothpaste, he noticed, like she had been particular about this before coming upstairs.

'Where's Anna?' he asked, his voice a croak.

Bennett pointed down through the floor in reply. She put a finger to her lips in a signal for him to be quiet. Then she kissed him.

Kovac felt her hand on his hip before it dropped to his groin. He felt himself react. It wasn't a good idea, of course. But then again, it wasn't his idea. He was a passenger on this particular ride, and who was he to argue with Bennett? He reciprocated. He kissed her back. All of it in complete silence, start to finish, though silence became harder to maintain as things acquired a tempo all of their own. It was instinct, a thirst for connection.

He climaxed just after she did, and by that point what Anna could or couldn't hear was the very last thing on either of their minds.

There was smiling and suppressed laughter, and a lot of rolling over one another and touching, all of it more tender now, less urgent, as they luxuriated in the feel of one another's skin. Purely physical, Kovac thought. Stress release at its finest. He hoped Bennett could say the same, and it seemed she could because she didn't linger. She rolled out from underneath the blankets, beginning the process of dressing herself before she was even standing.

Kovac kept one eye on the stairs, just in case Anna came up to see what all the fuss had been about. 'Don't worry,' Bennett whispered. 'She's asleep down in the kitchen. She rolled out a futon there.' Bennett paused, studying his face in the dark for a long moment.

'What?' he asked.

'She told me what you did, Kovac.'

'What do you mean?'

'At the business hotel.'

Kovac stayed where he was, admiring Bennett in return now. Was there anything more beautiful in the world than a naked woman? Yes, he realized – an unexpectedly amorous naked woman. 'That's it?' he asked in a whisper, grinning. 'You going to leave cash, too?'

'Shut up. You loved it.'

Bennett didn't come back down for a final kiss. Though Kovac could hardly see it, her face seemed to turn serious. 'Are we going to survive this, Kovac?'

Maybe that had been the basis of the drinking, too, he thought.

She was terrified.

'Answer me. Yes or no?'

'Yes,' he said. He reached for her hand and gently kissed her broken fingers. He kept his eyes on hers.

She pulled her hand away but sat back down on the edge of the futon, facing away from him. She pulled her knees to her chin, twisted and held his eye. He could see she desperately wanted to reason her way through this.

'Where do we go from here, Kovac?'

'I don't know. I like you a lot. I do. But I feel like at some point things started moving really fast between us, and I'm just not –'

She laughed despite herself and gave him a gentle punch. 'You know what I'm talking about. You don't know our next move, or you just won't tell me?'

'I don't know our next move.'

She got up abruptly. 'I think I'd prefer you not trusting me than having no clue what to do next.'

He rolled onto his back, tonguing one cheek. The abrupt interrogation had thrown him a little. This was why he normally worked alone. Bishop was right. Enjoyable as it had been, this was a bad idea.

She headed downstairs, leaving him to his thoughts. The calm he had felt in her arms went with her, replaced with growing unease.

What *was* his plan? He didn't know, because he didn't have an employer anymore. He was in uncharted waters.

He listened to Bennett in the kitchen for a few seconds, then rolled over on the futon and reached out across the cold, hard tatami. He got his fingertips to Masuda's phone and walked it closer, until he could jab at the screen. It had a signal here.

He rolled onto his stomach and went through the incoming messages. Everything was in Japanese, except for a string of texts from someone called "Chen". The texts ran back a long way. They were entirely logistics. Meet here at such and such a time, meet there. Kovac flicked through with his thumb. Masuda had been meeting Chen – whoever Chen was – for three years. And almost always in and around Kanagawa. Kovac saw there was a meet scheduled for later in the day today, and he thought back to what Masuda had said in the business hotel.

Masuda had been planning to meet Peng today. Peng, and possibly a fund manager?

Kovac used Masuda's phone to research Kanagawa and saw the prefecture had several large ports. The largest three looked to be Yokohama, Kawasaki and Yokosuka.

He put the phone down and shut his eyes. It made no sense to go after Peng. If he was going after anyone, it should be King. If he decided to vanish, King was perhaps the one man on the planet who had any hope of locating him. And Kovac knew how to hurt King. That familiarity cut both ways.

But just because he *could* go after King wasn't reason enough to do it.

Going after neither man was the smart move. It seemed like King and Peng were aligned, and Kovac couldn't go up against two billionaires and expect to win. Peng had a criminal army, and Bishop would hire mercenaries. Even with Kovac's knowledge and skills, reality was a cold, heartless bitch.

Vanishing was his only option now.

He would live on the run because it was better to live on the run than die fighting. Ditto any thought of revenge.

He listened to Bennett moving around downstairs. No one had made any promises. Not even a tumble under the sheets changed that. But he would honor his promise to himself in that dungeon of Peng's. He would help Anna and Bennett because he owed them that much at least. Only, he would do it on his terms. At some point between the dungeon and now, the romantic idea of helping them restore their old lives had given out to the cold reality of survival. Kovac wasn't proud of it, but he was an assassin, not a charity worker. He would turn them into new people, help them start new lives with no family or friends. Lonely, isolated lives. Lives like his own. But that was the best he could offer. *What they did with that gift would be up to them.*

He checked his watch. He wanted to give Anna more time to sleep, but so long as they were a group of three they needed to keep moving. As a group of foreigners, they were too easy to find, especially up here in the Japanese mountains. This area was practically monocultural.

He set an alarm for two hours and gave into sleep.

CHAPTER 50

After he woke, Kovac gave them five minutes.

Anna roused herself quickly and headed upstairs to get her stuff. Kovac followed and handed her the empty Colt 1911.

She took it, holding it limply, like she had expected it to be lighter. 'I have no idea how to use a gun.'

'That's fine.'

'How is that fine?'

'It's not loaded. It's just for show.'

'So… I just point it?'

'At bad guys, like it's loaded.' He paused and glanced downstairs. Then he lowered his voice: 'How did you meet Bennett?'

'The police called her. Why?'

'I just never asked you, that's all.'

'I told them I didn't have any family in Japan. They rang Resolute, which –'

'– is Bennett.' He nodded to the gun to change the topic. 'Point and act like you don't want to shoot but will if you have to.'

She practiced pointing it, aiming at Kovac. 'I heard you and Bennett, by the way. Sounded pretty hot. That a thing or…?'

Kovac swiped the pistol away with the back of one hand. 'Quit messing around, Anna. Get whatever you're bringing, and get downstairs. Time's up.'

He checked what was left over from the rucksack. It was mostly just an assortment of bug out crap now. He spread it haphazardly on the tatami floor. A first aid box, a fire starter kit, a compass, a shemagh, and a pair of binoculars. Then came his earpiece and a small, wireless directional mic, both independently powered and connecting back to his phone. A phone he no longer had.

He sifted through small cases of lethal drugs in disposable syringes, a key fob and about a dozen MREs. He was looking for disposable wipes. He wanted to wipe down the obvious surfaces before leaving this place. But there were no wipes and he figured he didn't have time anyway.

He counted the sux syringes – or succinylcholine to give it its full name. They were all present and accounted for. Sometimes he carried the drug disguised in a pen, but that meant a single lethal dose. Where possible, he preferred a collection of disposable syringes like this. It gave him options, so long as he kept track of the dose.

On the weaponry side, he was down to the two .38s with six rounds between them, and two useless Colt 1911 .45s. He also had ammunition for a rifle he no longer owned, ammunition for a pistol he no longer owned, ballistic goggles for a helmet he no longer owned, and a mini scuba tank with a mouth-piece, which was still completely useless here in the mountains.

Kovac gave up working through what he would and wouldn't need. He decided to keep it all – even the mini scuba tank.

He grabbed an old duffel bag from a nearby cupboard and bundled it all in.

Anna had gone back downstairs. She called up, telling him she was ready to go. Bennett said she was ready, too.

'Okay,' he said, grabbing the duffel bag and taking the staircase three steps at a time, 'we're out of here.'

'Going where?' Bennett asked.

He gave her the spare .38, sans its one remaining round. This he kept for his own .38. 'Tokyo.'

'This loaded?'

'No.'

'Good. Why Tokyo?'

'More foreigners, more buildings, more places to hide.'

'That's your plan? To just hide.'

'If we find a new vehicle and survive the journey, yeah. This is Peng's home turf. We're not going to survive another night here. It's time to retreat.'

Kovac led them outside and used the key fob from his duffel bag. It opened pretty much any vehicle in the States, but was a bit more hit and miss here in Japan. He tried opening the first few cars they saw. No luck.

He eventually had success with a Toyota Prius.

He wrenched open the door and slung himself down into the driver's seat. He tossed his duffel bag onto the floor in front of the passenger seat. He located a big blue power button and pressed it, then looked for a handbrake.

There wasn't one. Nor could he hear an engine. 'Electric vehicles,' he muttered grumpily.

The dash was all lit up, which he figured was a start. There were gauges and menus of all kinds, like the cockpit of a commercial plane.

Anna and Bennett got in: Anna into the back seat, Bennett into the front. If they were scared, they were doing a good job of hiding it.

Or maybe they just didn't fully comprehend what they were up against.

Kovac found the handbrake. It was down with the accelerator and brake pedals – a footbrake. He released it, then put Masuda's phone on an inbuilt car charger. He used a little blue gearstick to choose "D" and started driving.

The gas engine kicked in, carrying them with new zip through a maze of side streets and out onto open road. They drove in silence for about ten minutes before Bennett picked up Masuda's phone. She switched it to her damaged hand so she could peck and crab-claw with her good hand. 'This phone belongs to Ken Masuda,' she said.

'You can read Japanese?'

'I went to school here for a while.'

'Let me know if you find anything interesting.'

They drove for close on two hours: Kovac steering and getting Bennett to translate road signs; Bennett going through Masuda's phone; and Anna sleeping in the back. It was all open highway. Mountains with tunnels, paddies, then more mountains, more tunnels.

And snow.

Kovac was getting sick of snow.

Eventually, he spotted an isolated restroom building for truckers, with nothing but amenities and vending machines. He stopped and parked beside a Prius that was identical to theirs save for the paint job. The country was seemingly lousy with the latest hybrids.

He scanned for sniper perches and, finding none, went into the restroom. There were a lot of vehicles stopped and a line up even for the urinals.

Returning, Kovac heard a phone ringing in the Prius. It seemed like Bennett had connected the device to the car's Bluetooth. He saw her take the call.

'Shit.'

He ran a hand across his throat, telling her to hang up. But then he heard an unexpected voice coming out of the speaker in the open car door. A voice he knew all too well. Megan Curzon.

'Hello?'

Bennett finally saw him. It seemed like she hadn't been expecting him.

Kovac got back in the driver's seat and grabbed the phone. He switched off the Bluetooth but didn't hang up. He got out again and walked until he was well clear of the car – back towards the cover of the restroom. Again, he scanned the flat parking lot and paddies for any sign of a sniper, but he was confident the terrain didn't allow it.

Once inside, he held Masuda's phone in his palm, wondering about the call. If he said a word, Megan would have his location. She would see it was a parking lot. There were plenty of cars and trucks, plenty of people using the amenities, and that worked in Kovac's favor. Curzon had never been comfortable with collateral damage. But there was a first time for everything.

He put the phone to his ear but still said nothing. She must have heard him breathing.

'Kovac?'

Like she was confirming his identity, he thought cynically.

The company didn't have drone capabilities that Kovac was aware of – and certainly not in Japanese airspace. Snipers remained an ever-present threat, but not here. He scanned yet again, looking for any sign of a reflection, but there wasn't one. The terrain here was empty in every direction, and all of it covered in stark white snow. If he was going to talk, now was the time.

He kept well back in the restroom, eyeing his own Prius and the one beside it.

'Kovac?'

'How did you know I was on this number?'

There was a long pause. 'Oh God,' she said finally, the words so soft and sad he almost failed to catch them.

'What?'

'I just recognized your voice.'

He understood. She was only just putting it all together. He was "Bishop's son", the boy she had grown up training alongside at the farm, the boy she had loved with all her heart, the boy who had had inexplicably cut all ties with her at eighteen and headed off to be a soldier. The boy who had died in a stupid diving accident.

So they didn't tell you, he thought.

He asked again: 'How did you know I was on this number?'

This time she didn't hesitate. Her voice recovered its strength and she sounded like she did when he watched her on the TV and internet. 'We heard about Masuda. We figured it was you. You shut us out. At least, that's what Bishop's saying. As a long shot, I tried this number.'

Kovac doubted he was getting the truth but she was a good liar these days.

All grown up, he thought bitterly.

She didn't dwell on the personal. She got straight down to it. 'Listen, we've got a situation here, and I need your help.'

Kovac knew everything there was to know about Megan Curzon, down to her gambling and disguised dating app profiles. But this was the first time he'd spoken with her since leaving the farm. He knew there was a new relationship to forge here, a new power dynamic to establish. 'I'm listening,' he said.

'Lottie's been abducted, Kovac.'

He leaned in a little, frowning as if maybe he had misheard. '*What*? From where?'

'Pemberton.'

'How's that possible? You've got a core and a –'

'She went out riding with Daniel. They both went to McCartney Gorge.'

He mouthed a curse. 'Who was it?'

'Peng Biao.'

Kovac thought about the girls in the video, about the dungeon with its rinse cycle. If Peng had Lottie, the little girl was in serious trouble. He said: 'I still don't see how –'

'Bell helicopters, mercenaries. State-of-the-art equipment. It seems like they were after Lottie specifically. Daniel came back okay. He said they targeted Lottie. After they had her, they let him go. They took off again, headed north. Tokyo.'

Kovac stared out at the desolate, snowy parking lot surrounding him. Anna and Bennett were sitting patiently in the Prius.

'Then you can't trust Daniel, Megan.'

'I know.'

'How do you know it's Peng? How do you know it's Tokyo?'

'Peng's interests have been clashing with ours recently. He's reached out. He's offering an exchange. 1:00 a.m. tonight, Kanagawa prefecture.'

'My time or yours?'

'Yours.'

Kovac shook his head at their nerve but managed to bite his lip. As far as Curzon was concerned, he was still an employee.

And for now, it suited him to indulge that belief. 'And these clashes you mentioned? Why don't I know about them?'

'You'd have to take that up with Bishop.'

'I'm taking it up with you, Megan.'

'Okay. Need to know. And it was felt you didn't need to know.'

'I see. Until now.'

'Until now, yes.'

He figured it was all of them. King, Megan, Daniel, maybe even Bishop. He wanted to tell Megan to go fuck herself. But at the last second, he thought of the video again, of the dungeon, of Lottie. He had never said a word to Lottie, but he had watched her grow up from afar. He adored her. With her wild red hair and crazy, pre-teen teeth, she was as he remembered Megan. And she was kind like Megan, too. He'd seen it a hundred times in his dealings with the family. Lottie held them together in ways they didn't even realize.

Goddamn it, he thought, knowing he couldn't walk away. Not now. 'What do you need from me?' he asked.

Megan gave him an address in Kanagawa. 'Lottie won't be there yet, but if it's legitimate she's en route. We need you to rescue her – and kill Peng.'

'Risky, Megan.'

'I know. But it's the only way we get her back.'

Kovac thought for a moment. 'Let's say a rescue isn't possible, nor a kill. What do I offer Peng in return for Lottie?'

'If it comes to that, you can agree to whatever he asks.'

This set off alarm bells for Kovac. 'That's not a strong negotiating position, and I strongly recommend you –'

'Kovac, listen carefully – if it comes to that, *whatever he asks*. He can have the entire company for all we care, and you can have whatever you want, too.'

He was insulted by the insinuation he would want cash. It spoke volumes about his newly strained relationship with the Curzons.

He needed proof Lottie really was in danger but saw no way to get it from Megan. 'Okay,' he said.

'You'll do it?'

'Of course I'll do it.'

'Thank you, Kovac. Honestly, thank you so much. I knew we could rely on you.' The hardness in her voice fell away. Her relief was palpable and convincing, which led Kovac to hate her all the more.

Like everything else in Kovac's world, Megan Curzon had changed.

He ended the call.

CHAPTER 51

Kovac checked Masuda's phone but couldn't see anything different on it from the last time he'd gone through its messages.

He strode to the car, still scanning for threats but finding nothing. 'We need a new vehicle,' he said to Bennett, trying the fob and selecting the Prius that was identical save for plates and paint color. It worked.

He memorized directions to the address Megan had given him, then left Masuda's phone switched on underneath the driver's seat in the old car.

He pressed the big blue button on the new Prius and drove straight out of the parking lot.

For a long time, they drove in silence. The road was dotted with tunnels, and in one long tunnel Kovac felt his ears pop as they lost altitude.

Getting close, he thought.

He was relieved. It had been a tedious drive from the mountains of Nagano back down towards the coastline, with nothing to break up his churning thoughts. Neither Anna nor Bennett had said much, and at some point Anna had fallen asleep again. She was snoring faintly in the back seat.

Kovac took the chance to ask Bennett about Masuda's phone. 'You find anything useful on it?'

Bennett shrugged. 'No. It was all business and all in code. Meet here, do this, do that.'

'Nothing about a company called Curzon International?'

'No.'

'What about King or Bishop?'

'No.'

'Daniel? Megan?'

She glanced at him. 'That's who you work for? Curzon?'

'That's none of your business.'

This killed off all conversation, and they were once again left with nothing but Anna's snoring and the monotonous droning of the car's tires. They finished their descent, and the road passed through a final tunnel and construction zone, after which the landscape opened up and flattened out. The sea fell into view.

Kovac stopped the car and got out. He stretched and studied his new surroundings. He had spent most of his life looking for threats and normally it happened at a sub-conscious level. But not right now. Not while he was going up against billionaires.

'Have we arrived?' Bennett asked.

'No.'

'Mind telling me where we're going?'

'It's better you don't know. And when we get there, you should think about striking out alone. Safer that way.'

'What about Anna?'

'She should do the same.'

He gave this a minute or two to register, then got back in and resumed driving. Bennett said nothing, but he could feel her resentment.

Bishop had been right. Kovac worked alone, and it didn't work any other way. He had to put himself first now and lighten up on the baggage. He would give them money and instructions but it had to happen sooner rather than later.

The road up ahead tracked the coastline around a small bay. On the left, there was an unappealing beach with slate-grey sand, brown winter reeds and abandoned dinghies. On the right, dotted houses. These backed onto steep, forested hills covered in concrete, presumably to guard against landslides.

The address Megan had given him wasn't going to be difficult to find. It was the address for a lighthouse, and this road was tracking the bay.

But the road didn't track the bay for as long as Kovac hoped. It veered inland, through a gap in the hills, and the residential density picked up again. The sea fell out of view, replaced by apartment buildings.

Kovac wondered if he had made a wrong turn. He drove slowly and was relieved when he saw a toll booth and bridge. He parked the car in a side road, not far from a bus stop. He saw Anna was awake again. 'This is where we part ways,' he said. 'There's a bus stop just down there, on the main road.'

He gave them 300,000 yen each and the name of a man in Tokyo who could get them new IDs, then got out of the car. He got his duffel bag from the trunk. 'I'm sorry I can't do more for you,' he said, returning to the driver's door. 'But don't come looking for me, and don't hang around here. You both need to get out of this country and start new lives. An ID and some cash doesn't feel like much, but it's enough. If you go back to family or friends, they'll find you and they'll kill you.'

They both had a lot of questions but there was nothing else to say. He put the loaded .38 in his belt at the small of his back and, feeling like shit, set out on foot. He kept to side streets, out of sight, headed for the bridge. He wasn't helping them, he was dumping them. But he couldn't help everyone. Lottie was just a kid, and he'd seen what Peng did to kids. She came first. The other two had made their choices. There had to be some accountability in this life.

The logic fell flat. But he didn't turn back.

The bridge eventually fell into view again. It was long and straight and almost flat. It led to Jogashima Island, which lay out ahead of Kovac as a long, rocky mass.

He used the binoculars from the duffel bag, doing his best to guard against unwanted reflections. He took in the old fishing boats and sea birds on each coast – first on the mainland side, then on the island side. He estimated it would take a full minute to cross the bridge in a car, maybe longer. And no alternative road.

If he was planning an ambush, he knew he would position himself at the statue on the far side of the bridge. It was a natural choke point. He studied it intently. With the binoculars, he had a good view of it.

If Megan was to be believed, he was early and Peng didn't know he was coming. He didn't necessarily believe that, but it was the same plan now whether he believed Megan or not. He wasn't going to call her bluff on Lottie, nor demand proof. He knew full well he wouldn't be able to live with himself if something happened to Lottie and he had sat on his hands. He didn't like it, but at the very least he had to take a look.

The hope of walking away was all but dead now. He was in this, and not by his choosing.

He kept back, completely shielded from view, and began the long wait. His mind went to Peng's file.

CHAPTER 52

The sound of the incoming helicopter surprised the Taiwanese fishing captain. He pulled on his red cap and went out onto the trawler's deck.

The big old Sikorsky helicopter came in low, lower even than usual.

He lit a cigarette and waited. He always liked this bit.

The sliding door on the side of the helicopter was pulled back and three little bodies were pushed out. One managed a pin drop into the sea. The other two flailed. The third flailed worst of all, screaming. She landed on her back.

Stupid little bitch, he thought, laughing.

He dropped his cigarette and stomped on it. He signaled for the trawler to pick the girls up, and a few minutes later his men were dragging all three in like tuna: each one coughing and spluttering. They were between ten and twelve years old, dazed, scared, the usual. It was always girls, because who wanted to search an underage girl for drugs these days?

A sailor approached, passing on a radio message from the helicopter. He was to deliver these three personally. A new location. Japan. No drugs.

No drugs.

It was a deviation from the norm. A pretty fucking big one. The Taiwanese captain had never been asked to deliver mules without loading them up first. What was the point? 'Take them on through,' he said, sensing an opportunity. 'Get them soup.'

He stayed out on the deck. It was a calm, oddly mild night. He watched the helicopter disappear back into the darkness, flying low to avoid radar, the sound of it the last thing to give out.

He was in the Sea of Japan. Based on his location and the Sikorsky's direction and altitude he figured it was using North Korea as a base to rendezvous with private jets. An airport somewhere in that shithole of a country, which didn't ask questions: there had to be good money in that.

And now he would play his humble little part. He would take these girls the last of the way into Japan.

The Taiwanese captain had never smuggled anything into Japan before. Last time, they had made him pass girls off to a Jap captain. The Taiwanese captain was moving up. He was gaining their trust. They appreciated his unsentimental approach, perhaps, or his dependability. Whatever the case, he decided this was his last job. This was the Gods whispering to him. Three girls dropping out of nowhere like this, available right when he had a use for them. Fate, he thought.

He went to the girls. They'd been stripped of their wet clothes.

No drugs.

What did that mean? He figured they were going to be prostituted, though they seemed a few years too young for that.

Maybe organs?

Yes, organs. For some rich man's little girl. Rich girls got sick too sometimes, but money could fix that. It could find just the right organ at just the right time, every time.

One of the three girls was white, which made him even more sure it was organs. A weird blood type, maybe. The Taiwanese captain had never been sent a white girl before. A few Latinos, sure, but mostly the girls he plucked out of the ocean were Asian.

He studied the white one carefully. She was a redhead. He pulled her lips back, like a horse. Messed up teeth. She looked drugged, but then they always did on arrival.

He went off his organs theory. He returned to smuggling. He figured the redhead had an American passport. Maybe that was the plan. Get her into Japan, tidy her up, and put her on a plane to the States. The other two would pose as friends, maybe. Some inspiring youth exchange bullshit as a cover story, helping all three slip into California with bellies full of meth.

He looked over at the table with the box of condoms and three bricks of heroin. The heroin was his, a side venture. He opened the box and unwrapped a condom. Then he unwrapped another. He showed the two Indonesian sailors in the room how to put one condom inside another. Then a third into the first two. There was a trick to it, he explained.

They both had a go at it and made it look difficult. He made a joke about their lack of experience and demonstrated again with three more condoms.

They had another go and this time did slightly better.

He put on a mask. He made his men put on masks, too. Then he showed them how to use the machine in the corner of the room, which filled the condom balloons with heroin.

They made that look difficult as well. Whoever replaced him on this ship as the new captain would need new migrant workers, smarter migrant workers.

The soup arrived, laced with drugs and oil. He made the girls drink it. Then he sprayed their throats with a little bottle of anesthetic and waited a few minutes for it to take effect.

It was boring, waiting. He didn't like it. He cut it short

and grabbed the redhead. Gripping her with a fistful of hair, he force-fed her a condom balloon. He was rough about it, so his men would understand the sort of strength required. She thrashed and choked and coughed and convulsed. But that, he explained, was exactly what they wanted. That was all just evidence they were doing it right. There was no gentle way.

A kid like this could swallow up to 100 balloons, he told them. Today they were only forcing down 25. Easy.

The balloons were a little bigger than he normally made them and there was a trace of blood from the redhead's throat after he got three down. But it was done. He told his men to force-feed 22 more balloons to the redhead and 25 to the other two.

The Taiwanese captain went out for a smoke. Now that his plan was underway, he felt nervous. But he had to commit. The sooner these balloons went in, the sooner they came out; and he would need all of them out the second they arrived in Japan. He couldn't pass these girls on until they were empty.

He decided he wouldn't bother with the tablets to inhibit bowel movement this time. He wouldn't even give them antacids. Sure, there was a possibility stomach acid could eat through the condom balloons. If that happened, he would lose his heroin. The girls would drop dead and, depending on where it happened, he would need to cut their stomachs open to get his other balloons back. That's what the antacids were for. To make a nicer home for the balloons.

But he couldn't risk them. Not this time. Some of these young girls clogged up just with the antacids. He didn't want to risk anything that might constipate. He'd been given instructions by powerful people, ruthless people. No drugs in the mules. And he would be delivering the girls personally. He had to have the heroin out on schedule, or he'd end up a corpse himself.

He flicked his half-finished cigarette into the sea. He would triple the dose of laxatives as they got close to Japan. Any he would put fifty balloons in each girl, not 25.

Fortune favored the brave.

CHAPTER 53

There was no ambush. Kovac had watched the bridge for close on six hours, studying every vehicle that crossed it.

In between long stints with the binoculars, he had also managed to obtain a few tourist pamphlets to study up on the island. By anyone's standard, the west side of Jogashima Island was lovely. It had hotels, restaurants, a fish market, even arts and crafts shops. The east side, in contrast, was desolate and windswept.

Unsurprisingly, the lighthouse he needed was on the east side.

To get to it by car, Kovac would have to drive over the bridge and continue until the road came to a dead end at the eastern end of the island. Then it was a walking path the last of the way. He had waited for dark and now had it, but he still didn't like this approach. It would take too long and leave him exposed.

While waiting and watching, Kovac had considered the likelihood of this being another ambush. He still couldn't bring himself to walk away, but with this new mindset, the lighthouse looked like a trap. It was out on the eastern tip of the island, with flat, sea-swept rocks all around. It was modern. It resembled a white espresso pot. But the pamphlet didn't say whether or not it had windows. Kovac needed to assume it did. He would be a sniper target on his way to it, and after he arrived.

Going by car was out. So too going in on foot. If he was going to do this, he needed another way to scout the area without being observed.

He returned to the Prius and wasn't surprised to find Anna and Bennett sitting in it, waiting for him. They were both scowling at him. 'Where the hell did you go, Kovac?' Bennett eventually blurted.

'I told you not to wait for me. Pretty sure I encouraged you both to get a new life.'

'Exactly,' Anna said. She was speaking to Bennett, and Kovac had the feeling he wasn't entirely to blame for all the scowling. He suspected he had interrupted a longstanding disagreement between Anna and Bennett – presumably about whether to stay or go.

He walked round to the back of the car and opened the trunk. He poured everything from the duffel bag out and spread it across the trunk's carpeted base. He noticed the syringes were gone. Someone had taken his sux.

One jab and he would be paralyzed and struggling to breathe.

Two and he would be dead.

He stared for a long beat, thinking, computing this new information. It had to have been before he left the Prius and set out to watch the bridge.

He returned to the driver's seat.

All he kept on him was the loaded .38.

He said nothing about the sux.

He noticed Anna still had her empty .45, and that Bennett was holding the remaining .38 – the one he had fired down the concrete shaft. He had emptied its one remaining round back in the mountains and kept it for himself, but he couldn't assume it was empty now. The same went for the .45 in Anna's hand.

'I didn't sign up to sit around like an Uber driver without a customer,' Bennett said. 'I signed up to actually make a difference. I can help you, Kovac.'

Part of Kovac was impressed. Part of him was suspicious. What civilian opted into a potential gunfight? What civilian risked her life for a crusade, and one she barely understood? Best case scenario, Bennett was mentally unhinged.

Anna must've felt the same way, because she said: 'I've been telling her it's safer to leave.'

He figured he'd watch both of them for a bit, see what they revealed. But with the missing sux, he wasn't taking any chances. 'Well, if you're both staying, don't say I didn't warn you. And of course I'll need to see your weapons. Standard procedure. A frisk, too.'

They grumbled about this never having been procedure before, but got out and let him take the guns. He frisked them one at a time, then checked the weapons. Nothing on them, and both guns empty.

Perplexing.

'Satisfied?' Bennett asked.

'Like I said, standard procedure.'

This was bullshit, and he could tell they knew it was bullshit.

Keeping an eye on both Anna and Bennett, Kovac drove to the nearby port and checked the time. Coming up on 10 p.m.. He wasn't counting on an exchange taking place at 1:00 a.m., but that was all he had to go on. If the time was accurate, he was early. More likely though, the time was a rough guide. Kovac's experience with this sort of thing had long ago taught him that everyone arrived early to an exchange but hung back. Everyone wanted to get a good look at whoever showed themselves first.

If this even was an exchange…

He got out and searched the port for a boat with fishermen on it. At first there was nothing. He waited. A few boats motored in, but they were too small and open for his needs.

He went on waiting, sending Bennett off to get food and fluids for all three of them. He made her leave the pistol and checked it again as soon as she was gone. It was still empty. She was carrying it for show, exactly as he had asked her to do.

He sat with Anna in the car.

Waiting, watching, thinking.

Anna started talking about her school days back in Europe. While Kovac searched for incoming boats, she told him she had been a good student right through until her final year of school. Something had gone wrong that year. Not even she was sure what. Some kind of stress reaction, some kind of mental paralysis. 'And?' he asked distractedly.

'I messed things up and missed out on the university course I wanted. Things went wrong from there.'

'That's it?' he asked, swiveling to look at her. 'That's your excuse?' She looked hurt by his question, but he figured she needed to hear it straight, and why not from him. 'You've messed up, Anna. We all do it. But you're young. Fix it.'

'How?'

'By getting clear of me, for one.'

'Bennett says I'm safer here.'

'Bennett's wrong.' Kovac was still searching for a suitable boat, still thinking about Bennett and King and Peng and Megan and Lottie. And then about Bennett again. The sleeping with him, the interrogation afterwards, the endless hours on Masuda's phone before taking a call from Megan.

Best case scenario, mentally unhinged.

He spotted a larger boat coming in. He watched it arrive as two men set to work tidying up and reorganizing their catch. A father and son maybe? Both were making jokes and clearly enjoying each other's company. This despite a long day and half a night at sea. The younger guy looked more like a snowboarder than a fisherman. He was wearing mostly Quicksilver alpine gear. The older man looked more traditional.

Kovac knew a little bit about fishing. Bishop enjoyed it as a hobby and had taken him out numerous times. A few jobs had required Kovac to study up on the industry, too. There was a certain craft to it, he knew – especially here in Japan, where there was a certain craft to everything. It was all about ritual and routine. These two men could work and joke because a lot of their movements were automated and unthinking. Day in, day out. Kovac figured they had probably started early in the morning, preparing ice and bait. Then they probably went a long way out to get to the fishing grounds. They would've been watching the tide all day, always looking for a better place to fish, always moving around and setting out hooks. An idyllic life in some ways, hard in most others.

And now here Kovac was, about to make it a lot harder.

'You're thinking of stealing that boat?' Anna asked, following his gaze. She had shifted position and was now lying on the back seat, her long, beautiful legs up, her feet on the glass windows. Like she was bored.

Kovac said nothing, as Bennett returned with food. He watched her in the mirrors as she approached. She was alone.

Down at the boat, a woman in her late fifties or early sixties showed up with food. She had two metal containers which Kovac assumed were *bento* meal boxes, and a newspaper. She went to the boat and handed the metal containers and newspapers over to the two men. They looked surprised, but pleasantly so.

Bennett got back into the Prius, and Anna sat up straight again.

'Need to frisk me again, officer?' she asked with put-on indignation.

'Nope.'

Kovac monitored Bennett and Anna's hands without taking his eyes off the fishing boat.

He figured the woman was the older man's wife, facilitating a quick resupply. She was possibly the younger man's mother, too. A family operation, no punching in and out, no timesheets, no GPS.

Kovac figured the two men would now stick to shallow waters, aiming at fish moving in to spawn. He guessed they would be out all night, only coming in for the morning auction. That was when they would finally land the boat, pack up the catch, and hose everything down. A 24-hour shift.

This was all good news for him. The fishermen had no backup save for the wife-come-mother.

He got out of the car and grabbed what he needed from the trunk, packing it in his duffel bag. 'Why are you really here, Bennett?' he asked, coming back around the side of the car and stopping at her window. He had the duffel bag on one shoulder. 'And don't give me that shit about really making a difference again. Save that for Facebook.'

He had aimed to surprise her but she was quick and confident with her reply. 'Why? Simple. Because you're looking to cut us loose.'

'Meaning?'

'You don't want to do it. I can tell.' She looked up at him, looked him dead in the eye.

'And?'

'And I'm guessing that's because you feel like shit about it and know we don't stand a chance.'

He had to hand it to her, it was a better answer than he had expected.

'Am I right?' she pressed.

He held her eye in return, looking for any tell. There wasn't one.

Unhinged, he thought again. 'Okay, if that's how it's going to be, help me with this boat.'

CHAPTER 54

Kovac waited for the fisherman's wife to leave and return to her car, then wandered towards the boat with Bennett and Anna. He tapped his chest, smiling. 'I'm a tourist,' he said in English. 'Allen. From New Zealand. My wife here is Alice, and this is my daughter, Kate. You have a beautiful boat. Really fantastic. Traditional Japanese fishing, yes? Can I come aboard? A quick look? Very quick.'

The men looked more irritated than wary, like tourists were a common pest in these parts – even late at night. The older man was nicer than the younger one, managing a grudging smile and the most perfunctory of bows. The younger one just glanced at Anna's legs then got back to work.

Kovac asked for a quick tour again. They declined, flapping their hands like they were waving off bugs. The younger one took a longer look at Anna's legs but still didn't initiate conversation.

Kovac hadn't wanted to take out the .38 here. Not out in the open like this. That was his reason for bringing Bennett and Anna to the boat – the pretense of tourism, of a family. But the fishermen weren't interested and he didn't have a choice. He checked the port area was deserted then took out the gun. He aimed it at the fishermen. They saw it, exchanged a look and finally stopped working. They raised their hands.

Kovac climbed down onto the boat and entered the enclosed cockpit. He left Anna and Bennett to point empty pistols at the two men, and both kept their hands up.

Kovac studied the cockpit. A round section of the window had a clear sight that looked like it could rotate at high speeds to throw off sheets of sea spray, and there was a bag of tangerines off to one side, ready as a snack. Things were carefully arranged in here. Everything was in its place.

He went below deck and found a bed and small Shinto shrine, as well as a medicine box and tools. He saw the metal *bento* boxes with food.

Everything in its designated place, he thought. Ritual and routine.

He opened the medicine box and emptied it onto the floor, sifting through it with one foot. He bent down and picked up gauze bandaging.

'Bring them down here,' he called back up to Anna and Bennett.

Anna led the fishermen down to Kovac, pointing the .45, which sagged a little in her small hand. Bennett followed with the .38.

Kovac tossed the gauze bandaging to the son. 'Tie your father up.'

Bennett translated.

Kovac watched the son do it, and when he was done Kovac tied him up with a roll of tape he had found in the same medicine box.

He was just finishing the job and ordering them down onto the floor when he realized Bennett hadn't brought the supplies. 'Go back for the food and drink, we'll need it. This could drag out.'

Bennett didn't argue.

Kovac told Anna to stay below deck and collect the prisoners' phones. He told her to keep a gun on them, then went back up to the small cockpit. It wasn't a complex ship.

Certainly less complex than the Prius.

He familiarized himself with the controls then freed the boat from the dock. Bennett saw him do this and paused in her journey back to the car. She seemed to figure out his plan, and she immediately doubled back. She jumped back on just in time and appeared beside him in the cockpit as he fired up the engine. He glanced at her and decided leaving her behind wasn't worth the fight. 'Turn around,' he said, 'hands on the wall there.'

He frisked her again. Still nothing.

'What the fuck, Kovac? You don't trust me now? Is this because of what we did up in the mountains? Are you like this with all women you sleep with? What are you even looking for?'

He checked the .45.

Empty.

He said nothing and steered the boat gently out to sea, though he didn't have to go far. Within a few minutes, he found himself staring at the dim outline of an espresso pot lighthouse.

Definitely the one he wanted.

It was hard to tell in the dark but it looked deserted. He couldn't see if it had windows or not.

'Where are we going exactly?' Bennett asked.

'Nowhere. We're staying here.'

The sea had picked up a little and the boat was rolling under them. Everything smelled of salt and sweat and fish guts, and Kovac battled mild nausea.

He used the engine to maintain position and sat bobbing, waiting. For fifteen minutes, nothing happened. He ate a tangerine. He ate another. He was invisible sitting in the dark in this cockpit, which suited him just fine. He went on making regular engine adjustments, keeping an eye on Bennett's hands.

Finally, he noticed something out near the horizon.

'What's that?' Bennett asked.

It was a ship of some kind, coming closer, throwing up a lot of water. A luxury yacht, Kovac decided, as it began to close the distance. Bright white against the night sky and sea.

He showed Bennett how to maintain their position, went down and got his binoculars, then returned to the cockpit. They were 8x magnification for a wide field of view, with big lenses for plenty of light. Thankfully they were waterproof, with nitrogen gas to prevent inside fogging. They were perfect for fishing, though he missed his night vision. He could really have used that right now.

He gripped the binoculars by the rubber armor and brought them up to his eyes. They were easy to stabilize with the lower magnification. He couldn't make out the name on the dark bow. But it was aft too, on the transom where it was caught in a splash of artificial light designed to illuminate the deck. With the binoculars, he could read it without straining. "Fun Manager".

'Fun,' he said, realizing his mistake. He had heard it wrong when Masuda said it to him in the business hotel. There was never a *fund* manager, only "fun". It was a joke, a play on words befitting a playboy yacht.

The yacht had looked out of place before he had its name. Now Kovac was certain. It was connected to Peng. He began to reconsider his ambush theory. Maybe he wasn't the focus here. Maybe this was an exchange. He had to keep an open mind. There was potentially a young girl's life at stake.

'Is that a... that's a luxury yacht,' Bennett said, figuring out what it was for herself.

Kovac said nothing. He was still watching her hands,

waiting, debating what to do next. He liked that she was now steering the boat and working the engines. It kept her busy.

He considered motoring much closer to the yacht, but that would invite suspicion and possibly gunfire. Patience was still the name of this game. He went back downstairs.

'English?'

Both men shook their heads.

'Bennett, translate.'

He had Bennett shout down from above, offering the men 100,000 yen if they went ahead and fished. That was all they had to do. Fish. Kovac wanted them out on deck baiting hooks and laying out lines. He offered another 10,000 yen to cover the damage to the medicine box. 110,000 yen in all, with one stipulation. If they did anything other than fish they needed to accept the fact Kovac would kill them.

The men argued in Japanese, then reluctantly agreed.

Kovac cut them free and made Anna pay them on the spot. Then he guided them back up to the cockpit and pushed them out onto the deck. They did exactly as he wanted. They started baiting hooks and laying out lines.

Ritual and routine, he thought.

He waited in the cockpit, using the binoculars to see what was happening with Fun Manager. Nothing was happening. The giant yacht had seemingly come to a stop.

Time slowed to a crawl.

Kovac began moving the fishing boat at regular intervals to keep up the appearance of real fishing. Time slowed even more.

Then, at 1:05 a.m. exactly, things started happening. And quickly.

It began with a boat coming from the port, just as Kovac had done. It turned out to be a Zodiac, one heavyset man sitting at the outboard motor. Kovac couldn't make out a face in the dark.

The Zodiac stopped dead in the water about 150 yards out from the lighthouse and about 300 yards from Fun Manager. Without bow spray, it was suddenly almost invisible in the dark.

Fun Manager responded. It slowly set course for the Zodiac.

Neither boat seemed to pay any attention to Kovac's Japanese vessel, with its two Japanese fishermen hard at work on the deck. Kovac was able to secretly monitor proceedings from the fishing boat's cockpit.

He let the fishing boat drift for five minutes, gently putting distance between himself and Fun Manager. He maneuvered subtly until he had a view of the luxury yacht's stern. He figured that's where the action was most likely to start, and he was rewarded for the decision more or less immediately. Two mercenaries stepped out onto the aft deck, carrying M4s. They eyed the fishing boat for a while but seemed to decide it was harmless. They refocused on the Zodiac, which had also made its way round toward the yacht's stern. There was hand signaling and the Zodiac cut its outboard.

The man in the Zodiac held up what might have been a phone.

On the yacht, one of the mercenaries held up something too.

Or were they just gesturing?

Kovac kept raising the binoculars, trying for a positive ID. But neither Peng nor the sniper, Sukhomlinov, felt like a good fit for the man in the Zodiac. He was too big, too beefy. Kovac couldn't see anyone inside the luxury yacht yet, either. The tint on the windows was too dark. He let the binoculars linger on the yacht's vast roof, aware Sukhomlinov could do real damage from a perch like that, even with the swell. He couldn't see much. There was too much sea mist and not enough moon.

The man in the Zodiac and the mercenary on the yacht went on signaling. But communications seemed to hit a snag, because the man in the Zodiac turned the boat around and pulled the cord to start the outboard motor again. He put some distance between himself and the yacht.

For a few minutes, nothing happened. Then Fun Manager's transom opened to reveal an oversize tender. Floodlights were switched on, and the mercenaries swung the tender around: from parallel with the rear of the yacht to a right angle. They spent a few minutes messing around with straps and a winch, then guided it down rollers, into the water. One of the mercenaries climbed in and fired up the tender's seventy-horsepower outboard. 'What are you doing?' Kovac asked under his breath.

A girl of perhaps twelve was dragged out of the yacht and forced into the tender. She was stooped and compliant. A redhead.

'Shit.' Kovac checked the shore again, including the lighthouse. No one up there, nor on the elevated ground back behind it, though it was dark enough to remain a possibility.

He checked the roof of the yacht.

Nothing there that he could see, either.

One mercenary got into the tender with the girl. He messed around with the outboard for a moment, then the tender started towards the Zodiac.

The man in the Zodiac signaled. The mercenary in the tender did the same.

Then both boats came to stop again, as if waiting on something.

Kovac did another sweep. The island, the yacht, the Zodiac, Bennett's hands. In the same way he knew a little about fishing, he knew a little about kidnapping and hostage negotiation. If this was an exchange, models of rational, self-interested action said both parties would want to keep things predictable. Now that the exchange had started, there would be a preference for steady, predictable progress. No one would want surprises. Surprises undermined trust and decreased the odds of a mutually beneficial outcome. Tests at RAND said so.

So what was this delay?

Kovac wondered if this whole thing was simply a transfer, not an exchange. Perhaps Peng was using his men to move Lottie to shore, into Japan? But that wouldn't necessitate a delay like this, and the timing was suspicious. Megan had said 1:00 a.m..

Anna entered the cockpit. 'I found something,' she said, handing over one of the *bento* meal boxes the fisherman's wife had delivered. 'I was hungry, I looked inside.'

It was a simple metal lunchbox. The lid was loose and Kovac opened it, expecting salmon, rice and pickles. In the gloom, he saw a white substance in brick form. Four bricks in all, taped as pairs with black adhesive tape. His first thought was drugs.

He took out one of the packages, turning it over in his hand. It was too dark to make out much detail, but he instantly knew it wasn't drugs. He pushed a thumb into it, and sure enough it was a putty.

He felt for wires and found them, following them from blasting caps at the ends of each brick to a small circuit board in the *bento* meal box. He didn't want to risk feeling round for anything more in the dark.

'Okay,' he said, managing to sound calm even as his heart rate spiked, 'bring up the other box, Anna. And let's call these fishermen in.'

CHAPTER 55

Kovac wasn't the one observing. This was a hit and he was the target.

He understood how it fit together now. Far from being a spectator, he was the cause of the delay. He was payment. Peng wanted confirmation Kovac was dead before handing over Lottie. And the man in the Zodiac wanted Lottie before condemning Kovac.

It was the second trap he had walked into in a matter of days. He was furious with himself, but also saw the pattern. It was as if Peng knew his past, his training, his exact thought processes.

He exchanged clothes with the younger fisherman. He made Bennett translate his instructions, slipping into the Quicksilver jacket as quickly as he could in the dark. Bennett grabbed the second *bento* box from Anna and checked it. 'This one's a meal,' she said. 'Rice and salmon, I think.'

Bennett gave it to him.

He looked and she was right. He tossed it aside, keeping just the first *bento* box – the one filled with plastic explosives. He sealed it tight, then pocketed his .38. 'Tell these fishermen, any unexpected moves, any waving, use of a flashlight, any light, *any signaling*, I'll –'

He cut himself short, realizing the younger fisherman was glaring at him in the dark as if working up the courage for an attack. And sure enough, an instant later there was an attack.

Just not the one Kovac expected.

CHAPTER 56

Bennett lunged at him. She seemed to be going for a pointless chest shove, and Kovac only detected the syringe at the last instant. He stepped left and twisted sideways, the syringe sailing straight through the space where he had just been standing. He drove the *bento* box hard up into the side of Bennett's exposed jaw, attacking her from the side as she overbalanced and lurched forward. She crumpled sideways, landing hard in the corner of the cabin. Kovac retreated a few steps, forcing Anna back in the process, and realized he had no choice. It would be like reaching down for a snake. The syringe could be anywhere in the dark, and he'd be defenseless against it. He took out the .38., aiming at Bennett's chest.

He hit something sharp behind him and turned the pistol on the older fisherman, confused. 'Outside,' he yelled, still gripping the *bento* box. 'Move it. *Now.*'

It was too fucking crowded in here, too fucking dark.

Bennett moved to stand and Kovac shouted at her to stay down. She groaned and slumped across the door, trapping him in the cabin. He had the *bento* box with the plastic explosives under his Quicksilver jacket, and he perceived Bennett's move for what it was. She was blocking him, locking him in here, sacrificing herself to make sure he died in the cabin along with the rest of them. He wondered what Peng had on her that would give her the strength to do this.

He couldn't move her without getting jabbed, nor could he get out of the cabin. The explosives under his jacket felt like they would explode any second. 'Goddamn it, Bennett.' He fired two rounds into her chest, before stepping over her. Anna shrieked, but Kovac didn't have time for her right now. He pushed the older fisherman back out onto the deck.

Kovac kept his head down, shielded from the lighthouse and yacht, and moved around the boat. He grabbed a bucket, disguising the move as work.

As soon as he was safely out of Fun Manager's view, he threw the *bento* box as far clear of the fishing boat as he could. Doing this would cost him his chance to escape via water. If he was submerged and Peng detonated, the increased density and viscosity of water would leave Kovac vulnerable to the shock wave. The sections of his body that contained air – namely his lungs, intestinal tract and ears – would all likely be destroyed.

If he couldn't escape, he would need to stay on the fishing boat. Stand his ground and fight. And if he was going to have any realistic chance of winning that fight, he would need to be brutal, just as he had been back in the cabin.

He had no choice.

'Fuck.'

He stumbled and slammed loudly into the base of the cockpit wall. He only just managed to steady himself. Something was off with his balance.

He dragged himself into shadow, still shielded from the lighthouse, yacht and Zodiac, and pulled himself up. He was able to see into the cockpit, and he saw Anna's silhouette holding the .38 in one hand. She had the gun's cylinder open. She was peering down in the dark. Kovac saw her slotting rounds in one by one, even as she checked the windows. She was loading the gun as if she was driving a car at the same time: glancing down to position each bullet, then glancing up and out the cockpit windows.

Looking for him.

The bullets hadn't come from Kovac. And they hadn't come from a store. Kovac was sure of that. He hadn't seen a hunting store in town, and the few fishing stores had all been shut. To get .38 rounds, Anna and Bennett had made contact with someone. And they had done it well before getting on this boat.

He realized something was hurting. It was his shoulder.

He reached around and felt a syringe. He pulled it free from the Quicksilver jacket and held it up, trying to make out detail. He didn't understand how Bennett had done it, until he remembered forcing Anna back as he took his pistol out.

Bennett hadn't done it.

Anna had done it.

Kovac slumped down again, defeated. It wasn't a full dose, but paralysis was still the likely outcome. He looked out to sea, where he'd thrown the C4. The fact it hadn't yet detonated told him Peng had other plans. Maybe the C4 was only ever a backup, a failsafe. Maybe Anna and Bennett had been Peng's plan from the start.

Kovac could see how it would end from here. Anna would come out when certain he was paralyzed and check for the explosives. Finding nothing, she would shoot him.

Or more likely just roll him into the sea.

He heard an outboard approaching, heard a gunshot, but he couldn't move much at all now. Eventually, somebody appeared above him, nothing more than a shadow really, until the light caught his face. The man from the Zodiac?

'We're going to need proof of death, Kovac,' Bishop said. 'This won't hurt. Hold still and stay calm.' Kovac saw Bishop crouch. His arm came out and there was another jab, this one to Kovac's thigh. He stared at Bishop's morose face. *How had he* – But Kovac's mind never finished the question. Bishop took something else out, aimed it, and the whole world turned a dazzling white.

CHAPTER 57

Lottie was terrified. They had come off the fishing boat just before dawn and had been taken straight to a waiting car. The three of them had been put in the back seat. The mean man, the man with the red hat who had forced the first three balloons down her throat, sat in the front seat. He had been smoking all morning. The driver was smoking as well. They had the windows up and Lottie could hardly breathe.

The driver seemed to want to avoid big roads. They kept to small side roads. The car always seemed to be turning into one road or out of another. There were a lot of tunnels.

The men were talking in a language she didn't recognize, a language she didn't understand. Lottie thought of home. She thought of Pemberton and wondered if Megan was looking for her now. Her family was very rich. She had recently become aware just how rich. Was that why she was here, in this car?

She felt the girl on her left reach for her hand. She glanced down. The girl's hand was limp. With her other hand, she was scratching at her neck. Her head kept falling forward, like she was falling asleep. She would jerk it back up, but then it would fall again. Lottie wanted to ask her if she was okay, but she didn't dare speak.

The girl seemed like she was hardly breathing. She had darkish skin, but it looked different now. The lips were bluish purple. The girl looked sweaty, even though the heater was off and the car was cold.

Lottie squeezed her hand tightly, trying to reassure her.

Trying to reassure herself.

After a while, the girl fell asleep. Which was a good thing, Lottie figured. If she was asleep, she wasn't worrying, she wasn't scared. Maybe it was car sickness. Sometimes Lottie got sick in a car still.

She exchanged a look with the girl on her right. Her mind went to the balloons. What was inside her? Her throat was very sore when she swallowed, and she could still taste salty blood.

She stared out at the signs again. She suspected it was Japan. She had watched some anime on Netflix. The writing had been the same in that as it was here.

Or was the anime from Korea? Maybe she was in Korea. She didn't know.

Somewhere like that.

A helicopter, a jet, another helicopter and the fishing trawler. She was a long way from home.

Another wave of fear hit, and now she did feel carsick. She felt as if she was going to vomit. She let go of the hand beside her and leaned forward. She retched.

The man with the red hat spun and grabbed her by the hair. He pulled her head up, staring into her eyes. Then he noticed the other girl, the girl who was asleep. He flung Lottie aside and reached back and peeled open the sleeping girl's eyes, one after the other. The eyes didn't move. The pupils were like two tiny black dots. The lips were almost black now, the fingernails, too.

The man with the red hat said something to the driver. The car stopped, pulling abruptly over to the side of the road. The man with the red hat got out. He dragged the sleeping girl out into the street. He looked around. He saw a small shed near a rice paddy. He went to it, dragging the sleeping girl who Lottie now knew wasn't sleeping at all. She was dead.

They sat like that for a very long time, in the cold car filled with cigarette smoke. The driver looked nervous. He kept lighting cigarettes and stubbing them out, glancing across at the shed every few seconds like he expected the man with the red hat to come out. But the man with the red hat didn't come out.

Lottie thought about jumping out and running away. The door was still open where the man with the red hat had dragged the dead girl out. Lottie didn't want to die. She had her entire life in front of her. She had plans. She wanted to be like her step-sister. She idolized Megan. Megan was the most glamorous person she knew, and the smartest too. Megan would be looking for her right now. If she escaped, if she ran, if she hid, Megan would find her. Her father would find her. She *had* to run.

But for some reason she couldn't convince her body to move. She kept thinking about what would happen, what these two men would do to her if they caught her trying to escape. She took the hand of the girl on her right, more to reassure herself than the girl. It was trembling.

The man with the red hat came out of the little shed. He had blood all over him. He was carrying the balloons; the same balloons Lottie had seen men force down into the girl's stomach. He shut the rear door. He got back into the passenger seat. He said something to the driver. The driver grunted, then he pulled back onto the road.

The man with the red hat took out a gun.

CHAPTER 58

Kovac came to. Sunlight was blazing into his eyes, fueling a splitting headache. He rocked back and slapped the tatami for a weapon, his adrenaline spiking. He was naked, lying on a futon.

He sat as best he could, squinting against the shaft of light coming through the open window. He saw Anna. Anna and Bishop.

He went at Bishop, driving him into the wall before pulling him clumsily down.

'Don't be a fool, Kovac.'

Kovac realized he was going to lose this fight. He couldn't seem to find his usual strength. His mind scrabbled for new angles of attack, but he wasn't as fast or as strong as usual. He wasn't fighting Bishop, so much as some kind of insidious hangover.

He went down – or was forced down, he wasn't sure which – and the room spun when he rolled and tried to stand. He was forced down again and his eyesight fluttered. He was screaming, until a hand over his mouth silenced him.

Small, female.

Anna's hand.

'Shhh,' she said. 'It's okay, Kovac, you're okay. You're safe here.'

He felt his body go slack. Bishop had him in some kind of

hold.

He had been wrong about being naked. He was in underwear, he now saw, but nothing else. He tried to roll, but he could no longer move in any meaningful way.

Bishop said: 'I'm not your enemy Kovac. If I was, you'd be dead.'

'Listen to him,' Anna pleaded. 'He's telling the truth. He's helping. He's been helping all along.'

Anna tentatively raised her hand from Kovac's mouth, as Bishop said: 'Pemberton's been compromised, but I think you know that. We're on our own here. I'm just trying to put things right, same as you.'

Kovac didn't bother to struggle. There was no point. Bishop's hold was iron-clad.

He looked around, recognizing the room. He was back in the Meiji-era house in the mountains, back in the room where Bennett had seduced him – *on the same futon, in fact*. It made no sense. 'What the fuck is this?' he snarled, recalling Bennett's crumpled form on the fishing boat.

Bishop tightened the hold.

'I knew you'd do this, Kovac.'

'I'll fucking kill you. You gave her the sux? You gave her *bullets*?'

'The sux was all I had to work with. I needed you paralyzed. Bennett offered to do it.'

Anna said: 'It's true, Kovac.'

'Bullshit.'

'I had to use Bennett. I knew if it was me coming at you with a syringe, I wasn't going to last two seconds.' Bishop released Kovac. Kovac scrabbled backward, pushing Anna clear and checking around him again for a weapon. He was trying to think.

'You weren't meant to make it to the lighthouse,' Bishop said. 'That's exactly what I was trying to avoid.'

'By paralyzing me? By helping Anna shoot me?'

Bishop sat down heavily on the opposite side of the room. 'Like I said, the sux was all I had to work with at that point. You left it in this house. I figured if I could paralyze you, I could at least talk with you. Maybe even fake a proof of death clip like we did in Egypt – something we could use to get Lottie back.'

'Bennett agreed to it, Kovac.'

Bishop held up his hands. 'Full disclosure?'

'Jesus, there's more?'

'I recruited her while you were at the business hotel. I explained the sort of men you were going up against. The extent of their reach and what they did to their enemies. She could hear the shooting at the hotel, Kovac. I told her I could protect her. And not only that, fund Resolute going forward. She knew she was out of her depth. It didn't take much convincing. I showed her where the sux was, what it was. I told her to act like she might sleep with you, win your trust, jab you in bed. She didn't. According to Anna, she lost her nerve. She was scared of you.'

Bullshit,' Kovac said.

'I tried communicating with her via Masuda's phone as you made your way down to the coast. I thought maybe it was still possible to stop you getting there. I was wrong.'

'She took a call from Megan. You expect me to believe your loyalty is to me – over King? You and Bennett helped Curzon set me up.'

'My loyalty is to Curzon *and you*. Bennett wasn't in contact with Pemberton. She took that call thinking it was me. She was waiting on a funds transfer – for Resolute. But once you knew about the exchange, everything went to hell.'

'She thought it was Bishop calling,' Anna confirmed.

To hell with Bennett, Kovac told himself. She'd chosen her fate.

'Is Lottie dead?'

Bishop rubbed at the back of his neck. 'It wasn't Lottie, Kovac. It was an Asian girl they'd... I don't know. It was a wig. Peng was planning to screw us all along. It seems he wanted to kill me, too.'

'How do you know it wasn't Lottie?'

'Because they killed her in the tender and dumped her. I pulled her out of the sea. It wasn't Lottie.'

'So it was you in the Zodiac all along?'

'I was following instructions just like you – direct from Pemberton.' Bishop sighed. 'I was there to collect Lottie after Peng received confirmation you were dead. He had a sniper in place.'

'So Pemberton *did* order my death.'

'They're under duress, Kovac. Nothing they say right now has any –'

'The sniper Peng had in place – was it Sukhomlinov?'

'I never confirmed one way or the other, but that'd be my guess. After things went wrong and Anna signaled, I fired up the Zodiac. I went for the fishing boat. I jabbed you, and I sent Peng proof of death. But –'

'– he didn't buy it.' Kovac felt the futon beneath him. He didn't want to ask, but knew he had to: 'And Bennett?'

Bishop averted his gaze.

'Me?' Kovac asked.

'You didn't know, Kovac – and that's on me.'

'You're right. It sure as hell –' Kovac stopped himself mid-sentence. It was a lie and he hated himself for saying it. He had shot Bennett in cold blood because he was rattled, because he had wanted security, certainty. That was the truth of it. He couldn't hide from it any longer. He had to face it. She was trying to help him and he had murdered her. 'The sux was gone, she attacked me with a syringe. I had no choice.' He felt a flood of regret, his throat locking up. He could hardly breathe. 'I searched her. Anna, too.'

Bishop said: 'I should've risked coming forward. I should've dealt with you directly. I…' He shook his head. 'I knew you suspected them, and I didn't know how to get you back on side without catching a bullet myself. I held the sux for them. I put it in the bento lunch boxes and paid a woman to deliver it to the fishermen – as a gift from the local union. Bullets, too. Bennett demanded them. By that time, she was terrified.'

Kovac sat blinking for a moment, taking all this in. Finally he said: 'Bennett never helped Peng? Never helped King?' He forced the words out.

'No. She was only ever helping me.'

'Goddamn it.' Kovac tried to stand. It took a few goes, but he finally managed it. He winced, trying to get his mind off Bennett. That line of thought would only lead to a darkness he wasn't sure he could overcome right now. 'What the hell did you jab me with on the fishing boat, Bishop? I'm like a fucking newborn foal here.'

'I knew I couldn't risk more sux, so I had to go with what I could get locally. It ended up a bit of a concoction sorry.'

'How long have I been out?'

'Nine hours, give or take.'

'Peng didn't follow us up here?'

'Peng wasn't on the yacht. He wasn't at the exchange. We don't know where he is. I don't have any new intel beyond what

I gave you originally – the intel that placed him here in the mountains.'

'And Lottie?'

'We don't know where she is, either. Or if she's alive. Pemberton is still under siege, so we can't trust a word they say.'

Kovac nodded to himself. Two things still bothered him.

'Why the C4 or whatever it was?' he asked.

'It wasn't C4. It was putty, some calculator innards and wires. I put the sux and bullets in the one *bento* box, under the food, and Bennett set up the other as a diversion. She wanted something that would really tie your hands while she got clear and the sux kicked in.'

'She was going to pretend she had a detonator,' Anna said.

'She needed a plan – to have the confidence to take you on. Anna was meant to show it to you. While you examined it, Bennet was meant to jab you. But it didn't go that way. It was dark, cramped, the timing was all wrong.'

'She kept freezing up,' Anna said, with obvious frustration even now.

'That's a stupid fucking plan.'

'It wasn't his idea, Kovac. It was Bennett's.'

'I knew it was too complex,' Bishop said. 'I said no to it – more than once – but Bennett was set on it. She fell in love with her own idea, she could see it going perfectly. I thought she was going to back out on helping me altogether, and I was trying to save you from Peng and Sukhomlinov, so I figured what the hell. What's the worst that could happen? You pretty quickly realize it's a fake, and by that time you're paralyzed. It was stupid, but I never saw Bennett getting shot. I even added the rounds for the .38, so Bennett could defend herself if anything went wrong.'

'So *I* end up getting shot?'

'No one was meant to get shot. I was trying to protect you, Kovac, get you out of there alive.'

Kovac wasn't so sure about that. But he managed to hold his tongue. Mouthing off wouldn't change what had happened. He forced himself to move on to his second concern, which was more future-focused. 'Why are we up in the mountains again? Why are we back in this place?'

Bishop stood. He opened the sliding door to one of the cupboards and Kovac saw three rucksacks. The first two were identical to the rucksack Bishop had given him in Takumimachi-Dori, Kofu. They contained the same basic but lethal civilian gear. The last was of a different magnitude. It was a tactical assault pack, which Kovac had painstakingly prepared himself. It was practically a load-out bag, coming in at almost forty pounds and leaving nothing to chance. 'That's what we need to discuss, Kovac.'

CHAPTER 59

Kovac wasn't ready to talk plans.

He told Bishop and Anna he needed to clean up first. He locked himself in the bathroom and ran the shower. He put it so hot it scalded his skin, then stood under it, gritting his teeth at the pain. He kept seeing it. The two shots, down into the dark mass blocking the fishing boat's cockpit door. Like he was putting down a sick animal. No more emotion than that. Cold, clinical murder.

He switched off the shower, got out and wiped a hand across the fogged mirror. The middle third of his face stared back: unshaven, hollowed out by drugs and pain.

To undo it, to reach back and change that split-second decision...

Kovac had never considered himself a murderer before. A killer, yes. But never a murderer.

And there was a distinction.

When had it become so easy?

He opened the cabinet with the mirror on it and checked for painkillers. There weren't any. The plastic shelves were empty, save for a rusted safety razor and two used candles.

He thought about his panic in Peng's dungeon, about the surge of irrational hope that had come from the idea of helping Bennett get free of this mess. And now, here was the reality of his world, his chosen profession. He shut the cabinet door and was glad to see the fog returning. He didn't have to look at himself.

He toweled off and dressed, as his mind ran back to a rainy New York day. He'd stood and watched that day as three Catelo members needlessly turned a mugging into a rape. He had known Bennett's death would stir up this memory, and sure enough here it was.

Right on cue.

Bishop had been observing Kovac that day, too, preparing to pull him out of Catelo. He had made contact with Kovac for the first time that evening, and he had referred to that event repeatedly during Kovac's time at the farm. He had listened to Kovac justify his inaction. Listened to Kovac talk about a Catelo code. Listened to Kovac rationalize and gaslight, until eventually Kovac had crumbled in the face of an awful truth.

Bishop had allowed Kovac to kill all three perpetrators. The boys had been grown men by the time Kovac got to them. Two had been human scum. One had been married, with a wife and four children. Kovac had killed him in a parking lot in Pennsylvania.

Kovac checked under the sink for painkillers but found nothing useful. Just old soap and an even older hairdryer.

He straightened up, closing his eyes and waiting for a bout of dizziness to pass. His head was throbbing.

He thought about the parking lot in Pennsylvania again. It had made no difference. If anything, Kovac had ended up more confused, more conflicted. He had swapped Catelo's fucked up code for Bishop's.

He hung the towel so it would dry, then stretched his back, which was stiff and sore.

Target discrimination...

Kovac could hear Bishop's voice, his footfall as he paced overhead on ramps at the farm, watching a teenage Kovac continually make the same mistakes. He would bark the same phrase from overhead every time. “Target discrimination. We don’t shoot each other, we shoot the bad guys!” For a few weeks, it had become a mental block for Kovac. He tried so hard to think his way through things, he started to overthink. And the more he did that, the more he failed to discriminate.

Bishop’s solution had both surprised and horrified Kovac. Bishop had asked him to clear an old hut in a forested section of the farm. Kovac had done it. He shotgun breached the door and entered, and found the rooms filled with mannequins instead of paper targets. He made it through the first two rooms successfully and entered the last to find two more combatants either side of a mannequin on a chair. He shot the combatants and paused on the mannequin in the chair, momentarily uncertain. It was just a split-second. Less than that. He wasn’t even sure how he processed it. He didn’t see the man’s face, he hardly saw the man’s clothing. He just knew. He didn’t shoot.

Bishop had stood up from that chair and rubbed Kovac on the head, like a pet. Then he had strolled outside and taken a long piss.

Kovac had never forgotten that wordless show of trust, but here he was now. From this new vantage, the whole exercise felt more like abuse.

He paused at the door to the bathroom, still with half a mind to kill Bishop. What did he owe Curzon? What did he owe King? They were modern-day feudal lords. This was all a game for them. They had even given themselves regal monikers, for fuck’s sake.

He cursed softly, then exited the bathroom and stood staring at Anna. She was at the kitchen table, flicking through a Japanese cookbook Kovac guessed was from the 80s. The writing was all in Japanese and Anna didn’t seem interested in the pictures, either. She didn’t look up. ‘Feel better?’ Her voice was slightly croaky. She looked numb and Kovac guessed she had been crying.

'Was Bennett sincere about wanting to make a difference?' he asked.

Anna nodded, still not looking up. 'She admired you.'

'And I killed her.'

Anna nodded again, gently closing the cookbook. She ran her fingers over the cover – over a picture of a smiling housewife. When she did finally look up, her eyes were red. 'What do we do now, Kovac?'

'Nothing,' he said. 'I'm done. I'm out.'

'They'll kill me. I'm witness to all this shit too, remember. Bishop told me about Peng.'

'I can't help you. Or Bishop.'

Anna slammed an open palm down on the table, startling him, waking him the hell up. 'So that's it? You make a mistake and you just give up? I need your help, Kovac. Fix it.'

He recognized his own advice being thrown back at him, but this was different. He wasn't young anymore. He wasn't Anna. And Bennett wasn't a fucking university course. 'You saw how that worked out for Bennett.'

Anna got up and walked through into the adjacent room. She sat down on a wooden chair that matched the one in the kitchen, pulling off her shoes and folding her long legs under her as if about to meditate. She put her elbows on her knees and propped her chin up with her hands. She stared at him, completely miserable, seeming to expect nothing. Eventually she looked away, out a frosted window. 'You really are a piece of shit, Kovac.'

No argument there.

'Where's Bishop?' he asked.

'He went out for supplies. He said you were free to leave if you wanted. It sounds like you do.' She gave up on the non-view from the frosted window and started picking at the faded pink polish on one toenail. Seeing her barefoot again, Kovac was transported back to the train in Tokyo, just before Sukhomlinov took his shot. *Before Bennett was dragged into all this*, he thought bitterly.

Bishop had been right about one thing: Kovac should have ditched Anna and Bennett in Tokyo. 'I'm sorry, Anna,' he said. 'For Bennett, for everything.'

He tapped the doorframe a couple of times like punctuation on his apology, then peeled back from the door. He started towards the stairs.

'And Lottie?'

He paused. 'Bishop told you about Lottie, too, huh?'

'She's a kid. We have to try. Bishop agrees.'

Kovac thought for a moment. 'I'll be upstairs, Anna.'

'And?'

'And nothing. When Bishop gets back, tell him I'm waiting.'

CHAPTER 60

While he waited for Bishop, Kovac found a generic burner phone in one of the rucksacks. He unwrapped the heavy-duty plastic packaging and fired the device up. He created a fake account, downloaded a VPN, then navigated to an English-language newspaper based out of Tokyo.

It was already in the news. Kovac read the article, able to see Bishop's handiwork in all of it. Two Japanese fishermen and a young British woman had been found dead on a fishing boat just clear of Jogashima Island. All three had been shot in what police were calling drug-related executions. The article said the name of the British woman was being withheld until authorities were certain her family had been notified.

Massaging his temple, and struggling to think past his headache, Kovac pictured Bennett's mother waking in the middle of the night to that phone call.

He should have been the one to call her, but that was never going to happen. *A coward in all the ways that matter,* he thought.

He heard Bishop come through the broken door. He heard him take off his boots and bang them, removing snow. He said something to Anna and she mumbled a reply, and a moment later he was coming up the stairs. 'This place smells like mold,' he grumbled. 'How is that even possible in winter?'

Kovac disagreed. It smelled like Bishop's deodorant, the same smell he'd detected and dismissed last time he was here. And how had he not figured out it was Bishop in the Zodiac?

'I'm out,' he said.

'If you were out, you'd be gone.'

'After Lottie.'

He paused. 'Okay. But King's not –'

'Screw King. And screw you, Bishop.'

Bishop shrugged and started unpacking food from a shopping bag. He threw Kovac a hot meat bun. 'Anna said you liked them. And this canned coffee shit. Did I get the right type?'

Kovac nodded, catching the bun and coffee and cracking the coffee open. 'You got a plan, any way to get to Lottie?' He took a long slurp.

'Not exactly.'

'And we can't trust a word coming from Pemberton?'

'Correct.'

'Has news broken of that yet?'

'The siege in central Australia? No. We've managed to keep it out of the press so far. Lottie's abduction, too. Curzon's share price is behaving normally, so I don't think it's even a rumor yet.'

'What about Anna?'

He lowered his voice. 'That's simple. Cut her loose, Kovac.'

'Sacrifice one girl to save another kind-of-a-deal?'

'We're not sacrificing anyone. It's safer. For us, and for her.'

'Bullshit.'

'I told you to cut Bennett loose, too.'

Kovac ignored this. He took another slurp of coffee then started on the bun. 'Where did the extra rucksacks come from?'

'I brought four in total.'

'I can see that. Why three extra?'

'I had four packed and ready to go, including the tactical pack. It was me in a private jet. I didn't exactly have a baggage allowance.' Bishop plucked headache tablets out of the shopping bag and threw them across.

Kovac caught them. 'So we have equipment but no target.'

'Correct.'

'You got nothing from the fishermen before killing them?'

'They didn't speak English, and from what Anna told me, you shot the translator.'

Kovac gave him a look of warning this time, and Bishop raised both hands to shoulder height. 'Hey, I'm not judging. I'm just saying what happened.'

Kovac popped the lid on the tablets and took three along with another long gulp of lukewarm canned coffee. Then he stood and crossed to the windows. 'I found something down at the apartment building Peng owns.'

'Found what?'

Kovac told Bishop about the dungeon, explaining how it functioned. 'Basically, it's a human washing machine,' he finished. 'A giant rinse cycle.'

'And that helps us how?'

'It's an endpoint. Masuda told me he had a meeting in Kanagawa. He told me he was meeting a boat there, Fun Manager.'

'The yacht from last night?'

Kovac nodded. 'And his phone suggested he did a lot of business down there, but also up here. Maybe a start point and an endpoint.'

'You think Peng's using the Yakuza to run girls from

Kanagawa up to his human washing machine?'

'Girls, boys, men, women.' Kovac nodded. 'Makes sense. Only now Peng's going to need to be more involved. The yakuza's lacking leadership. He'll turn to someone he can trust to get Lottie into Japan.'

'How do we know he's bringing her into Japan?'

'We don't.' Kovac drained the last few drops of coffee. But he's using Lottie to get to me and you, right? And we're in Japan. If she's bait, seems logical to dangle her here.'

'How do we know she's not here already?'

'He used a double. The girl with the wig.'

'There could be a hundred different reasons for that.'

'I'm going with the most likely – he had no choice because she hadn't finished the journey up from Australia yet. It's not like he can just fly her in on Qantas. There would be delays getting her into a jet, landing it somewhere with lax protocols, getting her onto a boat, smuggling her in.'

Bishop unwrapped a cold sandwich. It was pre-cut into two triangles that looked to be full of some kind of white sauce with ham and cucumber. He started eating the first triangle, holding it in big ugly hands, chewing with his big ugly jaw. He wiped at his lips after the first triangle and started on the second. 'That's a shit plan, Kovac. But that said, I can't think of a better one. They're under pressure. They'll stick to channels and people they know.'

'Peng will want to be a little closer, and he'll put someone in charge who can control the yakuza goons.'

'Sukhomlinov?' Bishop asked.

'Maybe. Sukhomlinov's got the language skills. Whoever it is, though, if we get them, maybe we get a path to Lottie.' Kovac crossed the room and put his trash back into Bishop's shopping bag. 'I think it's all going to happen here.'

Bishop nodded.

'Don't do that,' Kovac said, crossing back to the window and resuming surveillance of Peng's apartment building.

'Do what?'

'Act like this is all news to you.'

'Some of it is. The rest, I'm just interested to hear your take. No games.'

'You brought me here last night, Bishop. You already knew about the human washing machine?'

'I brought you here because it's Peng's last known location. But sure, I'll admit it, you're not the only one who had a look around up here. I was here, too. I found the apartment key glued to the rock. I didn't find the washing machine underneath. That was nice work.' He paused. 'But there's something here I did find, something you didn't.'

'What?' Kovac listened as Bishop finished off the sandwich.

'No – this one you need to see for yourself.' Bishop threw the plastic bag aside and went for the rucksacks. He dropped one at his own feet and threw the other to Kovac. It landed with a heavy thud in front of Kovac and the contents clattered. 'Gear up.'

Kovac nudged the rucksack with his foot, in two minds.

His rucksacks had small variations, but this was more or less a clean replacement for the rucksack he had lost at the business hotel. *A kind of military mulligan*, he thought sourly. But did he want to go down this path again?

'For Lottie,' he said. 'That's all. Then I'm out, Bishop. Promise me that.'

'Understood.'

Kovac threw the rucksack back. 'And I'm done with civilian gear – I'll take the tactical assault pack there.'

Bishop shook his head. 'Not yet. You won't need it for this first outing.'

CHAPTER 61

They couldn't afford to wait for darkness. Every minute they sat waiting was another minute Lottie's life was at risk.

They left Anna to keep an eye on Peng's apartment, and Bishop led Kovac out the rear door and on up into the trees. Kovac was back to carrying a collapsible AR-15, along with a new HK45. The HK45 was in a mid-ride holster. Everything the way he liked it, providing he wanted to keep the weight down and remain somewhat low-key. Everything except for his old hiking boots, which were already going to work on his half-healed blisters. He ignored the pain. Blisters beat frostbite every day of the week.

They used the forest for cover, but didn't follow the perimeter of the town. Instead, Bishop began to climb. The path he chose was steep. It was covered in crisp snow, and it weaved between towering cedars which sent down showers of ice.

It was a good hike. Kovac felt his heart speed up. He felt a subtle burn in his calves and then in his thighs. He watched his breath plume white, more and more of it as the incline increased. Everything smelled like pine, reinvigorating him.

After about five minutes, Kovac noticed Bishop was following small metal plates tacked into the coarse bark of the cedars. He was curious about it, but he decided not to ask questions. Not yet. Instead, he kept alert for danger and followed Bishop's deep footprints.

There were birds. There were trees. There was snow. Then

more of all three. There were no threats Kovac could make out, and halfway into this sustained climb his mind started to drift. It ended up on Bennett. He couldn't help it. He could hear her half-drunkenly telling him about the kind of men she came up against in Resolute. He remembered not seeking clarification about what she wanted to do to these men. He had written her off as a drunk, as depressing company. And later, as mentally unhinged.

In other words, he had sold her short. At every turn, he had judged her not on the courage she displayed, but on her upbringing and social media profile. He had chosen to see the worst in her, to suspect her. And because of that he had found it all too easy to shoot her. It was a failure, he now saw, that didn't just reside in Bennett's plan and his trigger happiness. It ran back to his first impressions and paranoia.

They reached a peak, and Kovac found himself staring down over a large, icy lake. It was huge, filling a vast valley created by a circle of similar peaks.

'Postcard views,' Kovac said. 'This all leading us to something, though?'

'Nothing pleasant.'

They started down, and the journey only added to the agony of Kovac's blisters. His feet slammed forward into hard leather with every step. He focused on the pain. Better that than Bennett.

They were still following the metal plates in the tree trunks, and it only took ten minutes to get to the lake. They cleared the treeline, and Kovac – happy to stop walking – found himself standing at the edge of the water. There was a long jetty, frosted with snow. It had car tires attached to each side and its wood planks looked slippery. To the left, there was a small aluminum boat with a light blue interior and outboard motor. To the right, out towards the end of the jetty, some kind of office.

This office was on pylons, Kovac noticed. It was the modern, pre-fab type: the sort which acted as offices and break rooms at construction sites. It had windows that were dark.

Beyond the jetty, at the center of the inky lake, Kovac noticed an island that looked to be deserted. It was just snow and pines. 'We're going out there?'

'No.' Bishop led him along the jetty to the small office. He put on gloves, produced a key and unlocked the door. He entered, holding the door for Kovac.

Kovac stepped inside, one hand on his pistol.

The interior was dark, until Bishop threw open a few sets of heavy drapes. After that, Kovac could see plenty. There was just the one room, with two long cut-outs in the floor. There was matting for people to kneel or sit either side of these cut-outs, and a lot of fishing gear. The place wasn't an office, Kovac realized, but somewhere to fish. A room protected from the brutal elements outside.

He could see the water through the two open cut-outs in the floor and hear it lapping at the pylons underneath.

That, and the sound of a man struggling against restraints.

The man was at the far end of the large room. He was naked and tied to a chair, his body covered in tattoos. He had a black hood over his head. 'Your handiwork?' Kovac asked, being careful not to touch anything.

Bishop nodded. He walked to the man and removed the hood. The man had adhesive tape over his mouth. His eyes were bleary, and he was groggy, as if he had been dropping in and out of sleep for hours.

'Who is he?'

'Local yakuza.'

'And this place, why here?'

'Found it online. It's available for groups to rent. The owner's down in Kyoto. He had questions, but once all the paperwork checked out he was happy to let us have it for a week. He warned me it was a bit remote this time of year. I told him that suited me just fine.' Bishop undid his rucksack and took out an aerosol can. He screwed a blowtorch on top. Kovac had seen these attachments in stores throughout Japan. They were used for cooking food here, tasty things like eel and crème brulee. Kovac doubted the smells would be anywhere near as enticing today.

Bishop fired it up. The gangster squirmed in his chair and tried to scream, but Bishop didn't hesitate. He turned the flame up and started tracing one of the tattoos on the gangster's thigh. The man's flesh sizzled and popped and he made a lot of noise, even despite the adhesive tape. He went on making a lot of noise after Bishop cut the flame, too.

Bishop returned to the rucksack. He took out the burner phone Kovac had activated. He typed into it, then showed it to the gangster. The man nodded frantically.

Bishop cut one of his hands free and placed the phone under it.

'No luck last time?' Kovac said, circling the man and noticing he'd already had one tattoo removed from his upper back. The skin was red raw and oozing.

'He didn't speak much English,' Bishop said. 'Actually, I eventually decided he didn't speak any English. That's what the phone's for. Translation. I only had my own last time, and I didn't want to risk it.'

Kovac didn't like torture. In fact, he loathed it. He could count on one hand the number of times he had resorted to it. But he knew sometimes it was necessary. Times like now, for example, when there was an eleven-year-old girl slipping into a criminal network of rapists and murderers.

Even so, that fact didn't make the stench of burnt human

flesh any more tolerable.

He watched the man try and type into the phone with one trembling hand.

'What are you asking him?'

'Peng's location.'

'Not Lottie's?'

'We'll get to that. But my guess is, this guy has no idea about Lottie. To find Lottie, we need Peng.'

'Why this guy?'

'He's been photographed with Peng in the past. He's close to Masuda, or was. There's even talk of him doing well out of Masuda's death.'

Kovac noted the priorities. Peng over Lottie. 'I'm going to be out on the jetty.'

'Suit yourself.' Bishop picked up the blowtorch again.

'And Bishop...'

'Yeah?'

Kovac wanted to suggest Bishop stop at a light searing, but he reminded himself of the stakes. 'Nothing. Take your time.'

It lasted another forty minutes. Kovac stood on the jetty, occasionally wincing at the muffled screams coming from inside. He watched for new arrivals in the trees, but there was nothing out of place. The water remained still and the sky was clear of drones, too.

Eventually he heard the single, silenced gunshot that told him it was over.

Bishop let himself out of the fishing office, locking the door behind him. He threw the key in the lake and took off his gloves. He pocketed them.

'Doubt you'll get the bond money back,' Kovac said.

Bishop of course didn't smile. He flashed the burner phone. 'An address. Turns out Peng spends most of each year up round these parts. He owns more than the apartment building. He owns most of this town, this whole area.'

They started back along the jetty. 'The address is what, his place?'

'One of them, yeah.'

'How do we know he's home?'

'We don't.' Bishop nodded back towards the office. 'But if the guy in there's to be believed, Peng will be. He's expecting company.'

'When?

'Tonight.'

CHAPTER 62

Sukhomlinov switched on his headlamp. He made his way across the parking lot, past a small, abandoned white van, and on into Aokigahara Jukai Forest. He had been tracking the Taiwanese captain. He understood the man's plan and almost admired it. The captain had been greedy. He'd tried to load up the mules, but he'd messed up. And now he was looking to hide three dead girls deep inside a national tragedy.

It was a good spot to dump bodies. The eleven-square-mile tract of woodland was on the northwest flank of Mount Fuji. Its name loosely translated to "Sea of Trees", but no one called it that. Most called it Suicide Forest, on account of all the corpses, clothing and macabre memorabilia strewn across its roots and slippery rocks. People walked out here, sat down and killed themselves, and animals got to the resultant corpses before police did.

Even if bodies were found, wounds were considered self-inflicted.

He checked his watch. Almost 9:00 p.m..

Sukhomlinov left the main path and hiked through the snow and sparse undergrown until he was sure no one back at the parking lot would be able to see the glow of his phone. He stopped, switched it on and checked the tracking device he had insisted Peng put on Lottie. She was half a mile ahead.

Moving. *Hopefully walking*, he thought.

He composed an update on his phone for Peng. He wrote it

all in Chinese, with two cold thumbs. He explained Lottie was no longer on the Taiwanese fishing trawler. She was in the Taiwanese Captain's care, and he was acting erratically. As if maybe something had gone wrong. As if maybe he was scared. Sukhomlinov told Peng about the girl he'd found in a shed at the edge of a rice paddy, gutted like a pig.

He left it at that. Peng wasn't stupid. He would know the signs of a greedy fishing captain when he saw them.

A twig cracked underfoot as Sukhomlinov shifted his weight, the sound muted by snow. He read back over the message. It was clear and logical, factual. He sent it.

He resumed trudging. It took him a little under twenty minutes to close in on Lottie's tracking device, and along the way he saw the forest's name wasn't without justification. He found an umbrella, then shoes, then a pile of clothes in a small hollow below a tree. Moving closer, he realized the clothing contained a human. A human that was curled up on a thick bed of dead leaves – and still breathing. This was no old person coming out into the forest to say goodbye to the world. The hair was young, black and matted with blood. A girl, her pasty chest shirtless. She had shoes on and a jacket laid out like a cushion at her final resting place. She had been left here half-dressed, to freeze to death.

Scattered around this girl were the Captain's "clues": a few scattered prescription pills, and a bottle of liquor.

They were staging a murder-suicide.

Sukhomlinov was getting close.

He switched his red-light headlamp off and crept forward.

It took him less than five minutes to find three men, all with flashlights. These men were in the middle of nowhere, in an eleven-square-mile forest in the dark. They weren't expecting an interruption, particularly not from an armed assassin maintaining light and sound discipline.

He was able to calmly approach with his pistol raised. The men were standing around a corpse, arranging it so that it appeared to have taken a seat at the base of a large tree. It was a full-grown man. *One of the migrant workers from the boat*, Sukhomlinov thought. They were arguing over which pose looked more natural for a suicide. They had more pills to scatter.

Two of the men looked Indonesian. One Taiwanese.

Sukhomlinov switched on his headlamp and said in Chinese: 'Whoever runs, dies.' One of them flinched. The other two stumbled backward.

So now he knew who spoke Chinese and who didn't.

One of the Indonesians who had stumbled backward now spun and started running. He managed a sort of small zig, before zagging and picking up speed. Sukhomlinov shot him twice in the back.

The other Indonesian was a classic illustration of fight and flight. He ran backward a few steps, then changed his mind and charged forward. It wasn't clear what his plan was. Maybe he was planning to tackle Sukhomlinov to the ground. Sukhomlinov shot him twice in the chest.

That left the Taiwanese captain, the only one of the three who had understood Sukhomlinov's threat.

The Taiwanese captain started making excuses. No one had instructed him not to fill the girls. He had done it because he believed it was his job. 'That's what I assumed,' Sukhomlinov said. 'Don't worry, no one's upset with you. They're just stupid whores.' He made his way to the girl. He stared down at her and mumbled a profanity. 'The balloons out of her?'

'No. She won't –'

'You sedated her?'

'Yeah. But she'll come good if you want to keep –'

Sukhomlinov shot him in the head. Then he stared up through the trees to the stars. He was cold and he was tired. There was snow on the ground, snow in the trees, and darkness in every direction. Even though he wasn't a superstitious man, this suicide forest was starting to give him the creeps.

Sukhomlinov, still stiff and sore from his flight into Japan, experimented with different ways to lift the girl. She was barely conscious. She groaned with pain but there was no screaming.

He positioned her over one shoulder, shot the other girl, then began the long hike back down to the parking lot. As he walked, he thought about Kovac, about the sinking, gnawing disappointment he had experienced milliseconds after squeezing the trigger: the certain knowledge he had missed.

The attempt at the lighthouse had been worse. He hadn't even managed a shot. Peng had ordered him to stand down when the man in the Zodiac went rogue. There had been a photo, proof of death supposedly. Sukhomlinov had been crushed. He'd missed his chance. It would be the end of his career.

But the photo was fake.

It wasn't over yet, he thought. Peng had made the wrong call, and now Sukhomlinov had the girl.

The girl, and his green light to kill John Kovac.

CHAPTER 63

As soon as Kovac and Bishop got back to the old house on the edge of town, Kovac went for the tactical assault pack. He undid it and laid everything out. Then he put on the vest and filled the front pouch with three M4 magazines, locking each in with rubber retention bands.

Anna arrived in the room and sat watching him as he unzipped a drop pouch on the left of the vest and put two more magazines in here, too.

'What is all this?' she asked. 'What are you doing?'

He decided to take the question literally. 'Weapons retention setup for this M4.'

He checked the gun's flash suppressor, then clipped it into the retention setup before creating another retention setup on the right side of the vest – this one for an M320 grenade launcher.

'And that,' Anna asked. 'What's that?'

'For grenades.' He glanced at her. 'Was there any movement down at Peng's apartment while we were gone? Anyone coming or going?'

'No.'

Kovac liked to carry the M320 like a breaching shotgun, back behind his elbow. He tried it, taking a few steps, and decided he was happy with it.

'Am I coming with you this time?'

'No,' he said. 'You're staying here.'

'Again?'

'Again. Same job. Watch the apartment for us. You see anything down there, you call it in.'

He kept the front of the vest flat and slick. If he was facing a firefight, which he suspected he would be at some point tonight, he wanted to be able to get flat to the ground. But he made use of the pouches on each side to add a KA-BAR knife, a Gerber multi-tool, a tourniquet, and a red lens flashlight.

He securely packed .40mm grenades for the M320, then gingerly peeled off his boots. His blisters were raw and bleeding through his socks. 'Painful?' Anna asked, wincing in sympathy.

'Better than frostbite.'

Kovac made a mental note: good hiking boots in the rucksacks and tactical packs in future. And as soon as he had this thought, he had another. *There wouldn't be any more rucksacks or packs.* This was his last mission. For Curzon, for anyone else. After this, he was out.

He didn't know how he felt about that. In one way, it was liberating. In another, terrifying.

To distract himself, he checked the helmet, which was fitted with full panoramic night vision. He unpacked and added fresh batteries. Everything was up to his standards, which wasn't all that surprising given he was the one who had prepared it.

In the pack itself, he put MREs, water, and extra ammo. Then he changed into the tactical pants and pulled on tactical gloves. Anna laughed. 'Sorry, was I meant to look away?'

'They're just underpants, Anna. Everyone has them.'

Reluctantly, he treated his blisters then put the cursed boots back on over fresh socks. The last item he stowed was his pistol.

With all this done, he took the vest off. He didn't need it yet. He carried it downstairs in one hand, the tactical pack in the other.

Bishop was waiting for him. 'Jesus,' he said, 'you look like you're in Afghanistan.'

'I figure at this point, fuck subtlety.'

Bishop had set up three new burner phones and deactivated the one from up at the lake, destroying it. He gave one to Kovac and one to Anna. He explained he'd programmed the numbers into each and showed Anna how to use a VPN.

'This house is full of guns now,' he said to Anna. 'Use the burner phone with the VPN. It's got data. Get online and figure out how to use what's here. And if you're in trouble, use it.'

'The phone?'

'The equipment.'

'That's it? That's the best you can offer me? You're ditching me again and I have to figure out how to defend myself *online*?'

'We're on the clock,' Bishop said. 'I'm sorry, you're safest staying here.'

'It's not just that,' Kovac said. 'I'm serious about watching that apartment. You see anything – especially a young girl with red hair – you phone it in. Phones all set to vibrate?'

Bishop nodded.

Anna stared at the phone in her hand. She wasn't happy.

'Focus, Anna. Getting upset won't change anyone's mind here.'

'I know.'

They said goodbye to her and headed out to Bishop's car.

Kovac threw his vest in the back seat and used a navigation

app on the burner. They drove to the other side of town and soon ended up in dark streets lined with neon. Every turn seemed to reveal yet more cabs, all parked with indicators flashing. *Waiting for Johns*, Kovac thought.

Bishop said: 'Definitely feels like a red-light district.'

They located the address they'd been given while up at the lake. It was a small, traditional building with a shingle roof. Little blue curtains had been hung above anachronistic, automated electric doors. The entrance was framed by trees that reminded Kovac of bonsai, and there were a few garden statues in grey stone either side of a rock path. Kovac drove a little past it and eased Bishop's Audi towards the curb. He parked across the street.

It wasn't what Kovac had been expecting. 'This a hotel?' he asked.

'A *ryokan*,' Bishop said.

'A what?'

'Like a guesthouse. You know, all traditional and...' He shrugged. '*Japanesey*.'

'Feels wrong.' Kovac shut off the engine, grateful for the dark tint on the Audi's windows.

He searched the street for any sign of trouble. There were a few young women around despite the late hour, presumably arriving for or walking home from shifts. But beyond that, not much. Just the waiting taxis.

Bishop, also on the lookout, started tapping his pistol in the palm of one hand. It was another 1911. But it was a different beast to the two Kovac had been using while in Japan. Kovac noted the small details that set it apart. Low-light BoMar sights, a flared magazine well for faster magazine changes, and ambidextrous everything. It also had a suppressor on a flush mount with a standard G.I. guide rod.

Bishop broke the silence. 'So what's the plan exactly?'

'We sure we're in the right location?'

Bishop double checked on the burner phone. 'Yep. This is what we were given. Room 22. Under the name Shiga.'

Kovac saw a young, impossibly slim woman pause outside the little guesthouse. She checked her phone then started up the rock path leading to the automatic doors. She was tall for a Japanese girl. Pushing six foot.

He watched her enter, then got out of the car. 'It's looking like our theory on Peng's correct. He's here to unwind and get some action.'

'Looking like it.' Bishop followed Kovac out.

Kovac grabbed his tactical vest from the back seat and put it on. He locked the doors with his key fob.

There were two plans. One for heavy security, which would've seen Kovac and Bishop stay in the car and stake this address out. And another for minimal security. They were going with the latter plan. Kovac knew there was a chance this was Sukhomlinov, knew there was a chance they were walking into a trap, but he had to risk that. A little girl's life depended on it.

CHAPTER 64

Kovac checked for traffic then crossed the street. Bishop covered him as he entered the guesthouse, and as he pointed his M4 directly at the face of the middle-aged woman working the reception. She startled at the sight of soldiers in her lobby, then scowled. 'Shiga,' he said. 'Give me the keys. Room 22. Slow movements.'

She passed him a fancy looking door card. It was plain white, no markings on either side.

'22,' the woman said.

She half-raised her hands, like some kind of reflex or afterthought.

'Phone,' Kovac said.

She offered him the landline phone on the reception desk, which he pulled out of the wall. He pulled the cord out of the handset, so that it was all exposed wiring. 'Your cell phone,' he said. 'Mobile. Whatever you call it here.'

She was confused.

Because he had Bishop covering him, Kovac risked going around behind the reception. He frisked the woman and found a cell phone. He smashed it on the corner of the reception desk. 'No help,' he said, pointing the M4 at her head this time. 'You stay here, you do nothing. Understand? Quiet. Silence. No help.'

She nodded, but from the way she had pronounced 22 and the confusion about the cell phone he doubted she had understood much. He hoped he'd made his point with the two devices, but he moved quickly, not sure how long he could depend on this woman's corporation.

The guesthouse had a simple layout: a corridor with a staircase at the far end. The rooms all came off to the left. They ran sequentially from 1-1 forward. The right-hand side of the corridor had no rooms because it was a solid wall.

Kovac advanced, Bishop covered.

Kovac figured the rooms upstairs followed the same layout, but starting with a 2- instead of 1-. He climbed the stairs. Bishop followed.

He was right.

He found himself at 2-12.

He walked fast, rolling his feet, heel to toe, keeping perfectly quiet. He walked past 2-16, 2-15, 2-14.

Bishop swapped to his pistol. Kovac stuck with the M4. With his body armor, the M4 and the M320, he was operating under a lot more weight than he was used to. But he found it oddly comforting, more like his SEAL days than anything he had done since.

He stopped outside 2-2.

Room 22. *Had to be.*

When they were both in position, Kovac slipped the card into the door lock. There was the tiniest click, emanating from somewhere deep inside the rectangular mechanism. He depressed the handle and resisted the urge to pause. That would violate two of the three core principles Bishop had drilled into him as a teenager – speed and surprise.

Kovac tended to move slowly when working alone, but now that he was one half of a pair he could take greater advantage of the element of surprise.

The remaining principle was violence of action, which

Kovac now looked to implement. Entering the room, he didn't need to pull down his night vision. A light was on.

Another simple layout. There was a hallway, with a large room at the end. Before that, about halfway along the hallway, there was bathroom. Its door came off to the right. Kovac could see and automatically clear everything except the bathroom and the front, righthand corner of the large room.

A silhouette rose in the open space in this room, more or less directly in Kovac's sights.

His immediate assumption was Sukhomlinov, but there was no gun, only a cigarette.

Kovac didn't shoot, though every fiber in his body screamed for it. Entering a room like this was always a question of blind courage. Or as Bishop had phrased it back on the farm, "seventy percent testicles". And that adrenaline rush could be a bitch. It led to trigger happiness. Because, truth be told, there was a final element – harder even than speed, surprise and violence. It was the element Kovac had neglected on the fishing boat, the element which had given him hell in his earliest days at the farm. Target discrimination.

The memory of that training served him well now. The silhouette was a young Asian woman in some kind of white, hotel dressing gown. Possibly even the woman he had seen enter earlier. She had been sitting on the tatami floor, smoking, an ashtray off to her left.

Kovac cleared the bathroom while Bishop covered him. Then they cleared the right corner of the large room. Kovac found a mattress laid out on tatami here, with a man lying motionless under heavy bedding.

It was Peng. There were prosthetics propped against the wall. He had his eyes shut, as if asleep. Bishop gestured for the woman to sit back down, which she did. He put a finger to his lips, warning her to stay perfectly quiet. Then he gestured for the woman to go on smoking.

If possible, they didn't want to disturb Peng.

It worked.

He remained sleeping.

Kovac risked another look at the woman. *An escort,* he guessed. An innocent.

Peng went on snoring.

CHAPTER 65

Kovac indicated for Bishop to keep an eye on the door, though no one had come to Peng's rescue. It was still just Kovac, Bishop, Peng and the escort.

Kovac took heart from this. He had expected at least one bodyguard. His best-case scenario here was a bodyguard without a key card; a bodyguard testing Peng's door and finding himself locked out. But not even that happened.

The room stank of cigarette smoke. So much so, Kovac's eyes began to smart. The escort didn't move. She didn't scream, either. She smoked in silence, watching them. The only sounds were Peng's snoring and the purring of a humidifier.

The escort had a phone near one knee, but it was off. No weapon – at least not that Kovac could see.

He took out the sux he had grabbed from Bishop earlier in the day. The little syringes were disposable, like the one Anna had jabbed him with.

He contemplated putting the first syringe into the escort. But she was compliant right now. That would end the second Kovac tried to inject an unidentified drug into her system. Compounding this, the drug would take at least a minute to have a noticeable effect. Sure, when it did kick in, the woman would have trouble moving her eyes, let alone smoking. Within a minute, she'd be floppy, nearly every muscle in her body at least partially paralyzed. But a minute was a minute. She'd be able to make a lot of noise in a minute.

He decided to leave well enough alone.

Given Bishop had his six, Kovac refocused on Peng, pondering dose.

Sux was more commonly found in hospitals. It was part of a rapid sequence protocol for patients needing intubation. There, sux helped get a breathing tube down a patient's throat.

Here, it would do a different job. For one thing, there would be no sedation first. Peng would wake to the jab of the needle and he would be conscious as the paralysis set in. Kovac remembered it all too well from the fishing boat. Sux without sedatives created a uniquely horrific sense of terror. Peng would feel everything, but quickly realize he was losing control of his body and even of his breathing. He would be trapped inside himself, reduced to a brain.

It was, by any measure, a horrible way to die. And with careful dosing, that horror could be drawn out.

Kovac swapped to his pistol, pointing it directly at Peng's temple as he slowly peeled back bedding. Peng was sleeping naked, his flaccid penis covered with a used condom. Presumably, he had drifted off after sex with the woman in the corner of the room.

Based on Peng's gut, Kovac guessed a weight of 200 pounds for a height of perhaps five eight – but that was five eight with the prosthetics on. He pulled the bedding the last of the way back. Given the absence of arms and legs, Kovac figured he was looking at something closer to 130 or max 140 pounds.

One injection to incapacitate. Two to kill.

Sux was rapidly metabolized by the body. While that made it difficult to detect in a tox scan, it also made the drug hard to dose. It was quick to fade, yet easy to over-administer. Kovac decided to play it safe. He injected Peng on the side of one buttock. Just the one syringe for now.

Peng woke up and immediately detected the pistol. He didn't

look particularly sleepy – at least, not after his eyes went cross-eyed to take in the muzzle. He looked down to just below his hip, as if for a mosquito bite. He said something in Chinese.

Kovac said nothing. He waited for the first symptoms of paralysis to set in, then whispered: 'Where is she, Peng? Where's Lottie?'

Peng spoke in Chinese again, with more difficulty this time.

'I know you speak English. Try and blink. Try and lift your stump arms for me. Not so easy anymore, is it?'

Peng tried to spit, but it ended up on his face, running down one side of a flabby jaw.

'Right now, you can still swallow, you can still talk. But I can take that away. I can finish you. Tell me where she is, and I leave. You have my word on that.'

The escort in the corner still hadn't moved. If she understood everything Kovac was doing and saying, she was controlling her emotions well.

Bishop remained on alert, clearly expecting someone to kick in a door or window. 'It's too easy,' he grumbled. 'We should get out of here. Bring him with us?'

Kovac shook his head. 'There isn't time for that. We risk it here.'

CHAPTER 66

Kovac waited. Soon, Peng's blinking stopped. That told Kovac everything he needed to know about the drug's progression. 'You can't say anything right now.' He put his hand over Peng's mouth. 'You can barely breathe.' He pegged Peng's nose between thumb and forefinger and lowered his palm gently over Peng's mouth. He left it in place for 25 seconds then raised it. 'When this starts to wear off, you're going to start blinking again. Shortly after that you're going to be able to talk again. And I'm going to ask you where Lottie is.' He lowered his palm once more, leaving it in place for thirty seconds this time. 'I know what's going on in there, Peng. You look calm, but inside you're terrified. Inside, you're screaming, aren't you? You think I give a shit about you? Give me what I want, and I walk. You get to live.'

Kovac flipped his hand over and held the back of it to Peng's mouth. The breath was so faint now as to be almost non-existent. 'You're dying Peng, but you just might make it through this first one. A second and you'll die. Exactly like this, frozen, trapped in there, screaming without a sound.'

The escort suddenly raised her hands and moved to stand. Bishop pointed the Colt at her and she sat straight back down, wide-eyed.

Kovac waited. It felt like an eternity but slowly Peng started blinking again. His breathing became stronger and eventually he tried to sit up. Kovac effortlessly pushed him flat again, another needle at the ready. 'Last chance, you ready to tell me where Lottie is? You won't survive a second one of these, remember.'

Peng struggled to speak.

'Fuck you,' he said in broken English.

The accent wasn't fluent with a hint of Swedish. It was rough, clumsy Chinese English. Peasant English.

Kovac gave Bishop a look. Bishop nodded. They had discussed this possibility on the walk down from the lake. The security was lax because this wasn't Peng. It was Peng's double, a detail Bishop had highlighted in the AFP report.

'You're wasting your time,' said the escort. 'He's an idiot, barely educated, chosen purely because he looks like Peng. They gave him a choice. Lose the arms and legs and live with every luxury available, or die. He chose to give up the limbs.'

The escort's accent was almost American.

'And you're what?' Kovac asked. 'One of the luxuries?'

'Correct.'

'You American?' Bishop asked.

'Singaporean.' The woman leaned forward, her face full of hate. She was clearly mixed race, and seemed to be wearing blue contacts to accentuate this fact. 'Do it,' she said. 'Let me leave, then kill him.'

'And the real Peng?' Bishop asked, ignoring her request.

The escort shook her head. 'We fuck the double, never Peng.'

'You ever serviced this double while he was working for the real Peng?'

She picked up her phone. Bishop pointed his 1911 at her again but she didn't so much as glance at him. She started tapping the screen, typing.

'Put it down,' Kovac said. 'And tell us where Peng is. Otherwise you die here tonight, too.'

The woman tilted the phone so Kovac could see the screen. 'Where Peng lives,' she said. 'The real one.'

Kovac took the phone from her. The search result was for "Shiromori Onsen". It was a hot springs by the look of it, a tourist destination, complete with reviews.

'It's on Tripadvisor,' Kovac said skeptically.

'It's a front,' the escort said. 'In this town, everything's a front. It's all Peng. There's a place on the edge, here.' She pointed. 'Big and traditional. It's separated from the rest by this river, see.' She pointed on the phone again, tracing the line of the river now. 'That's where he stays wherever he's up there, and lately he's always up there. I go up there with this fat gingerbread fuck.' She nodded towards Peng's double.

'And tonight?' Kovac asked. 'Is Peng there right now? Shiro-whatever-you-called-it?'

The escort looked from Kovac to Bishop and back to Kovac. She shrugged. 'Am I free to go? I won't talk. I've been saving up to disappear. I won't even be in Japan by this time tomorrow.' She paused. 'I know you have no reason to believe me, but I'm not going to help these assholes. And I'm not going to jeopardize my escape. I didn't sign up for this job and I just want to go home.'

Kovac knew what Bishop's answer to the girl's question would be. She could talk and compromise any attack on Peng's place up in the mountains. She was a liability, the same way the desk clerk was a liability. Nothing she could say or do would prove she wasn't.

Kovac didn't trust a word that was coming out of this woman's mouth, but he was tired of Bishop's way of thinking, of his morally bankrupt code. 'You're free,' he said. 'But first you tell us everything you know, starting with these hot springs higher up in the mountains.'

'Deal.'

CHAPTER 67

As he listened to the woman talk, Kovac thought back to what Bishop had told him about Sukhomlinov. Russian father, Chinese mother, British education and accent. And, as Kovac knew from the past few days, a fondness for elaborate traps.

Sukhomlinov always went for the ambush. First it had been Tokyo, then the lighthouse. Now Kovac suspected Sukhomlinov was creating a new trap. Kovac had been open to the idea that Peng's double was a lure tonight. He had been on the alert coming here, aware Sukhomlinov might once again chase a sensational kill to cement his reputation and drive up future fees. Kovac had half hoped that ambition combined with inexperience and a lack of strategic creativity would render Sukhomlinov predictable. It hadn't.

If this was a trap, it was an elaborate one. Sukhomlinov was biding his time.

It was also possible Kovac was ahead in this game for the first time since it began.

Bishop went on pointing his gun at the escort, who said: 'That's all of it, that's everything I know. Can I go?'

Kovac heard a distant motor.

'Reinforcements,' Bishop said.

Kovac was inclined to agree.

The desk clerk, he wondered?

'Who's coming?' he asked the escort.

She shook her head. 'I don't know.'

It wasn't a car engine. Kovac homed in on the sound and decided it was a bike. More than one bike, in fact. Harley's or Choppers, maybe, something like that.

Not the local racing variety.

A moment later, Kovac heard both engines cut out. They'd stopped just outside the guest house.

He waited, then heard footsteps. Two men arrived at the door to the room. He could hear them whispering just outside.

Kovac signaled for Bishop to keep his pistol on the escort, then swapped back to his M4. But Bishop didn't see. He was already moving, slipping into the bathroom that came off the hallway.

Kovac kept his pistol trained on the escort and signaled for her to move into the corner with him and Peng – the room's only blind spot.

The men had a door card. The door clicked and opened. Kovac heard them cautiously enter. One step, two, three – there was a single silenced shot from the bathroom and a heavy thud. Then Bishop's voice. 'Drop it or you join your friend there on the floor.'

Another thud, this one lighter, more metallic.

Kovac waited, and a few seconds later Bishop led the man into the main room. He nodded for him to stand beside the escort and Peng. The man stared at Peng's double – specifically at his limp, spent penis.

The man was a biker. So was the one Bishop had shot in the head from the darkness of the bathroom as he passed by the open bathroom door. They were both in black leather jackets with patches. The survivor was morbidly obese. The one with a hole in his head was trim, with a white beard. He was lying face down in a pool of expanding blood. Kovac could still see blood pulsing from the head wound.

The men had been carrying shotguns and wearing knuckledusters.

The fat biker let out a small cough, which became a longer cough and, finally, a coughing fit. He thumped his chest, as if disappointed in himself. Then, sniffing sharply, he said: 'You going to kill me?'

Australian, Kovac noted.

This didn't exactly surprise him. Peng had influence all around the world, but that influence was strongest here in the Pacific. It was logical that any alliance with global biker gangs would see those gangs supply him with manpower from the closest chapters. In this case, Australia.

Kovac figured the men had dressed nice and covered their tattoos to get into the country, and had been enjoying running amok within it ever since.

Until tonight.

Kovac shook his head. 'No,' he said. 'You're coming with us, fat man.'

CHAPTER 68

The moonlight was gleaming off a large barrier as Kovac wound his way up onto an elevated expressway.

He set the cruise control and checked the car's occupants again. The fat biker was the greatest threat. He was crammed into the passenger seat, aware any sudden move risked a bullet in the back. Bishop was sitting directly behind him. He had a pistol pointed at the back of the biker's seat, ready to pull the trigger at the slightest provocation. The escort was beside Bishop, directly behind Kovac. She knew any sudden moves would be detrimental to her health, too.

It was a strange collection to have in a vehicle, and Kovac was glad he had left Peng's double back at the hotel room. A drug-paralyzed man with prosthetic arms and legs was a bridge too far.

Bishop took out his burner phone and put it to one ear without moving his pistol. 'Yeah?'

Kovac knew it could only be Anna. He couldn't hear her voice over the tires and road noise, because they were driving too fast. He focused on the biker instead, watching the man's hands in his peripheral vision.

Bishop hung up. He said: 'I'm needed back in town.'

Kovac pulled over to the side of the road and positioned his pistol to cover the biker. Bishop got out. He came round to the driver's side window and spoke in a near whisper. 'Our third amigo. Movement reported.'

'What kind?'

'The sort we were hoping for. I'll take the escort with me, make sure she doesn't tip anyone off.' He nodded for her to get out.

'You'll go on foot?'

'We're not far out of town. I figure your gear's better for recon up at the hot springs, and mine for town.'

'Agreed.'

'You think you can run reconnaissance without me?' His eyes flicked to the fat biker.

'Yeah.' Kovac turned to the biker. 'You're driving.' He got out of the car and slid into the seat the escort had just vacated. He aimed the pistol at the back of the driver's seat as the biker made his way around the car to the driver's side. The biker eyed Bishop warily, before flopping down into the driver's seat. His weight forced the suspension down and it stayed down.

'I'll get back to you as soon as I can.' Bishop gave Kovac a tap on the roof and Kovac gave him a single nod in reply.

'Drive,' he said to the biker.

The biker didn't try anything stupid. He followed the directions Kovac gave him to the letter, and twenty minutes later they were pulling over again. Kovac led him into the trees, now relying on his phone's GPS. He was expecting to lose signal but didn't. He paused a few hundred yards in from the road and studied the terrain between him and the hot springs. Then he studied a tourist map of the hot springs themselves. There were eight buildings in all. The one the escort had pointed out as Peng's was indeed separated from the others by a river. It sat at the back of the clearing, backing onto forest.

Kovac wouldn't be able to come in via the town. For one thing, he wasn't dressed for it. But equally, he wouldn't be able to get across the bridge that connected Peng's building to the other seven. He would have to come down out of the forest behind Peng's place and hope the route wasn't heavily defended.

He told the biker to resume marching forward. If it was heavily defended, at least he was bringing his own human shield. Bishop had shot the right biker. This one was six four at least, and wide enough to protect Kovac from just about anything.

The area was remote and thick with trees and snow. Now and then, branches snapped, requiring Kovac to pause and listen. Eventually he shut off the phone, confident of his orientation, and lowered the GPNVG-18 quad NODs. They were white phosphor, per his preference, and gave him a 97-degree horizontal field of view.

Worse ways for Curzon to spent thirty grand, he thought, still scanning his surroundings. The sky was clear and there was plenty of moonlight, giving Kovac crystal-clear definition. He scanned for any sign of drones but saw nothing. Heard nothing. The trees provided decent cover anyway, and they would provide good cover against snipers when the time came.

They kept inching forward. As he moved in on his target, Kovac watched his footing in the snow and monitored the sounds of the surrounding forest. At one point, he heard something in the trees and looked up to see eyes staring down at him. His heart rate spiked before he realized they were just large monkeys. 'Jesus,' he muttered under his breath.

He pushed on, relieved when he finally heard the static-like sound of a river running hard and fast.

He was getting close.

Ignoring the biker's hesitation, he spurred the big man on with threats. Eventually, the building fell into view. It was two levels, and old. It looked more like a traditional Japanese temple than a building anyone might live in. Kovac detected smoke from a wood fire and could see it coming from a sort of chimney in the building's roof. Lights on inside.

His heart rate picked up a little and he felt his grip on the M4 tighten. He slowed and let the biker get far enough ahead to act as fair warning.

And that, as it turned out, was an excellent decision. A moment later, the forest exploded.

CHAPTER 69

Kovac was on the ground before he fully comprehended the nature of the threat. His best guess was anti-personnel devices hidden waist-high in the trees. The biker had triggered them and they had detonated in succession. Kovac's quick reaction had saved his life, but the biker was a mess of body parts and already bleeding out into the snow.

Kovac scrambled for cover. He had just surrendered the element of surprise, and long experience told him what was coming next. He didn't have to wait to be proven right, either. There was a burst of automatic gunfire from what Kovac was now thinking of as the temple. The rounds weren't exactly wide of the mark. He could hear them slamming into trees all around him and ricocheting off rock. He kept down, crawling through snow on his belly, and swapped poor cover for a large, fallen tree trunk.

So much for recon, he thought.

So much for waiting on Bishop, too. Like it or not, he was in this fight now and would need to find a way through it. He momentarily considered a retreat to the car, but counterintuitive as it was, the car was the wrong choice. He would be hunted down before he reached it, and now that they knew he was out here they would locate the car from the air. He would be on his own, on the move, and they would have his destination.

He felt his phone buzz. He took it out, but had to put it aside and lay completely flat as another burst of automatic gunfire rang out down at the temple. The bullets were mercifully wide of the mark this time. 'Yeah,' he said, putting the phone on speaker then blocking the light.

'That a gunfight?' Bishop asked.

'Yeah. Tell me you changed your mind and you're less than a hundred yards away right now.'

'I wish I could. You able to get clear?'

'Hoping to. You find anything?'

'You could say that. I'm back at the house. I'm staring at Sukhomlinov right now. He's got an IR dot on him, not that he's aware. Take the shot?'

'What's he doing?'

'He just came out of the apartment. He's making a call.'

'No signal in his dungeon,' Kovac said. 'He's coming out to call Peng.'

'Yay or nay?'

Kovac lay motionless, the snow burning at one cheek, even as his breathing melted it just in front of his mouth. He heard dogs barking down at the temple and figured Peng's soldiers were beginning their own reconnaissance. He was out of time and needed to either piss or get off the pot. 'No sign of Lottie?'

'No sign of Lottie.'

'You sure it's Sukhomlinov?'

'Matches the photo you sent through in every regard. Anna says he's been out to make calls twice already, but we're not guaranteed another go at this.'

This was Kovac's mission, and even though Bishop was technically his superior he appreciated Bishop letting him make the call. 'If he starts back inside, take the shot. Otherwise, let it play. See if Lottie shows up.'

'Understood.'

Kovac ended the call and switched off the phone. He doubted anyone down at the temple would be able to detect the signal, but he wasn't going to risk it now that he had taken a call. He kept crawling forward on his belly, until he found a natural depression in the snow with a large rock. He propped himself behind the rock and put the fire selector to semi-auto on the M4. He risked a quick look. There were windows but they were small and ornate. At this range, without a sniper rifle, they made almost impossible targets.

He had to get closer.

He stood and moved in a crouch down towards the temple. He didn't shoot, didn't do anything that would reveal his position or draw attention. He had the flash suppressor, but he didn't want to test it in a pitch-black forest if he didn't have to.

There was another volley of fire from the temple, but it was way off the mark now.

He got as close as he dared, found another sizable rock, then unclipped his M320 grenade launcher. He put a .40-millimetre high explosive round into it and used the night sights to take aim. He fired, then took cover behind the rock as bullets once again chewed up the bark around him and ricocheted off rock.

He waited until it stopped, then moved. He pressed on down towards the target building, moving slow enough not to roll an ankle, but fast enough to quickly put distance between himself and the first flash and thunk of the M320.

He found cover, reloaded it and raised his night vision to check on his first shot. It had fallen short, coating a rear wall with shrapnel.

Kovac fired again. Hid again. Moved again. Fired again. These last two shots were better. They struck at the middle of the building, lighting it up from the inside and limiting the return fire he had to endure.

He kept moving, half-running in a hunch now, still closing

the distance between him and the temple.

At one hundred yards, he noticed a lot of smoke coming from the temple. There was flickering light inside now, too. He'd started a fire and was able to make out the empty window frames. Possibly, the shooters were simply taking cover behind the frames. Or possibly they were well back from the windows. They were probably prone on tables or some such, Kovac figured, and if so they'd be difficult to kill. On the flip side, the windows were small. They would have a narrow range of fire.

Kovac decided not to waste bullets on them – not yet anyway. The real threat was closer to home. Five soldiers entering the woods with two dogs. He lowered his night vision again and saw his attackers didn't have NODs. He began traversing and swapped to the M4.

CHAPTER 70

Sukhomlinov could hear dogs barking over the phone.

'They're here,' Peng said in Chinese.

'You're well defended there.' Sukhomlinov surveyed the empty street outside the apartment. He started pacing to calm himself, walking towards the entrance to the underground parking lot, then turning and walking back. He was nervous. The girl was almost certainly full of drugs. If a condom burst inside her, he would be powerless to save her. And powerless to protect himself against Peng's wrath. Now, it seemed Kovac and Bishop had located Peng's stronghold – another strike against Sukhomlinov since he wasn't there to help mount a defense. 'Want me to come up there and hunt for them?' he asked.

'No. I need someone I can trust with the girl. Get footage of her now. Send it to me. Make sure it's disturbing. Have you found them yet?'

Chinese was practically Sukhomlinov's native tongue, but he always had trouble understanding Peng. Everyone did. The man's voice was guttural, clogged with phlegm. And the confusion went deeper than that, too. It was the way the man's mind worked, always pursuing multiple tangential lines of thought.

Sukhomlinov knew his redheaded girl was connected to Kovac, but he didn't know how exactly, what she was for, or what use Peng had for a video of her. It didn't matter. He filed the video request in a mental category labeled "doable". He could film the girl and send the footage through right now. It was the question "Have you found them yet?" that had him confused.

'You said they're attacking you.'

'Someone's attacking me. That doesn't mean you stop searching down in town. How is it you can't locate them there? I own that town.'

'We think they're in the old houses up near the treeline. They're being smart about it, though.' Sukhomlinov looked up towards these houses now, scanning them. Most were dark and deserted. 'That's really the only place they could be without anyone noticing and alerting us. But whichever house it is, they're maintaining light discipline. Without putting a request in to the power company to –'

'I can't do that. Find them, and send me that video.'

Peng hung up.

Sukhomlinov lowered the phone and scanned the houses one last time. There was nothing up there. Lived in by old people stubbornly seeing out their years in the family home, he thought to himself, then left to rot. It would take him hours to search them, clearing them room by room, and he would likely end up dead before he succeeded. *Too many dark rooms, too many blind corners.* He wasn't going up to those houses – not tonight, not ever.

The video he could do, though.

He turned back to the apartment door, remembering he had locked it. Peng had given him his own key for this place. He didn't need the communal one the drug runners all used. He ranked higher than that. He took his key out again and moved to unlock the door.

CHAPTER 71

Bishop took the shot. And kept shooting. He had the rifle on semi-automatic, and he put nine rounds into Sukhomlinov's corpse before pausing and looking for movement. With the night vision and IR, Sukhomlinov made a difficult target. But not impossible. The first round into center mass, then eight more after Sukhomlinov went down.

Bishop put the rifle aside and tried Kovac, but there was no answer. He didn't like it. The gunfight had sounded intense up at the hot springs and Kovac was on his own. Bishop would need to be quick with this, and he was just praying Lottie was within reach.

'Who were you shooting at?' He heard footsteps galloping up the staircase behind him.

Anna.

'I told you to watch the escort.'

'She's tied up. Who were you shooting at? Tell me.'

'The bad guy, the one you saw.'

'Did you get him?'

'Of course I got him.' Bishop stood. 'I'm going to need your help with this. There might be a young girl down there. If there is, she's going to take one look at me and scream. You on the other hand… you look…'

'Motherly?'

He frowned at Anna's unexpected choice of word. 'Hardly.

But cuddlier than me, I guess. Which is going to have to do. C'mon.'

He led her outside into the cold and down to the apartment. She paused at Sukhomlinov's corpse. Bishop took her gently by one shoulder and moved her on. 'You don't need to look at that,' he said. 'There's a key hidden over there in the rocks. Lift the rocks one by one. You'll know when you see it.'

While Anna got the key, he checked Sukhomlinov for a pulse. There wasn't one. Blood ran from his mouth. A lot of it.

Bishop put his hand to the back of Sukhomlinov's nose but there wasn't any breath.

One less bastard, he thought.

Anna walked back with the key. She slotted it into the door.

'No,' he said, finding a key on Sukhomlinov, too. He saw her shoulders sag a little and he felt bad for the sharpness of his tone.

She didn't know what was going on up at the hot springs, or what they were walking into here.

'I should go first is all.'

He used Sukhomlinov's key. Gun up, he cleared the apartment one room at a time. It was all just as it had been last time he was here. It still had the strange smell of eucalyptus, reminding Bishop of a hospital.

He followed Kovac's instructions to get into the dungeon. Anna stood with her arms folded, looking uneasy. She watched without saying anything as he dragged a chair into place to keep the trapdoor open. 'I'll go down first, okay. Then you follow.' He was on his knees at the hatch. He looked down into it but there was no sign of Lottie. He called down. Lottie had never spent any time at the farm with Bishop. She had never even met him. 'I work for your father, Lottie. I heard about what happened at Pemberton. I heard you were out with

Daniel when the helicopters came. The man who was here, the man who was keeping you prisoner, he isn't going to hurt you anymore. But your parents and your step-sister need our help, so does Mollie. Ask me any detail you like about Pemberton, I'll be able to answer it. I'm a friend, Lottie.'

There was nothing.

Bishop dropped his head, hoping for an empty dungeon now. Devastating as that would be, it was infinitely preferable to finding a corpse.

Then a timid voice said: 'What kind of dog is Mollie?'

The voice was young and female, with an Australian accent. Lottie's voice.

'Kelpie,' Bishop said, feeling his face break into an uncharacteristic smile. 'Someone needs to train her, too, starting with licking fingers. And she's a menace with tennis balls.' He paused, unsure what to say next. 'You're never going to beat Megan by working on your serve. She's terrible at the net. That's why she's warning you off volleying. She's not a coach you can trust. She likes winning too much.'

Lottie appeared at the bottom of the shaft and craned her head back to stare up at him. Her hair was straggly and lifeless, and her face was pale with no color in the lips. 'They forced balloons into my mouth. They're inside me still. I can't...'

Bishop nodded, hiding his concern at this information. 'Okay, we can sort that out. Do you want me to come down and help you up, or can you climb up?'

'I can climb.'

'Okay, but take it gently. We're going to take everything gently, okay?'

She started up the ladder, moving nice and slow. 'Are they dangerous?' she asked as she reached the top.

Bishop tossed the chair aside. 'No,' he lied. 'Not really. But we still need to get them out.'

'How?'

'Hospital.'

'Will they cut them out.'

'No.'

Lottie saw Anna. 'Who's she?'

Anna smiled. 'Hi.'

'She's another girl these people tried to hurt.'

'Is the man still here?'

Bishop hesitated. He realized he should've moved the corpse before coming in. He wasn't used to having minors in the field with him. 'He's outside.'

'Under arrest?'

'Kind of. Like I said, he won't be hurting anyone.' Bishop offered his hand and she took it. He carefully pulled her the last of the way out. 'You did good,' he said. 'Just the hospital to go, and then we get you home.'

'Why do you have a gun?'

'Precaution is all.'

Bishop gave Anna a look and she led them back outside. 'You cold?' he asked Lottie as soon as they had locked the door and returned the key. Bishop kept Sukhomlinov's key. 'You want my jacket?'

'No.'

She was cold. He could see that. She was underdressed for this weather, though it was clear Sukhomlinov or someone else had given her extra layers. She looked like a small fisherman. But he didn't push it. He didn't want to force her into anything she wasn't ready to accept.

Bishop got out his phone and searched for the nearest

hospital. The town didn't have a hospital but it did have a health clinic with a 24-hour desk. It was less than ten minutes on foot. He deliberated and decided walking wasn't any more likely to rupture condoms than a vehicle, and calling a vehicle would only cost them time. It would also potentially expose them to additional danger. 'It's a short walk. Ten minutes. Fifteen at the most. You okay with walking it? We'll take it nice and slow. You tell me if you feel sick or sleepy.'

She forced a smile and then surprised him. She gave him a big hug. 'You're Bishop, right?'

He pulled back, surprised. 'How did you know that?'

'Megan told me about you.'

'She did?'

'She told me you taught her how to fight. She told me she'd ask – that maybe one day you'd teach me, too. I want to learn.'

He nodded as she broke off the hug. She thought for a moment, then rubbed at her goose-bumped arms and said: 'One of the girls died. She fell asleep and then she died. They took her into a little shed, and when the man came out he was covered in blood. The other girl they left in a forest. I don't remember that bit so well.'

Bishop turned her gently in the direction of the health clinic, giving up on any last hopes he held of getting to Kovac. This was too important to put on Anna's shoulders alone.

Lottie started walking, still thinking out loud. 'She also said you taught her tennis. That true?'

'Megan? Yeah. Like I said, you've got to get up to the net with Megan. She'll tell you it's all about the serve, but you've got to volley. I'll show you when we get back to Pemberton. There's going to be plenty of time to play, Lottie. Plenty of time.' But even as he said this, Bishop realized an uncomfortable truth. Pemberton was still under siege. The future of the property, the future of Lottie, the future of Curzon International itself –

it all now hinged on Kovac.

CHAPTER 72

Kovac had killed two of the men coming for him. The remainder – noting his accuracy, and sensing themselves ill-equipped for a gunfight in the dark – had called off their dogs. They had retreated through the snow, back to Peng's stronghold.

Since then, someone had cut the lights inside the temple.

All fine by Kovac. He loved playing in the dark, especially with a good moon hanging overhead and thirty thousand dollars' worth of panoramic night vision.

He finished traversing through the forest to the river. Looked up it, looked down it. It appeared shallow. Here and there, it had sections churned white by rocks. It swept down past the temple, and at one spot the river and the temple met. At this point, there was a stone wall. The wall supported the temple. It compensated for the fall in the land as the land dropped away down to the river, like a giant stone wedge. Because of this, the edge of the temple sat almost flush with the river's shoreline, albeit much higher.

Kovac knew this would be his best point of entry. It was a near-vertical foundation wall, difficult to observe without leaning out from the temple overhead. He felt confident few if any guards would be monitoring it. Best of all, the treeline continued to the wall. He could get to it unobserved.

He kept to the trees but followed the river now. When he hit the wall, he checked for cameras then waded into the icy water. It covered the sound of his tread as he moved over loose rocks, along the base of the wall.

He picked a good spot, then began a vertical climb. It was easy. The giant stones jutted out unevenly and he was spoilt for grips. Even with his hiking boots and his screaming blisters, he felt secure pushing up off every new toehold. His tactical gloves spared his fingertips all pain.

The wall was perhaps ten feet high. As soon as he was atop it, Kovac checked for cameras again. Still nothing.

He ran along the narrow stone pathway that the top of the wall provided. He did it in a crouch. The temple was on his right now, so close he could touch it. There were glass sliding doors, but all with heavy drapes drawn. He had an eave overhead, blocking his view above. But he knew there was another level, another line of windows.

No one leaning out, and no one shooting at him.

He made it to a corner, where he found himself staring out over a large pond. Or really, more of a lake. A faint breeze sent ripples across its surface. It was beautiful, ringed with stone gardens and spidery Japanese trees. Kovac saw that the building he had just climbed was in fact one of two identical buildings. An ornate, red bridge crossed the pond at its widest point, connecting building one with building two. From the air, he figured the complex looked like the letter "H", with the bridge as the center stroke. He had started a fire in one building, but was now looking at another that remained impervious to his attack.

It was all so much larger than he had dared believe. The fire wasn't going to spread across the pond. Which meant he hadn't necessarily forced Peng into evacuating, as hoped.

For all Kovac knew, the man was in a core not unlike the one at Pemberton.

Kovac had an excellent view across the pond to the matching building on the other side, and he watched a guard enter this building midway along. The man stopped to remove his shoes and take slippers from a locker at the entrance, before vanishing inside.

Not exactly panicking, Kovac noted.

He decided to go up one more level, and he checked for cameras again. There was no sign of them anywhere. There was apparently just no room for bulky CCTV units in a complex as old and zen as this one; it seemed aesthetics came first here.

He climbed at the corner where it was easier. Reaching the second level, he found a wood sliding door. He put one gloved hand to a bronze handle bearing some kind of traditional wire motif, and – M4 up and at the ready – slid the door back.

He entered.

No cameras in here, either. And no electrical light.

The room was on the same scale as the rest of the place. It was cavernous. It had pictures of the emperor and empress, and a welcoming flower arrangement. But beyond that it was largely empty. The floor was tatami, start to finish, and there were three long tables, all no more than a foot or so off the ground. The sixty or so chairs for these tables were wooden, with cushions but no legs. Clearly, anyone using them was expected to sit cross-legged.

Moonlight seemed to filter in from every conceivable angle. Most of it streamed through interior skylights that looked as fragile as balsa, with thousands of small white squares of nearly translucent paper.

Kovac crossed the room and reached the far end. He was trying to be silent, but the M320 was giving him grief. It had come loose since he used it, and was flopping around now. He made a mental note. He needed a custom-made holster. And he needed a longer buttstock, too. The existing one had been too short.

He caught himself.

After this, he didn't need anything.

After this, he was done. Gone.

He paused and listened carefully. He could hear voices now, men calling out in Japanese. He could smell smoke, too.

He moved out of the large room into a corridor with shiny hardwood flooring. The pond side of this corridor was made entirely of wood-framed glass, giving an uninterrupted view of the water. Kovac kept away from the windows. He kept to the inner wall, blending into the shadow of its wallpaper.

No one hassled him.

It felt as though they were watching the forest and maybe the hot springs, but not this pond. They were giving him a clear run from the center, but a clear run to what?

He paused.

That was the real challenge now. How to find Peng in this place?

CHAPTER 73

The hallway ran the inner length of the building, perhaps one hundred yards end to end. The side with the wallpaper, the side Kovac was on, had sliding doors coming off at regular intervals. These doors, Kovac figured, led to rooms with windows. Smaller windows. The small windows he had seen from the forest. If there were snipers lying prone on tables in there, watching the trees for any movement, Kovac had just effortlessly found a way in behind their positions.

He decided not to clear these rooms. They weren't the mission. He watched the far end of the hallway fill with smoke and tried to put himself in Peng's shoes – which meant prosthetics. The man was a quadruple amputee. Perhaps he would stick to the lower levels, avoiding stairs. But Kovac knew of men who had lost both legs in Afghanistan and Iraq, men who had gone on to master rock climbing. Peng would be able to walk, stairs or no.

As for the hands, Kovac didn't know for sure. Technology could compensate for a lot, and Peng would have access to the best of the best. Maybe they would be simple prosthetics, like the double back down in town. Or more likely something robotic.

Kovac was interrupted mid-thought. There was suddenly movement down below.

He watched as a gaggle of men led one, heavyset man across the bridge. Kovac couldn't make out the faces. They all had their backs to him. But the heavyset man at the center had a strange gait. Kovac couldn't be sure at this distance, but the man also looked to be wearing gloves.

Kovac stayed where he was, watching. He was trying to reconcile the anti-personnel mines in the forest with the lax security in this building. His best guess was a last-minute addition, a hurried bolstering of defenses out in the trees. He doubted Peng would allow the mines under normal circumstances. Tourists wandered. It was their job practically. And even if the grown ones followed the rules, their offspring normally felt an obligation to explore. Peng could hardly have tourists finding their children headless in the forest.

Had Peng had been on this side of the complex to see the fireworks as Kovac came down out of the trees?

If so, he hadn't counted on .40-millimetre grenades dropping out of the night sky.

Kovac felt his hopes lift a little. Peng had been in this building, but now it was on fire. He had been forced to risk a move to the building on the other side of his pond, and he had risked the bridge. No one in the group had night vision. They believed they were moving under cover of darkness. They believed the threat was outside, up in the forest maybe, or down in the touristy section of the hot springs. But not here. Not *between* the two buildings, watching their every movement in crisp shades of blue.

Kovac counted six men. They were all carrying guns and there was a pattern to the protection. Small and Asian at the core of the group, moving out to larger men at the circumference. The two men flanking Peng – if it was in fact Peng – were small with straight black hair. A couple of little Jackie Chans, both carrying pistols. The others were foreigners. One was a biker, thinner than the one Kovac had used as a meat shield, but otherwise identical. He had the same jacket with the same patch. Matching shotgun, too.

The remaining two looked like a pair of Eastern European

powerlifters now gone to seed.

Kovac figured Peng was keeping similar men close, and putting the foreigners at the outer ring. Perhaps his Association wasn't as harmonious as he made it out to be.

Kovac watched them clear the far side of the bridge. They followed an ornate stone path, up towards decking. They were going where the guy with the slippers had gone, suggesting he had been a scout, a test run.

Kovac had a decision to make. Launch an attack from here and surrender his position, or maintain stealth. If he attacked, he could expect to be attacked by anyone who remained in this building. If he didn't attack, he'd have to somehow get across to the other building, find a way in and take it room by room.

Kovac raised his M4, sweeping the building on the opposite side. He could see the full length of each hallway because, as with this side, both the upper and lower hallways were designed to provide a view of the pond. There was a staircase at each end, connecting the upper hallway with the lower. But no staircase in the middle.

Peng's group swapped shoes for slippers. Even the Eastern Europeans did it. Kovac heard the little wooden lockers closing.

Still not panicking, he thought.

They cleared the locker area, then entered the building's lower hallway. They started along it. Kovac watched the biker move ahead and pull back a sliding door. They were all going to step through, and after that Kovac wouldn't be able to see a thing.

Kovac would have to assume Bishop had failed and Lottie was here somewhere, which was a good reason to go easy on the grenades. To opt for stealth. But then he noticed that the Eastern Europeans had rifles like his own, and he instantly changed his mind. He loaded the M320 and lobbed one of his two remaining grenades across the pond into the lower hallway. *Thwomp*. He looked away and reloaded. He heard it explode, heard shrapnel, glass and wood, even as he raised the M320 and fired again from muscle memory.

Still he didn't look. He didn't want to ruin his night vision.

Kovac dropped the now useless M320 and swapped to his M4. He checked back the way he had come, but no one emerged behind him. Doors opened up ahead, though. Two men came out, guns down, like they were curious to see what all the commotion over the other side of the pond was about. Kovac shot them with short bursts, before retreating to the staircase at his end of the hallway.

He took the stairs carefully and entered the hallway below, but no one took a shot at him.

In an ideal world, Kovac would've finished what he started with the M320, using the M4. He would've made use of his perch to send bursts of fire across the pond. But the battlefield was never ideal, and this one was no exception. He had no one backing him up over here. He needed to move.

Kovac's breath was up now, and he felt his heart thudding hard. After the stillness of the hallway upstairs, things were happening fast. He let himself out via a strange, interconnected boathouse. For a moment, he considered slipping down into the icy, ink-blue water. He could cross the pond underwater. But he dismissed the idea as stupid. He wasn't about to sacrifice night vision.

He was going to have to go around the pond or – if he had the balls for it – across the bridge.

CHAPTER 74

Kovac opted for the bridge. It was exposed, sure, but it was even terrain. That meant he could run with his M4 up, his sights on the building Peng and his entourage had just entered.

He checked the building behind him one last time, then sprinted to the bridge. As soon as he was on it, he shifted his focus to dead ahead. It went exactly as planned. He got across the bridge without anyone firing so much as a single shot at him.

He did the math as he cleared the last of the icy wooden slats. He had counted ten hostiles so far, including Peng. He had killed two back in the forest and two in the first building, and now he needed to see what the grenades had accomplished. He pulled up the night vision and entered the second building. He focused on the hallway, satisfied with what he saw. The second grenade had fallen short, but the first had created the sort of carnage .40-millimeter grenades were famous for. The biker and at least one of the Eastern Europeans were no more. He saw body parts everywhere in the gloom, and the rounds had set off a fledgling fire.

Six down.

The bridge had been risky, but it had been the right call. Kovac had made it into the second building quickly. If this one had snipers, he had made it across before any of them got their brains into gear and thought to turn 180 degrees.

He could now clear the upper level, or go after Peng. But he couldn't do both.

He knew he wasn't going to get any backup here, and there was no telling what Peng was doing. But more than likely, he wasn't going to sit and wait for Kovac to whittle down his defenses. After the second round of .40-millimeter grenades, Peng would be doing what any sane human did in such circumstances. He'd be looking to get the hell out of dodge.

Which meant Kovac had to go after him now.

Gun up, night vision back in place, Kovac paused at what little remained of the balsa and paper sliding door – the one Peng had passed through before vanishing from sight. He cleared one corner of the room beyond it, before stepping cleanly around the shattered door frame and clearing the other.

No one.

They were definitely on the move.

By Kovac's calculation, the group was now Peng, the two Jackie Chans, and one Eastern European. This powerlifter was the only one with a rifle, and easily the greatest threat.

Kovac pressed on, keeping to the walls to conceal himself and moving at carefully calculated angles. The room he was in was a bedroom, with bedding folded in two neat squares near the center. There was another sliding door at the far end, which was open. A flat-screen TV near this door had been knocked over. Kovac looked for tripwires of any kind. Years of training meant his body complied with ease, his movements pre-programmed and automatic.

He noticed splotches of blood on the tatami and even on the edge of one set of bedding.

He had them on the run. But he wasn't naive. He knew nothing good lay beyond this room. He took another ten steps, then ten more. He entered another cavernous room, but where the original one had contained tables and chairs, this one had scattered, modern sculptures in some kind of Japanese wood. They were small towers, consisting entirely of wooden triangles, and they came up to Kovac's shoulders. He moved past them via one wall, double-checking each, ready for an attack that never came.

He was still following the trail of blood, and it eventually led him left, on through to another hallway.

Crouching, gun still up, he took a quick look around the corner. This was where Kovac would mount any last stand if he was on the run. The walls were narrow here, channeling him into a sort of architectural canyon.

He crouched, because if this was an ambush his enemies would be aiming at chest height. He was right. It was the powerlifter with the rifle, and the instant it took him to realize Kovac was lower than expected cost him his life. Kovac put a round into his silhouetted head.

Seven.

Kovac sucked in a deep lungful of courage and went again. No one opposed him this time, and he fired into the powerlifter once more before jumping him in one clean movement and sprinting in another crouch. He made it to the building's tall, ornate front door. It was wide open, but after his experience with the powerlifter there was no way he was exiting there.

He ran on, all the way to the end of the building. The windows were small here and ideal for his needs. He spotted one that would work. He moved towards it, keeping below the window line, then came up and risked a glance. He saw the man who resembled Peng getting into a car, one of the Jackie Chans helping him in and shutting the door. The other Jackie Chan was already in the driver's seat.

Eight nine ten, Kovac thought.

He switched to full auto, took aim at the car and emptied the magazine before crouching and moving to a new window. He pulled another magazine from the front of his vest and did it all again. The car was a luxury European model, but not bulletproof. He saw the glass and metal giving out and the Jackie Chan who had just shut Peng's door slumped on the ground like an athlete doing seated hamstring stretches. Blood ran from his mouth.

Peng's window was all but gone and so was the driver's windscreen. Kovac went on shooting, holes appearing in Peng's door like bright blue stars.

When he finished, the car was rolling with the engine idling, but no one was driving it. The horn was blaring.

It soon ran off the road, into a Japanese garden, where it picked up speed. Kovac saw it was heading for the river, which swept round the front of the building. He watched it enter the water and strike rocks in the shallows, finally coming to a stop. The horn was still blaring.

Kovac checked the door behind him as he reloaded, then returned his focus to the car.

No one got out.

CHAPTER 75

It had been national news in Australia, and had made most of the international papers, too. Kovac read about the siege at Pemberton, which had been abandoned after Peng's death. And he read about Lottie Curzon's hospital stay in Tokyo and safe return to her family in Australia. Social media had been awash with the usual mix of opinions about billionaires, but Kovac didn't waste time on opinions. He stuck to the facts. And the facts in this case were clear. Curzon International was safe, Lottie was safe, and Peng Biao was dead.

Now, The Association was splintering and turning on itself. Peng's death had left a power vacuum like no other, and the battles to fill it were playing out in countless Asian cities. Drive-by shootings in Shanghai, cafe killings in Melbourne, honey traps in Hong Kong. Even a bombing in Indonesia.

It all felt a world away from where Kovac now sat, because it was.

Cell phone in hand, he looked out over a turquoise sea.

So this was what retirement looked like. He had been here for a week now. He was a new man, with a new name, in a new country. He had spoken to no one since killing Peng. Not King, not Bishop, not Megan, not even Anna. He had kept his promise to himself and enacted his exit plan, and it had led him here.

He was a ghost, a memory.

Kovac watched a young girl of ten or eleven dive and come up with handfuls of sand. Over and over. He was sitting in the

Pelican Bar, a hut made from scrap wood on a sandbar. He was a mile off the Jamaican coast, in Parottee Bay. He had kayaked out here at dawn and had seen fishermen and tourists come and go by boat since. It was now going on lunchtime and he was in no rush to leave. In fact, he was more inclined to order another Red Stripe beer. Either that, or slip down into the water for another swim.

He watched a few locals playing dominos, and thought again about the look on Peng's face as he put his M4 to the dying man's head. Abject terror.

Kovac had pulled that last trigger only after clearing the top floor of the temple and risking a brisk walk out to the car in the rapids. Both the Jackie Chans had been dead. It had just been Kovac and Peng.

Kovac had been right about the hands. Peng had indeed owned NASA-worthy robotic hands. No gloves. He had reached out with one of these hands, and Kovac had heard tiny motors as it swiveled and turned palm up, a final appeal for mercy. None had been given.

Kovac punched Bishop's number into the burner phone in his hand, only to delete it again. He had done this perhaps a dozen times this morning. The curious thing was, he didn't know why. Did he want to find out who at Curzon betrayed him? If so, to what end? He wasn't going to do anything about it. Or did he simply miss his old friend? Was it as simple as wanting to tell Bishop about this bar?

He typed the number again.

Deleted it again.

He looked up at the thatched roof, filled with flags from all around the world. Mementos from passing tourists. He had been to all of these countries and could put a name to every flag. He could give the population in most cases, along with the key cities and industries. He knew the languages, the police procedures, the criminal gangs, the easiest place to get weapons and the best place to dispose of a body. But he had never visited any of them like this. His last two trips to Jamaica had ended with hits in Kingston, one to start a gang war, the other to end it. Now, here he was, torn between swimming and another beer.

Could he do it?

He'd managed seven days without breaking a sweat.

Could he do a month?

A year?

A lifetime?

A young tourist in a pretty, patterned dress caught his eye. She looked away, then looked back. She gave him a shy smile. She said something to her friend, who glanced over at him. The friend wasn't so different from Bennett in appearance. Tan face, hazel eyes, lipstick. Kovac put the phone away and stood. He pulled his T-shirt back on and crossed to the bar. He ordered three beers. One for him, and one for each of the girls.

It wasn't going to be easy, this new life. But his old life had consequences. It did damage, real damage, mostly of a kind that couldn't be undone. It was time. He owed it to himself to bury John Kovac. And damned if he wasn't going to try.

CHAPTER 76

Megan looked at the speakerphone at the center of the conference table, hoping Bishop would provide some kind of explanation. He didn't. As ever, the soft static quickly began to feel like a rebuke.

Why had Kovac's identity been kept from her until it was too late? She thought about their first kiss, a spontaneous thing as kids while swimming in one of the farm's three dams. Kovac – as she was now trying to think of him – had dragged her down into the reeds and mud. Hardly romantic, yet still the most meaningful and memorable kiss of her life. She wasn't going to top that on dating apps.

She stood, pushing back her chair. Last time she had been in this room, she had felt like the only female. She had felt like she had to fight against the unspoken belief she would forever be vulnerable to idealism, to emotional outbursts. Where had those worries gone? They had evaporated seemingly. Now, she knew her place. She would take over from her father. She would cease speaking for the company and instead chart its course.

She glanced at the seat her brother had once occupied. He was now the one who was excluded. He no longer worked for Curzon. He would be given a gilded cage, and he would wither in it. She felt nothing but contempt for her brother. He had gambled with Lottie's life.

She poured herself a coffee and crossed to the boardroom's floor-to-ceiling windows. She looked out beyond the familiar stone fence, into the desert. Her ears weren't ringing from the stress of the meeting this time, and there would be no exhaustive workout to erase stress afterward. She knew exactly who her enemies were now, and what she needed to do to defeat them.

She realized she was squinting. She let the muscles around her eyes relax, let her whole body relax, as she took a sip of coffee. She thought of the look on Daniel's face, the miserable figure he had cut as Peng's helicopters abandoned him on Pemberton's sprawling back lawn...

'Biogen,' she said. 'Why did we acquire it in 1995, given the risk?'

'It was promising,' her father said. 'Biogen's new treatment to relieve muscle ailments worked.'

'But it also contained botulinum toxin Type-A.'

'In trace amounts, yes.'

'A product that can and has been diverted for weapons production. And with our fingerprints all over it.'

'Yes.'

'Who has that weapon now?'

'We don't know,' Bishop said. 'Maybe no one. Peng's death has muddied the waters.'

His choice of phrase took Megan back to the dam on the farm again. She said: 'And Kovac? Any word on whether he'll come in voluntarily? Are we any closer to finding him?'

'Jesus,' Bishop said. 'Let him go, Megan. You want to know why I didn't tell you who he really was – this is why.'

Megan's father leaned forward. 'Letting him go isn't possible Bishop. You're as familiar with bioweaponry as I am. And if it isn't this, it'll be something else. We're a target, as ever. You know this.'

Bishop sighed through the speakerphone. 'He served us well. Doesn't he deserve retirement?'

'No.' Megan was in no doubt now. She needed Kovac. 'Find him. And get him back.'

'He thinks you betrayed him. He'll want assurances, and he may well want revenge. I vote we let sleeping dogs lie.'

The static again, but not a rebuke this time. A plea.

'Noted.' Megan drained her coffee, impatient for the caffeine hit. She looked for a sentence that would end the discussion and settled on it effortlessly. 'Curzon International owns John Kovac. He's either working for us, or…' And here she faltered.

Or what, she thought.

She didn't want to explore that ultimatum just yet, but it was coming. She crossed to the speakerphone and positioned a finger just above it, ready to terminate the call. 'Just get him back, Bishop. And get the farm operational again. I'll be down there Monday week with Lottie. I've got a lot to revise after my dismal performance here, and she's got a lot to learn. She's fragile, but we can't pander to that. What she's just been through has to become fuel. It has to shape her into something stronger.'

'Understood.'

'I'm counting on you Bishop, on a lot of fronts. Don't let me regret it.' She punched the button and terminated the call. She had never spoken to Bishop like this in her life, and knew she would never speak to him any other way again. It was part of the job now.

Her father stood and gestured to his chair at the head of the table. She met his eye. 'You're sure?'

'Might as well get used to it. It'll be official soon enough. Just remember, Megan, no more gambling.'

She dropped down into the chair and studied the conference

table from this new vantage. She realized she was exhausted.

Her father moved to Daniel's old chair, looking old and morose in it. He rubbed at his stubbled chin with the knuckles of one hand. 'He'll want assurances,' he said, thinking out loud. 'If we ever find him, that is. You know him well, Megan.'

She nodded. Her mind was back at the farm. In the dam again, but another day, training with Bishop. She had kneed Kovac in the groin to take him down a notch, only to have him almost drown her. 'And Bishop's right,' she said. 'He'll want revenge.'

Her father couldn't seem to get comfortable in Daniel's chair. He stood again, his body stiff.

'Your God Committee of one,' Megan said under her breath. 'You said no matter how I attempt to frame it, how I attempt to rationalize it – it's never more complex than the needs of this company against my own conscience.'

Her father nodded.

'You told me to feel it, to be at peace with it.'

He waited. When she said nothing more, he gently prompted her. 'And?'

She looked up. 'And that's why it has to be John Kovac.'

Thanks so much for reading. Your time is valuable, so it means a lot to me.

If you're open to becoming part of an advance team who get my books for free before they go up onto Amazon, I'd love to hear from you at:
davidcarisbooks@outlook.com.
And of course, thrilled to hear any other feedback via email or reviews, too!

Take care out there. And again, thank you.

David – January, 2021

Printed in Great Britain
by Amazon